MYCROFT
HOLMES

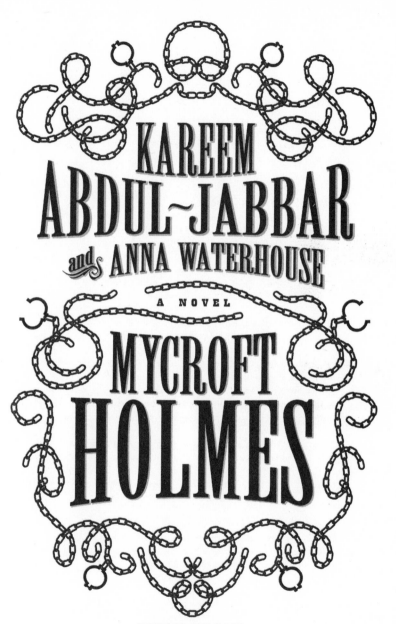

KAREEM
ABDUL-JABBAR
and ANNA WATERHOUSE

A NOVEL

MYCROFT
HOLMES

TITAN BOOKS

Mycroft Holmes
Paperback ISBN: 9781783291540
E-book edition ISBN: 9781783291564

Published by Titan Books
A division of Titan Publishing Group Ltd
144 Southwark Street, London SE1 0UP

First paperback edition: June 2016
1 3 5 7 9 10 8 6 4 2

A CIP catalogue record for this title is available from the British Library.

Printed and bound in the United States.

PROLOGUE

Outside of San Fernando, Trinidad, 1870

THE OLD MAN HAD HEARD OF THEM, OF COURSE everyone on the island had heard of them. A few had even seen the evidence—imprints in the sand—but he never had.

Not until the children began to die.

Emanuel stood on a promontory overlooking the sea. His mule was beside him, packed and ready to go. The sun was descending, painting the sky crimson as it disappeared below the horizon. A moment before, the humidity had been nearly intolerable, even for him, and he had lived on this island all eighty-seven years of his life. But with darkness came the wind, whistling through the crevices. He took out a handkerchief and wiped the damp sweat off his neck and forehead.

Still it chilled him to the bone.

Behind him stood a dozen small wooden houses. Each of them had once been alive with families. Each was now shuttered and abandoned, his neighbors having fled the horrors they had witnessed. He himself had been stubborn, refusing to turn his back on his home and his land, praying that the *douen* would simply go away.

But they had not gone away. Instead, they had become bolder.

He could still picture the first little body he'd seen, lying on the sand below as if it were still there, as if it hadn't already been buried in the small white cemetery that would be destined to be filled with more. So many more.

It had been sunset then too, not red like this one but golden and sparkling—a beautiful sky beneath which no one ought to die, especially a child.

The little boy's name was André. He had just turned six, an active little rapscallion, with skin as brown as a cocoa bean and curly hair bleached nearly white by the sun.

André had been the only living soul on the beach, a few feet from the underbrush, a tangled jungle mass that the villagers would periodically cut back, only to see it crop up again here and there, unwanted but persistent. He was skimming rocks into the water. Emanuel had been on the headland above, gathering sticks for his pot-bellied stove. No one understood how he could get so cold once the sun went down, but he was the elder of the village. No one there was yet as old as he.

Just wait! he thought. *Just wait 'til you're old and see how it is…*

He could not recall how long he had remained at his task, bent over as he collected the kindling into a respectable pile. He was nearly done when he thought he heard a commotion below, by the shoreline.

When he peered down onto the sand, André was no

longer visible. Instead, something was thrashing about in the underbrush. He saw, or perhaps imagined, the glint of a knife.

The old man turned and called out for help, but his throat was dry with fear, and the wind simply swept his voice away. He was in no condition to make the winding trek down the steep incline to the shore, but he would have to try.

Carefully, one painful step at a time, he made his way down the trail, past the little white cemetery in its patch of grass that had long since been burnt by the sun.

"I am coming, André," he called out. "I am coming—do not be afraid!" He wondered if the last few words were as much for his sake as for the boy's.

Step by painful step he went—*oh, what a madness to get old!* When at last he reached the sand, he was very nearly relieved, for he could see André quite clearly now. The boy was lying face down on the sand.

Perhaps it is the game, he thought hopefully. It was a favorite game of the children, to lie perfectly still and wait until the old man walked up to them, at which time they would jump up suddenly, to try to scare him. He would always pretend to nearly collapse of fright, and they would laugh and laugh.

But as he approached, André did not move at all.

Then, he spotted the footprints.

At first, it seemed as if some child had simply walked backward away from the body—except that the right foot was where the left foot should be, with the left in place of the right. Small, backward-facing footprints that seemed to lead to the boy and away from him at the same time.

The douen.

He knew then with terrible certainty that André was dead. The *douen* had called him out to play, and the *lougarou* had finished him off.

Shaking and crying, the old man turned the little boy onto his back. His skin was white, deadly white. Some blood had pooled in the sand beneath him, staining it an ugly copper, but most was gone, stolen away by the *lougarou.*

The old man had cried out again, loud enough at last that he heard voices calling back from the promontory above. They came running then, scrambling down the path and gathering around the little boy's body, horrified by what they were seeing.

Praying that they and their children would be left alone.

But that one sacrifice had not been enough. Nor had two, then three, then more. The *douen* had continued to call to the children, enticing them to come out and play. After which the *lougarou* had done the rest, draining the little bodies of their blood and then leaving them on the sand to be gathered up by their grieving families like so many wilted flowers.

The old man had helped to dig too many graves. He could no longer bear to look at them. This was not the place for living human beings, not any more. The breeze began to blow harder, as if pushing him away. So the old man wrapped his smock-frock around his long, thin body.

"Come play!" he thought he heard the *douen* say.

"There are no more children here!" he called out with

the last bit of rage he could muster. "There are no living beings here at all!"

With effort, he mounted his old mule and clopped away.

1

AS THE REED-GREEN WATER LAPPED GENTLY AGAINST the banks of the Thames, spectators on Putney Bridge and along the shoreline crowded shoulder to shoulder and craned their necks, vying for a better view. They were mostly boys and men, though the occasional crinoline and parasol could be seen—for the day was unseasonably warm, which prompted even the ladies to venture out, giddy with anticipation.

On this sixth day of April, the great annual race between the Oxford University and the Cambridge University boat clubs was about to commence, as it had without fail for forty years. Both sets of rowers were known as "the Blues"— Cambridge in their light blue and Oxford in a darker hue. "Betting on the Blues" was a time-honored tradition.

Among the spectators was Mycroft Holmes. Boat racing held no intrigue for the twenty-three-year-old secretary to the Secretary of State for War, nor was he keen on some bloke with an errant drink or waving cigar spoiling his brand new topcoat. And he certainly did not think himself a gambling man—a fair assessment, as he'd never made a wager in his life.

Yet today was different.

After a tediously gray and frigid winter, spring was finally in full and glorious bloom, making even the most practical sort of man—and Holmes ranked himself as such—a bit lightheaded.

He heard a voice at his side:

"You have wagered on Cambridge? *Indeed?*"

He turned to see a string bean of an ancient beadle, pale as milk, gawking at him.

"Beg pardon?" Holmes responded.

"I am asking, young sir, if you are a Cantabrigian!" the churchman repeated in an accusing tone more suited for oratory. "For there can be no other reason for your wager." He pointed his rather prominent chin toward Holmes's wager receipt, which peeked out of his lapel pocket, and which was marked with a telling line of light blue.

"Yes," Holmes responded coolly, "I am a Cantabrigian. I take it you wagered on Oxford?"

"Oxford University has won every race against Cambridge for a solid nine years running," the string bean huffed, pulling a soiled-looking kerchief from his pocket and wiping his brow underneath a cocked hat, as if the day were sweltering. "Or are you not aware of that fact?"

"I am indeed." Holmes smiled.

"Well, then," the beadle spat as if it were a personal affront, "why wager on a losing team? Is it affection, sir, that moves you?"

"I assure you," Holmes replied, "that it is not."

"Then what does?" the beadle demanded.

"Profit," Holmes asserted. "Pure and simple."

"Profit!" the beadle guffawed. "Well, if it's profit you

seek, then you are seeking in the wrong arena. Yet I suppose I waste my breath—most young men disdain the advice of their elders…"

"But if Oxford should win yet again," Holmes parried, "you shall not stand to gain much, for it is a certain bet. Whereas going against the odds will yield me twenty times the original sum."

"You, sir, are a dreamer," the man asserted.

"I assure you, sir, I am not," Holmes said quietly, turning and walking away.

"Then you are *arrogant*, sir!" the beadle called out. "Yes, an arrogant young whip."

That, I can accept more readily, Holmes thought, as he could not imagine the great sin in that. *But a dreamer? Hardly.* He prided himself on his practicality. It was an asset that, along with his intellect, he particularly prized. It was, in fact, the very combination of intellect and practicality that had brought him to this juncture in life.

His position as secretary to the Secretary of State for War was sound, placing his career on an upward path. His monthly stipend was more than adequate, his future promotions certain. Most important, after a full year's engagement, he was still madly and passionately in love with the prettiest, most intelligent, kindest woman in the world.

That was why, on this bright April day, Mycroft Holmes the non-gambler, the frugal civil servant whose future and parameters were set, had made a wager that went against good judgment. One that he hoped would add substantially to the nest egg he was stowing away for his wedding and his new life.

It was love that moved him—something an old churchman could know nothing about.

It was a risk, but a calculated one.

For he had a *plan*.

He crossed the field to the area that separated fans from athletes. Removing his coat, he folded it neatly, placed his hat on top, and proceeded to scale the barrier blocking the little beachfront where the crew prepared to depart.

"Say! You can't be here!"

Holmes looked down. It was nothing but a student masquerading as a guard. He paid him no mind, continued his clamber up, and dropped to the ground on the other side. Brushing himself off, he sauntered over to Cambridge's deputy rowing coach, one Stephen Tidwell.

Like Holmes, Tidwell had enrolled at both Eton and Cambridge. And though Tidwell was Holmes's senior by two years, he'd been one of the so-called "Mycroft's Minions"—a group of boys so taken with Holmes's powers of observation, and what Holmes referred to disparagingly as his "memory tricks," that they followed him as one might follow a conjurer or a magician, perpetually waiting to be entertained.

Tidwell recognized Holmes immediately and swallowed his surprise. Before the coach could utter so much as a syllable, Holmes pinned him with his gaze, ran a hand through his hair as if beyond exasperation, and leveled a finger at one of the rowers.

"*Tidwell*," he spat as if the name itself were accursed.

"You had the boys doing calisthenics only moments ago, and look at the bowman. Not a drop of sweat on him, yet he is dehydrated, and will weaken in the stretch—or worse!" he added for effect, then waited for his prediction to reach its desired result.

After a bewildered silence the rower in the bow laughed, with a few others joining him.

"Dehydrated?" the young man responded derisively. "Have you the foggiest how much water I consumed to get my weight up?"

Holmes did not grant him so much as a glance but continued to train his accusing glare on the coach.

"I know *precisely* how much he drank," he thundered at Tidwell. ""He was, what, eleven stone and seven pounds at the weigh in, and now he's eleven stone five. This 'bulking up' has depleted his reserves."

It was, Holmes knew, a trick that any carnival huckster could perform. All one had to do was gauge how much liquid a lad of that particular poundage, height, and musculature could retain in, say, a week. Then factor in the loss via sweat and other cruder forms of elimination. Given enough time, a carny might arrive at an accurate computation, while Holmes could do so in the proverbial blink of an eye. Calculation was almost as natural to him as breathing.

Recognizing that the numbers were true, the rower seemed to swallow his tongue. The laughter ceased.

And still, Tidwell hesitated.

"Cambridge has lost *nine in a row*," Holmes continued, his voice dripping with disdain. "Care to make it ten?"

And that, he mused, *will strike a nerve.*

The rowers eyed their coach and noted the hesitation there. Holmes had succeeded in making them as skittish as new colts. Tidwell had no choice.

"Randolph, take his place in the bow," he snapped to another man.

"Just a moment, Tidwell." Holmes wasn't finished. "There's no gain to be had from making matters worse." He turned to face the crew.

Employing a trick he'd learned from a friend of his father—an astute physician by the surname of Bell—he commanded the rowers to stand in a queue and hold their hands steady in front of them, while he scanned the line and noted the essentials: calluses on fingers, slouching shoulders, even the tucks of their chins.

"Stuff and nonsense!" seat seven grumbled as he held his arms extended. "Our strength is in our legs, everyone knows that! How our *chins* could possibly factor in—"

"Your chin *is* connected to you, is it not?" Holmes replied, overhearing. "And so has a vote in how your body functions. A peculiarity you shall notice in your later years, should you live long enough. Name?" he inquired.

"Lowe," the man replied sullenly.

With the point of his shoe, Holmes tapped on the hull of the boat and watched the manner in which it rocked in the water.

"Lowe," he repeated, as if he didn't much care for the sound of it. "Will you be so kind as to move from seat seven to seat five. Phelps, you are now at six, not four, swapping with Spencer. And you there—"

He pointed to another rower.

"Strachan, sir," the man said, properly intimidated.

"Strachan, yes. Right. You are at seven, not five. As for you…" He indicated the coxswain, Gordon. "Don't let your stroke man push too hard before Hammersmith. Keep an even pace at the start. You shall still get ahead."

The rowers took their positions with a glazed look, as if they'd been scrambled by a typhoon—while the dumbfounded Tidwell uttered not a squeak of protest.

Good, Mycroft thought. *Disorientation will force them to focus on nothing but the task at hand.* He stood back and examined his handiwork with satisfaction.

"Let victory be its own reward!" he said aloud, and he turned back the way he'd come. As he clambered quickly over the barrier and past the student guards, he heard the disgruntled Faulkes calling after him.

"Pride goeth before destruction," the young man shouted. "And a haughty spirit before a fall!"

Haughtiness? Holmes thought. *Not at all! I am simply correct in my assumptions!*

Still, it was the second time in a day that he had been so reprimanded. As he retrieved his coat and hat, dusted them off in turn, and moved quickly back toward the spectators, he thanked the heavens that he was not the sort of man given over to superstitions.

Once he had rejoined the throng—none of whom had a clue as to what had just transpired—Holmes checked his pocket watch and calibrated how long it would take him to ride to the end point of the race, Chiswick Bridge. There he would meet his friend.

Too quickly, he thought. *No challenge there.* So he lingered, enduring the crush of humanity, the cheers and the jostling as both teams got on their way.

After a sufficient time, whistling Rossini's "Figaro," he sauntered past the throng, back to the post where he'd tethered his horse.

He was looking forward to a final bit of fun.

2

"EASY, BOY, EASY," HOLMES MURMURED TO HIS HANOVERIAN, stroking his flank. A warmblood, Abie was not the swiftest of foot, but he had an intelligent gaze and an unfussy nature. Like many of his fellows, he was balanced, sturdy, and well proportioned. Holmes had purchased the five-year-old gelding for forty guineas—an excellent price, as the beast was easily worth twice that.

When Georgiana had first laid eyes upon him, she'd laughed.

"Ah, what a handsome lad," she said. "Dark blond hair, a good, strong chest, a keen and brilliant eye, and a steady disposition... much like its owner!"

Holmes hadn't known, at that moment, whether to be pleased or not, though upon further reflection he had decided that the horse indeed resembled him, and that since he liked the horse, and Georgiana liked him, she had meant it as a compliment.

Unlike his younger brother Sherlock—tall, dark, impossibly thin, with facial features that reminded one of a bird of prey—Holmes had been told since childhood that he was "a strapping lad." Tall enough, well muscled, with a pleasing yet noble profile. That last, he supposed, he owed to his mother—if little else.

In any case, he and Abie would race the rowers to the finish line, from Putney Bridge to Chiswick Bridge, four miles along a snaking obstacle course. That would make his journey nearly two miles longer than the rowers'.

A fair fight, Holmes asserted, *is the essence of competition.*

Though fully aware that it might be a tactical error, he lit a Punch Habana and allowed the delicious smoke to expand, tasting it, accepting the risk of missing the finale whilst secretly congratulating himself on this bit of recklessness—not one of his usual traits. Abie did not protest. He seemed perfectly content to stand in that spot of sun a few moments longer, shooing the occasional fly with a twitch of his tail.

Holmes waited a full eight minutes. Then, cursing the little war in Cuba that was pushing already unreasonable tobacco prices through the roof, he put out his cigar and swung up on Abie's back.

A kick of his heels, and they were off.

Horse and rider moved as if they knew every little knot and turn of Greater London. They avoided squalling flower peddlers, clanking boardmen, groaning mule carts, spitting bootblacks, shouting paperboys, lollygagging costers, and the occasional pair of oxen, missing each by a hair's breadth. All the while they nosed out the cleanest thoroughfares and most deserted byways, as if they and the city were gears in the noblest Swiss watch.

Holmes delighted in Abie's easy athleticism, and his

own. Just as the rowers were passing the Chiswick Eyot, where the river ran both straight and deep, Holmes took the time to lean down and scoop up an errant hat that had been plucked from the head of its owner by a fine spring wind, flinging it back to the startled but grateful little man—all without breaking Abie's canter a whit.

Just as they were turning onto Chiswick Bridge, a sewer worker blinded by sunlight poked his head up from a manhole right into Abie's path. The street was so narrow and the turn so tight as to make a collision unavoidable... but for a plank of wood, listing precariously from the back of an old abandoned cart on the side of the road. Holmes shifted Abie ever so slightly and sent him galloping up the plank, across the cart, and over the head of the startled laborer, who looked up in time to see the hooves and belly of a flying horse.

"Good lad!" Holmes said, patting Abie on the neck as they continued on.

At Chiswick Bridge, the crush of onlookers was even greater than it had been at Putney. Holmes was pleased—though not surprised—to confirm that the teams had just broken the sight line and were in the final leg. He quickly dismounted and handed his hat and reins to a very tall, distinguished-looking black man of forty or so, who took both without a word as Holmes jostled through the shoulder-to-shoulder crowd.

Holmes found a spot that gave him an unimpeded view of the finish line, and sat down. The black man, his skin the color of cinnamon, appeared at Holmes's side without a sound and stood by as the teams glided over the water in two faultless lines.

Still watching, he bent low toward Holmes.

"I thought you would never make it in time," he murmured.

"Well then, Douglas, you thought wrong," Holmes replied. Then he added with a smile, "Not for the first time, I am sure. I take it you placed a wager, as well?"

Cyrus Douglas nodded.

"I do as I am told," he replied.

"Oh, is that a fact!" Holmes said with a laugh. "And when, pray, did *that* commence? For I surely would like to be alive to see it."

The strokes of the rowers' blades were long, smooth, and steady, in spite of the pressure to win. Both teams were behaving to the last like gentlemen.

As the noise of the crowd swelled to a deafening roar, the Cambridge team performed exactly as Holmes had estimated, edging out its rival by a length and a half. Cries of dismay and exultation rose up so loudly that Holmes was convinced they could be heard all the way back to Putney Bridge.

In the tumult, Douglas dared to steal a sidelong glance at Holmes, and noted a smug little smile.

"So... you had a hand in this!"

"A small one," Holmes replied, "though for my trouble I was cursed with Proverbs 16:18."

"'Pride goeth before destruction, and a haughty spirit before a fall?'" Douglas quoted.

Holmes laughed. "Imagine anyone thinking me proud."

"Indeed," Douglas said evenly. "But if you knew the remedy, why not use it before?"

"I'd never wagered before," Holmes replied.

"I see." Douglas cocked his head and smiled, as if privy to a secret. "A handsome topcoat. Is it new?"

"Well, of *course* it is new!" Holmes snapped. "Did you expect that I'd purchase it used?"

In truth, he wouldn't have bought the wretched thing at all—it had cost more than his last two suits combined. But it had so pleased Georgiana that he felt he would break her heart if he let it go.

Douglas handed over the hat with no further comment. Holmes placed it once again upon his head, stood to leave, and motioned for his friend to follow. Douglas resumed his more servile demeanor, and the two pressed through the crowd to the place where a stout bookmaker with a scraggly black mustache stood behind his portable betting table. There was no rush to him, since most of the assembled had lost, and the few winners were anxious to watch their victorious team throw their beloved coxswain in the Thames, as tradition demanded.

The bookmaker, now a whole lot richer, counted out Holmes's winnings, and Douglas's, as well, all the while humming a merry tune.

"You bet handsomely, I see," Holmes said to Douglas as he received his share. "Though I cannot begin to fathom the looks of pity you endured when you placed your wager. For what rube, what deluded fool, would dare to bet on Cambridge after all these long and losing years?"

He breathed deeply, looking quite content.

"Care to wager how I shall use a portion of my winnings?" he continued.

"Oh, I think I have a notion," Douglas responded, clapping his friend on the shoulder.

That friendly act was an error in judgment that did not go unnoticed. A knot of Oxford fans stood nearby, well in their cups and aggrieved by the cash that would never line their pockets. In simpler words, they were itching for a fight. They had been glowering as the winnings were being counted out, so when one occasioned to see the familiarity between Holmes and Douglas, it provided them with the impetus they sought.

"That h'aint no valet!" one said.

"It's like they's *chums*," another replied.

Douglas was too intent on pocketing his money to observe the half-dozen ill-kempt drunkards pushing through the crowd and spitting out insults. But Holmes did. They seemed to him large and porous, as if nursed from childhood by ale, and their grooming left much to be desired. Several had tufts of hair protruding from their ears. And one was gifted with an eyebrow that went from right temple to left without a break in between.

Then he noted something more alarming.

Their fleshy hands held sticks and bottles.

They'd come prepared.

"Did you bring your pistol by chance?" Holmes nervously asked his friend.

"It seemed excessive for a Cambridge–Oxford race," Douglas replied, glancing at the men moving toward them.

As Holmes stood his ground, ready to fight, Douglas waited another moment, as if trying to discern what to do.

Then he ran off as fast as his long legs could carry him.

This caught the Oxford fans by surprise. They slowed slightly, muttering in derision.

"All cowards, every last mother's son of 'em," one jeered.

"But his friend there," the one with the eyebrow observed, "'e looks primed for a beatin'. And no good'll come in wastin' a perfectly good bottle!" With that, he sucked out the last drop of ale, and then held it like a cudgel in his hairy fingers.

"This otter improve 'is aspect somewhat!" he said, wiggling that long eyebrow up and down for emphasis.

Holmes dropped into a defensive stance.

"Take a look at that!" another guffawed. "That one fancies hisself a pugilist!"

Emboldened, they began to squeeze around him like a large and angry fist.

Suddenly, the unmistakable sound of hooves... and a moment later Douglas—astride Abie's back—charged into their midst, scattering them long enough for him to extend a hand.

Holmes grasped it and swung up behind him.

The two galloped away.

The passel of drunks was momentarily stunned but quickly recovered. Dragging themselves up onto their own mounts, they kicked and whipped the horses into a lather and set off after their quarry.

* * *

The din of their pursuit grew louder. Holmes knew only too well that poor Abie, with two astride him, would never be able to maintain a lead.

"We'll tan yer ugly hide, we will!" a lout shouted from behind.

"A real batty-fang, lads!" another called out.

Passersby and carriage horses became a blur as the chase went on. A few bottles crashed to the right and the left of them. One missed Holmes's head by a centimeter, yet found its mark just as Douglas was turning to see how much the men had gained.

It shattered against his left temple. Blood spurted from the wound, dripped down Douglas's cheek and neck, and stained his white collar a deep and ugly red. He lost consciousness upon impact, and began to list precariously portside.

The stomping of hooves grew in volume, as threats of a beating turned to promises of killing... and worse.

Steadying the unconscious Douglas with his knees, Holmes strained past him and grabbed hold of Abie's reins. Startled by his master's familiar touch, the beast mustered a burst of energy that bought them a moment's respite. His left hand on the reins, his knees still clenching Douglas on either side, Holmes reached into his breast pocket with his right hand, and pulled out his pocket watch.

He squinted, damning the sunlight he had praised so assiduously just an hour before, and finally managed to read the time.

Twenty-nine past the hour, he thought, abruptly changing course. *We have four minutes.*

If only they could reach St. Giles in time.

3

THE ROOKERY OF ST. GILES WAS A DESTINATION CHOSEN by no one—at least, no one with sense in their heads or a choice in the matter.

The sides of its looming old tenements had been patched and re-patched so often that it seemed that repairs alone held them up. The windows were so grimy with soot and dust that even spring had not yet made its mark, for the sun had been all but shut out. Accumulated piles of refuse stood in the center of the street, like stacks of hay left to rot, and the air smelled stale, as if even the breeze dared not venture therein.

It was the sort of place where smallpox and fevers took hold and never let go, where toothless hawkers extolled the virtues of flowers that proper housewives had discarded days before, while other hawkers—with no virtue left to extol—sold their own wilted bodies to any passing stranger.

Whatever else it was, St. Giles wasn't fit for fine gentlemen with overpriced topcoats. Once a person found himself at St. Giles, it was best to tread lightly, and to hold onto his wits and his wallet with equal vigor.

As Cyrus Douglas began his slow ascent back to consciousness, the first thing he smelled was St. Giles in all its damnable glory—a stirring aroma of piss, dung, and rotting flesh. And the first thing he heard was the echoing sound of Abie's hooves thundering down the broken, battered street as he and Holmes jostled violently from side to side at a pace that threatened to send them both tumbling arse over turkey.

What the bloody deuce are you doing, *Holmes?* he tried to say aloud, though he still couldn't find his voice. *Are you determined to get us killed?*

Then he heard another sound—one that froze his blood. It was the pounding hoof beats of their pursuers, mingled with jeers and laughing.

Holmes must have taken a wrong and fatal turn, Douglas thought. But rather than speed up, he was slowing Abie down to little more than a trot!

All the while, the sounds were coming closer.

Faster, Holmes, he thought frantically, though he still could not speak. *Faster, for the love of all that is holy!* Perversely, he could feel his friend pulling back on the reins, actually *slowing* their pace. It was such a mad choice that even Abie seemed reluctant to comply.

"Easy, boy… easy…" Holmes repeated.

The thugs were so very near that Douglas was certain he could feel their breath at the back of his neck.

He dared to glance behind, and immediately wished he hadn't. The villains had their sticks and whips and bottles raised high into the air. Those same mean weapons with which they beat their poor nags, they now planned to use on their unarmed quarry. And with the blow to his temple still so fresh and throbbing, Douglas was in no condition to fight. There would be little for him to do but roll up into a ball, take the blows, and hope that death came quickly.

A murder of crows, ragged and cawing, swooped down upon them. As if they were some celestial signal, Holmes suddenly prodded Abie into a full gallop, until the horse was flying over the gouges and ruts, the birds' caws melding with the men's laughter.

They approached a mews that led to nowhere, with carts and makeshift stands and garbage consuming every inch of the street. Yet Holmes continued on, prodding Abie so close to a tenement wall that it nearly scraped the poor thing's side. The pursuers began to ride two by two, so as to allow no room for escape.

Douglas finally unlocked his jaw to speak.

"What the deuce are you *thinking*, Holmes!"

Suddenly, above their heads, a half-dozen windows burst open at the same time, and several large, chattering women leaned out, upending enormous buckets of slop onto the street below.

The filth missed Abie and his riders by less than a length, but the ruffians behind them barely had time to cry out when they were drenched in a pungent mix of offal, rotting vegetables, bone, gristle, piss, and shit. Their beasts skittered on the slime, and the ruts proved lethal.

The assailant in the lead, the one with one eyebrow, went hurtling over his nag like a projectile and landed head first in a fly-infested, maggot-encrusted dung heap. Others went down hither and thither until all were crawling about in the muck, trying to regain their footing only to slip into it again, all the while cursing loudly.

Pulling again on the reins, Holmes turned Abie and trotted him past a confusion of upended horses and men while the crows nonchalantly swooped over the lot of them, eager to ferret out their breakfast.

The sight gave Douglas new vigor, and he resumed the reins. Though they had to pass through a baptism of grime, it was a sprinkling, not the immersion their pursuers had endured. And though Holmes's topcoat and his own were likely ruined, their bodies were more or less intact.

You are a lucky man, Holmes, he mused. *Has there ever been an individual so blessed by fate as you?*

They rode on out of St. Giles and into a more genteel section of town, neither man uttering so much as a syllable until they reached their destination—an inviting little tobacco shop on Regent Street.

Holmes and Douglas left poor exhausted Abie, his coat steaming from exertion, in a spot of shade, giving him fresh water and a pat on the flank for a job well done, which seemed a mean substitute, Holmes acknowledged to himself, for apples or oats.

As they hobbled up the stairs to the entry, he eyed the establishment as a pilgrim might eye Mecca. Over the front door hung a sign.

REGENT TOBACCOS
*Importateur de Cigares de la Havane,
de Manille, et du Continent.*

Some months before, Holmes had accompanied his beloved Georgiana to the London docks to pick up letters from her family back in Trinidad. The docks were a grimy affair, and occasionally a dangerous one—he had always insisted that she not go it alone.

As they passed a ship unloading its cargo, he had spotted several crates of the most elusive cigar of the year, that delectable Cuban the *Principe de Gales*. Owing to the never-ending skirmish between Cuba and Spain, the cigar manufacturer had relocated his factories to the United States, which was just recovering from its own civil war. All that shifting about had made it impossible for *Principes* to be found in London, even for ready money.

Yet there they were!

A tall black man with a sprinkling of gray at the sideburns of his otherwise ebony hair was supervising their unloading. After a bit of cajoling, that man—Cyrus Douglas—directed Holmes to Regent, the little tobacconist that employed him.

Holmes had been frequenting the Regent ever since, and upon each occasion had felt the giddy elation of a child on Christmas morning. Yet, he could not recall a moment when he'd been so glad to see it as this one. His hands were red and swollen from holding the reins so long, and pain was cramping his legs.

Twenty-one steps, he thought. *Twenty-one steps, and we are inside.*

4

GERARD PENNYWHISTLE STOOD BEHIND THE COUNTER of regent Tobaccos, tortoise-shell lorgnette in hand. He was so short that, though he was fully upright, he looked as if he were sitting down, for the surface of the counter reached to the middle of his chest.

He was going over the morning's ledger, and the lorgnette was meant to overcome his myopia, presbyopia, and astigmatism.

Ava Pennywhistle—a healthy head taller than her husband—was using a duster on the chandelier, though there wasn't a speck of dust to be had. When the doorbell tinkled, both looked up and smiled, though Mr. Pennywhistle could see nothing beyond the length of his own arm.

Mrs. Pennywhistle lost the smile the moment she laid eyes on Douglas.

"Coo, love, what's happened to *you*, then?" she said, hurrying over.

Then she stopped short.

"Ooof! And what is that *aroma?*" she inquired, dramatically waving the duster in front of her nose.

Douglas attempted to explain, but Mr. and Mrs. P. fussed over him so much that he could hardly get a word in. The miniscule Mr. P. was holding onto the much taller Douglas as if he half-expected him to collapse like a soufflé to the floor, while Mrs. P. ran back and forth with what appeared to be an entire pharmacy of bandages, salves, and balms.

Holmes observed all this with a bemused expression while doing his best to stay out from underfoot. He hung his now-spoiled topcoat on a hook, trying to forget what it cost, and allowed himself an exhausted but satisfied sigh.

Almost everything in the store delighted him, from the grain mahogany of superior quality that comprised the shelves to the polished glass of the displays. An aromatic, nearly hypnotic scent wafted from every nook, for the selection of tobaccos—sheer heaven! Somehow or other, little Regent always managed to find those elusive brands that even larger stores—like Jimenez & Sons on Fenchurch Street—couldn't ferret out, and could secure the best price possible for premium Cubans like La Meridiana.

And if one cared for cigarettes—which he himself did not, though he wouldn't disparage those who did—Regent carried La Honradez, with its intricate, colorful labels printed with the latest technology in the effort always to be one step ahead of the counterfeiters.

Of course, the place wasn't perfect. Holmes did not care for the new tin boxes that contained American cigars. In point of fact he was fearful that Regent was beginning to stock too many blends. But his deepest sigh of disapproval was reserved for a corner of the glass counter display filled with meerschaum pipes, made in Vienna by one Simon Schild, a meerschaum carver.

They were all the rage that spring in St. James's. And though Holmes really did think the world of his favorite little tobacco shop, he had to admit that it wasn't above catering to the whims of fashion.

He hobbled over to his personal cabinet. It was fairly modest compared to some others, as it contained only two hundred cigars: seventy-five Partagás, twenty-five formidable La Meridiana and an even hundred of his beloved Punch Habanas. He hoped to make the leap to a five-hundred-cigar cabinet, and if matters with his employ progressed as he anticipated, the goal should be easily achieved by the following spring.

He chose two Partagás—appropriate, he thought, considering what he and Douglas had endured. The latter, his head now nicely bandaged, brought him a cigar cutter.

"You'd best sit a while, dearie!" Mrs. P. called to Douglas. "We'll enjoy some free time tomorrow—you're in no shape to mind the shop today."

"Nonsense," Douglas replied in his most soothing tone. "I am perfectly fit to work. It's a beautiful spring day—you must take advantage of it."

The expression on Mrs. P.'s face said that she was having none of it, but Douglas persisted, and she finally relented.

"We'll put out the 'back in thirty,'" she said, "but we'll make it sixty," she added in a conspiratorial whisper, "so you can get yer proper rest!"

"Oh, and do feel free to imbibe!" Mr. P. called out a bit too loudly, for he was never entirely certain of anyone's location. "A few shots of the spirit'll set you aright, put some color back in those cheeks!" Then, as he opened the door to his wife, he chortled, "You hear what I said, Mrs. P.? Color, said I. In a black man's cheeks!" He repeated it for good measure so that they might enjoy a few more chuckles before it was done.

Douglas watched as the two of them waddled down the steps and onto the street, and shook his head with bewildered affection. Then he turned to a row of fine old bottles and ran a finger across the labels, making it clear that he intended to pull something from an inferior brand.

"Don't even think about it," Holmes said firmly, and he slapped his wallet on the counter. "We won a wager this day, and we have earned the right to enjoy the spoils of war." With that, he pointed to a fifty-year-old Saint Christeau Armagnac.

Douglas cast him a long look.

"Who are you," he said in somber tones, "and what have you done with my good friend Holmes?"

"He's still here," Holmes declared. "Though a bit worse for wear."

Douglas pulled down the Armagnac. They chose two comfortable old leather chairs by the fire. He uncorked the bottle, sniffed it, and declared it to be perfect. Holmes lit their cigars, and Douglas raised a toast.

"To the women of St. Giles, and their bloody good timing!" He looked at his friend with meaning, and added, "You are one lucky mobsman."

Holmes raised his own glass.

"To Dickens, may the good Lord heal him," he said. "And to Kingsley, and Mrs. Gaskell, and William Makepeace Thackeray!"

"I will gladly toast authors," Douglas replied, "but why those in particular?"

"For the miseries they catalogue! *They* are the ones who led me to St. Giles, 'with its nests of close and narrow alleys and courts… that have passed into a byword as the synonym of filth and squalor,'" he added, paraphrasing Henry Mayhew.

"Everyone knows the perils of St. Giles," Douglas huffed. "I don't see what *that* has to do with…"

"My dear Douglas," Holmes interrupted. "You cannot possibly think that a half-dozen women, leaning out of six fourth-story windows, at the exact same time, did so out of *coincidence*?" He shook his head at such brazen folly, and took a sip of his Armagnac.

"My dear *Holmes*," Douglas countered, "how could it not be? The bulk of the residents of St. Giles cannot even *tell* the time. And surely Dickens and Kingsley, and Mrs. Gaskell, and even the formidable Thackeray never wrote of those women!"

"No," Holmes admitted, "they did not. But, if you will indulge me a poetic turn, I set out long ago, utilizing those authors as my guides, to explore our city, traveling to those places in which gentlemen hardly set foot—unless, of course, said gentlemen are given to perversions.

"Which I most certainly am not."

"In that, we agree," Douglas said in a tone so wry that Holmes wondered if he meant it as a slight.

"In any event," Holmes continued, taking another healthy sip of Armagnac and waving the glass like an orator, "how are we to protect our fair and, I grant you, occasionally foul city if we do not know its every highway and byway? So there in St. Giles, among other strange and mostly sad facts, I discovered that its women had the odd habit of casting out their slop at the same time each day. Ten thirty-three in the morning, to be precise.

"I went back two weeks running, then three months after, just to be sure, and then a year after that. So punctual are they that they have trained the local birds to fly in for their breakfast." Holmes sighed as he took a pull of his Partagás. "Rich or poor, Douglas, we are all creatures of habit."

With that he sat back and awaited a reply, and perhaps a bit of applause.

"Stunning," Douglas said. He held his own Partagás aloft, as if he'd intended to take a puff, but forgot midway. "Creatures of habit," he murmured. And he stared into the distance, past the wall, past the street, across an unseen gulf.

"You have just described my family in Trinidad," he added.

Douglas wasn't a man given to easy confidences—nor did Holmes himself accept them easily—but their unusual friendship had just been shaken by adventure, and then stirred by fine spirit and cigars. So when Holmes showed interest, Douglas went on.

"My relatives are creatures of habit," he clarified, "who write me faithfully each week…"

"Your parents?" Holmes interrupted.

Douglas shook his head no.

"My parents died some years ago," he said quietly. "No, I have an older, widowed sister, two young nieces, and three cousins who are like my siblings, in that we grew up together. As I was saying, they write me faithfully each week. But now it's been more than a month since I've heard from them."

"That *is* worrisome," Holmes said, for lack of better. He could hear elements of Douglas's native tongue woven through his West London clip, like a jaunty spot of crimson on a somber black suit. Holmes hadn't heard that Trinidad cadence in a good long while, so seldom did Douglas relax.

What a world we live in, he mused, *where a good man like Douglas cannot find a moment's ease…*

"They are frightened," Douglas continued, and Holmes's curiosity was piqued. "Or rather, *were* frightened, the last I heard."

"Of what?" he asked, pouring them another.

Douglas nodded his thanks and took a goodly swallow, while Holmes tried not to calculate the cost per drop— though of course he knew *precisely* what it was.

"Some of the locals have… now, I know it seems odd, Holmes, but they have disappeared. They might be out fishing, or mending their nets, and then they simply *vanish.*"

"One? Two? How many?"

Douglas shrugged. "Ten near my village."

"Ten?"

"But not just my village. I've heard that it is happening up and down the coast. I'd say fifty or more are gone, in all."

"Fifty?" Holmes took a moment to digest the number.

"Fifty people *disappeared?* What on earth do the authorities say?"

"What *would* they say about fifty Negroes disappearing?" Douglas laughed, though he was not amused. "Good riddance, I suppose."

His expression soured. "And there is something else. Three children were found dead, the blood drained from them."

"*What?*" Douglas's words shook Holmes out of his mild and pleasant stupor. "Who in the world could do such a thing?"

"The villagers believe it is a *lougarou…*"

"A… a *werewolf?*" Holmes stammered, then quickly amended. "No, wait. In the Antilles, a *lougarou* is thought to be a giant mosquito that sucks the blood out of children—is that not the case?" he added out of politeness, though he knew perfectly well it was.

Douglas nodded, then he sighed.

"There is more. The lougarou have… 'companion demons,' if you will. The *douen.* According to legend, they are children who died before being baptized, and are therefore condemned to walk the earth forever on little backwards-facing feet."

"An ugly fate," Holmes muttered. "Not to say impractical."

"Whatever the cause, the killings seem to occur along the waterfront. People are staying well away from the water's edge. By now I am so concerned for my family's well-being that I am considering going."

"Going? Going where? You cannot mean Port of Spain.

Nonsense, my good man, think of the journey! Eight or more days there, the same to get back—provided you get back at all. And in any case, what would your employers say?" Holmes asked, allowing a certain edge to creep into his tone. "I cannot believe Mr. and Mrs. P. are prepared to lose you for so long."

He saw in Douglas's expression that these last words had hit their mark.

Douglas flinched. "You smug little sot," he replied, inhaling a last sip of Saint Christeau. "How'd you know?"

Holmes took another long drag of his cigar.

"I am not a *little* sot," he protested. "I'm quite nearly as tall as you, though I grant I'm seventeen years younger…"

"*How did you know?*" Douglas insisted, enunciating each word.

Permitting himself a slight smile, Holmes leaned forward and peered at his friend.

"You worked on freighters that shipped sugar and tobacco to the British Isles. Since you speak fluent Spanish as well as Portuguese, it's a safe assumption that you used those stretches of time to form ties in each of the best tobacco-producing countries." He leaned back and took another drag, exhaling the smoke at a leisurely pace.

"You save your money, that I know—I am not the *only* parsimonious soul in the room. And when you purchased this fine little establishment, you hired trusted people of, shall we say, an *alternate* color to masquerade as the owners. Thus, you ensured that you would not find your cigar shop burned to the ground some unhappy morning."

"You built your assumptions on such shoddy evidence?"

Douglas exclaimed. "Very superficial of you, Holmes." His tone was droll, but he was staring at his friend with unfettered curiosity.

"Naturally," Holmes replied, smiling. "I'd be a fool to rely on that alone."

"Well, if there's one thing you are not, Mycroft Holmes, it is a fool," Douglas responded. "One feels quite underdressed in your presence. Pray, enlighten me further."

"Thank you, I will." Holmes sat forward in his chair and narrowed his eyes. "Your employers do not have the aggressive manner an owner frequently employs in dealing with an underling. Indeed, they make eye contact with you whilst speaking, to the point that it seems as if they are waiting for nonverbal cues.

"Moreover," he added as he ran a distracted hand through his blond hair, "the first time I met you on the London docks, and asked about that shipment of Cuban cigars that you were unloading, your response was much too specific. It required insights into the political turmoil that affects both affordability and availability, quite a neat trick for a mere hensman and clerk."

With that, he folded his arms and sat back with what he hoped was an air of triumph.

Defeated, Douglas stared at the empty glass in his hand.

"I was always planning to take you into my confidence, Holmes," he said, sounding contrite. "But I fear old habits die hard."

Holmes nodded. "You are permitted to keep your secrets, Douglas," he said. "But you must forgive me if I ferret them out. And now that you have admitted you are the owner, what shall we do about those ghastly meerschaum pipes?"

"They sell beautifully," Douglas countered with a smile.

Holmes rolled his eyes, then returned to the topic at hand. "So. Was it your acquaintances who sent news of the vanishings in Trinidad, or was it your suppliers?"

"Both," Douglas answered. "And once the suppliers confirmed the rumors, I had to take them seriously."

"Well," Holmes said crossly. "Before you disappear off the face of the civilized planet, allow me at least to determine whether or not any new reports have come in to the office of the Secretary of State for War. I shall rifle through in the morning." He paused as a new thought crossed his mind. "And this evening, Georgiana and I are off to dinner," he added. "Perhaps *she* has heard something."

"Perhaps," Douglas murmured, though his tone indicated that he wished to say no more about it. Holmes thought it an odd reaction to an offer of assistance.

"Are you suggesting that my asking her is futile?" Holmes said uncertainly, finishing his drink.

"Not at all, Holmes," Douglas assured him. "I simply fear that, when she is around, your keen perceptions become woefully impaired."

Holmes could feel the last sip of Armagnac burn his cheeks, tinting them an unbecoming shade of pink, as was happening with alarming frequency whenever Georgiana's name was brought up.

"Is it true?" he said to Douglas after a moment. "Does love really make people so blind as all that?"

Douglas leaned toward his friend.

"There are three poisons to sound judgment," he said, "love, hate, and envy. I do not see that you are much in thrall to the latter two, but I do ask that you be careful with the first."

"I never suspected you of reading Petrarch," Holmes teased. But indeed he *was* feeling rather vulnerable. He shook it off as nonsense—that combination of fear, exaltation, and exhaustion their little ordeal had provoked. He put out the cigar and rose to his feet, then slipped on his topcoat, and tried not to flinch again at its rather estimable odor.

He turned as he reached the door.

"Have you never been in love?" he asked in a voice that sounded entirely too plaintive.

Douglas stared into his empty glass again.

"That, my friend," Douglas said, "is a story for another time."

5

FUELED PERHAPS BY BRANDY AND BY A WALLET LINED with fresh cash, Holmes continued his uncommon spending spree. First, he splurged on a brand-new coat, not as costly as the old, to be sure, but handsome enough. Then, he rented a brougham when an ordinary hackney cab would have done.

Finally, he sent a messenger with a tip to guarantee a table at an exclusive West End restaurant with the reputation for a particularly hearty turtle soup. The entire affair would cost him as much as five guineas, but as this was the one-year anniversary of his engagement to Georgiana, surely it was worth every sou in his pockets.

On the way to fetch his beloved, Holmes stared out the window at the nightmare of London traffic, a bottleneck growing worse by the day. Roads built in the last twenty years, from Victoria to New Oxford Street, were already proving less than up to the task. There were so many carriages, carts, horses, mules—even the occasional team of oxen or flock of sheep—that getting across town in a timely fashion was all but impossible. Given the great number of Adam's spawn in the streets, he had to assume that every house, hovel, tenement and pub in London must be deserted.

As his carriage lurched around and through the madness, Holmes was struck by a disconcerting thought. *Why wasn't the War Office alerted to the disappearances in Trinidad? They could presage some tribal conflict, at the very least... What else is being kept from us?*

The notion that Britain's War Office might not have pertinent information sent a chill through him that began at the nape of his neck and traveled south, tightening his stomach with anxiety.

How absurd, he thought. *I cannot take personally every mystery transpiring across the globe, or my career shall be quite short-lived.*

Yet, in spite of his best efforts at rationality, he still felt very much out of sorts. When he could not eradicate the feeling, he chalked it up to the Armagnac. It brought to mind that line from *A Christmas Carol,* when Ebenezer Scrooge first laid eyes upon the specter.

"'You may be an undigested bit of beef, a blot of mustard, a crumb of cheese, a fragment of an underdone potato. There's more of gravy than of grave about you, whatever you are!'"

"Sir?" the cabman called out inquisitively. "Is you be wantin' sumfin', then?"

"No, no!" Holmes replied—mortified to realize that he had been quoting Dickens aloud. "Carry on!"

He sighed. *What is the matter with me?* He could only hope that this last thought, he had kept to himself.

He leaned his head back on the seat and was gratified to note that it did not, as in lesser carriages, stink of pomade, sweat, and old perfume. Thus appeased, he tried to think of something more edifying.

Georgiana immediately sprang to mind.

Just her name created an image so clear that she could have been sitting beside him. Blond, with cream-colored skin, pink cheeks and sparkling blue eyes, Georgiana Sutton was the quintessential English rose. Nothing about her hinted she'd ever been outside of London proper, or had endured any jostling about at all. But in fact, beneath that very proper British exterior, she possessed something of the exotic. She had been born and bred in Port of Spain, where her ancestors had resided for more than 200 years, and where her parents still ran the family's large—and by all accounts prosperous—sugar plantation.

Holmes recalled with pleasure the day of their engagement.

Georgiana was wearing a peau-de-soie dress the color of fallen leaves, cinched at the waist, her hair done up high. He had pulled the ring from his jacket pocket, declaring his intentions. She had looked down at it and drawn a breath, her eyes brimming with tears.

"Oh! How lovely!" he recalled her saying.

"From South Africa," he'd confided. Then, to her astonished look, he'd explained, "Indian mines are close to failing these days, my love. In a few weeks' time, this African cache shall become public knowledge and Cape Colony awash with prospectors. But for the moment…"

That is when he had slipped the diamond onto her finger.

"…it helps to be a secretary in a war office!"

He'd assumed this little bit of knowledge would delight her, but she had remained silent, pondering the ring, studying it. He wondered if perhaps she thought it wasn't up to the quality of Indian gems, and if he should hint as to its worth—though he could not imagine how to do so without sounding vulgar.

"Cape Colony, you say?" Georgiana murmured.

"Yes, dearest. So far, the bulk of the diamonds has been found on land owned by two Dutch farmers, surname de Beer…"

She'd looked up at him then, eyes shining, as if she'd just had the most improbable, the most beautiful thought in the world.

"Mycroft!" she said. "Wouldn't it be exciting to invest in a diamond mine?"

He had laughed.

"Dearest," he'd said. "You of all people should know that I am not given to speculation when it comes to money. Even on so-called 'sure things.'"

"Yes, but this one time," she'd replied. "It seems a certain bet, and think of the good we could do with the earnings."

He had taken her in his arms.

"Georgiana," he'd murmured, brushing his fingers across her cheek, "perhaps I am too ordinary, or perhaps too risk averse, but that is something I cannot bring myself to do."

A shadow crossed her face, just for a moment, one that had given him a small shudder.

"My dearest," he had assured her, "I cannot promise you a terribly exciting life, but I can promise that you shall be greatly loved."

He took her hand and turned it palm up. On the band, engraved in the gold, was the outline of a small key.

"There you have it," he'd said. "The key to my heart."

She had thrown her arms about his neck that day. Her tears and embrace were all he'd needed.

The following week, when Holmes had informed his brother Sherlock of the engagement, the lad had looked down his long nose.

"She hails from Port of *Spain?*" he had sniffed, one eyebrow cocked as if Holmes had just confessed that his betrothed worked as a heaver on the London wharves.

"Georgiana is better educated than many of her peers," Holmes protested. "A year at Cheltenham Ladies' College, now a transfer to Girton!"

"Girton! So terribly *avant-garde!*" Sherlock had opined.

Yes, it was true—Girton dared to teach men's subjects such as Latin, Greek, and mathematics to the weaker sex. And though it pained Holmes that Georgiana was, in certain circles, frowned upon as a libertine for pursuing an education at all, he was proud of her nonetheless for daring to venture forth in that manner—and proud of himself, too, for holding such progressive views.

He told Sherlock as much, making it clear that he would abide no foolish talk when it came to Georgiana. But Sherlock could be like a bloodhound on the scent.

"She is pretty too, I'll wager," his younger brother muttered, spitting out the word "pretty" as if it were a pejorative. "Marrying a pretty girl is the height of folly. You shall never have a moment's peace."

But his brother was wrong. Holmes was sure of it.

Georgiana was pretty, yes, but she was no femme fatale. Men did not swoon at her feet. Yet though they might not vow to die for her, several had vowed to live for her—and she had rejected them all, choosing *him*.

Now he was determined to spend the rest of his life ensuring that she would never for one moment regret that decision.

Then again, this day's small luxuries will have to last a while, he thought with a sigh. His first and most important duty in Georgiana's regard was to save for their future home, for they could not marry until that was secured.

Within eighteen months, he would have enough for a terrace in Pimlico, with perhaps two maids, a cook, and possibly even a coachman. Once their future children were born—Holmes was hoping for three: two boys and a girl—they would relocate into one of those new, semi-detached villas in St. John's Wood, with their own small gardens, and bathrooms that were being constructed as separate rooms altogether.

Thus strengthened by his musings, Holmes dared to peek out the window of the cab again, only to notice a beggar with his hand out. The carriage was snarled in traffic, and Holmes could easily read the wretch's sign:

Former Sailer, Majesty's Fleat

If that is a former sailor, Holmes thought, *I am the King of England.* As if giving proof of what he had surmised, the old man spit deftly out of the wrong side of his mouth. *There you are, spitting to windward,* Holmes thought impatiently. *A thing no sailor on earth would ever do.*

But there it was, another shiver—as if that filthy creature were a harbinger of something, instead of some silliness he had spotted in the road.

The brougham began again and was making a bit of headway when, through the window, Holmes spied two funeral mutes standing sentry at the front door of a residence, dressed in black from head to toe. They stared straight ahead, holding brooms draped in black crepe, impassively silent, as they were paid to be. An expensive way to "announce" that someone in the home had died.

For the third time in that rather short trip, Holmes felt the now-familiar shiver travel down his back.

He shut the curtain impatiently. Then, when the carriage finally took a turn off Glamis Road in the East End, he suddenly felt more hearty, more like himself.

What in the world possessed me? he wondered.

And thank heavens it is done with!

6

GEORGIANA WAS JUST SETTING FOOT OUTSIDE AN OLD workhouse when Holmes's carriage pulled up. She was demurely dressed, with no elaborate overskirts or bustle. She wore only a simple little hat placed rather low on her forehead, hair piled up underneath, ringlets peeking out.

Holmes thought those blond ringlets were most becoming, as was the mauve shade of her frock and hat. As he stepped out of the cab, he eyed the mangy group of boys, aged twelve to fourteen, whom she had just finished tutoring, and who all looked adoringly upon her. And why wouldn't they? Teaching children to read, especially children such as these, was no easy task. The great majority already served as pauper apprentices to some overseer or another, and would never be required to read much more than their own indenture papers.

Yet Georgiana fervently believed that society could be better than it was, that the past did not have to define the future. Holmes was as delighted with the earnestness of her beliefs as with the exquisiteness of her face and silhouette— though he himself was uncertain that the world was likely to change much.

If at all.

As she laid her hand upon his arm, he could just detect, under the frilly sleeve of her blouse, the only visible symbol of her native homeland. It was a bracelet intertwined with red and black seeds. Even more noticeable, however, was the small but exquisitely cut diamond on her ring finger.

As he walked her to the waiting carriage, the boys called out "Evening, Miss Sutton!" in Cockney so thick it made his jaw ache to hear it. And they seemed thrilled down to their thrice-mended shoes when she waved and called back in kind.

Inside the cab, Georgiana leaned toward him and rested her hand gently on his bicep. He was immediately conscious of flexing that bicep, of the ridiculous longing to impress her with his sculpted physique—which to this point in his tenure on earth was more nature's endowment than his own doing, more the luck of the genetic draw.

Yet for all he possessed, from pleasing appearance to his acumen in worldly matters, he seemed forever at sixes and sevens when it came to Georgiana. Simply put, she unnerved him. And if a bit of bicep flexing could help equal the score, thus it would have to be.

"So. Eyes shining, distracted, either you've made a good bargain of something, my dear, or you're a bit in your cups," she said, appraising him.

"Well I… in truth, I won a nice little wager earlier this morning," he replied without mentioning the Armagnac. "But that was not what I was thinking at the moment." Then, because he couldn't very well confess that he'd been contemplating his bicep, he added, "I've just left my friend Cyrus Douglas."

"Oh, yes…?"

As he and Georgiana bounced lightly on the padded seat, Holmes tried to sum up Douglas's concerns, downplaying some of the more bizarre aspects of his tale, such as children's bodies drained of blood and left lifeless on the beach. But Georgiana honed in on the very portion he had chosen to brush past.

"Did you say there are *douen* involved?" she asked. "They are calling children to come out and play?" Her voice was entirely earnest.

"Well, yes…" Holmes admitted.

"You are saying that children have died?" she demanded in harsher tones. "Mycroft, please, I am aware of the culture, and I am not so very fragile—you cannot keep such things from me!"

"Well, yes," Holmes said again, "that is the rumor, but I hasten to repeat that it is *only*—"

"How many?" she said, interrupting him.

"How many children?" Holmes asked. "Well, three, but…"

Georgiana turned very pale. She seemed about to speak, but then covered her lips with her hand.

"Douglas has written to his suppliers," Holmes said, seeking to reassure her, "and he hopes to receive letters with further insight."

"Suppliers?" she asked. "You mean suppliers at various ports of call…?"

"Why yes, dearest, whatever else could I mean? I'd hoped that you had heard something that might put his mind at ease, as well, so he does not do as he has threatened, and make that wretched voyage back to Port of Spain."

Georgiana nodded, looked away, then back. She smiled weakly.

"Well, how… how very strange," she said. "Such turmoil, and no, I haven't heard a word!"

"Ah!" Holmes said, smiling. "And so whatever is taking place there, it cannot be as bad as all that."

"I wish it were that simple, my love," Georgiana responded, and his smile faded. "But Douglas's family and mine are on opposite ends of the island. Though Trinidad is small, and people inclined to talk, it is just as likely that the left hand, in this case, has no notion what the right is doing. I can only *hope* it is fuss over nothing…"

She seemed suddenly distracted, even a bit impatient.

"Oh, what a lot of traffic! Where are we headed, then?" she asked vaguely, glancing out.

It was to be a surprise, but the evening wasn't going as planned.

"A lovely little establishment with wonderful food but an unfortunate view," Holmes responded, "in that it catty-corners the Tower of London, and I am not the sort who appreciates gallows humor."

He expected Georgiana to laugh. Instead, she looked at him, quite pale, then glanced out the window again.

"Oh! How lovely the water looks," she said, "with the moonlight playing upon it. Would we be so desperately late if we were to get out and walk a bit?"

"My dear, you have lived in London four long years—does the Thames still charm you?" Holmes asked. The river was lined with wharves, and crammed with so many ships and boats and barges that the water itself seemed an afterthought. The city's commercial vigor could certainly be called impressive, but romantic it was not.

"And there's barely a moon at all," he added for good measure, "what with the fog rolling in. A week from now, nine days to be exact, it shall be full. Perhaps then we could—"

"My love," Georgiana interrupted tersely. "I could use a bit of *air.*"

They were still in a less-than-wholesome part of the city, nearing the decrepit Westminster Bridge. Holmes could smell coal fires, glue from a distant factory, even a brewery or two. He was about to counter that the air here was probably in short supply, but Georgiana looked very nearly done in, and in truth he could deny her nothing.

So he reluctantly called out through the trap door for the cabman to halt, hoping his now-grumbling stomach would wait without acrimony. The driver pushed the lever that released the doors, and Holmes held out his arm to help Georgiana down.

7

HOLMES AND GEORGIANA STROLLED ALONG THE riverbank. the fog lifted off the water, then rose to quickly obscure what little moonlight there was. He could feel Georgiana's pulse racing underneath his fingertips, as if he were holding a tiny bird in his hand.

She was quiet at first, confessing only to a sudden headache. But as they reached the yellow light of a gas lamp, she at last turned to him and, with haunted eyes, confessed.

"My parents *did* write me of mysterious disappearances. They are quite concerned…"

Holmes was taken aback. "But then why not tell me immediately, my love?"

"Because I assured them it was nothing," Georgiana declared, "for that is what I fervently hoped." Holmes watched as her tears fell. She looked so gloriously beautiful that it was all he could do to keep himself from kissing her that very moment.

"When you gave me the news," she went on, "it startled me. My mother is prone to mild histrionics, as I may've mentioned in the past, and so the hope did not seem unfounded. But surely Douglas is not given to flights of fancy, nor to groundless panic."

"No," Holmes acknowledged. "He is as steady a chap as can be."

"Yes," she said quietly. "He is that. So now I know what I must do."

"And what is that?" Holmes said, taking her hand and holding it to his chest.

"I must leave for home immediately!" she replied, staring into his eyes.

Holmes could not have been more shocked had she announced she was joining a nunnery.

"Home? You mean *Trinidad*?" he said. "But—"

"Oh, don't you see?" Georgiana said, interrupting him. "*I must.*" Without giving him a moment to respond, she snatched her hand away and waved for the carriage. "Cabbie!" she called out, and she hurried off.

Holmes ran after her and took hold of her arm.

"I do not understand any of this!" he cried.

"Mycroft, please," she protested. "Let me go."

Reluctantly, he released her arm, then followed mutely behind her as she reached the carriage. The driver dutifully released the lever and opened the doors, and she began to climb aboard. Then she turned back.

"Forgive me, my darling, I am quite resolute."

"Georgiana," Holmes said, "but what of your life here? What of your studies?" *What of me?* he wished to add, though he did not.

Georgiana smiled sadly. "Why, my love, have you not heard? 'Girls ought not study at all, for it leads to mental illness.'"

"Georgiana, if you are joking…" he replied.

"Yes, my dear," she said. "Yes, I am joking, but I am also in all earnestness. It is only a matter of a few orals before I finish. I have been faithful and diligent, surely Girton will allow latitude for a family emergency."

"Then I shall go with you," Holmes declared, stepping aboard.

"No." She laid a hand on his arm, on that same bicep that, moments before, he had been so proud to have her touch. "The people of Trinidad believe in demons and spirits," she said. "The world of the unseen. *Something* has shaken them! They will not talk of such things to most of our sort, but my family's workers have known me since birth, they *trust* me—and so may confide in me in a way that they cannot with others, even my parents.

"Your presence would do no good, and could actually do harm. Besides, this will allow me to speak to my father of our engagement. You know how I longed to do it in person, rather than by post."

"Yes, but to put yourself in harm's way…" he protested weakly.

"Mycroft, *please*." Georgiana seemed to be growing impatient with him. "I am simply going back to see my family to ascertain that all is well! Why, just this year, we women have been given the right to keep our own inherited property, and our own earnings. Surely we can be trusted to travel on our own accord."

"Let me at least accompany you back to your flat," Holmes offered helplessly as she recited her Hampstead address to the driver. But she shook her head.

"No," she replied. "No, I could not bear it. If you do

not leave now, I shall lose my nerve."

"Then I shall never leave," he said.

Georgiana kissed him lightly on the lips. Then she took a cameo brooch of herself from her purse and pressed it into his hand. It was small, carved in lava, and set in silver.

He stared at it as if he could not quite believe it was real.

"This was to be a surprise for you tonight, in honor of the one-year anniversary of our engagement," she murmured. "Now it shall be a keepsake 'til I see you again. You have the address of our plantation outside Port of Spain. You must promise to write to me each day without fail." With that, she turned. "Driver, go!"

Holmes dropped the cameo into his pocket and stumbled out of the carriage. He heard the cabman click his tongue, heard the wheels rumble, and then watched as the carriage followed the Thames for a few hundred yards before it turned a corner and was out of sight.

After that, if forced to do so, Holmes might have remembered hailing a second cab, this one unlicensed, for it was the first to come along. Of giving the soused and sour-smelling driver the address of Regent Tobaccos. Of alighting more or less in one piece at the destination, then walking inside.

In truth, he felt no part of his own well-ordered life until he found himself sitting in his favorite chair, where he finally felt comfort at the familiarity of it all.

It was half past seven. He heard Douglas announce to the Pennywhistles that they could end their shift a half-hour early. He saw Mrs. P. holding firmly onto Mr. P. so that his poor eyesight would not cause him to stumble into the furniture. The couple bid their goodnights and then strolled off arm in arm, Mrs. P. leaning into Mr. P. as if it were he who was forging the path for her, and not the other way round.

An old couple still in love, Holmes mused.

He watched Douglas as he waved goodbye, lowered the front door shade and flipped the "Open" sign to "Closed."

Given how poorly Holmes seemed to be faring, Douglas opened a bottle of Trinidad rum. While he swizzled it with syrup and Angostura bitters, he endured various permutations of "I cannot believe Georgiana would do something so foolhardy!" After that, he listened quietly as Holmes came up with a scheme that seemed every bit as foolhardy as anything Georgiana could possibly concoct.

"I shall go to Port of Spain, and you shall go with me," Holmes declared as if it were already a fait accompli. "I shall travel as a representative of the Secretary of State for War, and you shall be my trusted assistant."

"I shall be no such thing, Holmes," Douglas said aloud—though in his mind he was calculating how he could possibly leave his business for six weeks, to check on his family's well-being.

"What is it that I am drinking?" Holmes frowned mid-sip, though the glass was already half drained.

"Never you mind, it'll put some hair on your chest," Douglas replied. "Drink up."

Holmes peered down at it with distrust, but did just that.

"Give me your word that you shall think about it, at the least," he amended. "For I am resolute."

"And what of Cardwell? He has agreed?" Douglas asked, referring to Holmes's superior.

"He shall," Holmes thundered, "once I am done with him!"

Douglas sighed. "Very well, then. If you can persuade the Honorable Edward Cardwell, then you might be able to persuade me."

"That would be too easy a win," Holmes countered, "as you were already contemplating the journey."

"Yes," Douglas admitted, "but not with you. I have found that dragging a white man around Port of Spain tends to muck up the works."

"Not to worry, Douglas, there shall be no dragging involved," Holmes assured him. "I shall not embarrass you in the land of your birth." Then, smiling a little, he lifted a hand. "As a matter of fact, I give you my solemn promise as a gentleman that I shall pull my own weight every step of the way!"

Douglas briefly considered dissuading his friend. But he remembered all too clearly what it was like to be young and desperately in love—what that did to the mind and the soul. And because it was an unpleasant, even excruciating memory, Douglas decided to say nothing, though he sensed—as perhaps Holmes could not—that this particular adventure might not be destined to end at all well.

8

EDWARD CARDWELL DRUMMED HIS FINGERS IMPATIENTLY on his desktop and stared out the window of his Cumberland House office. Pall Mall was filled with people strolling by— the whole of the human race represented, it seemed, on this one street. He could hear the horses' hooves clopping along, and could see them toss their manes as if they knew that spring had finally come, even to London.

Yet here he was, in his large, musty office, waiting for a subordinate who'd failed to do his duty as required.

It was enough to make his digestion go sour.

As the Secretary of State for War, Cardwell had for the better part of a year now relied on his man Mycroft Holmes to bring in the morning's reports and to pinpoint the world's trouble spots with the deadly accuracy of a champion archer. And young Holmes, with his strange, steel-gray eyes and that shock of dark blond hair, was usually as punctual as the great clock of Westminster itself.

What in the world could be keeping him this morning?

Cardwell yawned, revealing several blue spots on his tongue. In truth, he hadn't eaten or slept well in three days, not since Oxford's unfortunate loss to the much inferior Cambridge. How on *earth* the Oxford crew could lose after nine solid years of wins, he had no notion, but it had injured his digestion all the same—even more than his assistant's tardiness.

Hellfire and damnation, Holmes…

He tapped the nub of his pen against his bottom teeth, and raked his other hand through his silver hair, which was already standing this way and that, as if a great wind had blown through it. He tugged at his fulsome muttonchops, fiddled with his speckled bow tie, cleared his throat, and tried to keep his growing temper in check.

Cardwell could bear many hardships, heaven only knew, but a change in schedule wasn't among them.

"*Holmes!*" he called out, full-voiced this time.

Holmes was bent over his desk, feverishly completing a chart. To his left was a window that overlooked Pall Mall. In front of him stood the closed door that led to Edward Cardwell's spacious but rather dreary office, and hovering nervously above him was Cardwell's junior clerk and errand boy, seventeen-year-old Charles Parfitt.

He could feel Parfitt's eyes on his back, could hear, by the boy's breathing, that his mouth was slightly agape.

If not quite a friend, Parfitt was Holmes's ally. It was Holmes who had secured him the post to begin with, thanks to the prompting—one might say the goading—of Holmes's landlady, Mrs. Hudson. For Parfitt was Mrs. Hudson's nephew, one of a baker's dozen all birthed by one sister and "her no-'count souse of a husband," to use Mrs. Hudson's own words. Thus, when Cardwell had expressed the need for an errand boy and junior clerk, Holmes had placed Parfitt's query at the top of the pile.

What was more, Holmes had neatly cured Parfitt of his stammer. When Parfitt had first come aboard, the entire office would hear Cardwell thunder, "Get *on* with it, man!" each time the lad was in the inner sanctum. Holmes had taught Parfitt to picture the words in his head before saying them, thus lessening the stammer.

He had even prescribed the calendula oil mixed with sandalwood that had brought his skin eruptions to heel. Parfitt proved to be quite the passable-looking young chap, once his skin condition cleared up.

The diminutive clerk returned the favor by being bright and eager to learn. He made it a habit to read through some of the more tedious correspondence that came into the office, then pass on to Holmes only what was pertinent. Parfitt proved himself to possess a keen nose for chicanery. Under more felicitous circumstances, Holmes was certain that he would have made a good magistrate.

As it was, he was the only one of thirteen siblings to be employed at all, and he owed it all to Holmes.

"Mr. Holmes, *please…*" Parfitt begged with an anxious whisper.

"Do you have the research on Trinidad I asked for?" Holmes muttered, looking up. The lad nodded and handed Holmes a sheaf of papers.

"Holmes!" the unseen Cardwell thundered, this time to the sound of his fist smashing onto his desk. It was the sound Holmes had been waiting for. He had set Edward Cardwell to simmering, and now the man was at a full boil.

So he put the finishing touches on his chart, rose from his desk, and followed young Parfitt into the inner sanctum.

"Terribly sorry for Oxford's loss, sir," Holmes said the moment he stepped through the door, thus effectively establishing the subject while giving Cardwell the first jab of pain meant to unsettle him further.

Cardwell blinked away surprise, then his sorrow.

"Injured my digestion for a full day and a half, I guarantee it," he replied. "You do not follow crew, I take it?"

"Not really, sir, no," Holmes responded. "But the news is everywhere."

It is not a complete lie, he reasoned. Then he stood there, fumbling through the sheaves of paper in his hand, allowing Cardwell plenty of time to grow impatient yet again.

"*Well,* Holmes?" the man demanded.

"Yessir?" Holmes blinked at him innocently.

Cardwell sighed. "Holmes. Are you quite with us? Have you given further thought to our discussion of yesterday afternoon?"

"Oh that, sir. Yes, sir, I have," Holmes said. "But I must point out that you have already made such wonderful strides in this arena. You have abolished flogging the soldiers, you have abolished the receiving of bounty money for recruits, surely no one can expect more from you than—"

"Nonsense!" Cardwell rose to his feet, planted his hands on his desk and leaned over it, the better to be heard—though Holmes assumed he could be heard perfectly well the entire length and breadth of Pall Mall. "It is unreasonable for men to serve, with no notion into whose regiment they are going, or into what county or district," he asserted. "To be away from their homes, family, and friends for *years* at a time. And to be horsewhipped for good measure.

"No! It will not do," he continued. "And what's more, I am the only one at liberty to say what is enough and what isn't, and I shall not be satisfied until we alter general military service inside of this calendar year. All I ask of you is an idea—a small notion—as to how we might bring this about.

"Would that be too much to ask?"

"Yes, sir," Holmes responded. "I mean no, sir, it is not, which is why I took it upon myself to… well if you'll permit me, this might be what you would propose." With that, Holmes handed Cardwell the chart he held in his hands.

"What's this, then?" the older man asked, picking up his spectacles from his desk and peering through them.

Holmes explained what Cardwell could see with his own two magnified eyes.

"By utilizing county boundaries and population density," Holmes said, "I have divided Great Britain into sixty-six brigade districts. Every line-infantry regiment would become two separate battalions. These two battalions would share a depot and a recruiting area. Then, while one battalion serves overseas, the other remains in country to train. If the area is populous enough, we could form a third battalion—a militia, if you will…"

"A militia?"

"Yes, sir."

Cardwell stared down at the chart in wonder.

"How long have you been toiling at this, Holmes?" Cardwell asked, his voice suddenly small.

"A while now, sir. Since early morning, I'd say."

"Since early... *morning?*" Cardwell repeated. "You are referring to *this* morning?"

"Yes, sir."

"I see. Well, I... I will have to give it some real consideration, Holmes. Some real consideration indeed. You may have just propelled the military, lock, stock, and barrel, into the next century. I must say that I am... impressed."

"Thank you, sir."

Holmes did not depart.

"Is there anything else?" Cardwell inquired.

Holmes nodded. "Yes, sir," he said. "There seems to be a looming storm in Trinidad."

"A what?"

"Looming storm, sir. In Trinidad. Port of Spain, specifically. The emerging Negro middle class seems to be articulating a national ideology, just as *we* are promoting the indenture of Indian workers."

"Bloody bad timing, that," Cardwell grunted as he sat down again, though his eyes were fully on the chart.

"Yes, sir. And with the Indian population on the island now hovering at twenty-five percent, plus new immigrants from China, the white minority is becoming quite jittery."

"An incipient revolt waiting to happen, you think?"

"Possibly. Now they—the white minority, that is—are divided among English Creole, faithful to the Crown, and French Creole, who might begin to question why they should be subject to a British queen at all."

"There you are! Did I not say an incipient revolt waiting to happen?"

"Yes, sir, you most certainly did." Holmes watched Cardwell rise to his feet once again, only this time he began to pace, one fist in his hair, the other rubbing at his muttonchops.

"We must nip this in the bud, Holmes. The last thing we need is another West Indies Federation on our hands— four million people suddenly deciding they are no longer subjects of Her Majesty. Or Jamaica, five years back. How many rebels did we have to execute?"

"Four hundred, sir."

"An excessive use of force," Cardwell said solemnly. "Still, the Crown *must* preserve its territories."

"Yes, sir." Holmes knew that he had to tread carefully with this next move, as its only relevance was to push Cardwell further into high dudgeon. "And of course, with that French Creole problem in Trinidad," he said, "should France spar with Prussia and prevail…"

Cardwell's great eyebrows shot up nearly to meet his hairline.

"France! Over *Prussia*?" he cried.

"I only mention the remote possibility of—"

"Never, sir. *Never!* 'Though on the face of it, Britain must remain neutral, I for one shall not lose a wink of sleep if noble, patient, deep, pious, solid Germany should weld itself into a nation over the objections of vaporing, vainglorious, gesticulating, quarrelsome, and oversensitive France.'"

Cardwell, done with quoting Scottish philosopher

Thomas Carlyle, stared daggers into Holmes, as if daring him to continue.

"What I am suggesting, sir," Holmes began, looking properly chastised, "is a diplomatic scout-about to Port of Spain. A steamship leaves the day after tomorrow. Perhaps someone could…"

"No, no, no—not 'someone,' Holmes," Cardwell said. "This requires delicacy. Tact. Who governs Trinidad at the moment?"

Holmes consulted his documents, though he had no need to.

"Baron Stanmore, Sir Arthur Charles Hamilton-Gordon," he said.

"Hmm. Name sounds familiar. Oxford man?"

"A Cantabrigian."

"Ah. As are you, Holmes. I know now whom to send." And just like that, Cardwell was seated again, pen in mouth, tapping his teeth, scattering blue blotches. "You shall travel as my secretary, of course. That should provide you cachet. And do take along a valet of some sort, courtesy of this office."

As Cardwell bent over his work, Holmes smiled to himself.

"Oh, and I shall importune my dear friend Sir James Clark to give you a thorough going over," Cardwell muttered as he wrote. "Physician to Prince Albert and all that, retired now."

"Too kind, sir," Holmes protested. "But…"

"Tut, Holmes. As a representative of Her Majesty's Government, we cannot have you traipsing about in ill health."

Holmes's smile disappeared.

Moments later he hurried out of Cardwell's office, and almost immediately encountered Parfitt. The boy's eyes were wider than ever.

"Is there anything I can do for you, Mr. Holmes?" Parfitt inquired.

You can learn to exhale through your nose, Holmes thought crossly. But what he said was, "No, Parfitt. That is, yes. I shall be leaving for Port of Spain the day after tomorrow. Kindly make the necessary arrangements on the West India and Pacific Steamship line bound for Barbados. Do not put me 'tween decks, for pity's sake, but take care that the cabin is economically priced. No view, nothing fancy, room for two.

"Oh, and there's this," Holmes said as he handed back the research on Trinidad. "One item I found puzzling. Has to do with large sums of money making their way from Luxembourg to Jamaica via Colonial Bank, an adjunct of the Bank of England."

"Yes," the boy said, "I noticed it too. Did look a bit odd."

"Well, there's no need to make anything more of it, Parfitt. It's no doubt the usual corruption. Nothing obvious, and nothing much to be done about it. But we don't want to be caught off guard at a time of incipient war."

"No, sir, we do not," the boy agreed solemnly.

"If anything should be amiss, send word to me via the post in Port of Spain."

"Yessir, Mr. Holmes," the boy said.

"Oh, and would you be so kind as to see after my horse? You may of course ride him…"

"Yessir, Mr. Holmes," Parfitt said with a huge grin. "I would be delighted, sir!"

"Well, pray don't run him into the ground, Parfitt."

"Of c-course I shall n-not," the boy stammered nervously, but Holmes was no longer paying attention.

I shall have to purchase a third topcoat in as many weeks, Holmes thought sourly, *one light enough for the tropics.*

And just in case anything happens to me, he continued to himself, *I should probably go round and say goodbye to Sherlock.*

But first, he amended, *that* blasted *physician…*

Clark's examination room was off the main parlor of an old edifice on Borough High Street. It boasted the frilly architecture meant to suggest the Italian Renaissance, but it was so faded—and its masonry so crumbled—that it looked more like a layer cake left in the sun too long.

Holmes followed a housemaid, who looked nearly as ancient as her surroundings, down a decrepit hall. He had to open his eyes wide to take in what little light could be had. She led him into the examining room and left with a grunt, as if he had importuned her somehow.

Everywhere he looked, boxes of surgical instruments were open and had been left untouched for so long that dust had settled upon them like the sprinkling of some inferior grade of flour. Lining the shelves were moth-eaten books, along with rows upon rows of jars, many with something or other floating within. Even his quick eye and sharp brain couldn't discern what those uniformly gray masses were or might be.

Sir James Clark—ninety if he was a day, stethoscope in hand—toddled in. With no word of greeting, he set off to explore Holmes's chest, all the while wheezing in a most unpleasant manner, then stared at Holmes accusingly with his cloudy blue eyes.

"Did you have rheumatic fever as a child?" he asked.

"Aged three," Holmes replied. "Why?"

"Your heart is not the better for it." Clark placed the stethoscope in another spot and listened more closely. "Not a pleasant sound at all—like water sloshing in there, Mr. Holmes." He straightened up with some difficulty. "And you say you are going where?"

"Trinidad," Holmes replied. "Port of Spain."

The physician leaned closer, holding up the stethoscope next to Holmes's lips. "Once again!"

"Trinidad!" Holmes said into the stethoscope.

The physician recoiled as if he had been struck.

"Nonsense!" he cried. "That will not do at all. You must avoid uncivilized places as if your very life depended on it.

"For it does!" he added.

Yet Holmes would not give in. He promised to take every precaution, and accepted Dr. Clark's quinine compound as a prophylaxis—if not Dr. Clark's offer to inject it right then and there, for the physician's hands were trembling so that he could have been put to work churning butter. Then he bid the good doctor a hasty adieu, sprinted back outside into the sunshine with an overly dramatic sigh, and rode on to Westminster to say hello and goodbye to his brother Sherlock.

9

HOLMES TIED ABIE ALONGSIDE OTHER HORSES LINED UP in the shadow of Westminster Abbey. From there, he crossed the lawn toward the Royal College of St. Peter, where Sherlock was to graduate in a year or so—at least, that was the hope. He was an indifferent student, which aggrieved his brother no end.

It was stunning how dissimilar two brothers could be.

Holmes resembled their mother, with her strange grey eyes and spun gold hair, whereas Sherlock took after their father, all dark lines and angles, as if he were a Gothic building that, while handsome enough, had a few joints out of alignment.

Holmes had embarked upon a civil career because he wanted to be of service to Queen and country, whereas Sherlock had no such notions. He was, Holmes thought with aggrieved affection, one of the most singularly self-centered individuals anyone could ever meet. And while Holmes had been a Queen's Scholar and was popular with fellow students, Sherlock had few friends—perhaps none at all.

The sole advantage of this last was that Sherlock could always be reliably located in one of three places: the dormitory, for no other boy would be caught dead in such a dank and humid place unless a blizzard threatened; the theater, where Sherlock was sure to be positioned at the back of the auditorium, carefully observing the activities upon stage; or the library, his nose pressed into a book that never had anything to do with his studies.

Holmes settled upon the library, and was successful upon his first try.

There he was, his long, angular face obscured by James Cowles Prichard's *Researches into the Physical History of Man*. His spider-like fingers were turning the pages gently but swiftly, as if he were absorbing the information, and not merely reading it. Holmes knew that the click of his steps across the marble floor would make no difference to Sherlock—and indeed, he didn't even glance up.

"Sherlock," Holmes said when he finally stood just inches away from his brother.

He looked up with an expression as casual as if they'd only seen each other minutes before, rather than weeks.

"It's fascinating," Sherlock said, nodding to the book in his hand.

"Yes," Holmes responded. "I read it years ago." For that was how the brothers greeted each other, eschewing hellos.

"*Naturally* you did," Sherlock countered. "When one has a seven years' advantage from birth, it is not a fair fight now, is it? You will therefore recall Prichard's theory of moral insanity. He posits that there are some human beings devoid of the common thread of human decency. I posit that our mother might be one of them."

"And I posit that you might be another," Holmes replied, taking a seat across from him. "The question remains as to why you are reading Prichard. Something propelled you to investigate moral insanity. What was it?"

"William Sheward is *torturing* me," his brother exclaimed dramatically. "That fifty-seven-year-old tailor who sliced his wife's throat with a straight razor, cut her up into manageable chunks, boiled the pieces, then scattered them all over Norwich... a thumb here, a foot there, her entrails clogging up some poor innocent's drain. And of course they never did manage to locate her head..."

"Why the gruesome and the macabre fascinates you so, I cannot fathom," Holmes interjected. He had heard of the story, of course—everyone had, as it was strange indeed. The murder had occurred some eighteen years back, and the man had escaped punishment. In subsequent years he'd not only remarried, but had become the proprietor of the Key and Castle Public House in Norwich.

In spite of that, on the first of January, 1869, he'd walked into a London police station, confessed to the murder of his first wife, and had promptly been hanged for his trouble.

Sherlock leaned across the table. "If there is moral insanity," he said in a conspiratorial whisper, "then there may be the reverse, a moral sanity, if you will, that comes upon one suddenly, like a fever. In thrall to this moral sanity, Sheward may have been compelled to come clean. It was, after all, the first of the year—a time for resolutions and whatnot. Later, when the fever passed, he tried to recant, but by then it was too late."

"You look a mite feverish yourself. Do you really believe that?" Holmes asked, smiling.

"Of course not, it's perfectly daft," Sherlock responded sourly. "Nonetheless, the facts of the case are even more absurd than my theory. I've been wracking my brain, trying to conjure up a reason for his behavior."

"Well, you've been wracking it too thoroughly," Holmes said. "Think more simply. What grieved him? What prompted arguments with his wife? It was in the papers…"

Sherlock shrugged. "What prompts most arguments amongst couples? Money."

"Yes. But you dismissed that clue out of hand, because you yourself dismiss money as beneath you. You allowed your feelings to get in the way of your deductions."

"I did no such thing…" Sherlock protested, but his tone betrayed him.

"And the time of year?" Holmes went on. "What of that? Once again you dismissed a clue because you are not fond of holidays and celebrations."

Holmes watched his brother's face and could almost see the gears in his brain turning.

Sherlock's eyes opened wide.

"The Key and Castle!" he exclaimed. "Perhaps it was undergoing financial difficulties… Perhaps their New Year's Eve was not up to snuff, did not meet expectations…"

Holmes nodded his encouragement. "Go on," he said.

Sherlock did so, his excitement building.

"He was now remarried," he said, "and found himself

in the same situation again, bickering with the wife over money. He'd had too much to drink the night before—perhaps had been drinking all night. He knew perfectly well what he was capable of, yet perhaps he loved her and did not want her to meet the same end as her predecessor. With age comes regret, and he was older and wiser.

"So, in order to stop himself from doing her great bodily injury, he confessed... and then he sobered up! Once again in control of his faculties, he tried to take it back, but it was too late."

He stood up, very nearly vibrating with energy. "All I need do is make a quick trip to Norwich and ascertain how the business was faring a year back," he continued. "Interrogate the wife about whatever bickering they did—"

"Though I am certain she would love nothing more," Holmes interrupted, "you have your studies to think of."

Sherlock frowned, sat down again, and fell into a sullen silence.

"But before you get on with that," Holmes added, "how about a nice round of boxing? It'll put some color in those sallow cheeks." Sherlock didn't look any happier at the prospect. If anything, he looked less pleased.

"Have you not read, dear brother," he said in that slightly annoyed cant that he always affected, "that 'bodily exercise profiteth little'?" Nevertheless, he shut the book with a definitive *clap* and stood to depart without protest.

Holmes smiled.

Sherlock was rarely so amenable.

I have had an impact on him, he thought, secretly pleased.

* * *

The two brothers faced each other within a rectangle of ropes set up on the main floor. Their hands were wrapped in strips of leather so musty that they threatened to turn to dust.

"Hands high," Holmes commanded. "Elbows low, head moving. And for pity's sake, chin down!"

As if to emphasize his point, he thwacked Sherlock on the jaw.

Sherlock put his chin down but continued to study his brother, as he had been doing since they'd first entered the gym.

"And now that you have solved my riddle," he said, "I think it only fair that I solve yours."

"And what riddle might that be?" Holmes asked.

"What, pray, is that fervor in your eyes?" Sherlock demanded. "Surely it's not simply from buffeting me about. Is it some intrigue or other that disquiets you? Perhaps an undertaking having to do with human suffering, along with the possibility of circumventing it? If so, it would be the least inspiring subject I could imagine…"

"Speak less, box more," Holmes said.

"…which leads me to assume that Georgiana has something to do with it. Did you not announce, some months back, that you are beginning to look at social inequities not as curiosities to be catalogued, but as wrongs to be righted?"

"It's true," Holmes said evenly. "I do owe that to Georgiana."

"She has made you *weak*, brother mine," Sherlock sneered.

Why, you ungrateful ninny! Holmes thought. *Here, I solve your insipid crime, and you insult me?* He jabbed his brother a bit too hard on his exposed septum. Sherlock flinched—but was on the scent and would not be deterred, even by a cuff to the nose.

"Yes, perhaps it is love that… *aha!* You see there? You pursed your lips! As if not wanting some secret to escape."

"I pursed my lips because I would like you to shut up and box," Holmes said dourly.

"Nonsense, you are disquieted," Sherlock shot back. "Discomfited. Why, I would even go so far as to say that this secret distresses you."

"Rather than alliterate, kindly practice turning your body *into* the punch, not away."

"I am turning away so you do not hit me!" Sherlock protested. Still, he was not about to let it go. "Wait," he mused. "Has something gone awry with the sainted Georgiana?"

With that, Sherlock began to hum "La Donna è Mobile" from *Rigoletto*. Holmes was familiar with the opera, and knew precisely what Sherlock was inferring.

And he didn't like it one bit.

"You *must* use height and reach to your advantage," he said in a vain attempt to take control of the subject. "Utilize your entire body, not just your arm. Like this!" He demonstrated, catching Sherlock in the ribcage. The boy expelled his breath, but was again undeterred.

"Yes!" he gasped. "The problem is with Georgiana. Perhaps one of her street urchins is in mortal danger. Forced to use a present negative subjunctive when a plain old subjunctive would do!"

"You are insufferable."

"So I've been told," Sherlock said, "more times than I care to recall. Though I do, unhappily, recall each time."

"Short uppercuts and hooks, short rights, *long* jabs," Holmes said, trying to keep the conversation on track. "Not short jabs—and long everything else!"

"Tell me, Mycroft, why'd you appear today? Surely not for a boxing lesson. And why did you comment, as we strolled here, that you shall be 'frightfully busy this summer,' when I have not seen you in weeks? June, July, and August could easily slip by without my noticing your absence. What need would there be to announce it?"

"Curiosity is a good thing," Holmes countered. "Pray be judicious about it, and not simply sarcastic. And breathe *out* when you punch. Eye your target. Chin *down!*" Holmes tapped Sherlock a little harder than necessary on his jutting chin, and Sherlock once again lowered it.

"Let us not forget that I am not, like you, ambidextrous," Sherlock said.

"Not naturally, no," Holmes said. "But you can practice to become so."

"If that is an attempt to sidetrack me, it will not work. Summer is a slow season for the War Office, as even subversives need a respite now and again. Odds are, you won't be 'frightfully busy' at all. So why say it, other than to excuse a long absence? Or to draw attention to it."

"Nicely done," Holmes admitted, though he sighed to himself. Why had he always been so keen on helping his brother develop his observational skills when he wasn't at all certain that Sherlock would use them wisely?

Because his mind is a Stradivarius, he quietly reminded himself. *He simply needs to pick it up and learn how to play it.*

"Now, think of everything," Holmes said. "Odors, clothing, carriage… good God, why are your eyes darting about? I meant *my* carriage, Sherlock, how I comport myself. For pity's sakes, keep focused!"

"Odors, yes," Sherlock mused, sniffing the air. "Formaldehyde. Either you've been pickling mice, dear brother, or you've had a visit with a physician. You are hale, I take it?"

"Never better," Holmes responded tightly. "What else?"

"Your hair smells faintly of tobacco. Or, rather tobaccos—surely more than can be smoked by one man, even you. Most likely that means long hours at the tobacconist, scheming something up. With your friend Douglas, or someone else?"

"I shall concede Douglas," Holmes admitted. "Now put it together."

Sherlock frowned, a movement that caused his nose to drop down toward his lips so that he looked like a perturbed hawk. "It's not very sportsmanlike, this game you have played with me since I was a child," he protested, "as you already know the answer."

When Holmes did not reply, Sherlock's frown deepened.

"Mycroft, can you not simply *tell* me?"

"Oh, for the love of heaven, don't stand around *waiting* for me to hit you. Throw something, even if it does not land. And no, I will not 'simply tell you.' You need to work it out."

Sherlock began to flail about, with little conviction.

"Very well," he said. "In truth, you seem out of sorts. Sad, as if you've lost your wallet. No, not your wallet, something closer to your heart, although I strain to imagine what that could be, if not your wallet. And that new traveling coat," he added, pointing his very vulnerable chin in the direction of the hook on which the coat now hung. "Dull but practical—bargain-priced, no doubt, light enough for the tropics.

"The tropics… Wait. *There* is something! The tropics, and Douglas, whose origins are in Trinidad. And… given Georgiana's family background—yes! Something's afoot in Trinidad, and that is precisely where you are heading. Mycroft, you have come to say goodbye!"

Just as Holmes swung, Sherlock lowered his guard. Holmes tried, but could not pull his punch in time. He hit his brother squarely in the nose. Sherlock buckled to his knees, and though he arose quickly enough, he was bleeding profusely.

This was not the impact I had in mind, thought Holmes. He quickly unwrapped his hands, then reached into his pocket for a kerchief, which he proffered.

"Chin up," Holmes instructed. "Chin up!"

"Chin down, chin up… kindly make a decision," Sherlock snuffled crossly as he held the kerchief to his nose.

The boxing lesson thus terminated, the brothers walked across the main square to a cavernous dormitory that held 150 beds. Holmes could tell immediately which was his brother's by the mess around it, as if someone had tidied the entire quarters to a fare-thee-well, but had forgotten one small spot for a decade… or perhaps three.

"The headmaster makes no mention of this?" Holmes asked, staring askance at the piles of papers, books, and curios jumbled there.

"Well, naturally he does," Sherlock said. "Westminster holds thrice-weekly inspections—has done so for some centuries now, I believe."

"Well then…?"

"This is all new, d'you see. I have added to it only since last night."

"Cleanliness is next to godliness…" Holmes began, but Sherlock wasn't paying him any mind. He had somehow located his tin of shag tobacco, and was rolling himself a cigarette.

"You did well, by the way," Holmes said. "Not with the boxing, perhaps, but with the deductions. I must admit I was impressed."

Sherlock lit the cigarette and exhaled a cloud of acrid smoke. "And what, in your estimation, am I to accomplish with such gifts? Eh? Become a detective? An Inspector Bucket? Is that how you perceive me, dear brother?"

"If you refuse to take a compliment—" Holmes began, but Sherlock interrupted.

"I have no qualms with compliments, when I hear them. That was not one."

Cigarette in hand, he dove into various piles of detritus, avidly searching for who-knew-what.

Glancing about, Holmes spotted a document that stood out from the rest, and lifted it up. The pages were so yellowed and stained, the text so faded, that the only thing he could even make out was the Latin phrase, *nullius in verba*. Roughly translated, it meant "Take no one's word for it."

He was about to dispose of it in a proper trash bin when Sherlock prevented him.

"Halt!" he cried. "I might need that."

"Need it? You can't even *read* it!"

"Precisely," Sherlock said. "I thought I might experiment with different ointments and tinctures to see if I could bring up the ink again… aha!" This last came as Sherlock dug into a mound with intent, and pulled out a fine old walking stick.

Holmes stared at it. "Father's walking stick!" he said, trying to keep the accusation from his voice.

"Correct," Sherlock said. "Mother is ill again—'medicated' is the genteel term, I believe—and Father is avidly ignoring it. This," he said, indicating the walking stick, "is his appeasement, for want of a proper wife."

"Be quiet," Holmes countered quietly. "She *is* our mother."

"On occasion, yes," he shrugged. "Then there are the more frequent occasions when she is nothing of the kind. Though she *has* taken to heating the mixture herself—I am told that cooking reveals a maternal instinct, of sorts."

With that, Sherlock tossed the stick to his brother, who caught it on the fly.

"Bon voyage, brother!"

Holmes shook his head no. "Father gave it to you. Taking it is the last thing I would want."

"Nonsense. The last thing you would want is to lose a limb, or to perish in some freakish manner in a foreign land where hospitals are appallingly ill-equipped."

Holmes sighed, silently conceding the point. In truth, he didn't want the blasted thing at all. He considered it cumbersome, if not downright pretentious. On the other hand, it was a touching gesture by a younger brother from whom touching gestures were all but unheard of. And so he accepted it graciously.

"Thank you," he said with a slight bow.

"In exchange," Sherlock continued, "you shall endeavor to keep a mental record of your adventures. Mind, however, that it slant toward individual peccadilloes, and not some larger 'view of humanity.' Or, God help us, political intrigue, governments falling—that sort of thing.

"As to my walking stick," he added as his brother made ready to depart, "it is to be returned to me in one piece. As are you yourself, of course," he added.

Well, mused Holmes, as he shut the door behind him. *Though my well-being was most definitely an afterthought, he spoke of it, nonetheless. It is progress!*

It seemed a most agreeable start to his journey.

10

WAITING AT THE LIVERPOOL DOCKS WAS THE *SULTANA*. the 3,500-ton steamer boasted three masts and an iron hull, and could accommodate 200 first- and second-class passengers, with another thousand shoehorned into third class. She was agile, able to reach speeds of thirteen knots, and was "majestic in countenance"—or so claimed the advertising graphic clutched in Holmes's hand.

Now that he was actually about to board, he had to admit that the plaudits seemed accurate enough.

> She is built to impress, from the height, thickness and strength of the bulwarks; to the heavy wheels and pinions connecting it to its steam-power; to the immense blocks and tackles hooked to the rigging; to the vast efficiency and force with which the passengers' heavy trunks are run up by machinery into the air, and then lowered rapidly into the hold.

When he showed the advertising brochure to Douglas, the latter laughed and reminded Holmes of the points it failed to mention. Somewhere below decks and hidden from view, stokers known as the black gang—aptly named for the color they quickly assumed—would be shoveling a backbreaking five hundred tons of coal per day to keep the ship moving at a steady clip. The black gang consisted of trimmers, who shifted the coal, coal-passers, who carted it in huge barrels to the boilers, and firemen, so called because they tended and stoked the furnaces.

"Hell hath no fires that burn hotter than those," Douglas proclaimed.

Upon the deck itself, a bit of the heat might have been welcome. The morning was overcast and cold, with a pervasive mist that—especially in late spring—often gave Liverpool its slightly yellow hue.

The dense fog obscured a great crush of strangers from all parts of England, from the very rich to those so poor that they carried everything on their backs, including bedding. There would be no comfortable bunks to be found for the third class, also known as "'tween decks." Indeed, between those decks they would be entombed for eight long days, with no light and precious little air.

Holmes easily spotted the dreamers among them, the ones with a bit of light still in their eyes. The ones who dared to hope that their children, or their children's children, might someday join the ranks of the burgeoning professional class—physicians and barristers, owners of businesses, perhaps even what Holmes himself had become: a civil servant on his way to a political career.

For many, their hopes were buoyed by the Prime Minister himself. William Ewart Gladstone was a non-aristocrat like them. The fact that he was a millionaire many times over, with massive holdings of land, did not quench the pride with which the "common folk" clutched him to their proverbial bosoms. Like Georgiana, those poor wretches were certain that progress was just around the corner.

Holmes wished with all his heart that he could believe as they did. But a war was looming. And war rarely did the poor any favors.

The captain of the *Sultana*, James Miles, walked past Holmes and Douglas as he hurried aboard. He sparkled in his uniform and wore very well his other emblems of authority, including side whiskers so fulsome that they would have made Edward Cardwell weep with envy. As he went, all eyes were upon him, for twelve hundred passengers relied on him to get them through gales and mists, past treacherous tides and small islands of floating ice, safely to their destination.

As the fog grew thicker and more pronounced, guards took their positions at the hatchways and companionways and spoke ominously of heavy waves that would soon be crashing over these pristine decks. As if on cue, a great bell sounded and the steward cried out.

"All ashore!"

This prompted another jostling and unsettling of the great throng as non-passengers said their final goodbyes, then hurried off the ship across the heavy bridge that connected the *Sultana* to the pier.

A second bell sounded, and the massive engine came alive. Water at the stern suddenly became a whirlpool of boiling surges as the vessel slowly moved away from the pier. As she picked up speed, and the city and its waving denizens became smaller and smaller, everyone aboard felt the thrill of knowing that they were at long last underway.

Some passengers hurried to secure seats on the promenade deck, where they would wrap themselves in blankets for warmth and watch the shoreline recede. Others strolled to their staterooms to unpack and relax in peace. The poorest of the poor scrambled down the rough-hewn wooden ladders to steerage, to claim the hard wooden planks on which they would sleep—the only alternative being the harder deck.

Holmes and Douglas moved through and past the throng, searching for the one passenger who had set this entire adventure into motion. From the moment they'd arrived—more than three hours before—Holmes had been craning his neck, hoping to spot Georgiana. The bouquet of irises and yellow roses that he'd purchased from a street vendor had by now been crushed so assiduously by strangers that it looked every bit as crestfallen as he felt. He found himself growing so desperate, in fact, that if he could have climbed upon Douglas's shoulders to have a better look round, he surely would.

As the two men kept up their vigil, a handsome but severe-looking man in his mid-thirties with light brown hair, a neat handlebar mustache, and rather intense hazel eyes, took particular note of them.

Then he melted into the crowd.

Douglas and Holmes both caught a glimpse of him, but as they could think of no particular reason why someone should be observing them, they granted him only a curious glance. Then, when he disappeared, they thought no more about it.

Douglas, in his usual guise of valet, was handling Holmes's bags along with his own. As a result, he would have loved nothing better than to locate their cabin and put them down at last, but Holmes insisted they first go to the steward's office. Since he understood Holmes's anxiety, Douglas acceded to the request.

Armed with his credentials, Holmes demanded to see the passenger list, adopting a tone that said he would countenance no response but the affirmative. When the steward quickly complied, Holmes ran his finger down the pages filled with names.

"Sutton… Sutton…"

Searching for Georgiana was no easy task. There were hundreds of passengers aboard. As was standard, the list had been compiled, not in alphabetical order, but in order of boarding, with extended families at times grouped together under various surnames.

Douglas helpfully pointed out a Sutton that Holmes had missed.

"That is a *Sully* Sutton, aged fifty-five," Holmes grumbled.

"Could the person you are seeking have boarded an earlier ship?" the steward inquired meekly.

"The last ship to depart for Trinidad was three weeks ago," Holmes snapped. "Don't be absurd!" At which point the steward found something else that demanded his immediate attention, while Douglas quietly proposed a different explanation.

"Perhaps she changed her mind," he offered, "and had

no manner of contacting you."

"Nonsense, Douglas," Holmes muttered. "She is quite resourceful. Had she wished to get a message to me, she would have done so."

"Resourceful or not," Douglas replied, "she is most certainly not aboard."

Holmes stared at the list, very nearly undone.

As they walked out of the steward's office, he looked toward the strip of land that seemed now so thin that it might have been the paring of a fingernail.

"What now?" he asked of no one in particular.

Before Douglas could reply, a gaunt woman dressed all in black came rolling toward them. Deathly pale, she rode in a rickshaw-like wheelchair, supported by pillows and attended to by an Indian maid, and was looking around languorously. As she glided past, her eyes fell upon Holmes, and she smiled a hello.

But when she caught a glimpse of Douglas, she reared back as if he might take it into his ebony head to abuse her, there and then. She clutched possessively at a plum-sized black pendant that hung about her neck.

Douglas ignored the insult and would have walked on, but Holmes was in no such mood.

"He is not interested in your jewel, madam," Holmes said scornfully. "He has two of his own—larger, I am sure, and much more dear to him!"

The old woman looked shocked, while behind her the Indian attendant struggled not to smile.

"You *cannot* say such things to an elderly woman," Douglas hissed as they continued on their way.

"She deserves no special consideration," Holmes replied crossly. "She's the sort who finds *Oliver Twist* seditious. I will not allow you to be abused by someone like that."

"Please allow *me* to decide when I shall be abused," Douglas retorted, "and by whom. And the next time you wish to berate someone in public, kindly leave my 'jewels' out of it. Now, may we please find our cabin and be rid of these bags?"

"One more detour, Douglas, I beg of you."

"Holmes, she is not here!"

"Perhaps she is traveling under an assumed name…"

"An assumed name? For what reason?"

Holmes could think of none. Yet he would not be deterred. He was so agitated, while at the same time bullish about their mission, that Douglas simply sighed and followed him—bags still in hand—to the grand saloon.

11

THE GRAND SALOON, SET APART FOR FIRST- AND SECOND-
class passengers, was neither grand, nor was it a saloon in the
traditional sense. It was a large, plain room with walls covered
in cedarwood, a dozen long cypress tables in the center, three
beds on wheels in one far corner, and four large gas lamps
that hung from the ceiling, as the room let in little natural
light. Its plainness was by design, as it was meant to serve a
variety of functions: parlor, study, dining hall, drawing room,
and even—should it prove necessary—invalid chamber. All
around it were ventilated doors that opened onto the nicest
staterooms, so that the passengers therein could have the
luxury of going directly from their cabins into the saloon
without having to set foot outdoors.

When Holmes and Douglas walked in, ladies and
gentlemen were already selecting their preferred places at
the long dining table in the center, pinning their calling
cards upon the seats to mark them as reserved.

One of these was the intense brown-haired chap who'd
been eyeing Douglas and Holmes. As they walked past,
Holmes glanced at his card.

MR. ADAM MCGUIRE

Once again, Holmes paid him little mind, noting only that his mode of dress and bearing indicated he was American, and that he'd been—at some juncture—a government official or military man. While scanning the crowd for a glimpse of Georgiana, Holmes noticed that there were perhaps half a dozen government officials from various countries lingering about... and that they all seemed to be avoiding one another.

He whispered as much to Douglas.

"How do you know they are government officials?" Douglas inquired.

"Because *I* am a government official," Holmes replied. "Do you not know other purveyors of tobacco when you see them? Surely I can suss out my own kind."

"Be that as it may," Douglas countered, "people can eat with whomever they choose." But Holmes shook his head.

"There is something about this that I find unsettling."

Douglas considered pointing out to Holmes that he was already unsettled, and might be fabricating excuses to become more so, but he decided to hold his peace.

In the meantime, Captain Miles—he of the fulsome side whiskers, for they extended to the top of his breastbone— hurried in and waved a jovial hello to the passengers. Clearing his throat, he announced that, should they choose to stroll out onto the quarterdeck, he would be briefing them on the ship's progress for the day.

But it was bitterly cold outside, and the quarterdeck offered no barrier against the biting wind, so most passengers stayed where they were, chatting in little groups, or celebrating to the steady sound of popping champagne corks. Since there was no sign of Georgiana, however, Holmes and Douglas decided to hear the report, after which they would locate their quarters…

Then something caught Holmes's eye.

Seated on a straight-backed chair, a small portable writing apparatus unfolded before him, was a boy of fourteen or so, not homely but not particularly attractive, laboring intensively on a document of some kind. His concentration was such that Holmes, some twenty feet away, couldn't help but notice, though he had no way of seeing what the boy was writing.

"Ah, he is saying his final farewells to a girl," Holmes whispered to Douglas.

"Or perhaps he is writing down a description of his surroundings," Douglas countered, ready to move along.

"Nonsense," Holmes scoffed. "He isn't scanning the room for detail. Rather, from his point of view, the room seems to have disappeared. You see how his eyes turn down and to the right? That is a sure sign of the poetical, rather than the practical thought. And the florid way he composes each and every letter? No, it is a schoolboy crush gone awry."

Douglas was keen to continue on their way, but Holmes planted himself squarely in the middle of the room, so that others were forced to flow round him like eddies of water.

"It is an inferior paper stock," he said, his eyes still fixed on the boy, "mixed with too much hemp. What does that tell you, Douglas?"

"That he cares little for this girl you are imagining?" Douglas muttered.

"That his family has few resources," Holmes corrected.

"The fact is supported, too, by his attire. Curious, however, in that the writing apparatus is... aha! Note the flourishes on the capital 'A'." With that, Holmes began to spell out a name, letter by letter, as the boy wrote.

"A... n... a... b... e... l. His beloved's name is Anabel!"

"Or his mother's," Douglas posited.

"Nonsense, Douglas. One does not 'flourish' one's mother's name unless one is given to moral turpitude..."

"Enough, Holmes, it's not appropriate to peek into someone's private—"

"Your duffer!" Holmes interrupted.

"Pardon...?"

"The boy signed it, 'Your duffer'."

"'Your duffer'?" Douglas repeated, suddenly curious. "Perhaps because she stole his heart?"

"Since it is street parlance for 'pickpocket,' she would then be *his* duffer, would she not?" Holmes said.

"In any case," he added as at long last they moved on, "I hope I have convinced you that he is *not* writing to his mother."

"You have not," Douglas said. "We read no actual words, Holmes. For all I know, you assumed the word to be 'Anabel' while the boy was writing that he is particularly fond of apricots."

As the two of them walked out of the saloon and toward the quarterdeck, bickering back and forth on a subject of little relevance, three rough-looking characters kept a close eye on them.

One was small of stature but wiry, with the pointed, alert face of a ferret. The second was very large—or at least he seemed that way to Holmes, who appraised him out of the corner of his eye. The large man moved as if the air was molasses, and it was his ponderous duty to push through it.

The third, with bright red hair, was equally large, but seemed more sure-footed and treacherous. The scar that ran across his forehead made it look as though his cranium had been popped open, and then closed again.

A fourth man joined them. He was short, like the first, but so stocky that his chest seemed to rise to his chin with no neck in between. His eyes were two agate stones sunk into flesh. His head was shaved bald, with small cuts and scars suggesting that the straight razor was not his friend.

"Have you your revolver?" Holmes whispered to Douglas.

"In my bag," Douglas replied.

"Well, you may want to keep it handy from this point on," he said, and Douglas nodded.

In truth, Holmes knew no one besides Douglas who carried a firearm as a matter of course—not even his employer, the estimable Secretary of State for War. Yet he understood Douglas's need for protection, and was glad that his friend kept with him the American-made weapon. Already it was proving to be a comfort to them both.

When he and Douglas headed to the quarterdeck to hear the captain's report, the men did not follow.

"Much ado about nothing," Douglas said, relieved.

"On the contrary, Douglas—it *was* something," Holmes corrected. "I'm certain of it."

"What?"

Holmes sighed. "I fear that that part has yet to be determined."

12

HOLMES AND DOUGLAS STOOD ON THE QUARTERDECK
and heard the sorry news from the captain's mouth. Fog
and foul weather, Captain Miles was explaining, were
causing the great ship to move more slowly than had been
planned, so that she was making less progress than they
would have hoped. And they were about to hit some even
fouler weather, which should send all but the hardiest
among them to the shelter of their cabins.

Amid the small knot of people was a fashionable
dowager, wearing buckets of jewelry and a bustle so large
that each time she turned, she threatened to send one of
her companions sprawling headlong across deck. As the
captain spoke, she tapped the deck with the tip of her
umbrella, periodically adding a melodramatic sigh.

"How *vexing*, how very *tedious*!" she declared when he
was done. "And this was supposed to be a fast ship. Is there
no recourse at all? No route that would enable us to avoid
this bothersome delay?"

"Oh, there is much to be done!" Holmes said before
the captain could utter a word or Douglas could stop
him. "Here we are with immense furnaces under our feet,
burning with furious fires—a boiler pent up with sufficient

force to blow us all into the air in an instant, and howling gales and storms violent enough—if they assail us—to send us to a watery death.

"So long as we are still safe and headed toward our port," he continued, irritation evident in his tone, "so long as all the fire is shut up in the furnaces, and all the force held in the machinery, and the winds and seas allow us to move on steadily through them, then we should not utter a word of complaint, simply because we are only proceeding at twelve and a half knots, instead of thirteen!"

The aggrieved dowager began to stutter out a protest, but it was drowned out by applause. Captain Miles tipped his hat to Holmes in thanks before hurrying away—for he could not be seen to be taking sides.

"Brilliant," Douglas said darkly. "You have now offended two older women in the span of twenty minutes. I would venture to guess that is some sort of record."

"These new-fangled fashions," Holmes muttered as he watched the dowager waddle off. "How she even stands erect is a mystery of science."

"I believe the jewels at the bow serve as ballast for the bustle at the aft," Douglas offered. "And, speaking of aft, I must admit that was a poetical turn back there, Holmes!"

"Tosh," Holmes countered. "I read it in a magazine earlier this year, thought it was well phrased, is all."

Douglas smiled. "So you memorized a speech assuming that you would—what, have use for it some day, on the chance that someone might complain about a ship's speed?"

"Don't be daft, why would anyone bother to do a thing like that?"

"Then you memorized it for no reason at all," Douglas persisted, bewildered.

"I don't know what you mean, Douglas, by 'memorize' it. I simply read it."

"You read it once? And it stuck?"

"You must stop staring at me as if I were a specimen in a jar," Holmes huffed as he led the way to their room. "It is a family gift. Or curse, if you will. My mother and brother, too, are capable. In my mother's case, it drove her quite mad. In my brother's... only time will tell."

Douglas, bags in hand, followed, shaking his head.

At long last, they reached their room. Even after nearly two decades in England, Douglas found that he suffered cold more thoroughly than did most Englishmen. And damp cold was a particularly onerous kind, insinuating itself to bone and marrow, and forming little icicles in between. He put down the bags, massaged his cramping hands, and waited impatiently for Holmes to open the door.

When the door swung open, Douglas half-hoped he would shut it again, for the room did not look promising in the least.

"It is rather plain," Holmes said, studying it.

That would be lofty praise indeed, Douglas mused.

Though portside, it had no view at all. It contained only two bunks and, against one wall, a wooden medicine box with mirror, a basin for shaving, and a pitcher of water. It was, in other words, just as Holmes had no doubt requested, for Douglas knew only too well his friend's reluctance to spend money.

"I doubt *you* will fit in here, Holmes, never mind me," Douglas said, all the while recriminating himself that he hadn't booked his own quarters. "And look here—what good is a pitcher for water, with no glasses?"

Holmes had just put down his small bag and his walking stick when, through the open doorway, he spotted the same four ruffians who'd been eyeing them on deck. They were hastening down the narrow passageway toward them.

And there was no way out.

"At least there are four this time, and not a half-dozen," Douglas muttered.

Holmes thought to pick up the walking stick again, though in a small space it might be more trouble than help. On the other hand, the small space also meant that four men could not use their superior numbers as effectively.

"Choose!" Holmes said to Douglas.

"Darkies oughtta be 'tween decks, not here amongst us proper folk," the wiry leader shouted.

"Choose *quickly*," Holmes amended.

"The red one," Douglas declared. "And the big one."

"Which big one? There are two big ones!"

"The figgy pudding…"

Before Douglas could finish, the men were upon them.

As the stocky bald man—the "figgy pudding"—lumbered toward Douglas, the redhead's fist connected with Holmes's cheek. The ring on his pinkie opened up a gash that immediately began to bleed.

Holmes jerked his head away to avoid a second fist, and landed his own right upper cut to the redhead's jaw, followed by a roundhouse left that dropped his assailant to his knees and sliced his chin with a well-drawn line of blood.

Douglas, for his part, gave better than he got. As the figgy pudding lurched his way, he leaned sideways and kicked, his leg parallel to the floor—and broke his assailant's nose with a crack that reverberated down the passageway. The man collapsed in a puddle of blood and snot while Douglas twisted that same leg toward their wiry leader, shifting his foot from first to fourth position like a ballerina, nailing him neatly in the throat.

The leader fell in a heap, struggling to breathe, while the big man with the cobalt eyes rushed at Holmes with a roar.

Holmes ducked.

His assailant tumbled over him.

Using the man's own momentum, Holmes pushed him into the figgy pudding, who was just rising on wobbly legs when his partner toppled him again like a bowling pin.

The wiry leader, still gasping for air, fled first, running as fast as the narrow passageway would allow. The others limped away soon after, and Holmes and Douglas made it to their cabin in one piece, bolting the door behind them.

"You said *you* would take the redhead," Holmes muttered. The gash on his cheek was bleeding profusely. He held his handkerchief to it, trying to stanch the flow.

"I think he chose you first," Douglas replied. "I noticed you used the move I taught you. Momentum is a gift."

Holmes nodded. "You're not half bad yourself, for an

old man. All that spinning and flailing about does come in handy…" He stared at his reflection in a mirror on the wall. Douglas stared at it, too, and frowned.

"That is a nasty wound you've got there, Holmes. Perhaps the ship's physician…"

"Tosh," Holmes replied. He opened the medicine box with its mirrored lid. Inside were a used strop and straight razor, along with a little jar of carbolic acid.

"I have no clue what 'tosh' means in this regard, Holmes. That is a bad cut—you must see a physician!"

"Tosh means tosh… ah, here we are!" Holmes exclaimed. "Ask, and you shall receive!" He mixed a handful of carbolic crystals with a few drops of water from the pitcher.

Then he frowned.

"Something doesn't sit quite right," he muttered.

"Beatings seldom do," Douglas opined.

"When you mentioned that the redheaded man *chose* me, Douglas, you were unintentionally correct. He did choose me. A ruby, cabochon cut, did this. But they weren't the sorts who could afford a ring at all, much less a cabochon! You noticed, yes?"

"The cabochon? Or the redhead?" Douglas asked. "I have to admit that I did not."

"He wore it on that sausage he no doubt refers to as his 'pinkie'." Holmes frowned. "And it barely fitted."

"What are you saying, Holmes, that someone *gave* it to him?"

"Lent it, most likely, yes."

"Whatever for?"

"To cut me."

"A knife would not serve?"

Holmes grimaced. The carbolic acid was beginning to sting.

"With a knife, it is too easy to slip up, do real damage," Holmes explained. "Whoever arranged this did not want me dead—merely warned."

"Warned of what?"

"I haven't the foggiest."

"What good is a warning if you are not certain what you're being warned about?" Douglas protested.

"You fought them, Douglas, and yet you ask such a question? They were back-alley fighters, at best. Clearly not professional killers—merely incidental. Our presence here has disrupted a plan of some sort..."

"Your presence, you mean," Douglas corrected. "Secretary to Edward Cardwell. I would be of no consequence to them."

"Perhaps."

"You say 'perhaps,' but you do not know what sort of plan," Douglas said.

"Of course not," Holmes shot back. "How should I? I am a secretary in an office! D'you think this sort of thing happens to me every week?"

He stared again at his face in the mirror. It was an ugly cut, running from the top of his cheekbone nearly to the top of his lip. Bearing the sting, he applied more carbolic acid, hoping it would heal properly, and not leave too prominent a scar.

In truth, he was thinking of Georgiana. If she was in

any way displeased with his appearance, he feared he could not bear it.

And where in the world is she? he wondered.

"If Georgiana is aboard, under an assumed name or otherwise," he said aloud, "I must find her. In the morning, I shall do a thorough search of the ship—"

Suddenly the *Sultana* pitched, interrupting Holmes's thought and sending both men scrambling to hold onto something solid, while the cabin creaked and groaned as if it were in agony.

Douglas peered around with concern.

"I am afraid the captain's prediction was right—we are hitting a patch of very bad weather," he said. "Searching a ship in a storm is not the soundest plan, Holmes."

"Nevertheless," Holmes responded with great determination, releasing his handhold, "I must."

The ship pitched in the other direction, sending him skittering into Douglas.

"Beg pardon," Holmes muttered, touching his forehead as though they were two strangers who'd bumped each other on the train.

Then he sat hard on his bunk.

"Strange," he said. "Even when the ship is not pitching, my head continues the movement…"

"You might have a touch of seasickness," Douglas posited. "Understandable, under the circumstances."

"Tosh…" Holmes replied. But he nevertheless put his head on the pillow and closed his eyes.

* * *

Douglas left Holmes napping in their cabin and hazarded a trip up on deck to judge for himself just what sort of quandary they had stumbled into. He doubted that he would encounter the toughs again. They were street ruffians, not sailors.

None but a damn fool would walk the promenade on a night like this.

Nevertheless, he tucked his Smith & Wesson top-break, single-action Model 3 into his coat, just in case.

The damn fool might just be me, he thought wryly.

13

BESIDES PASSENGERS AND CREW, THE GREAT SHIP carried a full cargo of tobacco, leather goods, and lard. Douglas thought she was less than six years old, from the looks of her, and as fit as any vessel put to sea. Then again, he doubted that her mettle had been tested in a storm of such magnitude.

He watched her bow rise and dip over angry black water that seemed not so much beneath as all around her, while above her the twilight sky was a patchwork of mist and fog and flying scuds of rain, so that there was no respite to be had, either above or below.

If she sank beneath those fulsome waves, succumbing to a watery grave, the only thing left afloat would be the lard.

He walked back to their cramped quarters, having discovered nothing of import. Neither he nor Holmes had a notion what the next move might be, but one thing was certain. Since they could not discern friend from foe, for the time being they would keep the assault to themselves.

"I say we go to the saloon and have some dinner," Holmes said, "as if nothing had transpired. We simply keep our wits about us, and judge if anyone is surprised to see us there."

"Our other alternative is to remain where we are," Douglas said, only half joking, as he already knew how that suggestion would be received. Holmes frowned his disapproval and put another round of carbolic acid and water on his wounded cheek—after which the men silently dressed for dinner and exited the room.

The moment they stepped outside, the wind seemed to want its pound of flesh. It howled through each crack and cranny of the long, dank passageway, whipping up whorls of dust like ghosts rising up and taking form. They could hear the water slosh against the great ship's sides as she forced her way through the swells.

Douglas bent his knees to lower his center of gravity. He had long grown accustomed to the motion of a ship, and could anticipate the *Sultana*'s moves and coordinate them with his own. Holmes, on the other hand, was attempting to ride her, to beat her, to wear her down. He treated every sway as combat, pitting his balance and reflexes against her feints and jabs. Watching him, Douglas became concerned that his young friend would soon land upon his head—so he decided to act the role model.

He grabbed the handrail.

"You will find this to be of service," he said, hoping his tone would carry a warning.

Holmes assiduously ignored him.

Douglas abandoned the futile effort and let go.

No use providing an object lesson, he mused, *when the student pays not the slightest heed.* Not to mention that the effort to stay upright actually seemed to be having a positive effect on his friend. It was the first time he'd seen Holmes act even remotely carefree since they'd boarded.

At that very moment a shadow crossed their paths, quick and fleeting. Douglas instantly laid a hand on the gun in his coat pocket. The move did not slip by unnoticed—Holmes glanced at him, curious, especially once the shadow proved to be a play of the light, and nothing more.

Douglas laughed. "There's nothing like a ship, once the sun has set," he said, "to give true meaning to the term *eerie*."

"You are allowing your nerves to get the better of you," Holmes said, and he smiled. "Though I grant you this journey has not been terribly peaceful thus far—"

"Your cut is bleeding, Holmes," Douglas interrupted, proffering his handkerchief. Holmes took it with a gruff "thank you," and then pulled the jar of salve out of his pocket.

"If a bit is good, a great deal more is best," he said wryly.

"I am not certain it works that way," Douglas responded. "But if it makes you feel better…"

"A bit of normalcy would make me feel better, but that seems to be in short supply at present," Holmes said, shrugging.

Just as they reached the door to the grand saloon, the weather rewarded them with a temporary lull. Even so, there were plenty of seats to be had at the long table. Usually, passengers who were tardy had nowhere to sit, but on this night most everyone had elected to remain in their rooms.

Douglas counted. Fewer than fifty were present. Nevertheless, that meant one hundred eyes, all critical of a tall, somber black man in his middle years, who—though he might be staring humbly at the floor—seemed too self-possessed to be a servant. Especially since he stood next to a young man of no more than three-and-twenty, with a fresh and ugly gash upon his cheek.

Bound to attract attention, Douglas mused, subtly scanning the room. But it seemed the passengers were concentrating entirely on their meals, as if by focus alone the soup would remain in its bowl where it belonged.

They had crossed into international waters, so Douglas would be permitted to sit next to Holmes at dinner. Indeed, one of the advantages of ship life was that people were forced to share the same small space with others from many different parts of the world, including persons of darker hue.

"Quite fascinating, really," Douglas opined. "What might at home be considered inappropriate is here accepted as exotic."

Holmes raised an eyebrow.

"You would be exotic, then?" he asked, eliciting a raised eyebrow in return, along with a nearly imperceptible smile.

"Only in comparison to you, Holmes."

The attendants brought them the first course, a hearty clam and oyster stew, and then poured what looked to be a rather anemic white wine into a crystal decanter.

Holmes tasted it and grimaced.

"A pox on *phylloxera!*" he muttered to Douglas, referring to an aphid that for twelve long years had been ravaging the great French vineyards, particularly Languedoc. Owners of formidable wineries whose origins dated back hundreds of years had been left devastated. They were now forced to graft hardy American vines onto their native plants. The results so far were promising, though French pride had taken a beating.

"Poor France," Holmes said. "First their wine, and now a war."

"It's not a war—not yet," Douglas countered.

"No, but it shall be. Good thing you doubled up on Armagnac and Cognac shipments. Those, at least, shall be spared."

Douglas kept on eating, enjoying the lull, however brief it might be.

"I wish I could have done the same with human beings," he muttered. "Saved a few. Especially the children. They suffer most in times of war…"

Holmes stared into his soup and said nothing, and Douglas did not like the look of him. Perhaps his discomfort would be eased by an after-dinner brandy, which he hoped would not be too second-rate, and a fine cigar.

He had barely harbored the thought when, as if on cue, the *Sultana*'s respite ended. She began to lurch about. More and more diners went green at the gills and succumbed, excusing themselves. But Holmes was determined to remain steady. Peering around the room, he raised his eyebrows in a way that played on Douglas's last nerve.

"You look as if you were Temperance herself, caught in the presence of drunkards," he grumbled. "Do you consider seasickness a moral lapse?"

Holmes seemed stung by the reproach.

"You misread me," he said. "My frown was not brought on by passengers who are present, but by those who are not."

Douglas took another sip of wine.

"You are speaking of Georgiana, then?"

"Georgiana, yes," Holmes confessed with a shrug. "But also those government officials who earlier seemed uncannily intent on avoiding one another. I was calculating the odds that they would all be taken ill at once, and they are long odds indeed. I am quite put out that they are not here, as they were my most likely suspects."

"Though you have absolutely no reason to think so…" Douglas began when Holmes continued.

"As to 'moral lapse,'" he said, "I think nothing of the sort. There's nothing 'moral' about an unruly stomach. No, what these passengers are experiencing is a perfectly normal biologic function, brought about when the brain repeatedly loses its equilibrium, and then recovers it.

"This effort leaves the mind bewildered and fatigued," he continued. "The digestive organs—most especially the liver—begin to be affected, bringing on nausea. People then attempt to cure this orally, say with milk of magnesia. Yet as the nausea is only symptomatic, and not the root cause, such remedies must inevitably fail."

"You missed your calling," Douglas said with a laugh, "for surely you should have been a physician."

"Ah, what a dreary, dull life that would be," Holmes replied, "to spend one's days palpating human beings and cataloguing their ills. No, Douglas, I would have made a perfectly wretched physician, in that patients would have made a perfect wretch out of me." He paused to take a tentative spoonful of soup, and did not care for the taste.

"As for seasickness," he said, pushing away the bowl, "the only cure is to have perfect control over the origin of the difficulty, and that is the brain. It's really quite simple, you see. You must focus, with great control, on objects in sight that are fixed and stable…"

"That's quite the challenge," Douglas interjected, "as everything that is seemingly 'fixed' is on the boat, and therefore rocking alongside you."

"Granted, that may cause a difficulty or two," Holmes admitted. "One must keep one's gaze on the horizon," he added, "and perhaps assume a prone position."

He paused again, and frowned.

"By doing so…" he said, "you will diminish the… the…"

Rather than finish his thought, he doubled over. His stomach began to heave—not quietly and politely, but loudly, like an orphaned baby seal. It was only Douglas's swift reflexes that kept Holmes from regurgitating his clam and oyster stew all over his shoes.

With apologies to those seated beside them, he quickly helped Holmes to his feet, and back to their room. As they went, Holmes managed a few more words.

"I wish to die," he muttered. "Kindly let me die."

Holmes at last lay in his berth, in between his moans and explosions of vomitus. Douglas did his best to wipe up the mess on the floor. But even in the throes of illness, Holmes could not abide having his friend and traveling companion cleaning as though he were a scullery maid.

"There will be none of that," he said, lurching out of bed. "I shall not allow you to… *aaaaahhh!*"

Douglas turned from his mop in time to see Holmes slip on his own effluence and land on his backside, legs akimbo. He hurried over to pick him up. As they made their unsteady way back to the cabin, Holmes looked up at him with a weak smile.

"Pride goeth before destruction," he quoted, "and a haughty spirit before a fall."

"You may indeed have been cursed, Holmes," Douglas said wryly. He helped Holmes out of his soiled clothes, situated him back on the bed, and then finished cleaning up both the floor and himself. Thankfully, it seemed as if his friend had nothing left to expel.

Crawling into his own bunk, he put out the gas light—although he ended up staring at the dark ceiling for a good long while. The tiredness was overwhelming, yet sleep would not come.

Here I am, he thought, *in the exact situation I said I would not abide—dragging a white man about…*

In truth, he enjoyed Holmes's company. But he had never quite known what to make of this good-looking, brilliant young man, so very British in bearing, pedigree, and character, who somehow found pleasure in the friendship of a forty-year-old native of Trinidad. He supposed there must be a purpose to it, this fate that brought them together.

Certainly, over the course of a year, Holmes had proved a dear if somewhat exasperating companion. And, because he was so inordinately intelligent, it was difficult at times to remember that he had been out of his teens a mere four years, that he had gotten into few scrapes outside the boxing ring, and that he had never before traveled outside of England.

I must endeavor to be more patient.

At midnight, he heard the wail of the steam whistle on deck, which meant that the blackness and the mist were now so thick that the sound was all that stood in the way of their colliding with whatever else happened by. But as he had traversed this particular waterway many times before, he knew that the one true danger for a ship this size was an iceberg.

And that icebergs were particularly impervious to steam whistles.

Holmes, too, was not asleep—at least not in the healthiest definition of the term. Rather, he was very nearly comatose.

And hallucinating.

"Moral insanity." That was what Sherlock had spoken of—the idea that some humans were devoid of the common thread of human decency. The words wove in and out of his consciousness, along with the mutes who'd been standing guard over the house of the dead, and that false sailor spitting out the wrong side of his mouth.

Moral insanity.

That particular form of madness, Holmes knew, consisted of a morbid perversion of natural feelings. It was a *manie sans délire*—a mania, without delirium—that deprived the subject of the sorts of ethics most people would consider constant. It was a state in which intellectual faculties remained unaffected, while emotions were so profoundly damaged that patients were carried away by "some furious instinct."

An instinct so fierce that the destruction it wreaks is incalculable.

This bleak thought was followed by images—*lougarou* sucking children's blood, mutes laughing soundlessly as they stood watch over the dead, their teeth blackened, their mouths opening up like a grave, threatening to swallow up Holmes and all he held dear.

14

THAT FIRST NIGHT OF THEIR VOYAGE WAS AN IMPOSSIBLY long one for Douglas. His instincts for survival, given everything he had endured in his life, were quite strong, as was his nose for small problems that could easily turn deadly.

That nose had been twitching since they'd first come aboard.

What in the world are we in the midst of? he wondered, and not for the first time.

"The key to my heart…" he heard Holmes mutter in his sleep.

He is dreaming of her, Douglas realized as he stretched his long body on the cot to try to get comfortable.

He had met Georgiana a handful of times. Each time she'd struck him as the sort of girl whose prettiness masked a fierce intelligence, and an equally fierce determination. Their first meeting had been at the London wharf.

Douglas had just returned from a harrowing voyage, much like the one they were enduring at present, with storm upon storm granting no reprieve to passenger and sailor alike. He was tired and filthy and in a hurry to unload the latest shipment when, out of the corner of his eye, he spotted a well-heeled young man and a rather stunning blond hurrying toward him. She was so slight and so pretty that she looked as if someone had painted her, and then set her as a lark in the incongruity of those drab and dreary docks.

Having no reason whatsoever to speak with them, he returned to his labor until the young man stood in front of him so that he could no longer be avoided, and pointed to a crate of Cuban cigars.

"Where in heaven's name did you find *those*?" He spoke the words with such wonder that he might as well have been referring to the Holy Grail. "They are *Principe de Gales*, are they not?" the fellow added in a tone that was very nearly accusatory.

"They are indeed," Douglas said with a smile and a slight bow of the head.

The young man was about to say something else when he was cut off by his companion's delighted laugh.

"Port of Spain!" she said, just as eagerly. "Is that where you are from?"

Douglas confessed that it was so.

She held out her hand for him to shake, an action Douglas found both unusual and endearing, as she was ignoring both the color of his skin and the dirt that covered it. That was when he noticed the jumbie beads bracelet that she wore under the sleeve of her ruffled white blouse.

The young woman caught him staring, but she just laughed again—the easy, bright laugh of the young and carefree. It made him melancholy—not for her, but for something he had lost…

"I've had it since I was a child," she said, interrupting

his thoughts, "and am loathe to give it up."

Douglas nodded.

"Had one too," he confessed. "Wish I had it still, for they remind me of home."

The young man introduced himself as Mycroft Holmes, and the young woman as Georgiana Sutton. They chatted for a short while longer, and Douglas gave the young man the address of his little tobacco store. He suggested that Holmes stop by, and he would put a few *Principes* aside just for him, whereupon Holmes looked as delighted as a child at Christmas.

They left, and Douglas went back to work.

From that point on, Holmes had visited at least thrice weekly, taking in all the knowledge Douglas had about cigars. Now that Douglas thought about it, Holmes could recall every word that was said, down to the smallest jot and tittle. He had absorbed in a handful of weeks what it had taken Douglas years to glean and digest.

Some three months later, Holmes brought Georgiana into the shop to announce their engagement.

"Douglas would have been my best man, were it not for… a certain luck of the draw," Holmes had told his fiancée. Then he'd added, rather mournfully, "As it is, I suppose I shall have to make do with Sherlock."

"Georgiana!"

He heard Holmes toss in his berth and call out her name.

Holmes was so very tender with her, treating her as if

she were made of the finest crystal and liable to shatter at any moment. To Douglas's mind, however, she didn't seem inclined to do any such thing. She seemed equally careful with Holmes, however—squeezing his hand, being the first to laugh when he said something witty, or listening intently when he waxed eloquent—sometimes at great length.

She seemed blissfully unaware of his tendency toward superciliousness, yet she was no shrinking violet. She spoke her mind both well and forcefully. She was the sort, Douglas mused, who believed the entire world could be saved, if one only went about it with intent and resolve.

She and Douglas frequently spoke of Trinidad— something they held in common, though Georgiana came from wealthy planter stock and Douglas's family, while literate, was poor as dirt. Over a glass of brandy or two, Douglas had given her and Holmes a few morsels about his upbringing.

"It was only my putting out to sea at the age of twelve, learning by hook and by crook to make a living, that allowed my family to survive at all, and even, eventually, to thrive," he'd explained.

"We are not so different, Mr. Douglas," she had replied—and what she'd said next had remained with him ever since. "You come from slaves. Well, so do I. My great-great-great-grandfather and his bride migrated from Britain to Trinidad in 1640. Though they were white, they became indentured servants, doing hard labor for five long years. She did not survive it, and he did.

"For his troubles, my ancestor was given 'freedom dues.' Ten British pounds, plus ten acres to farm. It forms a portion of the land that we still own to this day. It was from those humble beginnings that my family built its fortune."

Douglas had nodded.

"Yes," he said, and he frowned. "Similar to the forty acres promised to American slaves, some five years ago."

"Well, that doesn't seem to be going as promised," Holmes commented. He looked ready to say more when Georgiana interrupted him.

"Surely the *intent* is there," she had said. "I loathe the idea that 'the road to hell is paved with good intentions.' What do we have, after all, but what we intend?" She paused, looking thoughtful. "Then too, most of what we value—from the Great Pyramids onward—was built on the backs of the poor and the vanquished. I do wonder what society would be like without the blood, sweat, and tears of those forebears…"

Now, lying in a too-small berth across from his very sick friend, Douglas felt an unpleasant tingle at the pit of his stomach. He wondered just where Georgiana was. Had she taken an assumed name? Could she be hiding aboard the ship?

And if so, whatever for?

I am too exhausted to ponder it now, Douglas decided with a yawn. *It shall have to wait 'til morning.*

He finally drifted off to sleep to the sound of Holmes's fitful snoring.

* * *

When Douglas awoke the following morning, the first thing he did was to check on his friend.

Holmes was still asleep, but not pleasantly so. He was tossing and sweating, though the room was far from warm. He opened his eyes only long enough to ask for the carbolic acid, which Douglas mixed with a bit of water and brought him. Holmes slathered it on his cheek with little finesse, as if his hand were a mitt.

"Be careful," Douglas said, taking back the dish, "or you'll use it all up."

Holmes began to mumble.

"Can't feel my extremities at all…" he said.

Then he promptly fell asleep again.

For four full days, Holmes remained thus, wanting nothing but a sip or two of water, and the carbolic acid. When asleep, he continued to agonize in his dreams about Georgiana.

During his years at sea, Douglas had seen seasickness in all its permutations, even masquerading as a bad influenza now and again. And with the ship still pressing through a mighty storm, this was no time to try to rally Holmes. All told, it was best to let him sleep on.

Douglas himself did little besides read. He was grateful that he had packed Alexandre Dumas's *The Fencing Master*, mostly to practice his French, as well as *Oliver Twist*, though he knew it nearly by heart. Every so often he would wet a rag and place it upon his friend's burning forehead and quote Dickens' immortal lines to himself.

"The worm does not work more surely on the dead body,

than does this slow creeping fire upon the living frame…"

When Douglas did venture out, the decks were empty, and the sick were hidden behind locked doors. Everyone else aboard seemed to be as ill as Holmes, and this assuaged Douglas's worries for his friend. Still, if the symptoms were to persist for another day, Douglas would be forced to call the ship's physician, regardless of any feeble protestations to the contrary.

On day five, the *Sultana* at last hit a patch of good weather. The pitching finally ceased, the sun shone intermittently, and people began to venture out, gaunt and sallow, but alive.

Yet Holmes was no better. The few sips of water he permitted Douglas to pour down his throat turned immediately to sweat. He mumbled incessantly and incoherently, and he snorted most unbecomingly, as if he were breathing underwater.

Armed with a list of Holmes's symptoms, Douglas went to pay a call on the physician. But when he got there, both the ship's doctor and his assistant were otherwise engaged. He spoke with the former's secretary, a hearty fellow of fifty or so.

"They're making the rounds," the man said. "No telling when they'll be back." He had an accent that Douglas could not place. Possibly Australian. When Douglas gave him their room number, the fellow took it, staring down at it as if it were hieroglyphics.

"I'll pass it on," he said dubiously, "but with nearly three-quarters of the passengers down, the doc may not get to 'im 'til the morrow." He looked up at Douglas. "Please pass along my best to your employer, beg him be well!"

Though it was said in good spirits and accompanied by a hearty slap on the back, Douglas was in no mood.

If begging him to be well would do the trick, he thought crossly, *I wouldn't need a physician.*

On his way back, Douglas passed by a cook's assistant and importuned him for some bread and a pat of butter, along with a cup of tea. For the bulk of the journey, Holmes had missed all five meals normally served on a ship— breakfast, luncheon, dinner, tea, and supper. Though breakfast had long passed, Douglas hoped it would tempt him into sitting up, at the very least.

After a few moments, the scullion returned with a tray, garnished with a frilly serviette. The bread was stale, the tea was lukewarm and bitter, and the butter more than likely colored lard, but the man was kind, giving him what he had on hand.

Douglas had nearly reached the companionway when he noticed a strange sensation, or possibly a lack thereof. The very few times he'd been out and about, he had fought unease, waiting for the inevitable moment when someone would confront him with a, "Say, who d'you think you are, wandering about like this?"

But this morning, he did not feel that prickle at his back, that sourness in his gut. He'd finally found an answer for the challenge of "wandering about like this." Looking down, he realized to his chagrin that it was the tray that did it. Carrying the tray marked him once and for all as a manservant.

He continued on his way.

As he crossed beyond the companionway, Douglas walked past the slats that separated the rest of the *Sultana* from the so-called 'tween decks. If the "above-ground" passengers looked bad, then the poor souls who'd had to endure these catacombs looked positively wretched. They were poking their heads up like so many scraggly, starving moles.

Douglas handed a little boy a bit of Holmes's bread. He was no more than five, and wearing what looked to be a collection of rags. He stared at Douglas with wide, suspicious eyes, snatched at the crumb with a tiny claw-like hand so tough it could have been made of leather, and then disappeared once again into his hole. Immediately ten other children took his place, and the resulting uproar forced Douglas to retreat.

He had almost reached the long, narrow hall that led to his room when he overheard two deckhands discussing a burial at sea that was to take place within a half-hour's time. Two passengers, it seemed, had succumbed to dysentery.

"Big men they was, prime o' life!" one rough-hewn hand confided to the other.

The second man exuded an aura of confidence. He was smaller but somehow tougher, as if he had been constructed entirely of brown cables. He appeared more seasoned than his fellow.

"Pikuliar 'ndeed! It's usually women and children what go first," he said knowingly. "You seen 'em then? The dead 'uns?"

The first deckhand rubbed his nose by way of acknowledgment.

"I thrown my eye over just one," he said. "Ginger hair he had, a full head of it! And a cut acrost 'is fore'ead looked fresh shorn. Musta stung a mite when 'e got it."

"I'll wager it don't sting now!" the second man responded. And the two deckhands laughed as if it were the funniest joke they'd heard in their lives. They gave Douglas the evil eye, however, as he passed, to show the colored man who was who and what was what. Then they went on with their chortling.

Back in the room, Holmes wasn't aware that Douglas had left. He wasn't aware that the storm had abated. He was focused on one thing and one thing only—the vision in his mind's eye.

Through the roiling clouds of delirium, he saw Georgiana's diamond ring. The delicate stone began to thicken and darken like a tumor until it morphed into a large red ruby on a fat pinkie. The vision was so terrifying that he forced himself awake—and found he was sitting bolt upright in bed.

It was only a dream, he assured himself, and for a moment he felt relief.

Then he touched the wound on his cheek.

It was all too real.

Hurting from his toes to his hair follicles, Holmes stared at the medicine box. His brain was trying to deduce something, though he couldn't quite grasp it. His unfocused gaze settled upon three containers, although he was fairly certain that there was but one, and that the true one was in the center. He decided that, as long as he was already sitting up, he should probably attempt to stand.

The box, no more than ten feet away, may as well have been on the moon. Nevertheless, he planted one foot, then the other, on the very cold floor, and shuffled toward his singular goal step by step.

Wheezing, heart pounding, he reached it at last. He unscrewed the lid on the jar, silently chastising Douglas for having put it on so tightly. Then he wet his finger, dipped it into the carbolic acid crystals, brought them up to his face—and licked his finger.

As soon as he did so, he *knew*.

15

UPON RE-ENTERING THE CABIN, DOUGLAS SAW BEFORE him a very odd sight indeed. Mycroft Holmes, flush with fever, was standing semi-naked at the medicine box, his index finger jammed into his mouth.

All thoughts of burials at sea went right out of his head. He put down the tray.

"Holmes!" he cried as he rushed toward him.

Holmes, his red eyes wide, held up the jar in triumph.

"Laudanum!" he announced, as if that said it all.

Then he began to sway. Douglas caught him before he crumpled, and held him upright.

"Here, let me help you to bed," Douglas mumbled as Holmes regained his balance.

"Laudanum, carbolic acid!" the latter exclaimed, while not allowing Douglas to steer him in the least.

"What the *deuce* are you going on about?" Douglas demanded. "And we are getting you back into bed this instant."

"There is laudanum mixed in with the carbolic acid," Holmes explained. "It is seeping through the cut, directly into my bloodstream."

Douglas peered at him, then at the jar in Holmes's hand.

"Absurd," he said.

But Holmes persisted.

"It is bitter like opium," he explained. Then he looked uncertain. "Based, you understand, on what I have *heard* of opium…"

Douglas snatched the jar away.

"If this has been tampered with," he said, "then kindly do not *eat* it."

"I am not eating it," Holmes corrected. "I am *tasting* it."

Douglas stared at him silently. He was nearly certain that Holmes was hallucinating.

But if he wasn't?

He bit his bottom lip. He could not believe what he was about to do. Wetting his own finger, Douglas put it in the jar, and tasted. His face registered both surprise and recognition.

Holmes looked positively giddy.

"There you are!" he said. "Laudanum."

But Douglas shook his head and stared down at the jar in wonder.

"Not laudanum," he said. *"Abrus precatorius.* A vine native to Trinidad."

"Not laudanum?" Holmes repeated, in a tone that suggested that being wrong was something with which he was thoroughly unfamiliar.

"Its jumbie seeds carry a toxin—" Douglas went on, when Holmes interrupted him tersely.

"*Jumbie* seeds? Just what do you mean, Douglas, by jumbie seeds? What the deuce are you implying?"

Douglas realized that Holmes was referring to Georgiana's bracelet.

"No, no," he said. "Do not hasten to a conclusion.

Jumbie seeds, from which the beaded bracelets are made, are as common as dirt on the island. It just so happens that, in powder form, they make a walloping good poison."

But Holmes was no longer listening.

"What a *fool* I am!" he berated himself. "She's had that bracelet for as long as I've known her… I simply assumed they were pretty beads!"

"And why on earth would you assume otherwise?" Douglas protested.

Holmes groaned from the strain of standing after such a long time in bed. His legs gave way. He found himself on his knees on the floor.

Douglas helped him to his feet again.

"Tell me all you know about them," Holmes demanded. "Leave nothing out."

Douglas sighed.

"Their toxin is deadly. The dosage in the jar is by necessity small, as it has to blend with the carbolic acid. Had you kept applying it, however, it certainly would have killed you. And in large enough quantities, it would have done so within twenty-four hours."

"And why would you be familiar with the taste?" Holmes asked.

Douglas raised an eyebrow.

"It is essential knowledge in my profession," he said. "Witch doctors on the islands sometimes use it to… let us say, *dispose* of some poor wretches their clients are not fond of. And I am in a business that occasionally makes enemies. But the taste is distinct, and hard to hide."

Holmes reached for the jar.

The latter held it at bay.

"What are you doing?" Holmes protested. "I merely wish to taste it again."

"I realize that," Douglas responded. "But surely you have enough in your system."

Yet Holmes would not be deterred. "I may not know the taste of abrus," he replied, "but I know carbolic acid. Based on that, I can deduce what percentage of abrus was used. Which is something we must know, and something you cannot do."

Douglas was astonished.

"You know the taste of carbolic acid?" he asked. "Whatever for? Your personality cannot be so egregious that you expect to be poisoned at any moment."

"I worked one summer for a physician... Douglas, please. I have no energy for stories at the moment." He insisted with his open palm that Douglas hand over the jar.

A reluctant Douglas did so.

Holmes tasted the contents, and frowned.

"I would say two... perhaps three percent foreign substance." He tasted again. "Closer to three," he said. "My guess is that this was meant to keep me more or less unconscious throughout the trip. But not to kill me."

Douglas shook his head, trying to make sense of it all.

"So the carbolic acid was placed in the medicine box," he said, "in advance. Possibly at the same time as the used strop and razor, to make certain nothing looked amiss..."

Holmes nodded and finished the thought.

"Then I was cut," he said. "And whoever hired that man to cut me knew that the first place I would seek aid was the medicine box, a natural conclusion…"

He staggered a bit.

"…and now, might you help me to sit?"

Douglas did so. Then he emptied the salve into the chamber pot, reiterating the point he'd been attempting to make at first.

"Well, whatever else you may think, Holmes, Georgiana is not the only one who keeps a jumbie bead bracelet."

"No," Holmes admitted. "But she is the only one in my life who does."

"And why would she want you hurt?" Douglas pressed. "Or murdered? It makes no sense."

"No, it does not," Holmes agreed. "In no way, shape, or form does it make sense—yet, there it is."

A series of thoughts occurred to Holmes.

Georgiana has been taken.

She has been brutalized.

She has been killed!

Her bracelet is the only thing left of her… now someone is using it, making her out to be a murderess.

He said as much to Douglas.

Douglas listened, deeply concerned. Holmes's words were spilling out in a way that seemed frenetic and unfocused. He wondered if the poison had affected his reasoning, as well as his body. Nevertheless, he decided he must tell Holmes his own news, whether he was of a mind to hear it or not.

"At least one of our assailants is dead," he said. "Of

dysentery. The redhead who cut you."

Holmes looked surprised. Then he let out a skeptical laugh.

"That fireplug, dead of dysentery? Not bloody likely! Perhaps our assailants are being disposed of."

Douglas admitted to the same thought.

"Yet by whom?" he said. "Why would we have assailants at all, much less a mastermind *behind* the assailants, doing them in? In any event," he added, "the redhead's burial at sea, along with another man's, is to take place in half an hour's time."

"Well then, that is where we shall be," Holmes announced.

"But you can barely walk!" he protested. "And surely I cannot be seen traipsing about by myself. Even here in international waters, I will attract undue attention."

"Naturally," Holmes sniffed. "We cannot have some mental dullard, acting under cover of darkness, toss you overboard for sport. No," he declared. "You shall drag me along. With this."

With a grunt of exertion, Holmes reached into the bag at the foot of his bed and held up his cravat.

A bird's-eye view of Holmes and Douglas that evening would have been a sight indeed. In the foreground stood a handsome young man with a shock of blond hair and a strange, shuffling gait, as if he were performing an ungainly but slow-moving jig, while leaning upon an ornate walking stick.

Behind him, uncomfortably close, was an elegant

black man with one hand tucked inside his waistcoat, à la Napoleon Bonaparte. That hand was the sole reason that the blond young man could stand at all.

Holmes had undone several inches of stitching from the back hem of his topcoat. He'd wrapped his waist with his cravat, and then pulled the ends through the newly made hole. Behind him, Douglas held both ends of the dark blue silk. By lifting the ends upward like a leash, he could keep Holmes more or less upright.

"Surely we could have come up with something more efficient," Douglas growled as he took the reins.

"Not in five minutes' time," Holmes countered, "and with my brains so addled."

As it turned out, the solution was not half bad. In the daytime, the cravat would have been clearly visible. But under cover of night, in the tight quarters of the ship, and wearing topcoats, they managed well enough—as long as no one attempted to step in between them. That would not have been likely, as few people were keen on wandering about in the dark after a storm. Fewer still to approach a tall Negro whose shooting hand was hidden inside his vest.

"My knees are giving way," Holmes hissed as they crossed the deck, and he lurched about like a marionette with a new handler. "Can you not sustain me a bit more?"

"Not with one hand," Douglas shot back. "As it is, I shall end up with a right forearm that is thrice as large as my left."

* * *

The two deckhands were approximately where Douglas had last seen them. They turned out to be as pleasant to Holmes as they had been boorish to Douglas. And after Holmes introduced himself as secretary to the Secretary of State for War, they became positively deferential—though Douglas guessed they had never heard of Cardwell, nor known that such a position existed at all.

"Poor unfortunates, they was," the more seasoned of the two opined with dramatic nods and tilts of the head. "Come out o' steerage. We holds they services at night so's as not to disturb the uppers."

He pointed somberly to heaven, but in fact was referring to the upper decks, to the genteel folk who might be discomfited to realize there were dead people aboard—especially ones who'd succumbed to dysentery.

"Big men, they wuz, prime o' life!" the younger one said. "Pikuliar they wuz..." he began, when the older man interrupted by stepping in front of him while at the same time elbowing him deftly in the ribs to quiet him down.

"Pikuliar, yes," the older one intoned. "It's women and children what go first, not hale men such as them two."

"You saw them, then?" Holmes asked.

"Not me, guv'nor," the older one admitted. Then he reluctantly ceded the attention to his fellow again, frowning as he said, "This one 'ere laid eyes on 'em."

"I din't see 'em in death as wuz..." the younger one clarified.

"Why, you rum creature!" the older one protested. "You sworn you cast your eye on 'im."

"And so I did!" the other yelled in his own defense. "But

he wan't dead-dead when I did so, simply ailin', as wuz."

The older man objected with a cuff to the ear of the younger man—who then pled his case to Holmes:

"I *knows* one of 'em, guv'nor, and I knows it h'ain't kind to speak ill of the dead, but *wicious* he wuz, 'im and 'is friends, what's always itchin' fer a brawl. Bright red hair, he had, and a gash here…"

He made a line with his pinky that cut his forehead in twain.

Holmes nodded. "And who takes care to wrap the corpses before burial?" he asked.

"Oh, the cap'n do that, sir," the older man said. "He's partickler about it, yer might say… then he has 'em brung out when they is wrapped tight about."

Holmes thanked the men, then hurried off in his strange shuffle-step, Douglas hovering like a shadow behind him.

The younger man stared after them.

"Gadzo, talk about pikuliar…" he muttered, but his elder poked him deftly in the ribs once more.

16

THE NIGHT WAS STRANGELY QUIET. AFTER FIVE DAYS OF storm, the absence of a strong wind made it seem even more so. Fog blocked out the stars but amplified every sound, including the *Sultana*'s easy slices through water that was, for the moment, smooth as glass.

All told, quiet is preferable, Holmes thought. Standing on the spar deck, he checked the direction of the wind, the better to hear. Then he and Douglas remained a respectful distance from the goings-on, and watched.

Two bodies lay on the gangplank.

Each was wrapped like a mummy and covered with a Union Jack. A young clergyman approached. He looked round wide-eyed, as if something untoward might be descending upon them at any moment. After that, he turned back to the corpses, and performed the funeral rites.

When he finished, the captain lifted one finger. The gangplank was lowered, the two bodies slid into the ocean and then the captain, the clergyman, and the little knot of deckhands went their way without so much as a look back.

"Did you hear it?" Holmes whispered to Douglas. "The bodies falling into the water?"

Douglas nodded, and Holmes went on.

"Too light for those large men, wouldn't you say?" he opined. "They were under their original weight by a tod and a stone. Each."

"The men died of dysentery, Holmes… "

"Be sensible, Douglas!" Holmes snapped. "They could not have lost so much as that in a few days' time."

"Five," Douglas corrected. "It has been five days since you were cut. Did the shrouds on the gangplank appear small to you?"

"Two mummies wrapped in Union Jacks, viewed at a distance, in the dark? Do you imagine that I am superhuman?"

Douglas almost laughed at that.

"No," Holmes went on, ignoring his friend's amused expression. "It was the *sound* they made upon entering the water that was instructive. The amount of water they displaced. Water never lies.

"I have no idea who was buried at sea just now, but it was not our assailants," he concluded. "This was done for *our* benefit—the clue of the redheaded man, all of it. Someone is trying to frighten us into believing that our enemies will stop at nothing—not even murder. Though in truth they have not reached that waypoint yet."

Douglas sighed, sounding exasperated. "Suppose, for a moment, that I accept your theory. Would 'our enemies'— whomever *they* are—not need to dispose of *four* bodies, then, since it was four who attacked us?"

"Oh, I am certain the other two will be accounted for soon enough. But they cannot simply pretend to kill four large men with dysentery. That would raise tremendous suspicion. No," Holmes mused. "We are here for a reason, Douglas. Here on deck, I mean—I am not speaking metaphysically. Someone *knows* we are here, and they are taking great pains to—"

Suddenly he stopped speaking. He stared up at the smokestack, belching coal. Some smoke descended upon them, obscuring their view and causing them to cough.

"*There* it is," he said happily. He wet his finger and held it up, again gauging what little wind there was. Then he hobbled over to an unobtrusive spot on deck that he declared was "proper for our needs," removed a kerchief from his coat pocket, and laid it out.

"What now?" Douglas asked, watching him.

"Now we return to our room. Two hours hence, you shall kindly fetch my kerchief, and bring it to me."

Douglas frowned, but said nothing.

Two hours later, in their cabin, Holmes inspected the handkerchief via a magnifier he had improvised using a broken piece of glass and a few drops of water. With his fountain pen as a pointer, he indicated bits of fabric that seemed to match a shirt one of their assailants had worn, along with ash that appeared—to Douglas's naked eye— somewhat more elaborate than coal dust.

"You see there, Douglas, the gray and white, the dark gray, and this, yellow in color? That is unburnt trabecular bone with its internal latticework. Nearly impossible to destroy. Distinctly human."

"I suppose it does no good to ask how you know that."

"No, no, I am glad to oblige this time, as I feel a bit stronger, and to give credit where it is due. I spent a few summers assisting a physician friend of my father, in his laboratory. I was to serve as no more than an errand boy, but Dr. Joseph Bell took a liking to me, said I had 'the gift.' I assume he meant the gift of observation. And so he allowed me to attend whilst he conducted various experiments. He believed that nearly everything can be deduced on sight, as long as one knows what one is looking for, and that the rest can be broken down into mathematical equations."

"Or taste," Douglas added with a smile, recalling the carbolic acid.

"Yes. That, too. He was constantly placing all sorts of herbs and potions and chemicals on the tip of his tongue, then lifting his eyes as if he were dissecting a particularly fine wine."

"What luck that we happened to be standing underneath the smokestack at the precise moment that bodies were being burnt down below," Douglas parried. "Yet you will no doubt claim that it wasn't luck at all…"

Holmes shrugged. "If bodies were indeed tossed into the burners, those smokestacks would be emitting miniscule quantities of human for a day and a half before they were done. But yes, we happened upon a good deal of it. With the average man rendering seven-point-four pounds of matter, two of them would be belching out fourteen-point-eight pounds, with the rest residual. How much comes out depends, of course, on when they were placed in the furnace, which is also a matter of simple mathematics."

"So, two of our assailants were poisoned, two more tossed in with the coal?"

But Holmes did not respond. He was frowning down at the handkerchief.

"What is the matter?" Douglas asked. "Not enough detritus?"

"On the contrary. A great deal too much, I'd say." Holmes looked over at Douglas with feverish eyes. "You must go to the furnace room. Now, Douglas, and on your own, as I would slow you down!"

"Nonsense," Douglas protested. "I cannot be seen mucking about…"

"You must! For we cannot proceed further until you do."

"And whatever shall I do when I get there?"

"Breathe," Holmes commanded.

It was no small feat for a man of Douglas's stature and color to make his way through the bowels of the *Sultana* without attracting attention of a negative sort. But he was a man of no small means. He had been more or less on his own since he was a child, and as he had learned to survive by making himself all but invisible to the rough-hewn men who would hurt him for sport, he managed to arrive at his destination with but one small incident in his wake.

He had almost reached the door of the furnace room when a deckhand spotted him. The man seemed quite put out that Douglas was in an area closed off to passengers. A strapping lad of twenty or so, wielding a mop, he didn't even inquire as to what Douglas might be doing there. He simply grinned in a way that spelled trouble, held onto one end of the mop, and with the other moved to bash a hefty dent into Douglas's skull.

Douglas watched the grin turn to shock when a blow from an upraised leg cracked the mop in half.

Refusing to admit defeat, the boy grabbed his broken mop and came at Douglas with the jagged end, intent to put out an eye. Douglas moved aside as efficiently as a cat, and as his assailant lunged past, he reached out and snagged the boy's neck in the crook of his arm, increasing pressure until he went limp.

"Pray forgive the headache you shall have when you awaken," he muttered as he laid the young deckhand gently on the floor.

Then he opened the door to the furnace room.

Inside, two dark-skinned coal workers were feeding flames that seemed too hot for any mortal to withstand. When they heard the door, they turned and stared in surprise, but made no move toward Douglas.

And so the latter did as instructed—he took a deep breath, inhaling through his nose. Then, feeling quite foolish, he nodded to the two gaping men.

"Right, then. Carry on," he said before hastening out again.

Douglas returned to the room to find his weak and ailing friend lying comfortably upon his cot, legs crossed at the ankle, reading Douglas's copy of Dickens. Holmes looked up from the book.

"So? What did you smell?" he asked mildly.

"A furnace room," Douglas answered, annoyed.

Holmes put down the book and sat up. "And there you have it!" he said, as if he had been vindicated.

"Holmes," Douglas said as equitably as he could manage, "I have neither eaten nor slept properly in five days. There are people trying to kill us, or possibly not. The least you can do is give me a decent explanation for your request."

Holmes sighed patiently.

"We have already ascertained that the first two did not die as advertised," he responded. "Now, thanks to you, we know that neither did the second two."

"And how, pray, do we know that?"

"I shall not insult you by replying," Holmes said.

"Insult me," Douglas responded crossly, "and be quick about it."

But Holmes remained mute. Although Douglas was in no mood, his curiosity forced him to play along. All he could do was state the obvious.

"Burning bodies have a foul odor, but I smelled nothing," he said.

"Precisely!"

"But that is impossible! What of the bone and gristle on the kerchief?"

"Peculiar, I will admit," Holmes conceded.

"You do not know how it came to be there?"

"Of course not, Douglas—how should I? And another

thing, did you note the curious emotion the clergyman showed as he performed the funeral for those two corpses on deck?" Holmes asked. "He seemed more than green. He seemed positively unnerved. Perhaps he knew that whatever else might be wrapped in those shrouds, it was not two men recently dead of dysentery."

"So we *don't* have two corpses, much less four," Douglas muttered. "Maddening."

"Is that not what I have been saying? In the meanwhile, I—as it turns out—am rather famished," Holmes said. "Might your hands survive another walk to the grand saloon?"

"If you are hungry at last, as it is a problem I am able to solve, I am glad to attempt it," Douglas said. He helped Holmes to his feet, handed him his walking stick, took hold of the reins in his left hand this time, and opened the door.

They had just emerged when Douglas felt a large sack drop down from on high, covering him completely. It was damp burlap. He could smell it, and could see just enough through its loose weave to make out that Holmes was suffering the selfsame fate.

Then the blows began.

Sticks. Clubs. Fists.

All coming at him in rapid succession. Douglas thanked the heavens that his topcoat provided a bit of cushion, while his arms did their best to protect his face and skull.

The beatings went on and on until he was certain he could take no more. He was feeling himself slip into unconsciousness, falling into that pleasant netherworld where the pain is no more… when he realized that he was being dragged across the ground. It lasted only a moment.

He was just wondering where Holmes might be, when he felt the weight of another burlap bag against his, then heard a door slam shut.

And voices, growing fainter by the moment.

"That big black 'uns a tough old bird!" one said.

"Shut yer yap, Rickets!" another shot back.

Moments later, or perhaps hours, Holmes emerged from the burlap bag to find that he'd been dragged back into his room. Douglas, too, was struggling out of his sack like a huge butterfly from a dark and bloody cocoon.

The two of them were a cut-up, banged-up mess, with barely the strength to crawl onto their respective beds.

"One was named Rickets," Douglas groaned.

Holmes nodded. He had heard the same thing. Then he noticed something on the floor, close by Douglas, and pointed to it with a shaky finger.

Douglas reached for it, picked it up.

"What is it?" Holmes whispered.

"A *douen*," Douglas said. His voice sounded strangled.

His arm shaking from the beating he had endured, he held up the little plaster figurine.

It was of a child with empty eyes and backward-facing feet.

Holmes sighed. "So this is about you after all," he said. "They are trying to frighten you!"

Douglas laughed weakly. Then he grimaced and laid a hand on a bruised rib.

"They know me poorly, then," he said. "They assume I am African, but my people are half African, half Indian, or *dougla*—it's the origin of our surname. Roughly translated, it means 'bastard.' I was not raised to believe in either *douen* or *lougarou*."

"But dead children are understood in any culture," Holmes replied.

Douglas nodded.

"Yes… it is what frightens my family," he mumbled.

"Thus far, we have been poisoned and beaten, yet are no closer to the truth than when we first left London," Holmes said back.

Then he groaned and shut his eyes.

17

NEITHER HOLMES NOR DOUGLAS POSSESSED A HOT-tempered disposition—both were sanguine in nature. And so they did not attempt to seek vengeance, as that would have been foolhardy. They understood that in order to be any use whatsoever for the remainder of the journey, their bodies must first heal.

At least, that was how Holmes comforted himself when he mourned all the time they would waste.

After discerning that they had neither broken bones nor torn ligaments, and that their eyes and brains were still safely ensconced in their skulls, they decided to set up defenses. First they confirmed that they had an empty chamber pot and enough water in the pitcher, then they dragged Douglas's bed directly in front of the door to prevent easy access. From there, they gave themselves up wholeheartedly to the most important task at hand.

Sleep.

They slept so well and so soundly that watches were left unwound. Day and night merged—and in any case, there was no porthole in their room to tell them otherwise.

They arose from slumber only when necessary. Finally,

Holmes regained enough of his senses to survey his surroundings.

"The *douen* is gone," he noted in alarm, as he did not comprehend how that could be possible.

Douglas shook his head no, then stopped and grimaced with pain.

"Only in a sense," he said. Dragging himself out of his bed, he rummaged around the floor near the doorway, then held up what remained of the little figurine. "When we moved the bed in front of the door, it was crushed," he explained.

Most of it was powder now—all that remained were its two little ankles, with those feet that pointed in the wrong direction.

"There, you see?" Douglas said. "Not even evil spirits can survive our chaos."

Holmes took the little feet and dropped them into his coat pocket, which hung over a chair.

"It's not quite a good luck charm, Holmes," Douglas opined, watching him.

"It is whatever we make of it," Holmes countered.

Neither wished to sleep any longer, so with some difficulty they dressed. Too exhausted even to speak, each assisted the other with more onerous tasks, such as fitting arms into sleeves.

Then they stumbled outside, hoping the day would bring a respite to the violence that had transpired thus far.

Holmes's head was pounding as they made their way to the deck. He dearly wished that the fault had been cognac and cigars, rather than blood, bruises, and bile. An arrogant sun stabbed his eyes, rendering him momentarily blind. When he dared to look out again, he discerned crowds of people, most with luggage at their feet.

"How long did we sleep?" he asked in wonder. But all Douglas could manage was a weak joke about Rip Van Winkle.

They peered past the assembled bodies. The *Sultana* seemed to be approaching a shore of some kind. Holmes had perused maps of all the islands they would pass on their journey, further studying whatever paintings, sketches, and albumen prints were available. Yet an actual landmass, in full and rapidly hastening color, disoriented him. No amount of squinting served to make it any clearer. So he took his best guess.

"Barbados…?" he offered.

But Douglas shook his head no.

"Must've passed that two days ago," he responded. "We have entered the Gulf of Paria. You are staring at our destination. Port of Spain.

"Trinidad."

Holmes marveled at the very thought. They had endured five days filled with storm and poison—then three, perhaps four, barricaded in their room…

"I had best get our bags," Douglas said beside him, "as we are about to disembark."

"You cannot carry them all," Holmes objected. "Not in the state you are in. I shall go with you."

Douglas held up a hand to stop him.

"Do we not attract attention enough with our battered

appearance?" he muttered. "Add to that a white man in charge of his own bags, and we will find ourselves drawn, quartered, and thrown overboard."

Holmes, still blinking furiously so that his eyes would adjust to the light, watched with some trepidation as Douglas hobbled off.

Then he saw something else that drew his attention.

Three of the "government types" he'd noticed that first night were standing nearby—not so close as to arouse suspicion, but close enough—and they seemed to be paying him particular mind. With them was the finely mustached American whose name he recalled as Adam McGuire.

By way of experiment, Holmes turned toward them a time or two, peering over their heads as if more taken with the approaching scenery. Each time he did so, they turned away, as if suddenly preoccupied with other matters. The moment they thought they weren't being observed, however, they looked his way again.

He heard a woman shrieking.

It came from behind him, and he glanced over his shoulder. It was the fashionable dowager who'd complained of the storm. Her chatelaine bag was tied securely to her belt, as was the norm—but she was holding it so that all could see that the bottom had been cut.

"Empty!" she cried aloud. "My money, my jewels… gone!"

A few puzzle pieces suddenly snapped into place.

He looked around and spotted the ship's purser. Though not far off, he seemed to be unaware of this kerfuffle. His gaze was up and to the right, and his mouth was working ever so slightly.

Making good use of his walking stick, and trying not to wobble, he propelled himself in the man's direction, and then slowed.

Would a purser be anxious to mark the words of a disoriented young man, covered with scabs and dried blood? he wondered. *Not likely.*

He would have to impress him first.

"I do not mean to disturb whilst you are tallying the crew's pay," he began.

The purser looked startled

"How'd you know…?" he started to ask.

But Holmes could not respond. He was fighting for air as if he'd swum across deck, instead of walked.

"Jostled about a bit, are we?" the purser asked kindly. "Might you be needing assistance, then?"

Holmes rethought his strategy. Perhaps it was best to get right to the point.

"Here… aboard, is a boy of fifteen or so…" he began, trying to force air into his lungs. "This boy… referred to himself as a duffer."

The purser frowned. "Duffer?" he repeated. "And however'd you come to be aweer of this fact?"

"I… it would take too long to explain," Holmes said. "Please. You see that woman there? Her purse was cut, her jewels and money taken."

The purser hesitated only a moment. Then he pulled out a whistle hooked to a cord about his neck, blowing it loudly.

"*Pickpocket aboard!*" he bellowed. All the men within

earshot immediately patted their pockets to ensure that their wallets were where they had left them. But Holmes's eyes were trained on three men in particular.

Satisfied in his assumptions, he gave the purser a description of the boy so that he could recount it for the security detail.

"Oh, and might you recall an elderly woman," he asked, "dressed in mourning clothes, being pushed about in an ornate carriage by an Indian nurse?"

The purser shook his head no. "But if she be an invalid, she'll be at the front of the line by now," he replied, and he pointed to the moveable railing where the gangway would be set for disembarking.

Huffing like a locomotive, Holmes pushed past the crowd until he saw the old woman at the railing, her Indian assistant by her side. Upon reaching her, he walked behind her wheelchair, carefully extended his hand to the back of her neck, unclasped the plum-sized locket, and pulled it into his palm. Then he opened the locket, ran his pinkie inside, and drew out a dusting of ash.

At this juncture, both the servant and the old woman had realized there was something amiss, and stared up at the young gentleman whose face was yellowed by healing bruises.

"It seems your consort… has had an impromptu burial at *sea*, madam," Holmes wheezed. "I am afraid this is what is left of him." With that, he flicked the bits of ash from his pinkie into the receptacle again before dropping the locket onto her lap.

The old woman opened her mouth to speak, or to scream—but by this time Douglas was at Holmes's side.

Upon seeing him, she opened her eyes wide, just as her mouth clamped shut.

"Come along, Douglas," Holmes said imperiously.

He turned on his heel and strode off. Douglas followed suit, though he managed to call back over his shoulder.

"Dreadfully sorry for your loss, madam!"

18

WITH NEARLY EVERYONE CLUSTERED UPON DECK AND
waiting to disembark, Douglas and Holmes found a quiet
spot inside the grand saloon. They took a moment to catch
their breath, and then Douglas spoke tersely.

"I am quite unsettled that I am once again forced to ask
this question," he said, "but what on earth was *that* about?"

"I have much to tell you," Holmes replied with a smile.
"But first, what do you infer?"

"Aside from the fact that you can be an insufferable
ass?" Douglas shot back.

"That aside, yes," Holmes replied equitably, folding
his thumbs together, his index fingers tapping against each
other.

"I *infer*," Douglas said, "that the elderly woman was in
mourning."

"Brilliant!" Holmes teased.

"Given the Indian motif on her bag, and the nationality
of her attendant, that her dead husband was a British
military man stationed in India," Douglas added. "And
when he died, she had him cremated in the Indian fashion."

"Very good. Thus far, you would do any schoolboy
proud."

"I *further* infer," he continued, parrying the insult, "that she had his ashes placed in that ghastly piece of 'mourning jewelry'."

"Precisely—though you neglected to mention that she was in her second mourning," Holmes clarified. "The nine-month period following the first. In the second mourning, one may still wear black, and may appear in public without a veil. Though normal jewelry is still not permitted, one may wear mourning jewelry, receptacles into which some portion of the deceased is placed, including snippets of hair and fingernail parings."

"And you Englishmen call us savages," Douglas muttered.

"Her husband's ashes were safely ensconced therein," Holmes went on, "until someone emptied said contents onto my kerchief, along with bits of hair and fibers—the latter taken directly from our assailants, most likely with their consent. After which, someone—perhaps the same person, possibly not—replaced the now-empty locket inside her stateroom before anyone could be the wiser."

"And how'd you know the ash did not spew out of the furnaces?"

"Because there was too much, and it was too evenly distributed. The wind is not so fair-minded as all that. No, Douglas, as you are well aware, there are only so many ways to dispose of a body on a ship this size."

"I don't like what you are implying, Holmes," Douglas said evenly. "How would I know the ways to dispose of bodies aboard a ship of any size? Although you are quite correct," he amended. "Short of cutting them up for stew…"

"...either they go overboard," Holmes agreed, "or up the chimney. Once our mysterious opponents faked the death of the two assailants, they observed our attempt to check the *other* viable method of disposal—the furnaces. When we laid out my handkerchief and left it alone, we made it easy for them.

"The trap was laid," he concluded, "and they fell in."

"The trap?" Douglas replied. "What trap? You never mentioned anything of the kind..."

Holmes shrugged. "It was a hunch. And had I been wrong, I did not care to show my hand. But I did know this—if they wished us to believe that someone had been torched, they would need to provide ashes. And so they did."

"Always 'they'," Douglas said irritably. "Though we still cannot fathom who 'they' might be."

"Now that is where I have *outstanding* news!" Holmes said as his smile grew. "You heard the purser call out the presence of a pickpocket, did you not?"

"Of course. Everyone heard."

"And what is the first thing you did upon hearing it?"

"Felt for my wallet."

Holmes nodded. "Standing near me, and feigning not to notice me at all, were three of the 'government types,' along with that other one, the American Adam McGuire. When the purser called out the warning, they seemed surprised, but made no move. They already knew a pickpocket was aboard, just as they knew that they would not be his marks.

"For they are the ones who had hired him."

"The boy?" Douglas asked. "The duffer?"

"There you have it!" Holmes replied, clearly pleased with his friend's deductive skills. He leaned in closer and lowered his voice. "It was that lovesick boy who broke into our room. Who put the poisoned powder in the medicine box. It was he who purloined the old woman's locket and emptied its contents, and then replaced it without allowing the woman or her maid to be any the wiser."

"And cutting the woman's purse?" Douglas objected. "Was that part of their plan?"

Holmes shook his head no. "Most likely that was from habit, or to impress someone with his cleverness. As I said, the men did register surprise. But they did not see themselves as victims."

"Of course, the larger question remains," Douglas persisted. "*Why?* Why any of it? Why attack us? Why incapacitate us through the course of the journey? And why try to make us believe that our assailants are dead?"

Holmes shrugged. "Perhaps they are throwing everything at us, hoping something connects. As I suspected when we were first attacked, they are not professional killers. Murder is their last resort. But I would say they are approaching that last resort rather quickly."

The ship's whistle sounded.

The *Sultana* had come into port.

Douglas rose to his feet and cracked his sore back.

"Forgive me for not being more impressed with your deductions, Holmes, though they are impressive," Douglas said. "I am tired, aching, and famished, and in spite of your good work, we seem to be out of our league—and certainly out of our element."

"True enough," Holmes replied. "But we are new at it. We shall get better."

Douglas looked at Holmes, surprised and a bit annoyed.

"I do not wish to 'get better'," he objected. "I enjoyed my life well enough as it was!"

Holmes arched an eyebrow. "Yes, but when one is given lemons, one must perforce make lemonade. Either that, or they shall make lemonade of us."

Douglas sighed his assent. Then he wearily picked up the bags again and walked toward the saloon door.

Holmes would have followed behind, but his nose had other plans. On a plate left next to the rubbish bin, he spotted a few slices of bread, along with a piece of smoked haddock.

He quickly secured the repast for himself and Douglas. Then they left the room and proceeded along the deck. They walked toward the gate, eating as they went.

"So now we are banged up like two soused old seamen," Douglas said ruefully, "and smelling like fish."

"True," Holmes agreed. "But a dried piece of fish has never tasted so good as this. And I have never been so glad to say goodbye to a ship as I am to the great *Sultana*."

19

THE TWO OF THEM SOON FORMED PART OF THE GREAT crush of humanity that was working its way down the gangway to the dock.

The sky was crystalline blue. In the distance, church steeples rose up here and there over the one-story houses and the green, sloping hillsides. Banyan and silk cotton trees swayed in a wind not yet sticky with heat and humidity. Trinidad would have another month or more of glorious weather before daily showers marred the tourists' fun and made life tedious for the locals.

The closer they got to the wharf, the more they heard the lilting sound of native speakers, as different from the clipped tones of Cumberland House as sand is from concrete. But then another sort of sound rose up—one that seemed as if it had been plucked directly from the gutters of East London.

It was the boy they had seen writing on the ship, the duffer. He was down below, on dry land. His wrists were bound, and on either side of him stood a ship's constable. As they were dragging him away, he was yelling back rather desperately toward the *Sultana*.

"I done all ya ast me!" he cried. "My kidsman'll tell ya, I h'ain't no duffer, I's a proper fine wirer!"

A stunned Holmes looked to Douglas.

"Do you know what this means?"

Douglas groaned. He was struggling to hold the bags in a way that would not send pains shooting up and down his spine. He'd had enough of questions and mental gymnastics.

Nevertheless, he responded dutifully.

"He protests that he is no mere thief, but an expert pickpocket. Clearly, he is hoping to impress someone aboard. Your 'government types,' I suppose, if they are the ones who hired him."

"Not at all!" Holmes declared. "The boy was in love, was he not?"

"So you said."

"Thus, he desires to impress but one person—his beloved Anabel."

Douglas frowned, his exasperation growing.

"You are saying this 'Anabel' is aboard the ship? Then why would he have bothered writing her at all?"

"Perhaps her family was not keen on having her courted by a scruffy younger male. There was an Anabel on the passenger list," Holmes said as they reached the dock. "Aged twenty, surname of 'Lynch.' But as there is no shortage of Anabels in the world, I assumed it was mere coincidence."

"Do you mean to say that you memorized more than one thousand names?" Douglas asked, and he let out a surprised laugh that made his ribs ache.

"Don't be daft," Holmes responded crossly. "What need would I have for that? I only noted the women who were aged seventeen to twenty-five. With the very good notion of seeing if... perhaps Georgiana was aboard."

He said her name with profound sorrow. *As if she were lost to him already*, Douglas thought. Then he put the notion aside. "And how many were there," he asked, "aged seventeen to twenty-five?"

"One hundred and thirty-eight," Holmes mumbled.

Douglas stood where he was, forcing Holmes to stop, and the stream of passengers to move around them.

"You memorized *one hundred and thirty-eight names*—in the half a moment it took you to read them?"

"I did not 'memorize' them," Holmes protested. "I 'noted' them."

"And what, pray, is the difference?"

Holmes sighed. "If you memorize something, it is in your brain forever, rattling around in there, taking up space. If you *note* something, you do not recall it unless something else brings it to mind. As did the boy's plaintive cries, just now. I noted something I had read, in relation to something I heard. Is that so very strange?"

"It is strange when the memory is word for word," Douglas responded. He thought a moment, then added, "So, for example, the speed of the ship brought to mind that magazine essay."

"Precisely," Holmes said.

"Fascinating," Douglas said. They began to walk again, saying nothing more until their feet had reached the end of the dock.

"We have made it," Holmes declared, glancing about.

"Yes," Douglas said. "For better or worse, here we are."

* * *

The wharf was filled with people of all colors, which meant that Holmes was able to take his bag from Douglas without arousing hostility.

Port of Spain's docks appeared no different than any port's, which was to say mostly they were dirty and noisy, with large wooden warehouses meant to facilitate cargo, and not to appeal to the senses. The water looked slick with oil, and crowded-in with ships and boats and tugs and vessels of all kinds.

Making their way through the throng was a chore. The thousand souls who had been trapped for nine long days 'tween decks were taking full advantage of their newfound freedom. No longer were they beholden to England's stuffy ways and her ideas of class. They and their children were running roughshod through the port.

Given the people disembarking from other ships, natives selling wares and trinkets, laborers and crew hastening for a meal and a drink, and painted ladies looking for a man for an hour or for the night, it was nearly impossible for Douglas and Holmes to move at all.

They had managed only a few steps when Holmes felt a tap on his shoulder. He turned, and was surprised to see Captain Miles.

He thought that the man looked haunted, or perhaps a bit drunk.

The captain glanced around quickly, as if about to do something untoward. Then, taking advantage of the mass of people on the docks, he sidled up so close that Holmes could smell the rye on his breath.

"I... I was aware of the goings-on aboard," he

murmured. "Some of it, at least. I never should have turned a blind eye. Never. This is… by way of apology." With that, he took a small envelope from his coat pocket and handed it to Holmes. "Inside is a list of names. Get to the governor's office, and do not open it until you arrive, as you shall need aid with what you find therein. Now that you are no longer on the *Sultana*, you are no longer under protection.

"Go quickly, for there is no time to spare."

He stepped away and moved to depart. Before Holmes could say a word in response, half a dozen crewmen surrounded their captain like a human shield and hastened him out of their sight.

"So. He was bribed to look away from whatever 'indiscretion' was transpiring aboard," Douglas grumbled. "We—most likely you—were a danger to that indiscretion, based on your position in government. He allowed us to be beaten, and you to be poisoned to within an inch of your life, and now the guilt consumes him. If that is how he protected us," he added, "then let us thank our stars that his protection has come to an end!"

Holmes shook his head no.

"He said 'under protection,' Douglas. Not 'under my protection.' Someone else was protecting us—someone who wanted us to be out of commission, but not killed. Whoever that was, his influence has waned. We had best get to the governor's office posthaste."

The two mingled again with the crowd, every one of them anxious to get away from the docks and begin their brand-new adventure in Trinidad.

* * *

The two friends moved past the warehouses to where the docks finally ended and Port of Spain began in earnest. In truth, however, the section through which they walked was still heavily indebted to the ships that came in and out of harbor, and most particularly to the thirsty men who worked long, hard hours to provide for themselves and their kin.

Just across from the docks stood a long row of wooden dwellings, each two stories high. Gaps between their mildewed planks gave the appearance of a mouthful of rotten teeth. Here and there, where the dwellings seemed ready to buckle, large, rough-hewn beams propped them up, with one end of the beam sunk into the roadway below. To add to the maze, there were wooden stairs that led to doorways—as well as occasional second-story windows. More stairs led below the sidewalk to basement doors covered by weather-beaten burlap of fading red, yellow, orange, or teal. None of these openings was tall enough for a human body to pass through without squatting.

"These 'habitations' look less than habitable," Holmes said, and he frowned to Douglas.

"That is because they are public houses," Douglas explained.

Drawing closer, Holmes could see that a few of the better ones—the ones with regular doors—sported such names as "The Anchor," "The Pig and Whistle," or "The Port o' Call." Many more were unnamed and very nearly invisible, but for handmade sketches of beer mugs announcing that drinks could be found therein.

"They serve only ale?" Holmes asked, indicating The Anchor. "Might we find quick sustenance there, as well?"

Douglas shook his head no.

"Stale bread or crackers is more like it. Or dirty water that someone will call a broth. Surely we are not that desperate." He nodded into the distance. "Once in town proper, there'll be nourishment aplenty. Might you survive 'til then?"

"If *you* can," Holmes muttered.

The two kept hurrying along, with Douglas trying to ignore his sour gut and aching head as he pondered the captain's words.

"So it is your assumption, to this point," Douglas posited, "that the captain had been paid or goaded into compliance, and that he in turn had made the priest complicit. For surely nothing happens on a ship without the captain's knowing."

Holmes nodded. "That priest, like the others, was not a professional deceiver. He was simply a man who found himself in the wrong place at the wrong time."

"This way," Douglas said, pointing. While still back in London, he had written ahead and secured a rig to take them wherever they wished to go. Plaza del Marina was to be the assigned meeting place.

As he kept up with his friend's long strides, Holmes recalled Douglas's plaintive words back on the ship.

I enjoyed my life well enough as it was.

As did I, he mused. *As did I.*

What a strange and unwelcome twist of fate. He never intended to be on a scout-about in Trinidad for the estimable Edward Cardwell. Nor did he intend for it to be a ruse to chase his fiancée halfway around the world, only to lose sight of her before the journey had even begun.

He never intended, for the life of him, to be assaulted, cut, poisoned, then beaten—and to drag his closest friend through the thick of it. It comforted him only a little to know that Douglas would surely have made the journey regardless of his involvement.

Though possibly not with strangers attempting to kill *him,* he admitted to himself. Holmes continued to believe that it was he—not Douglas—who was the lightning rod for all this misery. *Someone does not want me to follow Georgiana. Perhaps to find her.*

Perhaps to learn what she knows...

Holmes's reverie was interrupted when Douglas cleared his throat. He looked up to see his friend's chin pointing in front of them. But he could discern nothing beyond a phalanx of top hats spreading this way and that.

"What is it?" Holmes whispered without stopping.

By way of response, Douglas picked up his pace even more, pushing through the throng without so much as a "thank you" or an "if you please." Holmes followed as best he could, wondering what could cause his friend to behave in this very un-Douglas-like manner.

As the crowds scattered to their own destinations, Holmes finally saw what had so piqued his friend's interest. The man was stout. Hair like carrot shavings poked out from underneath his brown cap and curled down his thick neck. On his back and over one shoulder, he carried a rolled up woolen blanket. And when he turned to glance furtively over his shoulder, Holmes caught a glimpse of the ugly scar that split his forehead in twain and reached around to his ears.

Holmes indicated the blanket. "He is a swagman," he

muttered to Douglas, who nodded.

"And he is most certainly not deceased!" the latter added in a harsh whisper.

The man hastened across the street, impervious to traffic, and then hurried down a set of rickety steps that led to the doorway of an anonymous bar. Holmes was ready to follow when Douglas held him back.

"That is not a place for you, Holmes," he said. "Your skin is decidedly the wrong color."

"That redhead is whiter than I!" Holmes protested.

"No one could possibly be whiter than you," Douglas chided. Then, to head off any reply, he added, "He has his swag, Holmes. He is a vagrant, a traveler. He knows these parts, and they know him."

"Then you must go," Holmes said, but Douglas shook his head.

"I have a better idea. Come along." With that, he sprinted across the street, his hand lifted to halt horses and mules and carts.

Unlike London, where any attempt to circumvent traffic resulted in curses and perhaps a sound beating, people here seemed more kind, some even smiling at the two strangers, freshly arrived and still carrying their bags, who seemed in such a frightful hurry to procure a drink.

Once they had crossed, Douglas glanced around and found a place where his bags would remain unnoticed. Placing them out of sight, he climbed a ladder, then clambered in through a cracked window above the pub.

After a moment's hesitation, Holmes followed suit.

20

IT WAS AN INSUFFERABLY FILTHY ROOM, ABUSED BY AGE
and grime, but quite abandoned. Here and there the
wallpaper, which appeared to have once been decorated
with light pink rosettes, was yellowed as if someone had
thought of setting it on fire but then changed his mind at
the last minute.

"What is this place?" Holmes whispered.

"Was," Douglas whispered back. "Opium den."

"Ah," Holmes said under his breath, as if that made all
the sense in the world.

In truth, he had always had sympathy for the poor
wretches who found themselves addicted to some substance
or other. They had troubles enough, he felt, without being
demonized. His brother, on the other hand, was merciless
with habit and dependency of any sort. Sherlock dismissed
the fact that he smoked tobacco, however, as a peccadillo—
but then Sherlock made himself the exception to every rule.

He could still picture Sherlock waving to him from
that impossibly grubby corner he claimed for his own.
However strange the scene had been at the time—that was
how normal and even serene it appeared in retrospect. He
hoped he would remain alive long enough to tell his brother

all about this strange adventure he had embarked upon.

In the center of the room, among the whorls of dust that looked as if they had been created of spun cotton, was a wooden chair deprived of two of its legs. Douglas pulled it out of the way to uncover four knotholes in the floor— whether man-made or natural, it was hard for Holmes to tell, as the whole place appeared to be so very chewed up.

"There you see?" Douglas whispered. "A bird's-eye view into the bar below."

"Provided the birds can sink to their knees and stare through knotholes in floorboards," Holmes muttered as he squatted down.

It was nearly impossible to make out more than shadows, but as their eyes adjusted, they noticed their man taking an empty seat at the bar. He took off his cap, revealing hair of such orange-red hue that even the darkness could not subdue it.

To his left, and particularly difficult to discern, were two more men. By their casual demeanor, it was clear they all knew each other.

Then, a fourth man appeared. He was massive, every bit as large as the one that Douglas had labeled "the figgy pudding." In his hand he held a pot of ale, which he poured into three waiting mugs, while he kept the pot for himself. He took a seat to the right of the redhead.

The four men clinked, and drank. They spoke, but Holmes and Douglas could not hear what was said. One by one, however, they turned so their features could be seen, and before long it was certain—all four assailants were still quite alive.

A moment later, someone else entered Holmes and Douglas's sightline. He was small, thin as a stick, and barefooted. Even in the dark, he looked no more than ten years of age. He had the tentative demeanor of the chronically impoverished. His shoulders were raised up around his ears, his head pulled slightly back as if to protect himself from a blow that sooner or later would surely come. Around his neck hung a tray, affixed by a strap, laden with pies.

The boy tapped the redhead on the shoulder and held out his offerings.

"Rickets!" one of the men bellowed to another. "Why, here's a feast, my lad!"

Above his head, Holmes elbowed Douglas.

"Did you hear that?" he asked softly. "Rickets. The four men who attacked us in the passageway are clearly the same men who waylaid us outside our—"

"Meat pies," Douglas whispered back, interrupting him. "Minced beef packed with thyme, chives, garlic, onion, paprika."

"Enough!" Holmes hissed through gritted teeth. "My mouth is watering as it is—I do not need details. Meat pies, you say?"

Douglas nodded silently.

Beneath them, the redhead slapped his comrade on the shoulder and pointed a thumb the boy's way, and soon all four men had turned and were grabbing at his wares. When he tried to pull the tray away, the redhead cuffed him smartly on the ear, while another threw a few coins on the ground by his feet, all the while rising from the stool in a threatening manner to indicate that—whatever their cost—he needn't wait for more.

The boy gathered the coins and disappeared, his pies taken, and the men turned back to the bar to enjoy their food and drink.

Holmes kept watching, though the hard wood was playing havoc with his knees, which were still bruised from the beating. He felt in his jacket pocket for Georgiana's cameo—something that had become second nature to him—and wondered for the thousandth time where she was.

But then, next to the cameo, so comforting and familiar, Holmes felt something else—the backward-facing feet of the figurine. He pulled his hand from his pocket as if he had touched fire, and focused once again on the scene below.

In less than twenty minutes' time, the men in the bar had finished off the pies and downed nearly four pots of ale.

At this juncture, the redhead and the figgy pudding— the most visible of the four—began to act strangely. They touched their lips with their fingertips, and then squeezed their hands. The redhead cocked his head, as if he were listening for something. Then he wiped beer—or perhaps it was drool—that dribbled from the sides of his mouth.

Without warning, he clawed at his chest as if trying to dig something out.

The figgy pudding, with his hand laid gently over his heart, seemed to be trying to draw air into his lungs, to no avail.

Then all four men lurched to their feet, and began stumbling about in panicked distress, ripping at their chests, squeezing their throats, or rubbing hands and faces with increasing desperation. One by one, they fell.

Moments later, all four lay crumpled on the dirt floor.

Chaos ensued. Several patrons went near and checked the men for breath and heartbeat. Apparently finding neither, they assured the others in the bar that yes, indeed, all four were most decidedly dead. One of the patrons went to the entrance and lifted the curtain. Sun streamed inside.

Above, Douglas and Holmes recoiled back from the unexpected light, then resettled.

With newfound clarity, Holmes noticed a slender man who stood up from a nearby table, pulled a fur cap from out of his back pocket, and with his two hands—one of which was missing two fingers—placed the hat upon his head. Then, with a strange, shuffling gait, he walked out of the establishment without looking back.

Holmes was just glancing over to Douglas when the latter caught his eye.

"Edward Dedos," Douglas declared, "known as Three-Fingered Eddie. Port of Spain's most efficient poisoner."

"Ah," Holmes responded. The deaths had shaken him more than he cared to admit, and he could think of nothing pertinent to say.

The two dusted off their knees and headed for the window.

21

DOUGLAS AND HOLMES HURRIED OUT AND DOWN THE ladder again and did some scouting about as the lorry wagon arrived with its hand-cranked siren to pick up the bodies.

But neither the boy nor Three-Fingered Eddie were to be found.

They recovered the bags, which to Holmes's relief had remained untouched. Then they hastened toward Plaza del Marina, where they were to meet their cab.

"So," Holmes exclaimed in a tone that, to Douglas, sounded suspiciously like intrigue. "A poisoner for hire."

"You seem to be enjoying this part a bit too much, Holmes," Douglas said.

"Not at all," Holmes protested, though inwardly he wondered if he was, just a little. "It's purely scientific curiosity," he continued as they went. "Accounting for loss of sensation in the lips, fingers, and lower joints, culminating with paralysis of the diaphragm... would you say puffer fish?"

Douglas nodded. "A quick but painful death. Eddie milks the creatures that carry the toxins—puffers, toads, blue-ringed octopuses, certain types of angelfish. And he is diabolically good at placing the stuff where it can best be ingested."

"I can only thank the heavens, then, that he wasn't aboard ship," Holmes said in all seriousness. "Was that his boy?" he inquired. "The one with the pies?"

"Probably," Douglas replied. "But he never uses the same helpmeet twice. Most likely he provided both food and tray, along with a goodly payment for the young charge. Three-Fingered Eddie prides himself on being a generous, if only a one-time employer."

"Would he have poisoned those men out of a personal vendetta?"

Douglas shook his head no, then stopped and looked thoughtful.

"To this juncture, at least, it has never been personal with Eddie," he amended. "It is simply business. He hails from my own neighborhood in San Fernando—"

"So, it is as we suspected," Holmes interrupted. "Our swagmen were purchased aboard ship to torment us. That done, they became expendable. Someone here has deep pockets, Douglas. Forgive my brusqueness in Three-Fingered Eddie's regard, but I doubt if it is worth our while to try to find him."

Douglas nodded. "Even if we find him and demand to know who hired him, one does not survive as long as Eddie has unless one is tight-lipped, and with more hiding places than a gutter rat."

"We could try to guess who hired him," Holmes added, "but I think it would be best now to concern ourselves with why…"

He paused mid-thought.

Before they had even reached the plaza, he could smell

the food. It was a heady mix of aromas—Indian, Creole, African, Spanish, Chinese—fused with sea salt, seeming to cling to the humid air. Holmes felt his knees go weak with desire. At the plaza, he scanned the crowds until he spied the vendors. As his olfactory sense had promised, they were selling what appeared to be a cornucopia of tasty concoctions.

However, there were queues of hungry patrons, and they were long. Holmes calculated the shortest line— with an approximate wait time of two minutes and four seconds per each of sixteen bodies…

"Perhaps we had best get to our destination first," Douglas suggested.

For once, Holmes wished his emotions could best his logic. But he grunted his consent. Douglas tore his gaze from the vendors and their food carts and focused instead on the rigs for hire, spotting the one he'd retained.

The owner was a local of Chinese extraction. He was leaning against a two-wheeled gig, arms folded before him, eyes downcast to signal to prospective passengers that he was otherwise engaged. His face was as round as a penny, and of approximately the same hue. He looked up, almost as if a magnet had drawn him, and saw Holmes and Douglas. He stood up straight, clapped his hands like a child, and smiled so brightly that even Holmes exhaled with relief.

Douglas looked amused. "Huan has that effect on people."

Huan hurried over to them, clapping all the while.

"You had me worrying," he said to Douglas, looking as if he had never worried a day in his life. "Nico, too!" he added, pointing back to the mule harnessed to the gig. "The boat, she come ashore as she is bound to. We wait, as we are bound to. But no Cyrus Douglas." He stopped, and his smile faded.

"Ah! But what has happened to your face, old friend?" he added the moment he got a good look at him.

"Ah," Douglas said, his tone easily falling into the cadences of his homeland. "A bit of business to care for, is all!"

Huan nodded as if Douglas's explanation were entirely sufficient.

"May I introduce my dear friend, Mycroft Holmes?" Douglas continued. "Holmes, my good friend Huan."

The two shook hands.

"You have hair like the sun, my friend!" Huan commented. "And eyes like the ocean in a storm!"

Holmes was left speechless, for once.

They stored the bags, then Huan pulled down the back of the gig. Holmes and Douglas climbed in. Nico the mule stepped gingerly through the plaza, then quickened his step the moment they reached the packed-dirt streets. Pillows at the back made the journey only slightly less jarring.

And so it continues, thought Holmes as he held onto the sides of the contraption for dear life.

Port of Spain was nestled between low-lying green hills, with palm and mangrove and cacao trees in full fruit. One-story wooden shanties gave way to old mud-plastered Spanish *ajoupas*, some of which had seemingly crumbled into convenient dust to make room for a large, impressive Catholic church here, an elaborate Indian temple there.

As they traversed the city, Holmes marveled at the whirlwind of civilizations, of conquerors alongside the vanquished. The sun was sinking into a fireball that streaked the sky crimson and mauve. He had to admit he had never seen a sunset to match it.

From having perused the maps, he knew that the city proper was composed of eleven major streets in a straight grid that pushed from the foot of the Laventille Hills to the area that culminated in the Saint Ann's River. But like a waterway with endless tributaries, the streets split off into alleys and courts and cutaways and everything in between, as if the very nature of the place would not allow for conformity but somehow had to unshackle itself from the grid. The people themselves ebbed and flowed, making no allowances for vehicles at all, but simply walking where they pleased.

Huan turned in his seat and looked back at his passengers. "Everything here is done in the road," he laughed as if it were a game. "Walking in the road, eating in the road, dancing in the road. Trinidad, she likes to play!"

Even so, he seemed to know precisely which tributary to navigate so they might proceed with a minimum of fuss. In truth, he appeared to be as intimate with his own city as Holmes was with the London grid. And Nico was a bright-eyed young mule with soft, chocolate-colored fur. He needed next to no prodding, but seemed to discern what his master wanted even before Huan was fully aware of it.

It made Holmes ache for Abie.

I do hope Parfitt is taking proper care of him, he thought, though he had no reason to doubt it.

His musings were interrupted when one particular

building caught his eye. It was the color of a freshly plucked mandarin orange, with a courtyard and lovely fountain that reminded him of paintings he had seen of Madrid.

He gestured toward it, but when he turned to Douglas to ask about it, he saw that his friend's amber eyes had darkened. His skin looked sallow. He was glancing about, Holmes thought, as if unnaturally nervous.

"The Cabildo," Douglas said in response to Holmes's gesture. "Former seat of the Spanish colonial government, before the British set up their own government." Then he leaned forward and called out to Huan. "Why so few people in the streets, my friend? On such a lovely spring evening as this?"

Huan shrugged and glanced back.

"The *douen*, my friend," he said loudly enough to be heard. "They have arrived, and they have set up house. They call to the children to come play," he added for Holmes's benefit. "And then the *lougarou*, they finish the deed. Twelve children found dead, their blood sucked from their little bodies!"

"Twelve?" Douglas repeated in alarm. "I was told three."

Huan nodded. "Nine in the last week alone. The *douen* and the *lougarou*, they have been busy of late."

"Huan?" Holmes interjected. "You said the *douen* have been seen about. But seen by whom?"

"Ah, I did not say they had been seen," Huan responded. "You do not see them, only footprints in the sand. Made by little feet that move forward but face back."

"On sand..." Holmes repeated. "And are there other

prints around those? Human feet, perhaps? Lines? Markings of any kind?"

Huan shook his head. "Little backward-facing feet, is all…!"

As they jostled along, Holmes rummaged inside his jacket pocket and pulled out the little clay feet. He opened his palm and pressed them into the soft part of his skin, "walking" them from pinky to thumb and back again—then he stared down quizzically at his hand.

The governor's office wasn't grand, but it had a certain charm. There were no interior hallways—each door simply opened up onto an arcaded front. And the second story, with its own arcaded walkways and back-end balconies, provided shade for the offices below.

Shade was a necessity. Even as the sun descended, and though it was April, the heat was impressive. By nightfall, as the streets were cooling down, the buildings would have absorbed all the day's sun. Sitting inside would grow quickly so oppressive that the only businesses that stayed open past sunset were eating and drinking establishments, gambling houses, and houses of ill repute.

But the governor's office had been alerted that the secretary to the Secretary of State for War would be arriving on the *Sultana* on that specific day, and so—though they were past the point of their usual closure, the doors were still open to welcome Holmes in.

22

SIR ARTHUR CHARLES HAMILTON-GORDON, ALSO KNOWN
as lord Stanmore, was tall, with wispy gray hair, a long,
slightly crooked nose in an equally long, slightly crooked
face, and a good-natured, hearty disposition.

The son of a former British prime minister, he was too
well bred to mention their battered faces. For that, Holmes
was grateful, as it meant he had no need to explain. He
and the governor simply greeted one another as though
the obvious did not exist, and when Holmes introduced
Douglas as his aide-de-camp—a lofty title, given that
Holmes himself was little more than that to Cardwell—
Hamilton-Gordon did not twitch so much as an eyebrow.

There was a slight, black-haired man in his thirties—
Holmes assumed he was the governor's own aide-de-camp—
who was not so charitable. He looked askance at Douglas,
and when the governor requested a platter of biscuits and
three cups of rum, the aide could not hold his tongue.

"Three, your Lordship?" he asked, his tone making it
clear that he did not approve of Negroes imbibing with
their betters.

The baron frowned, and turned to Holmes.

"Has your aide other duties to execute at this late hour?"

he inquired. When Holmes assured him that Douglas was at liberty, the governor smiled.

"There you have it, Beauchamp," he declared. "Three glasses. Gentlemen! Make yourselves at home." He indicated two plush leather armchairs on the other side of his desk.

Douglas and Holmes did as instructed, sinking into them with gratitude.

As they waited for the biscuits and rum, Douglas dearly wished Holmes would get to the reason for their visit—which was, after all, of some urgency. But Holmes and the baron had first to observe the niceties of their class—talk of the weather back in England, the state of the British pound, even the health of the Queen.

If their toes were on fire, Douglas thought, *they would still spend a quarter of an hour on polite chatter before reaching for the extinguisher.* He sank deeper into the armchair, stared out at the enormous five-fingered tree that grew up and over the back balcony, and let it all evolve as it would.

For the next few moments, Holmes and the governor spoke of Cambridge, their alma mater. The baron recounted that he had spent six years as Lieutenant-Governor of New Brunswick before his 1866 transfer to Trinidad.

"The differences between this place and Canada are monumental," the governor confided, "and I do not simply mean the weather. It seems that Port of Spain runs on graft. It is to be expected, I suppose. When a country is poor, anything can be bought."

"Yes, we experienced a taste of that ourselves on the *Sultana*," Holmes said cryptically. "We also hear tell of… supernatural occurrences."

"They are a superstitious lot, Mr. Holmes," the baron exclaimed. "If we were to chase down every bogeyman that… aha, but here we are!"

His aide arrived with the tray of sustenance. The three men took their biscuits and rum, and toasted to Trinidad. The rum warmed Holmes's belly, but it was the biscuits he craved. He ate one, then another almost immediately. Only sheer willpower kept him from making a complete spectacle of himself with the third.

Douglas, he noted, was more circumspect.

Both his age and his coloring have taught him patience, Holmes mused, watching the restraint with which his friend ate and drank—even though Holmes knew full well that they were equally famished.

"Mr. Holmes?" Hamilton-Gordon was staring at him curiously. "The note I received from Mr. Cardwell mentioned that you wish to visit the French Creole section of the city."

"Yes, but, uhm…" Holmes managed to choke down his third biscuit. Then he pulled out the envelope that Captain Miles had given him.

"Forgive me," he said to Hamilton-Gordon. "Before we discuss my plans, this was entrusted to us with some urgency. We were asked not to open it until we reached you. Do I now have your permission to reveal its contents?"

The baron looked at it quizzically.

Then he turned to his young aide.

"That will do, Beauchamp," he said.

The three waited until Beauchamp walked out, shutting the door behind him. Then Holmes tore open the envelope. Inside was one sheet of paper, and on that sheet were hand-written eight names.

> Roland Traiters
> Adam McGuire
> Otis Oswald
> Richard Nelson
> Upton Bork
> Nestor Ellensberg
> Robert Bouvier
> Ben Quartermaine

Holmes recognized the first five immediately, from the calling cards that the men had used to reserve their places at the *Sultana*'s dining room table. He said as much.

"I assume the other three were aboard, as well," he continued, "but did not make their presence known. Might they be known to you? Perhaps they are criminals of some sort."

The baron stared at the names. Then he walked to his desk and opened a drawer, removed a file, and compared Holmes's names with a list in his hand.

Finally, he shook his head.

"If they are miscreants," he declared, "they have caused no trouble here."

Holmes noticed Edward Dedos—Three-Fingered Eddie—among the governor's list of criminals. There was also a Rickets, a Peter Rickets, but no others he recognized. So he turned his attention back to the list he had been given. There was something peculiar about the names...

The governor perused his list again, and compared it to Holmes's. "We have no records of them at all," he declared.

"That is because they are not criminals, merely businessmen," Holmes murmured. Whereupon he picked up his list, quickly tore the names into strips, then positioned them in a new order.

Adam McGuire
Richard Nelson
Otis Oswald
Nestor Ellensberg
Ben Quartermaine
Upton Bork
Robert Bouvier
Roland Traiters

As Douglas and Gordon looked at them curiously, Holmes explained.

"You see there? The first letter of each first name forms an acronym for the famous American vice president and seditionist, Aaron Burr. My hunch is that none of these men knew the others by sight before they embarked. Once they put down their calling cards in the grand saloon, any interloper would quickly be ferreted out, as his first name would not fit the acronym."

"Aaron Burr?" Douglas repeated. "An American vice president who killed Alexander Hamilton in a duel? Why pick him, of all people?"

"I am assuming," Holmes said, "that the names came first, that they are not pseudonyms. They would have utilized Hamlet, Prince of Denmark, if it fitted."

The governor cleared his throat.

"Forgive me for pointing out an error in spelling, especially at such a crucial juncture, but…" He placed his finger between "Adam McGuire" and "Richard Nelson," then continued. "Burr spelled his first name with two 'a's, not one," he said.

"Quite so——" Holmes began, when he was interrupted by a hard knock upon the door.

"What is it?" the baron called out impatiently.

His supercilious aide peeked in.

"All apologies, governor, but it is a matter of some urgency."

Holmes quickly gathered up the names and placed the pieces back in the envelope. The governor motioned Beauchamp inside, and the man handed him a note.

"From the chief of police in Port of Spain," he said by way of explanation.

When the governor read it, he turned as white as a sheet.

"By h… heavens," he stammered. "Not half an hour ago, your good captain, James Miles, was trampled in the streets by a runaway horse. He is, I am aggrieved to report, deceased!"

Holmes and Douglas glanced at each other.

"I most solemnly assure you," Hamilton-Gordon went on nervously, "that this sort of thing never transpires on our fine little island. The drivers here are kind, considerate…"

"I noticed as much," Holmes assured him as he and Douglas rose to their feet. "I am sorry to say, governor, that there is a conspiracy afoot. Have we your permission to interrogate a pickpocket, currently being held at the jail by the docks?"

"You have but to ask, Mr. Holmes. And whatever you discover, you may count on our full support," Hamilton-Gordon announced, waving his hand in an arc, indicating his entire office.

Holmes and Douglas moved for the door.

"Perhaps we might issue a guard, to ensure your safety," the governor suggested.

Holmes shook his head.

"Please do not take offense," he said. "But at the moment, I am afraid the only ones we can trust are in this room." He indicated the three of them, while clearly omitting Beauchamp, the aide who glared at them from the corner.

In the back of the cart, as the sky changed from violet to cobalt, the men's internal organs were once again rearranged by the jostling about. Douglas turned to Holmes.

"So tell me why Aaron is missing an 'a,'" he said.

"Because one name is not on the list," Holmes responded. "Someone whom they all knew by sight, so there was no need."

.

"Anabel Lynch?" Douglas guessed, though he didn't see the point.

Holmes nodded.

"The boy mentioned her specifically. Remember when he cried out, 'I done all you ast'? The men might've been the ones who paid him, but it was *she* who gave him his marching orders. He did it for her, Douglas. He did it for love."

"You assume all those men knew her by sight," Douglas said. "You think she is the one who gathered them there?"

"I would not go so far as all that," Holmes said with a shrug. "Perhaps it's simply that there aren't that many women involved in… whatever this is." He frowned, then continued. "Now all we can do is to see what the boy tells us."

"If anything at all," Douglas added pessimistically— for the mystery seemed to him to be deepening.

The West India Regiment's barracks was a crumbling limestone building. Large Xs in red chalk were scrawled here and there. Douglas explained that it had been marked for demolition, and a police headquarters would be put up in its place.

"So where does Port of Spain hold its detainees?" Holmes asked.

"There are still a handful of cells here and there, maintained for those awaiting transfer to various prisons around the island," Douglas explained.

"And security is lax?" Holmes inquired.

"Everything on the island is lax," Douglas said.

While Huan and Nico waited in the street, the two

men entered the barracks' dank little outer office. A gas light in the corner flared out what little illumination there was. The moment they stepped inside, a bored bailiff eyed them drily.

"If you seek the boy, he is gone."

Holmes was about to ask how he'd know whom they sought, but Douglas shook his head, as in *don't bother*.

"Port of Spain is a city," he muttered under his breath, "but when it comes to gossip, it is the smallest of small towns."

"Gone?" Holmes asked the bailiff. "Gone where? Was he transferred?"

The bailiff, with a pockmarked face and a permanent scowl, was seated behind an ancient desk that bore countless gash wounds upon its surface, along with a smattering of papers upon which a pair of handcuffs served as a paperweight, and a plate with what appeared to be the remains of a meal of chickpeas. He calmly finished picking his very white teeth with the pointed ends of a pair of scissors, wiped the blades on his trousers, stabbed them into the desk, and burped loudly.

"Bail," he said.

"Someone provided bail?" Douglas repeated. "And who might that be?"

The bailiff shrugged.

"Not my never mind."

In a flash, Douglas stood over him, his hand hovering over the scissor blades.

"We have come a long way," he purred menacingly. "We are tired, hungry and cross. I suggest you give us a bit more information than that."

The man stared up at Douglas.

"You are threatening me, mon?" he asked blandly.

"Assume what you wish, *mon*," Douglas replied, his look filled with meaning.

"You talk fancy for a local boy," the bailiff began. Scooping up the handcuffs that lay on his desk, he started to rise when he inadvertently glanced toward the door. His eyes registered surprise, along with a hint of alarm.

Douglas and Holmes followed his gaze.

It was Huan. He stood in the doorframe, grinning— one hand raised in greeting as if to the room at large. Then, with a shy bow, he ducked out again.

Without altering his expression a whit, the bailiff sat down. Then he turned his gaze upon Douglas and nodded pleasantly.

"Chestnut hair," he said. "Fine mustache, nice looking, strange talking."

"Strange talking?" Douglas said. "American, perhaps?"

The bailiff held up one finger. Then he balled the hand into a fist, and drove it into his solar plexus. This elicited a second, even larger burp.

"Might be," he said, shrugging again. "Might very well be."

Holmes and Douglas turned and hurried toward the door when he called out to them.

"Ah, and a woman!" he said loudly. They both stopped in their tracks.

"A woman was with the American?" Holmes repeated, turning around.

"No, mon!" He sounded exasperated, as if he had been

trying to explain the same point for hours. "I am saying that the boy would not go with him. Then the woman, she comes in…"

"Describe her!" Holmes commanded.

"Calm yourself. Blond hair, blue eyes—as I live and breathe, a fine-looking woman. She did not speak, but she has a bracelet under the sleeve. Jumbie beads, local girl, I think…"

"On her right arm or her left?" Holmes interrupted, his voice unsteady.

The bailiff frowned and held out his arms. He looked at both, as if trying to picture her.

His smile grew more lascivious.

"Right," he said. "It was her right." Then he began to chuckle. "And the boy, when he sees her? He starts to cry. *Now* he go with the mon! *Now* he go! Pretty young lady, very persuasive indeed!"

And the bailiff laughed as if this were the funniest thing in the world.

23

HOLMES FOLLOWED DOUGLAS OUT OF THE DANK LITTLE jail. he knew what the next stop would be on this very strange journey he was on. He knew it would answer some questions while raising more.

He also knew it would be a crucible.

What he did not know was if he could bear it.

"She was on board all along," he muttered to Douglas. "There would have been no other way into port. Georgiana is Anabel Lynch. That boy may've been one of the urchins she taught…"

"It certainly seems that way," Douglas responded. "But why would she do this? Why bring the boy on a journey she wasn't even planning to undertake until three days before the *Sultana* was scheduled to leave?"

"And why change her name? Why *any* of it?" Holmes groaned.

Douglas laid a hand on his shoulder but said nothing further. Holmes was grateful for the silence. After all, what was there to say?

Thick wisps of fog were beginning to appear as they approached Huan, who was leaning against the side of his gig, his arms folded across his chest. He eyed the two men warily.

"There are *douen* inside, then?" he said, only half joking. "For you have both lost your coloring—even you, Cyrus. You have gone nearly as white as your friend there."

Douglas quickly changed the subject.

"I take it you knew our good bailiff?" he asked, his thumb pointing back to the edifice behind them.

Huan grinned. "Never met the man!"

"Well, he must have known of you," Douglas responded, "for the moment he set eyes upon you, he suddenly became quite a bit more eager to assist."

"Glad to be of service," Huan said with a gracious bow— but he did not elaborate. "And now? Where do we go?"

Douglas looked to Holmes for the answer.

Here it is, Holmes thought. *The crucible.*

He removed his wallet from his pants pocket. Inside was a slip of paper upon which were written the words *Sutton Plantation*, along with a local address. He handed it to Huan.

"Do you know of it?" he asked.

"No," Huan admitted.

"A large plantation such as this?" Holmes pressed.

Huan shrugged. "Port of Spain is one plantation followed by another." He flashed a grin. "We will find it."

"Good. And as quickly as possible," Holmes urged.

Douglas shook his head no.

"It'll have to wait 'til morning, Holmes," he said. "There are no lights in the outlying areas."

"We cannot tarry..." Holmes began, but Huan seconded Douglas.

"Nico has many fine qualities," he said, indicating his

mule, "but not the eyes of a cat!"

"Nevertheless, we are not safe until we unravel this mystery," Holmes insisted. "For your sake, Douglas, if not for mine…"

He looked away, his expression completing the thought.

For what happens to me no longer matters.

Huan misunderstood entirely.

"Ah, if it is safety you are after," he chimed in, "I know just the place!" With that, he lowered the trap on the wagon and motioned them aboard with a welcoming hand.

"Where are we going?" Holmes asked, though if it wasn't toward the Sutton plantation, he didn't much care.

"You said safety? Safety is where we go!" Huan announced.

Then he smiled his brilliant smile.

This time, it had no effect on Holmes whatsoever.

They hastened to a section of the city that seemed darker than the rest. The crepuscular blue of the sky, which could linger for hours on islands like this, was not present here. There were no torches to light the way, no gas lamps.

From what Holmes could make out, it was a labyrinth of shanties more or less covered by shade trees and corrugated roofs. In spite of the gloom, it seemed the busiest of all the areas they had passed thus far. Hundreds of souls—rag pickers, from the looks of them, street vendors, and hawkers of all kinds—scurried from here to there, with their bounties atop their heads, or stuffed into buckets strapped to yokes laid across their shoulders. In all that scurrying about, they never entangled themselves in others' comings and goings, but sidestepped one another like dancers on a busy stage, or ants on an anthill.

Yet it was all strangely quiet. The only sound was the slapping of sandals on the hard ground. The humidity no longer smelled to Holmes of spices and meat, but of something else, something sour yet nearly sticky in its sweetness. And the eerie, low-lying haze that enveloped the place carried with it the acrid odor of shag tobacco.

Sherlock would be at home here, Holmes thought.

"*Ting ting*, Nico, *ting ting!*" Huan commanded.

The mule halted in front of what looked like an outdoor bar under an enormous silk cotton tree. It rose some eighty feet high, while its branches had the width and the breadth of a small-town plaza. A hunched little man wearing a *saipan* on his head was busily lighting colored lanterns. Other men were raising them by rope and pulley to their designated spots high in the air, until dozens were glowing like pinpoints underneath the branches, and illuminating what was beneath.

The panorama became clearer, but—in Holmes's estimation—not a whit more comforting. He and Douglas climbed out of the cart and drew closer.

Dozens of Chinese men of indeterminate age were finding spots on two long wooden benches, placed on either side of a long wooden table that held only chopsticks and pewter mugs. Most of the men were clean-shaven, though a few had thin mustaches that fell to their jawlines. They wore what Holmes recognized as traditional Chinese outfits known as *changshan*—printed silks in the shape of skirts that covered them from waist to ankle, while loose-sleeved shirts or shirt jackets, held in place by cloth buttons and knots, did the job from waist to neck. As for their feet, they were either slippered or bare.

To a man, they lacked Huan's gift for putting others at ease. They neither spoke nor looked around, but almost rhythmically alternated between drinking out of those pewter mugs and smoking the thin, reed-like pipes they held between their fingers, which accounted for the tobacco scent.

The hunched little man appeared again with a tray covered in dumplings. It seemed larger than he was. He reminded Holmes of a tiny leafcutter ant that somehow managed to drag an acorn five times its size back to the nest.

It's a question of balance, he thought. *Something the West has long forgotten.*

The men picked up the chopsticks and helped themselves without uttering a word.

"Hungry?" Huan asked, watching Holmes's eyes as he stood to the side and observed the goings-on. For the first time since his recovery, Holmes could genuinely say that he was anything but. His appetite had disappeared the moment he'd set foot outside the jail. Even the sight of food made him queasy.

"Sleepy?" Huan inquired again.

Holmes nodded, which was all he could muster.

"Sleep then!" Huan announced with a smile and a hearty slap to Holmes's back that threatened to send him stumbling over a bench and into the table.

Douglas, whose hunger had not abated, excused himself to take a seat among the men. Without acknowledging him in the least, they scooted aside so that he might join them. One pushed chopsticks his way, which Douglas took but did not acknowledge with so much as a nod of thanks.

This left Holmes no choice but to follow a gesticulating, grinning Huan down a dank little alleyway. Though he'd left his bag in the cart, he had brought Sherlock's walking stick, more to ensure that he'd remain solidly on his feet than for any protection it might provide. As they wandered about in the dark, having it as support seemed like the only sound decision he had made in a while.

"Where are we going?" Holmes asked dully, though more by rote than out of curiosity.

"Hotel. Safe hotel!"

They turned down an alleyway that was quiet except for the sound of their own shoes on the shale road, along with the gurgle of what looked like a thin river of green effluence that ran right in the middle of the street and seemed to be spreading slightly as they went. Above them were windows covered in cloths. Holmes could see dim lights behind one or two.

A moment later, Huan stopped. "Here we are!" he announced, followed by a hand gesture so extravagant that it would have been suitable to introduce the palace at Versailles. But this was no Versailles. This was a lean-to—a series of boards that had been nailed to the side of a shanty to form a right triangle.

Huan parted the burlap curtain that served as a doorway, and Holmes looked inside. There was a bed made of straw, with several moth-eaten blankets atop it. Beside the bed, a shipment container with a stamp in red that read CIGARILLOS served as an end table. A cheap and lavishly dripping candle in a dirty brass holder was the only source of light. Near the candle was placed the oldest, dustiest, most crumbling edition of the King James Bible that he had ever seen.

"Goodnight, Mycroft Holmes!" Huan said.

And he began to walk off.

"Wait!" Holmes cried after him. "What of the... the... facilities?"

"Facilities?" Huan repeated, as if the word were incomprehensible.

Then he grinned.

"Of course, no problem. Facilities!" he said. "Right outside the door. There!" And he pointed to the greenish effluence that meandered past.

To his own surprise, Holmes felt neither revulsion nor desperation at the thought of relieving himself in that filth. In truth, he would have welcomed either emotion as a reprieve to the numbness that enshrouded him.

Once Huan had gone, and with no better notion of what to do, he took off his topcoat and hat, kept the cane close at hand, unhooked the burlap door, and then lay down fully clothed on the hard straw mattress.

Deeply out of sorts, he picked up the Bible and flipped idly to one of the few verses therein that hadn't been torn, crumpled or soiled.

It was a passage from the book of Jeremiah:

> Stand ye in the ways, and see,
> and ask for the old paths,

> where is the good way, and walk therein,
> and ye shall find rest for your souls.

The verse, though not particularly comforting, was certainly curious. What were "the old paths"? What was "the good way"? He felt as if the words had nothing to do with him, and yet had everything to do with him.

He thought he had found a good way, once.

And a path carved specifically to bring rest to his soul.

Now it was gone.

24

EARLY THE NEXT MORNING, HOLMES AND DOUGLAS
were once again in the back of their rented gig, with Huan
at the reins. The hollow feeling in Holmes's stomach was
still very much present, though his hunger had been sated.
Douglas, ever thoughtful, had arrived at the lean-to with
biscuits and fresh tea. Holmes, who had awoken ravenous,
was so grateful that he did not think of inquiring from
whence they came—or even to wonder where his friend
had slept, if he had.

As they passed cocoa fields and sugar plantations—
miles and miles of them—and as the day grew hotter,
Holmes whistled to mitigate the dull anxiety in his head. He
noticed that Douglas glanced at him occasionally, arching
an eyebrow. Since he said nothing, Holmes continued
whistling, and it eased his inner torment somewhat. Until
Huan turned his head and looked squarely at him.

"Woman troubles?" the latter inquired.

"I beg… your pardon?" Holmes stammered.

At which point Douglas leaned in to explain.

"You have been whistling 'La Donna è Mobile' for the
last quarter of an hour," he said. "You end the verse and
the chorus, then go back to the beginning."

Holmes could not believe he was so fragile-minded as all that. It reminded him of the time he had quoted Dickens aloud in that London carriage. Was it possible that he was going mad? It certainly wasn't out of the question, as there were seeds of madness in the family, specifically his mother…

In any case, he would not whistle, hum or sing "La Donna è Mobile" again. But it was too late.

Huan had begun to hum the popular operatic tune. He kept humming it, much to Holmes's chagrin, until they reached their destination.

The Sutton plantation was comprised of acres and acres of wild sugar cane reaching upward of thirteen feet and more. It was lovely to look at, green and lush, but not at all what they were expecting.

"That cane has not seen a machete for at least a decade," Douglas said as they rode past. He pointed out the tracks of the cane carts. "They are there, you see? Barely visible. The *Saccharum* has reclaimed all available space."

The boiling house, when they passed it, was half torn down. Through the holes in the slats Douglas could see the brick furnaces, along with a succession of copper kettles of diminishing size, even the large cooling trough. Rats by the dozen skittered from the largest kettles to the trough as though it had been left especially for their amusement.

In a few more moments, the plantation house came into view, just beyond a dilapidated old barn.

It was a gracious affair in the American Southern

tradition, with stately pillars and a sprawling wraparound porch, but it was so run down that Huan said he was sure it was abandoned. Holmes and Douglas had to encourage him to keep going.

As they passed the barn, Douglas was the first to notice an ancient nag inside, eating her fresh allotment of hay.

"Something resides here after all," he said.

The men dismounted and peeked around the barn door, which was creaking on one broken hinge. Beyond the horse stall and the lone horse stood a carriage that had once been, if not grand, then certainly respectable. And from the tracks of the wheels, it appeared that it had been used fairly recently.

"Something resides here all right," Holmes repeated, "but *how?*"

Huan put Nico and the gig in a shaded area outside the building, and the three of them made their way toward the main house.

They climbed the stairs to the crumbling porch, taking care not to place a foot on splintered planks or rot. Holmes knocked upon the worn front door.

Nothing.

He knocked again.

Before he could knock a third time, the door opened a crack, and a woman appeared.

This cannot be Georgiana's mother, Holmes thought. *It must be a servant.*

She had told him that her mother was born in 1830,

which would make her no more than forty years of age, yet this woman looked to be in her sixties, perhaps older. Her face, which may once have been lovely, was crisscrossed with lines, as if both weather and sorrow had left their mark. Her hair, which was pulled up in a thin and untidy bun, was a dull, yellowish gray. Her eyes were filmy with cataracts.

"Yes?" she inquired curiously. Holmes noticed a slight American Southern accent in her speech.

"We are seeking Mr. or Mrs. Sutton…" he began. Before he could continue, she laughed, placing a withered hand in front of her mouth as she did so.

"Ah, that is rich!" she said. "Mr. Sutton, indeed! I am *Mrs.* Sutton. How may I help you?"

Holmes stared at her.

"I am Mycroft Holmes," he said, watching her carefully. But there was nothing in her expression that said she recognized the name at all. "And this is my… my associate, Cyrus Douglas," he added. "I am secretary to the British Secretary for Agriculture, and Mr. Douglas is an attaché of a large agricultural consortium based in the Antilles. We have been charged with informally querying landowners in this area on… the advantages and disadvantages of growing sugar."

Mrs. Sutton's face darkened.

"Sugar is the last thing I wish to speak of, Mr. Holmes…"

"We promise to take up very little of your time," Holmes pressed. But there seemed to be no need for assurances, as Mrs. Sutton brushed off his words with a wave of her hand.

"You should allow a lady to finish her sentence, sir. As

I was *saying*, Mr. Holmes, even though the topic is a painful one, seeing as how the company of other intelligent persons is more rare than gold these days, I shall gladly oblige."

"Thank you, Mrs. Sutton," he replied. "Might our man have some water for his horse?" He indicated Huan.

"Of course, Mr. Holmes," she said kindly. "There may be hay left over as well. Dixie's appetite isn't what it used to be." As Huan bowed and headed back toward the barn, Mrs. Sutton called into the darkened house.

"Maria! Tea for three, if you would! And pull open a few curtains for good measure! After all," she said, addressing the men again, "we can't have this lovely day going to waste."

She opened the door wider and motioned them inside.

The hallway and parlor were as grand and as shabby as the exterior. The wooden floor had been shined to a gloss, but the French crewelwork upholstery on the divan was coming apart, the satin drapes were shiny with age, the needlepoint on the chairs was bald in patches, and the lace doilies were threadbare.

Above the mantel was a portrait of a man in his early forties. The black velvet that draped its ornate gold frame had once been black, but had been streaked violet blue by a bright and unrelenting sun.

When Holmes saw it, he drew a breath. Though Georgiana did not own a daguerreotype of her mother, she did have one of her father. She had shown it with pride, as her father was a handsome, distinguished man.

And this most certainly was he.

"Are you quite all right, Mr. Holmes?" Mrs. Sutton asked.

"Yes, perfectly," he said, and he nodded. "Is that... Mr. Sutton, then?" he asked, as he did not wish to insult her by saying "your son."

Mrs. Sutton nodded. "My husband. Deceased these ten years, I'm afraid."

The two men were standing by the divan, which Mrs. Sutton indicated was the preferred spot for guests. She chose a chair across from them, and as she sat, so did they.

Holmes forced himself to sit up straight and to remain composed.

You are a gentleman, he admonished himself. *Behave as such!*

A moment later, to the shuffling sound of footsteps, a woman appeared. She was a toothless, ageless Creole—she could have easily been forty or seventy. She served them tea and lemon cake from a large silver-plated tray, which had been scrubbed clean so many times that most of its plating was gone.

"Had to sell all the silver, I'm afraid," Mrs. Sutton remarked airily. "Well, hard times come and go, don't they? Though this particular hard time has lasted more than I care for. Please, gentlemen, help yourselves to the tea and the lemon cake. It reminds me that I still do a few things well enough!" Then she picked up a pair of spectacles from an end table, put them on, and peered at her two visitors.

"Well," she said, "I am glad to see that the two of you have been in some scrapes. Much better, indeed, than the curse of bad skin. I have some salve that will help with those cuts and scratches," she added. "Were you set upon by ruffians, then?"

Holmes nodded vigorously. "On the ship from Liverpool, someone tried to rob us. Unsuccessfully, I am pleased to say."

"Oh! Isn't that frightful! Traveling is so hazardous nowadays! I myself never venture forth. Maria takes the trap into town for victuals, and nothing more. Poor thing is very nearly lame—I know I should shoot her, but I've grown quite attached."

When Holmes and Douglas eyed her with dismay, she spoke again with a laugh.

"I meant Dixie, my filly," she amended. "Not Maria! Good heavens!"

"That is a relief," Holmes said, attempting a smile. "As to the salve, we have plenty, thank you."

"Then you aren't particularly faithful in its application!" she chided, adding, "Ah, men!" as if that explained it all.

"In any event," she continued, settling into her chair, "you asked about growing sugar. I am afraid that the cost of help, the upkeep of land, and the injuries have proved prohibitive for most of us planters. And with sugar there are so many injuries! To be sure, no one wishes to work hard anymore, not even the locals.

"Now, some thirty years back, the British government realized our plight, and they tried to send us *white* indentured workers—Welsh and German and the sort—so it wouldn't look so much like slavery, d'you see. But all of 'em died, every last one, of some tropical disease or the other. I don't suppose white folk're as hardy as the nigras and the coloreds…"

When she said this last, she smiled at Douglas as if she

were paying him an enormous compliment. He smiled back pleasantly.

"You are built for this sort of work," she continued, still addressing Douglas. "That is what my husband always used to say. And the best thing one can do for a person is to turn him loose to the work he was born to do."

Douglas shot Holmes a look that said, *She is no longer of sound mind.*

And indeed, this was more than the "mild histrionics" Georgiana had occasionally mentioned. Mrs. Sutton was clearly no longer all there. It seemed unfair to trick her in this manner, Holmes thought, but the stakes were too great to do much else.

"Mrs. Sutton, have you heard anything about workers disappearing?" he inquired.

Mrs. Sutton laughed again. The more she relaxed, the more the sound turned high-pitched and girlish… and a bit eerie.

"Why, I surely can, Mr. Holmes. They disappeared the moment we could no longer afford to keep 'em! We were trying to get out of sugar, you see, and into cocoa, but Mr. Sutton—God rest his soul—thought to go a different way, purchasing land off the coast. But his deal took too long to put in place and, alas, it all fell to dust in our hands.

"My husband's great-great grandfather and his wife migrated from Britain in 1640," she said. "Indentured servants, they were, did hard labor for five years. He survived, his bride did not, and he was given 'freedom dues' of ten British pounds, plus ten acres of land, on which we are sitting. Now Mr. Sutton always said that if our own ancestors could be slaves, practically speaking, and still make something of their lives, well, so can they all."

It was the same story that Georgiana had recounted back at the tobacco shop—one that seemed to be quite important to their family.

"Mr. *Holmes!*" she declared suddenly. For an instant, he dared to hope that his name had finally rung a bell. "You have not had so much as a *bite* of my lovely lemon cake," she said. "Now do be a good lad and taste it, at the very least."

In truth, Holmes was feeling so queasy that he feared that whatever went into his mouth might come right back out again. But he did as he was told, cutting off the smallest possible bite that would suffice without giving offense.

"Quite delicious," he said, "with a delightfully subtle lemon tang."

"It is an ancient family recipe," Mrs. Sutton responded gaily. "From the proud state of Georgia! That is where my people are from, on both sides. And though we have been here for a few generations, we named our daughter Georgiana to commemorate that fact."

Holmes, swallowing with difficulty, could see no point in prolonging the agony. He dove into the fray.

"Mrs. Sutton, have you had word of Georgiana?"

Her filmy eyes grew moist.

"Do you know my girl?" she asked, surprised. "Do you know my Georgiana?"

Holmes wondered how he could possibly link himself—a chap from the agriculture department—with a girl who frequented Girton and taught impoverished youths.

"Well, I…" he muttered, when Mrs. Sutton interrupted him.

"Because if you do, then you must know that she is in London, Mr. Holmes."

"But on her way here, surely…?" Holmes stammered.

Mrs. Sutton laughed again.

"Here? Whatever for?" she exclaimed. "I haven't seen hide nor hair of the child in four years, not since she went off to university. But she's a good girl. Writes to me faithfully every single week—without fail!" With that, Mrs. Sutton rose and walked over to a roll-top desk on which sat a basket of letters, decorated with a faded red ribbon.

She brought it over, showing it proudly to them.

"You see? Without fail!" Holmes noted Georgiana's return address in the upper left corner. And written carefully in the center, in Georgiana's writing, was the name of the recipient.

Anabel Lynch Sutton.

Her mother.

25

THOUGH THE GREATER PART OF HOLMES WAS CONSUMED with suffering, a niggling part was still analyzing. As he and Douglas rode back to town in Huan's cart, cane stalks provided the lesson on the treachery of sentiment.

He was surrounded by green, tidy sugar cane. Even wild, it was an ordered grass—it did not shoot up randomly, but was upright in its bearing and rather precise in its arrangement. It grew best in soil that was bathed in sunshine, with air perfumed by the sea.

And yet, were he to give in to his emotions, Holmes could have sworn that he wasn't passing fields of sugar cane drenched in sunlight, but that he had, in fact, fallen into a ditch, becoming buried in the mud. That a shroud-like mist hung suspended over his head, while the snaking tendrils of some loathsome weed were insinuating themselves around his chest and arms, creeping ever closer to his exposed throat.

Threatening to cut off his breath completely.

When he tried to breathe, he felt a twinge in his chest, like a fist squeezing his heart, then abruptly releasing it.

"Ah, that one," he heard Huan say to Douglas. "He looks like his soul has already left his body."

Perhaps it was true. Perhaps souls truly could abandon living bodies.

Douglas put a hand on his arm.

"Holmes?" his friend said, nudging him. "Are you all square?"

Far from it, Holmes thought. But he said nothing.

After their visit with Mrs. Sutton, he had stumbled back into the cart. He had sunk into the pillows, hands grabbing the sides—not to secure a bit more comfort on the ride, but to keep himself as steady as possible… so as not to vomit.

Echoing in his head, over and over, was the litany of Georgiana's lies. Her "prosperous" plantation. Her father, long deceased, to whom she would speak "in person" about their engagement.

There are none so blind as those who will not see.

But there was more to it, he reminded himself silently.

The most deluded people are those who choose to ignore what they already know.

He said as much to Douglas, who shook his head.

"You are being entirely too hard on yourself, Holmes. Surely being poisoned, sickened, and beaten does nothing to sharpen your deductive powers."

"It was Georgiana," Holmes said dully, interrupting Douglas, "traveling incognito as Anabel Lynch, who did not wish me killed…"

"Yes, yes, so you have said. Rest your mind a moment," Douglas instructed.

"Rest my mind?" Holmes scoffed. "My mind has been entirely too much at rest! When we came unexpectedly aboard, she and her… *accomplices* were forced to improvise, hoping we'd be frightened by the thought that there were murderers who'd stop at nothing to—"

"But there *were* murderers aboard," Douglas objected.

"Yes, but I'm not certain that…"

Holmes paused.

Were the words he was about to utter led by blind emotion, or did he know at least a little something of Georgiana's nature?

For what seemed the millionth time, he mulled over his final encounter with her.

"Are you telling me children have died*?"* she had demanded. *"How many?"*

When he'd given her the number—three at that juncture—she'd turned ghostly pale. She'd opened her mouth, then quickly covered it with her hand, as if…

As if trying to keep a secret from spilling out. He recalled Sherlock's words in the gymnasium.

She had seemed to him unnerved. Now he was of the opinion that she'd been terrified.

He finished his thought out loud.

"I am not certain she knew those men were *capable* of murder," he told Douglas. "And as I intimated before, perhaps they did not yet know it themselves—perhaps they were still humoring her. In any case, *someone* was protecting us. The captain said as much. And I doubt it was the American. So who would be left if not… Anabel Lynch?"

He felt the tendrils tighten around his chest, continuing their inexorable advance toward his throat.

"She had always planned on leaving me, Douglas!" he said suddenly. "Your confiding in me frightened her, put her plan into motion sooner than she had intended."

"You cannot know that for a fact," Douglas said. "Besides, we still have no notion of conspiracy, other than the acronym 'Aaron Burr'—"

Suddenly, the contraption in which they were riding lurched to a halt, cutting him off and sending Douglas and Holmes skittering forward. They gripped the sides harder to keep from being pitched to the ground.

Nico had stopped of his own accord. He was braying indignantly at an obstruction in the road some four hundred meters away.

Peering out from where they sat, the three men discovered the cause.

It was a body, lying face down in the dirt.

The lad was stretched out on his stomach, forehead pressed to the ground in a most unnatural pose. Holmes leapt out first, and recognized the clothing immediately.

"Duffer!" he said. The young pickpocket.

Cart and horse tracks led to the body, then cart and horse tracks doubled back. Whoever had done this had ridden away, depositing him there.

Douglas knelt by the boy's side and gently turned him over. He was as gray as the dust he lay on. His eyes were staring. His shirt had been torn open. Blood was pooling at his stomach.

There were perpendicular slices in the soft flesh of his abdomen.

Huan reared back.

"*Lougarou!*" he cried.

The moment Nico heard his master's cry, he bared his big yellow teeth and brayed even louder. Holmes looked up, sheltered his eyes from the sun, and frowned at them.

"Nonsense!" he said. "Come here this instant and have a proper look. Nico! Be quiet!"

Nico obeyed.

Huan crept forward, looking askance at the corpse.

"Closer," Holmes commanded with an exasperated sigh.

Huan moved a few more inches.

"To begin with," Holmes said, pointing at the boy, "*lougarou* are vampire *mosquitos*, are they not?"

Huan nodded, his head still keening to one side.

"Then they would have a very large proboscis—a *nose*—and the cut would look like a puncture wound, would it not?" His tone demanded a reply.

Huan nodded again.

"These"—Holmes indicated the lines on the boy's stomach—"are not puncture wounds at all. They are uniform slices. In two sets of four. No, this was clearly the work of a scarificator."

"Who is that?" Huan asked in a quavering voice, glancing here and there as if it might descend upon him any moment.

Douglas laid his fingers against the boy's eyes, pressed his lids shut and answered quietly.

"It's not a who," he said, "it's a what. A medical instrument used for bloodletting. I have never actually *seen* one—"

"Carries eight lancets in two sets of four," Holmes interrupted. "Spring loaded. Each set of the four blades is parallel one to the other. Quite handy for small bloodletting, but, because the incisions are rather superficial, they are not usually deadly in and of themselves. So first they cut open the boy's aorta, you see there?" He indicated a large gash just below Duffer's breastbone.

Huan peered down through squinted eyes.

"Now that was done with an ordinary kitchen knife, one meant for cutting steak. That is, of course, what killed him. His murderers allowed blood to drain from the aorta into his abdomen—which it did fairly quickly, eight minutes or so, as I recall from my time with Dr. Bell. After that they simply sliced the abdomen with the scarificator, turned him over, and let him bleed out—again, a matter of minutes."

Huan turned to Douglas.

"It is not a *lougarou?*" he asked, stating the obvious.

"No," Douglas said. "It is only unnatural in the sense that there are human beings who can do this sort of thing to other human beings."

Huan breathed a sigh of relief, and Holmes appraised him.

"I confess I do not know you well," he said, "but you do not seem the fearful type. It is the supernatural, then, that causes you unease?"

Huan shrugged. "I do not like what I cannot fight. You are certain…?" he asked.

"Yes. As Douglas said, unnatural. Not supernatural."

* * *

Douglas enjoyed hearing the imperious tone in Holmes's voice. It was as if his friend was coming back into himself, and he was glad of it—until Holmes brushed the dust off his knees and climbed into the back of the cart again.

"What are you doing?" Douglas asked.

"What we should be doing," Holmes said. "Getting on with it."

Such a degree of coldness seemed unusual, even for him.

He is still in shock, Douglas mused, giving him the benefit of the doubt.

"We cannot simply leave him, Holmes," Douglas protested, pointing to the boy. "We must take him back to town."

"Back to *town*?" Holmes repeated. "So that while we wait for burial documents and sigils and stamps, whoever wishes to murder us might do a proper job of it? This is what they expect us to do! Even now, there's a welcoming party for us at the coroner's office. And what a very convenient place to do us in, wouldn't you say?"

Douglas stared at Holmes, incredulous.

"So fear should keep us from—"

"He is *deceased*!" Holmes shouted. "On our account, on *my* account! Because I was on that ship, I disrupted whatever plan Georgiana and these… *gentlemen* had concocted. The boy knew too much, the boy broke under pressure, the boy was murdered by people so heartless that they would draw all the blood from his body and abandon him in the roadway like an old cur!"

Douglas rose to his feet. A few long strides, and he was inches from Holmes.

"He had breath in him once," he declared. "He is to be treated with respect, no matter the cost."

"Now is not the time for empty ritual," Holmes thundered.

"Now is *precisely* the time!" Douglas thundered back. "When we ourselves are empty, it is the *ritual* that turns us human again."

Holmes looked as if he'd been struck.

"That boy," he said with difficulty, "will be tossed into a pauper's grave. And we shall be ambushed and murdered." He held back sobs. "Know this, Douglas—I believe fervently in an afterlife, and I am not afraid to die. Nevertheless, I find great confidence in facts, in the rational mind—most particularly in *my* rational mind. And no matter how I try, I cannot make... *sense*... of any of this!"

He struck his temples with the palms of his hands.

"Holmes. Holmes," Douglas said, catching his friend's hands in his. "You are brilliant. You can deduce *anything*, given hints or facts or even conjectures. But you are also twenty-three years of age. You have never even traveled outside of England proper, never mind to the depths of human depravity."

Holmes plucked his hands from Douglas's grasp.

"You are calling me naïve?" he said, sounding offended.

Douglas shook his head.

"You have an enormous arsenal of tools at your disposal, and you certainly know how to use them. But you have never encountered true evil, and in order to comprehend evil, you have to learn to think as evil does. Once you do that... you are never the same." He paused and added, "We cannot sink to evil's level."

Holmes considered this.

Finally, he nodded.

"Very well. Then we bury him here," he said tersely, climbing out of the cart.

Douglas procured an old shovel from the boiling house. He and Holmes found a spot underneath a row of wild sugar cane and took turns digging. The hole had to be deep enough that wild creatures would not unearth the boy's remains.

But the ground was tough and full of shale, and the day growing hotter and more humid. As Holmes and Douglas were still sore and undernourished, the work proved arduous and slow.

"What a fool I was," Holmes berated himself as he took his turn. "Blinded by love. It is as you said, Douglas. The small evils I encountered here and there in my life are nothing to the utter depravity I have now witnessed. I was unprepared. I swear on all that is holy that it shall never happen again."

Douglas nodded.

He was surprised at how morose he felt, how out of sorts. It was more than the sorrow one might experience when a dear friend is betrayed. It seemed to him that he was taking Holmes's heartbreak personally.

Perhaps Holmes's contentment with his life had given him a glimmer of hope that happiness was not a mirage but was, in fact, possible.

There is no fool like an old fool, Douglas quoted to himself. Holmes shook his head.

"So much better to be as you are, Douglas," he said. "A bachelor. Keen-eyed and keen-hearted."

When Douglas did not respond, Huan—who was standing guard nearby—grew suddenly curious.

"You have never been in love?" he asked Douglas.

Douglas paused.

"Yes," he said softly.

Holmes looked over, slightly resentful.

"It seems you are full of secrets," he muttered.

Douglas shrugged noncommittally.

Holmes shoveled a few more spades of dirt and then added quietly, "I would surely like to know, if you don't mind telling."

Both the request and the plaintive tone surprised Douglas. He took the shovel from Holmes's hands and began to dig.

"I was married once," he said.

26

HE HAD MET HER TEN YEARS BEFORE, IN 1860, TRAVELING to the United States from Trinidad to build his tobacco business.

"Annie was twenty-two, from Memphis, Tennessee," Douglas recalled. "I was thirty, and in love for the first time in my life. We married in Memphis, among her people. I brought her back to Port of Spain and introduced her to my family. They fell in love with her, too, as I knew they would. She had that way with people."

He rubbed his nose, leaving a trace of dirt across it, and then redoubled his efforts with the shovel.

"Of course then the American War Between the States began," he went on, breathing harder from the exertion, "and travel back and forth proved prohibitive. So I expanded into England. In the meantime, we had a son. I never much cared for the name 'Cyrus,' but she insisted. And so he was baptized Cyrus Nickolus Douglas the Second. My mother used to call him *El rey del Puerto de España,* the king of Port of Spain," he added with a wistful smile.

"Four years ago, mid-April, with the war finally over and my business prospering, Annie asked if she could go home to her family. Only for a month or so, to show off our boy. I wasn't mad for the idea, and I could not yet leave work for such a long stretch of time, but I knew how much it meant to her."

The hole had grown deep enough. He and Holmes gathered branches to form a sort of bier at the bottom.

"My parents had never been abroad, so I convinced them to serve as escorts. They docked at New York and from there took a train to Memphis. Cy was four by then. Good-looking, sweet, like his mama, learning both English and Portuguese."

Douglas stopped. He looked around for a moment, as if he had misplaced something, then he began again.

"What Annie and my parents did not know—could not know—is that there had been a skirmish back in Memphis, between Negro Union soldiers and police. They had only been in the city two nights when white mobs appeared. Protected by the police, the mobs attacked anyone they could find—men, women, children. By morning, forty-six people lay dead. My wife and child, my mother and father among them…"

His voice trailed off.

He'd been laying leaves over branches at the bottom of the hole. Now he finally looked over at Holmes and Huan. But their faces were so grieved that he could not bear it.

He looked down again and resumed the work at hand.

"Two years ago," he said as he tamped the leaves down onto the branches, "the United States passed the 14th Amendment to their Constitution—'equal protection under the law.' The same police officers who had supervised while Negroes were indiscriminately killed that night, in their own beds, were now sworn to defend them. Not quite soon enough for my family, I'm afraid," he concluded.

Holmes wished he could say something that would lessen his friend's pain. But if such words had been invented, surely he had never heard them uttered aloud.

It did explain, he thought, the melancholia that Douglas wore lightly, almost like a second skin—in spite of being one of the gentlest, most easygoing souls whom he had ever known. He recalled what Douglas had said when referring to the murder of their young pickpocket.

"It is only unnatural in the sense that there are human beings who can do this sort of thing to other human beings."

In silence, the three men lifted the boy and laid him into his final resting place. As Holmes and Douglas began the chore of replacing the dirt they had displaced, then tamping it down and laying rocks on top, Huan twisted a little cross out of sugar cane.

It was nearly dusk by the time they arrived into town again. Nico brayed his hunger, and this time even Holmes's stern voice could not quiet him.

Douglas and Huan agreed with Nico. The first order of business was to eat. And since both men persistently assured Holmes that the safest place in Port of Spain was the Chinese section, Holmes soon found himself seated at the long wooden table, shoulder to shoulder with his companions, while some fifty men sat hunched all around him, silently drinking and smoking, and brightly colored lanterns shone like multicolored stars overhead.

There were young men standing in the shadows— the oldest seemed barely out of his teens—all wearing *tangzhuang* jackets, the formal garb of Han Chinese. Their hairlines had been shaved back and their long black hair was gathered in *queues*, or braids. They said nothing, but stared impassively before them, like the Queen's guards.

Holmes did a quick head count. If there were fifty men seated at the table, then there were easily fifty boys, standing sentry here and there.

They seemed formidable.

"Who are they?" Holmes whispered to Douglas.

"They are the reason that this is the safest section of the city."

Holmes eyed them with a hint of dismay.

"For *whom?*" he quipped.

Douglas smiled.

"Then I am thankful they are on our side," Holmes added.

His friend shrugged. "Only if it suits them," he murmured—which was not at all the news that Holmes was hoping to hear.

While he waited with a sour stomach for the food to arrive, Holmes took a sip of the liquid that the hunched little man poured into all the mugs. It tasted like ethanol to which something vaguely sweet had been added. That did not mean that it was bad—it was simply something he was not used to, and did not care to learn to enjoy.

Beyond that, he had a maddening tickle at his throat from the shag tobacco that hung over the table like a blue canopy; while at the same time he could feel his first niggling desire for a nice Cuban cigar.

Unfortunately, he and Douglas had only brought enough provisions to last them through the journey on board, assuming they could replenish their stash once they arrived at Port of Spain.

If you wish to make angels laugh, Holmes thought, *tell them your plans.*

But when the very large bowl of dumplings arrived, he forgot all about Cuban cigars. For in truth, the smell was so aromatic that he felt giddy. He thought he might indulge after all.

His first attempts at transferring the precious little sacs of pork and duck from bowl to mouth proved unsuccessful. As one, two, then three dumplings plopped onto the table or the ground, an almost imperceptible muttering began among his fellow diners.

Douglas—with a quiet elbow to Holmes's ribs—demonstrated the technique. He held the chopsticks below the surface of the table so that Holmes might mimic his movements without making a spectacle of himself.

There was one more false start—a dumpling rolled off the edge of the table and plopped onto his lap—before he caught on. When dumpling number five finally made it to his mouth, even Holmes in all his sorrow had to admit that he had never tasted anything quite so delectable in his life.

By that time, the long table had grown noisier. Once

the eating had begun, so did the talking and the laughter. From what he could tell, they were speaking Mandarin. And although Douglas apparently knew enough words to join in here and there, Holmes was grateful to simply sit and not have to make conversation.

He looked around for the boys in *tangzhuang*, but they seemed to have vanished.

Just as well, he thought, as they did not exactly bring him comfort.

He let the hunched little man pour him another drink, then a third for good measure. Between healthy sips, he stretched out his arm toward the bowl, and with the long ivory chopsticks hooked one of those beautiful little morsels of meat, bringing it more or less deftly into his mouth.

Holmes was satiated and a bit drunk when Huan looked past him and casually asked Douglas if he had eaten his fill.

"I have indeed," Douglas replied, patting his belly.

"Very good," Huan said with a grin. "Then you are ready."

All of a sudden, a dozen young men in *tangzhuang* surrounded them.

Holmes could almost smell the approaching fight. As Douglas began to rise, so did he—but Huan placed a firm hand on his shoulder and in no uncertain terms pushed him down again.

He was no longer grinning.

A few more men placed their hands on Holmes's shoulder to underscore the message. Meanwhile, one of the boys pulled away from the group and bowed to Douglas, who bowed back.

Within seconds the lad was sailing feet first at Douglas's head.

The men at the table seemed to rise like a fifty-headed dragon, yelling what sounded like war whoops, cheering on the combatants, or maybe demanding Douglas's blood—it was impossible to tell which.

Douglas removed his shoes so quickly that Holmes barely saw how, and in a flash had his right foot on the boy's throat, pinching his gullet with bare toes. Though the boy's kicks were formidable, Douglas's long legs kept him safely out of harm's way.

Even so, his assailant was relentless. Choking and gasping for air, he finally managed to beat, kick, and pry Douglas's foot from his neck. As the two opponents continued their wild acrobatics, seemingly to the death, the whoops and the yells of the crowd grew. Money began changing hands, and this gave Holmes comfort in a way, as it had to mean that Douglas and the boy were sparring...

Then came a spray of blood from the boy's nose, as Douglas landed a roundhouse punch... along with a welt rising on Douglas's face where an elbow connected to his cheekbone.

Sparring or not, the wounds were all too real.

Their wounds from the journey had finally begun to heal, the bruises to discolor acceptably. Now Douglas would have a fresh batch to contend with.

Using his *extensor digitorum longus,* Douglas hooked the

boy's neck from behind. But this time, the boy was ready. Instead of trying to swing at Douglas—an impossible proposition—he simply dropped to the ground onto his back, using his momentum to throw Douglas off balance.

Douglas started to fall squarely into a double punch that the boy had readied. At the last second, however, he catapulted over the boy's prone body, and landed on his feet behind him. The boy bounced up from his prone position and flipped toward Douglas as if the dirt underneath him contained a springboard.

But he was one blink too late.

Douglas ducked… and as his opponent flew over him, Douglas landed a punch to his gut that expelled the boy's air all at once and left him on his back, as helpless as a tipped-over scarab.

The crowd cheered wildly.

A gong echoed from somewhere.

Douglas waited a moment until the boy caught his breath again, then he helped him to stand, and the two bowed to each other.

Another moment, and Douglas turned to Huan.

"I would not have recognized him," he said, breathing hard, "but for that pitted little scar just above his right eye—the bad case of rubella when he was five. We were all quite worried about you," he added, turning to the boy. "On our knees night and day, praying you would not die. Then again, I had no idea that you would grow up and attempt to murder me."

Douglas grinned at this last, while the boy smiled bashfully and bowed again.

"He is nineteen now!" Huan announced proudly. "Mycroft Holmes, may I present my son, Little Huan."

Little Huan, who was taller than his father by a head and a half, turned and bowed to Holmes, who bowed back, trying to not appear as befuddled as he felt.

Then Little Huan turned to Douglas.

"Welcome back, Uncle Cyrus," he said. "We have missed you."

"You have grown so much," Douglas said. Then he swept his hand to include all the boys, who seemed to have materialized around them once again.

"Mycroft Holmes," Douglas said. "It is my great pleasure to introduce you to the Harmonious Order of Closed Fists."

The hunched little man handed drinks in ceremonial cups to Douglas and Little Huan, and another round of bows began.

Douglas took a drink, then wiped his mouth. "It is not an easy life for Chinese immigrants in Port of Spain," he explained. "The Closed Fists perform as a sort of militia to ensure that… things are fair. In commerce, housing, whatever the need might be. They are trained in combat from the time they are very young."

"So I gathered," Holmes responded.

"Your skills have remained sharp, my friend," Huan complimented Douglas.

"I am very glad of that at the moment," Douglas said with a slight bow.

Holmes raised an eyebrow.

"Any other little secrets you'd like to share?" he asked.

"Don't much care for the taste of our own medicine, eh?" Douglas countered, grinning.

"It's a good thing you were already banged up," Holmes said. "As it is, you don't look much the worse for wear."

Douglas laughed, and Holmes joined him.

"In truth," he told Douglas, "that was a terrifying display."

Douglas nodded. "There is nothing quite so frightening as to have the human body come at you in some unexpected way. It is not simply the kicks and the jabs that strike fear, but—"

"Yes, I understand," Holmes interrupted enthusiastically. "It is what stories of gargoyles and monsters count on. The idea of something attacking you that is not upright, that is not facing you eye to eye. Things that crawl, things that fly... it is the odd angles themselves that can be terrifying."

He glanced around at the strange locale, and tried to pinpoint what he felt.

Though it had indeed been "a terrifying display," he also felt satiated, as one might feel after a hearty meal. Perhaps it was Douglas's small victory against a younger, stronger opponent. Perhaps it was the haze of alcohol. Or perhaps it was knowing that "the monsters" he had feared were actually friends, but he finally felt—if not the deep sense of safety that Huan and Douglas had extolled— then certainly a reconciliation with the environment that allowed him to breathe a bit more easily. Something he hadn't experienced since he'd left his flat in London.

He recalled Mrs. Hudson, calling out from her window. *"You be careful among the heathens, luv!"*

He wondered what Mrs. Hudson would make of all this.

"We know you have difficulties," Huan was saying to Douglas, "and we are happy to help you. Whatever you need, you have only to say so."

"I appreciate that, my friend," Douglas responded, "but our next destination is my family's land, and anyone there will already be quite traumatized. I am not certain that the sight of men with partially shaved heads and *tangzhuang* would assuage it."

"The offer is forever," Huan said.

Little Huan and the other boys nodded somberly.

Who are these people, Holmes wondered, *who will so readily sacrifice themselves for others, asking nothing in return?*

In his circle, he hadn't met very many like them.

27

DOUGLAS'S FAMILY HOME WAS LOCATED IN THE southwest part of the island, just outside of San Fernando. It was a day's ride by horseback from Port of Spain, as no trains ventured there. They leased twin mares for their journey. Though the horses weren't particularly fleet of foot, or terribly bright, they did their duty and did not spook easily.

This last was especially useful, as the hand-dug road would often abruptly end, eroded by rain and sea, or buried inside a mangrove swamp.

"Two steps forward, one step back," Holmes muttered sullenly as they sidestepped another dead end while trying to locate the next piece of road.

"So long as it's not *two* steps back," Douglas said evenly.

Holmes frowned. "Must you *always* put the positive light on things?"

"I do it merely to balance you out, Holmes. If not, we would surely have stumbled into a ditch by now."

Thankfully, Douglas knew the terrain and could always locate some alternate way for proceeding, and soon the sleepy little town came into view.

* * *

Founded some ninety years before, San Fernando had only one throughway, High Street, so baptized because its center was built upon the flanks of two hills. Its sloped appearance made visitors feel disoriented and slightly drunk. Though the buildings had a definite Spanish flavor, most of the inhabitants appeared to be Indian. In fact, Holmes recalled reading that San Fernando had become a hub for Indian immigrants who served as cheap but dutiful beasts of burden for sugar, cocoa, and tobacco growers.

"Spain has laid the foundation, and India has populated it," Holmes said, glancing about.

"The West Indian Petroleum Company has taken up residence here," Douglas added in a tone that implied he did not much approve.

"Another employer is surely a good thing," Holmes suggested. "I assume they are searching for pitch oil?"

Douglas nodded. "No one argues that this island needs employment, but it is ugly and dangerous work," he said darkly. "It spews filth into the air and water, and the death rate is quite high, especially among the Indian immigrants who must accept the worst of jobs. Yet it was from them that I learned my trade. What they knew or intuited about tobacco, I could never have gleaned anywhere else."

"I owe them my livelihood," he concluded a bit sadly.

A moment later, a quavering voice called out:

"Cyrus? Is that you, boy?"

"Emanuel!" Douglas called back as he halted his horse.

A toothless, ancient Amerindian waved to them from the other side of the road. Age had not so much bent him as it had whittled him down. He seemed light-boned, as if the most innocuous wind could blow him away. That sense of lightness was enhanced by the long smock-frock he wore that seemed almost as old as the man himself, and that blew like bat wings in any trace of breeze.

Douglas dismounted and lobbed the reins toward Holmes, then began walking to the old man, his arms wide.

"You tired old carcass!" he declared, grinning as he approached. "How happy I am to see you again!"

Emanuel remained where he was. Great tears began to roll down his worn old cheeks. He wiped them away with a hand that was so thin it was very nearly transparent.

"Whatever is the matter?" Douglas asked, quickening his step.

"Three-Fingered Eddie is dead," he declared. "I have been upstairs, comforting his mother and sister, for they are undone."

Douglas ran the rest of the way and grabbed the old man by the arms.

"How?" Douglas asked. "How did he die?"

"Local boys! On the road that leads from Port of Spain. He was carrying enough victuals to last a week. His throat was cut ear to ear."

"Emanuel, what are you saying? That local boys killed him?"

"Local boys?" the old man repeated. "No, no, they found him! As for who killed him, who can know? But they left him lying in the road like he belonged to no one."

Douglas looked over at Holmes, who shook his head.

Our amateur murderers are starting to become professional, he thought.

"Ah, such bad news all around, such bad news!" Emanuel cried. "First Eddie, then your family home."

"Wait," Douglas said. "My home... what about it?"

"Burned!" the old man said. "Burned to the ground."

At first, Douglas wondered if the old man had grown demented, but as a few more neighbors descended from their houses to greet him and to commiserate, he realized Emanuel was telling the truth.

"And my family?" Douglas asked. "Are they..."

He could not say the word. But he was quickly assured that his sister, nieces, and cousins were all safely inland, hiding with other neighbors.

"No one left in the village," the old man said. "Everyone too afraid. I myself am staying away from the sea. I cannot bear to witness the graves, day upon day." His voice broke. He began to sob again. "And all the other houses still stand." Emanuel mumbled between sobs. "Yours is the only one that burned."

Douglas and Emanuel, astride one horse, with Holmes on the other, rode the four miles from San Fernando proper to Douglas's family home.

Though Emanuel had referred to their destination as a "village," Holmes thought it looked like nothing of the kind. It consisted of a dozen small wooden houses built on a promontory overlooking the sea. Eleven stood, shuttered and all but abandoned.

One had been burned to its foundations.

Leaving Emanuel astride the mare, Holmes and Douglas dismounted and began to pick through the rubble, but there was nothing left, apart from a few iron pans lying next to an ancient pot-bellied stove, its flue still rising into the air.

"Why?" Douglas kept asking. "Why *my* house? What vengeance is this?"

"Perhaps it wasn't vengeance," Holmes offered. "Was there anything here that held interest? That revealed a clue of some kind? That had worth?"

Douglas looked at him askance.

"Anything of worth, or a clue," he repeated. "I swear to you that there is nothing—*was* nothing here of worth, unless one factors in the emotional…"

He looked around helplessly.

He could not go on.

It was obvious to both men that the fire had been set intentionally. Burned-out husks of wood, most likely removed from the pot-bellied stove, lay at strategic spots beside piles of clothing now charred beyond recognition. Handfuls of straw had been yanked from mattresses, along with any other flammable material that could be found.

Holmes surveyed the destruction.

"They certainly were thorough," he said.

"And did nothing to hide their intent," Douglas added.

Emanuel, who still had not dismounted, looked down.

"They?" he asked. "You know who did this, Cyrus?"

Douglas shook his head. "I will not speculate. But if you hear anything, no matter how strange or improbable, you will tell me, yes?"

"Of course!" Emanuel declared, looking slightly offended. "But no one could have known what happened. Only the dead know. Ten fresh graves in the cemetery, thirteen in all."

"So we heard," Douglas said vaguely.

"And more in other villages!" Emanuel proclaimed. "Yes! From here to Icacos. South."

The last bit of geography was for Holmes's sake.

"Nothing on the other side of the island?" Holmes inquired.

Emanuel shook his head. "Only this side. The *douen* leave the east alone."

"How many?" Douglas asked. "How many other children have died?"

Emanuel shrugged. "Three in Icacos, five in La Brea, another three in Point Fortin. Here in San Fernando, we have the most, but no one wants to talk. Because of the footprints."

"Footprints?" Holmes inquired.

"*Douen*," Emanuel announced miserably. "Below the cemetery. On the sand."

Underneath the promontory where the houses stood was a headland—another smaller point of ground that jutted out over the sea. Though a path of sorts led there from the promontory, Emanuel could no longer make the trek down the steep incline.

Which was just as well, Holmes thought. He and Douglas would traverse the path more quickly without him.

He took out his handkerchief and patted beads of

sweat from his forehead. Even the light traveling suit—the one that had provided fodder for Sherlock's teasing—was too tightly woven for this implacably damp weather.

As they drew closer to the cemetery, Holmes noticed grass growing, with brown patches here and there as silent witnesses to an unmerciful sun. There were several dozen graves in all, some bearing white crosses, others marked by a simple wreath.

"That grass does seem at odds with its surroundings," Holmes said.

"It is," Douglas responded as they continued down. "The village elders wanted a proper British cemetery, so they planted grass over Miocene rock and sediment, without much success, I'm afraid." As they drew nearer, Holmes could see that ten small graves had been freshly dug.

The children, he thought.

He fought back the sorts of "what kinds of animals" queries that have no immediate or satisfying response. For him to be effective at all from this point on, he reminded himself, he would have to dismiss anything in himself that was not pure logic.

Yet it wasn't just the size of the graves, or the pungent smell of new dirt that drew his attention.

"The grave heads point east," he said. "An old Christian tradition to be sure, but an odd one in a place like this, as they seem to be all but snubbing the sea."

"They point toward Mecca," Douglas said.

"Mecca? But why, when most bear crosses?"

Douglas shrugged. "There is such a mixture of religions here, and all of us are neighbors. Since Muslims are required to point east in death, and the Christians had no objections, the community elders declared that all graves would point toward Mecca, and all the families complied."

"Quite reasonable," Holmes admitted.

Then, looking toward the shoreline, he added, "Douglas, do you not find it curious that the *douen* have been calling children only on this side of the island?"

But Douglas did not answer.

He was staring at the sand below.

28

THE FOOTPRINTS COULD HAVE BELONGED TO A FIVE- OR six-year-old child. They traversed the sand from one pathway to another—some fifty yards apart—that led down to the beach.

At first glance, it appeared as if someone had simply walked backward, for play. It was only upon drawing closer that the anomaly became all too clear—the right foot was where the left foot should be, while the left was in place of the right.

"The prints are unusually well placed," Holmes remarked. "Far enough from the shoreline that the water will not take them, protected from the wind by that overhang in the rock, yet still visible from the little cemetery."

"An important element," Douglas agreed, "if they are meant to serve as a warning."

Holmes nodded. "They are the final convincing that people need." He stared out at the water. "It seems rather obvious," he continued, "that the *douen* and *lougarou* are meant to keep people away from the shoreline. But why?"

The two men scrutinized the footprints for any sign of tampering, then explored the area for indications of boats that might have docked with contraband. But there was nothing of the sort. It did not appear as if any boat had touched the shore at all, much less one laden with goods. There were only claw prints left by birds, along with the occasional flipper marks of leatherback sea turtles coming up out of the water, and then padding back into the sea again.

"No boats?" Holmes asked, stating the obvious.

"My neighbors pick cotton, tobacco, and sugar," Douglas said. "I know of no fishermen here."

Then he stared at the prints again. "I suppose someone could train a small child to walk backward with its legs crossed," he mused, "but the child would have to execute the maneuver perfectly the first time. For some fifty yards, with no assistance."

Holmes nodded. "And the prints would not be so perfectly weighted, nor so precisely equidistant. No," he said, "I believe I know how it was done, although the 'how' isn't really pertinent."

With that, he started back up the path leading to the promontory.

"Not pertinent?" Douglas exclaimed, watching him go. "It may not be pertinent to you, but it is very much pertinent to me!"

"To what purpose?" Holmes called back. "Since it is obvious to us both that the source isn't supernatural, what does it matter how the unscrupulous fool the gullible? It will get us no closer to the truth, and besides, you shall figure it out for yourself soon enough, if you will but think a moment!"

With that, he hurried along.

Douglas hastened after him.

"For the love of all that is sacred, Holmes," he growled. "Will you tell me what you know about the footprints?"

Holmes halted mid-step. When he turned to look at Douglas, one of his eyebrows was raised in a most superior manner.

"I do not know, Douglas. I only surmise."

"Well, surmise, then," Douglas said, an edge to his voice, "and pray do it quickly, for this is growing tedious."

Holmes took a deep breath, and exhaled.

"Very well," he said. "If we must waste the time to satisfy some morbid curiosity… think of *geta*."

"*Geta*," Douglas repeated. "You refer to the sandals that geishas wear?"

"Precisely. But instead of two horizontal 'teeth' that support the sandal, picture only one. Vertical, and molded like a little backward-facing foot—the right on the left, the left on the right. Once that is constructed," Holmes went on, "one need only possess marginally good balance to make the prints.

"Surely you noticed that they were heavier at the heel," he continued, "then heavier again at the toe. It was as if someone were rocking their foot forward, the way one does a stamp."

"Astonishing," Douglas muttered, looking back at the prints to confirm what Holmes said.

"If 'astonishing' refers to me," Holmes replied, "then I accept. As for the information itself? Useless. What is important now is what one can see from the beach that one cannot see from the promontory. Anything you can call to mind?"

"Nothing," Douglas responded. "Although we can have a look round and see," he added doubtfully as he followed Holmes up the path.

They returned to the promontory to find Emanuel still astride the horse, fast asleep. Douglas gently awakened the old man and helped him to dismount, though he did so carefully, as Emanuel was not only disoriented by being awakened but had grown quite sore from sitting so long with his legs splayed.

Then Douglas unsaddled the horse, propped up a blanket against a nearby *poui* tree, and settled Emanuel underneath its shade and gigantic yellow blooms.

That done, he and Holmes walked to the edge of the cliff and looked out.

The haze had dissipated. The sun was beginning to set, painting the sky green, gold, and violet. It was unquestionably lovely, but there was nothing unusual that could be seen from the beach but not the promontory.

"Effluence," Douglas said.

"Yes," Holmes agreed brusquely. "Detritus of some kind. That is what can be seen close up. But there was none on shore—at least, not yet." He turned and made his way back to the burned-out husk, then began to poke around again amongst the ashes.

Douglas looked out a moment longer, then joined him.

The two continued to poke about in silence for a while. Something was occurring to Holmes, and he did not like it one little bit—for though it might answer their latest riddle, it made him gullible, to say nothing of culpable.

"Were you expecting the letters from your suppliers to arrive here?" he ventured.

"Yes," Douglas said. "That is, no—they would first arrive at the post office in San Fernando, then a neighbor would pick them up and bring them here." By habit, he looked over toward the pot-bellied stove.

"The post is usually waiting at the kitchen table," he explained. "Emanuel is the one most likely to:..."

When he realized what he was saying, he stood up, brushed the ash off his knees and ran back to the *poui* tree.

"Emanuel!" he shouted so as to awaken him. "Did you collect my letters?"

"When?" the old man asked, gazing up at him with rheumy eyes.

"Did you collect my letters at any time?" Douglas repeated. "Any time in the last month?"

"Of course," Emanuel said. "That is what neighbors do."

"When was the last time…?"

"That I gathered your post? Not yesterday, so it must have been the day before… Why? Did I do something wrong?"

"No, no, you did everything fine," Douglas said, leaning down and patting Emanuel on the arm. "Get some rest. We will be headed back to town soon."

He returned to the ruined house and squatted next to Holmes, who was investigating broken crockery.

"The letters are one with the chairs and table," he sighed, indicating the mounds of ash by the pot-bellied stove.

Holmes felt a wave of nausea assail him.

"Georgiana knew about them," he said.

Douglas scrutinized him. "And how would she know that?"

"Because I *told* her." Holmes exhaled loudly and closed his eyes. "Whatever your suppliers may've written," he continued, "was threatening enough that she and those beastly men came to search the property. When they could not find what they wanted, they burned down the house so that no one else would find them."

"But I only asked them to report back on disappearances and deaths. Facts that can be easily unearthed, once someone is in this vicinity. So what could possibly be so terrible that—"

"Cyrus?" a quavering voice interrupted.

Douglas turned. Emanuel was standing behind him, smiling.

"Yes, Emanuel, what is it?" Douglas asked, forcing a smile in return.

"With all this commotion, I have not had the chance to congratulate you on your engagement."

"I beg your pardon?"

"Oh, what is *wrong* with me?" Emanuel said. "Never grow old, Douglas. Never, for it is a terrible fate indeed. Promise me you will not."

"Yes, yes, I promise," Douglas assured him. "But what were you saying about an engagement?"

"Yes, your engagement!" Emanuel repeated with growing enthusiasm. "I knew that in the midst of all this tragedy, there was a bit of good news. There I was, leaving the post office with your mail, and your fiancée, she was at the counter, asking about it, just as I was walking out. Ah, such a lovely voice! Like a little bird tweeting."

"What did she look like?" Douglas prompted.

"She looked like a beautiful woman," Emanuel declared with certainty. "She was at the counter, and I heard her say your name, and I heard her identify herself, and that you had asked her to fetch your post. So I say to her, 'Missus!' I say. 'I have them,' and I pulled them out from under my hat, thusly!"

He mimed the motion.

"And I gave them to her," he continued, "there and then. Oh, she was so grateful. She kissed me on the cheek. Here!"

He pointed to the spot.

Holmes stepped forward. "Emanuel. Please. What did she look like?"

"Pretty, I said," Emanuel repeated. "Blond! And young… too young for you, Douglas," he added with a wink, accompanied by a dark and toothless grin. "She wrapped them in a neat purple bow."

Douglas stared at Emanuel, then at Holmes, mystified.

"Cyrus?" Emanuel asked.

"Yes?" Douglas said, distracted, turning back to him.

"I think I shall go lie down again a little."

"No, old man, it's getting cold. One more moment, and I'll take you home."

Douglas turned to Holmes again. "But if she *had* the letters, then why *this*?" he asked, and he indicated the destruction all around him.

It took Holmes a moment of contemplation, a moment when the noise around him ceased, and he was alone in the depths of his mind, which appeared to him like gears endlessly turning. Everything he knew about Georgiana, about her character, about her ideals, sifted through.

Out came a hunch that made him feel both prescient and emotionally destroyed. He hurried over to the metal flue that was attached to the pot-bellied stove, tore it off of its foundation with unnecessary force, as it was no longer anchored to anything of substance, and dug around inside the tubing.

Along with soot and cinders, out came a packet of letters. The envelopes were blackened by smoke and curled with heat, but otherwise undamaged.

They were still wrapped in a neat purple bow.

Douglas's eyes were as round as two large coals.

"What on *earth*…" he began, but Holmes shook his head.

"I realize my feelings for her are absurd," he said quietly. "She *is* a monster, after all."

"You think Georgiana put them in there?" Douglas asked, astonished.

Holmes shrugged. "Who else?"

"What, is this a game with her?" Douglas shot back angrily.

"No," Holmes replied. "I think she is in over her head, and does not know how to get out."

"Ah, I see! She conspires in the murders of children, of adults, now she is rethinking it."

"Who conspires?" Emanuel interjected meekly. "Your fiancée? Douglas, is she a bad girl?"

The sun had set and a light wind was beginning to blow, lifting the cinders.

The old man was starting to shiver.

He looks as if the thread of his life is ready to be cut, Holmes thought.

"Emanuel," Douglas said, wrapping a protective arm around his shoulders. "I will take you home now, as I promised."

"You cannot think of leaving now," Holmes protested, holding up the bundle. "Not when we have these in hand!"

"There is a living creature here that I am responsible for," Douglas murmured through gritted teeth.

Holmes waved the packet of letters in the air.

"And who knows how many *other* living creatures might be saved if only we could suss this out," he countered.

"You are being irrational," Douglas shot back. "We are in ashes, and losing the light. How do you propose we read these precious letters?"

Holmes ran an exasperated hand through his hair and seemed ready to answer back in kind.

"Forgive me, Douglas," he said after a moment. "You are correct, of course. It seems I am mortified that my carelessness has added to your sorrows—"

Emanuel interrupted.

"Ah, my boys, is it a place of refuge you are seeking, then?"

"Yes, Emanuel," Douglas said patiently. "For you. The night is growing chilly."

"But I have a place here, Douglas," the old man declared. "It is not as spacious as your house was, as it is only one room, but it is large enough, with four sweet-smelling straw beds, hardly used, though we require but three. I have my own pot-bellied stove, and a stall for the horses, and hay…"

"I realize that," Douglas interjected, "but it saddens you to stay there."

Emanuel shook his head.

"If you remain with me," he said earnestly, "if you will not leave me alone, I can survive it one night. It will almost be as when you were little, hey, Cyrus? And you would stop by for Mariana's ginger-blossom tea. Do you remember?"

"Indeed I do," Douglas replied softly.

"He loved my wife's tea," he explained to Holmes. "Always such a good little boy. So well behaved."

"We would be honored to stay with you tonight," Douglas said, squeezing the old man's shoulder.

"Good, good." Emanuel smiled, clapping his hands. "Then it is done! And perhaps soon you will introduce me officially to your fiancée. Eh?"

Douglas and Holmes glanced at each other, dismayed.

"She is not my fiancée," Douglas explained patiently.

"I know, I know," Emanuel said somberly. "It is not so easy for one of our kind…" The old man rubbed his skin with a forefinger. "…to marry an Englishwoman. Times have changed, but not so much, eh? Well hush, then. Let it be our secret for now. Perhaps some day, people will not see color so much."

Douglas nodded. "Perhaps," he said.

29

EMANUEL'S HUT HAD ONE SMALL WINDOW FACING westward to the sea, but was set so high up that the view was all sky and no water. It was grimy with soot, and its top hinge was missing so that it could no longer be pried open.

There was a pot-bellied stove, but its front grate had been torn off, and it hadn't had a good scrubbing in years. The room itself was nearly empty but for a deal table and three splintered old chairs, a wooden chaise that looked like an instrument of medieval torture, and four mattresses with straw stuffing so old that some of it actually stood up in sharp little needles.

The mattresses themselves weren't quite so sweet-smelling as promised. Holmes could smell them from the moment he walked in—and "sweet" would have been nowhere in the description.

Yet the old man was kind and seemed very glad for the company. He generously filled his lamps with enough oil that they could have burned for a month. Then he expertly lit the stove and stood back, admiring his handiwork as the ancient old receptacle coughed plumes of smoke that painted another layer of soot upon that small high window and turned the room into a sweltering oven.

But creature comforts mattered not a whit to Holmes. He was anxious only about the letters. He blew dust off the deal table and took a seat.

Douglas, after ascertaining that Emanuel did not need his help, pulled up a chair across from Holmes, when the old man called out from across the room.

"I have no beer or wine," he said despairingly.

"That won't be necessary!" Douglas called back.

"Ah, you'll be playing cards, then. Hearts?" he guessed, squinting at them while removing his shoes.

"Now what prompted *that* idea?" Douglas asked.

Emanuel cocked his head, confused. "What other reason to sit up then, eh? When the beds are so comfortable? Here!"

He toddled over to one mattress, one with a particularly prominent hump, and sat upon it. Then he demonstrated how to stretch out upon one's back, as if neither man had ever attempted such a daring feat before.

"There, you see? I do not even need a pillow," he announced proudly. "Which is handy, as I have none. You simply lie here quietly…"

"If you are going to sleep," Douglas scolded, watching him, "kindly do not take the worst bed of the lot."

"And you will kindly be quiet before your elders!" Emanuel snapped. "Now, then," he continued as if in the midst of some difficult lesson. He pulled a moth-eaten blanket around him, up to his neck. "You simply close your eyes… thus…"

Within seconds, he was snoring lightly.

* * *

Douglas took the packet of letters from Holmes and cut open the first two envelopes, both of which bore a postmark from Honduras, both sent by the same correspondent, but five days apart.

As he scanned them, Holmes watched him expectantly, and after a moment began to drum his fingertips on the tabletop.

"I am too practical," he said, "to believe that somewhere in that stack lies the answer to all our problems."

"Far from it," Douglas replied sourly, "at least judging from these. They say nothing beyond the usual niceties. 'All is well,' not to be outdone by 'all is *still* well'…" He pushed the first two letters aside and tore open the third envelope, this one hailing from Jamaica.

"Might you include me from the first salutation?" Holmes asked drily. "For if not, I shall surely go mad."

At which point Douglas began translating aloud.

"'My dear Cyrus,'" he said. "'You shall be pleased to know that our little island has seen a rather peaceful month…'"

Holmes laughed mirthlessly.

"We are not pleased in the least," he said.

That letter, too, was shoved aside in favor of the fourth and the fifth. Holmes's hopes to the contrary, these were no more productive. Douglas showed his disdain by balling up both and lobbing them neatly into the stove's open maw.

By the time he'd reached the sixth envelope—this one hailing from Venezuela—it bore the brunt of his growing annoyance.

"Careful!" Holmes cried. "You nearly cut the letter in twain!"

Douglas scanned it with disgust.

"It says nothing," he muttered darkly. "The usual 'we hope your family is well and your business is thriving'—certainly not the sort of information one would torch a house to quell…"

He paused, and frowned, squinting over the letter.

"Although this," he mumbled, "I have no notion of…" Then his voice trailed off, and his frown deepened.

"What is it?" Holmes pressed.

Douglas translated:

"'Men of genteel but profitable employment, whom we have not seen in two decades or more, are now at our ports—'"

"What does he mean, 'at our ports'?" Holmes interrupted.

"Caracas," Douglas said distractedly, then continued. "'And they are wishing to repurchase merchandise at its former market value.'" He paused, then said, "What sort of merchandise could he mean?"

Holmes suddenly leaned forward in his chair.

"What is it…?" Douglas asked, eyeing him curiously.

"Dear heavens, Douglas. Keep reading!" he sputtered.

"Why? What do you infer from this?"

"Come, come, man—I grant that your supplier is being diplomatic to the point of cryptic, but, having worked in a war office, I am well versed in cryptic," Holmes exclaimed. "I am certain that the poor sod is too frightened to do more than hint."

"Frightened of what?"

"You know perfectly well what—"

"*HOLMES!*"

Douglas thundered his friend's name so loudly that Emanuel, lying in his bed, twitched and snorted, before drifting off to sleep once again.

"Whatever is the matter?" Holmes bleated.

"You must keep me apprised as we go along," Douglas blurted out. "God's teeth, man, you can make *anyone* feel like an idiot."

"Apprised?" Holmes stammered. "Why, of course! You needn't bellow, we *are* partners in this, are we not?"

Douglas leaned across the table.

"Perhaps it has not been made sufficiently clear to you," he countered tersely, "but someone has burned down my home to destroy *this*!" He waved the letter inches from Holmes's face. "This endless litany of 'we trust your family is well,'" he continued, "has cost my family and myself dearly. So, if you discern something of worth, pray tell me without a trace of smugness." He sat back and crossed his arms at the waist. "Because at the moment I cannot bear it."

"Smugness?" Holmes replied. "I am not *remotely* smug! But does 'genteel employment' suggest nothing to you?"

Douglas took a moment to breathe. He acknowledged to himself—not for the first time—that arguing with Holmes was useless. That he'd do what he would, and heaven take the hindmost.

"Genteel employment," he mused. "I suppose it reminds me of 'the genteel trade'."

"There you have it!" Holmes declared.

Douglas blanched.

"You are referring to slaves?" he asked, incredulous, as

if the very notion might spring out and bite him. "You think that slaves are the 'merchandise' of which they speak?"

"What *else* could they be speaking of?"

"Holmes," Douglas said, as evenly as he could manage. "I realize you are given to far-fetched notions…"

"All of which have been proven true thus far," Holmes reminded him.

"But *this* letter hails from Venezuela. The slave trade has been banned there for twenty-six years."

"Nevertheless, we are on to something," Holmes insisted. "Pray, keep reading. I have an inkling that this is the first major opportunity we have had."

30

THE SEVENTH MISSIVE, HAILING FROM PORTUGAL, subtly confirmed the one from Venezuela. It was more overt, referring to the slavers as "men of the genteel trade," and it ascertained that, after a good long absence, they'd suddenly begun appearing openly at various ports of call that had once been part of their routes.

"'Employment in the Caribbean is scarce, as you are aware,'" Douglas read, "'and merchandise tends to stay put.'" He looked up. "I assume that means ex-slaves continue to work for their former owners, there being no other work to be had."

Holmes, who was fanning himself with letter number one, nodded.

"'In exchange for a moment's distraction, merchandise is appropriated for three hundred British pounds per unit,'" Douglas read.

He stared at Holmes.

"So past owners are asked to identify not only the former slave, but his or her whereabouts, so that the slavers may kidnap them—to the tune of three hundred pounds per head. Three hundred per head..." he repeated, whistling.

Abruptly he rose and began inspecting Emanuel's drawers and shelves.

Holmes stared at him askance for a moment.

"What the *deuce* are you searching for?"

"Ah, thank heavens," Douglas gasped. From out of the recesses of an otherwise bare shelf, he pulled out a little brown burlap pouch of shag tobacco, along with a sheet of yellowed rolling papers. The tobacco was nearly as old as the straw in the old man's mattresses, but Holmes was every bit as glad to see it as was Douglas to have found it.

Both men rolled it up quickly, set it afire, and inhaled greedily.

"Brilliant notion, Douglas," Holmes complimented him after a long exhalation. "Helps one to think."

"It never occurred to me that you might need assistance in that regard," Douglas replied. "In any case, with the sugar and cocoa trades struggling, three hundred British pounds per head would, unfortunately, be wildly tempting to just about anyone."

He took a puff of the cigarette and exhaled the acrid smoke.

"On the other hand, it makes economic sense only to the seller," he mused. "Half of the twelve million slaves 'imported' from Africa were brought here, to the Caribbean. That's quite a bit of 'merchandise' for the slavers to repurchase, and for an awful lot of money. Imagine how long it would take to contact every former slave owner in—"

"Six years," Holmes interjected.

"Beg pardon?"

"It would take six years to contact them all."

"So you are saying they began this process six years ago?" Douglas ventured.

"I said no such thing," Holmes exclaimed, "and they are certainly not planning to kidnap six million former slaves. No, if they receive an affirmative from even one in one hundred previous owners…"

Douglas shook his head no.

"I realize maths is your forte, Holmes," he declared, "and not necessarily mine, but that is still sixty thousand former slaves they would be proposing to pay for, and then kidnap—which would be a chore in and of itself. And while it's true that some people consider the Negro expendable," he continued, "sixty thousand human beings vanishing into the ether may attract a bit of notice."

"Yes," Holmes admitted, "the monetary sum would be sheer folly, and the logistics of the kidnappings? Untenable, as you said. So, while our discovery is certainly momentous in nature, what we need now is direction."

Douglas stared down at the last envelope. It bore no postmark.

"Perhaps it contains a map," he suggested, only half joking. He tore it open, but there was no map inside, and no letter. Instead, there was the gleaming illustration of a steamship, with the words "seeds and machinery" penned above it in a printed hand that neither man recognized.

Holmes looked it over.

"It seems self-evident that the slaves would be transported by ship," he said. "That isn't the sort of revelation we need. And there's nothing here to indicate what the final destination would be."

"'Seeds and machinery,'" Douglas quoted. "'Any ship that carries seeds and machinery, regardless of the other cargo, is protected as a commercial vessel and is immune from search and seizure.'"

"That is a fact," Holmes acknowledged.

At that moment, they heard a hiss.

The old stove had finally burned its fuel down to embers.

"Thank heavens," Holmes declared, eyeing it with mild contempt. "I never thought I'd mourn the London chill."

"Have we been sitting for so long?" Douglas marveled. He rose and checked his pocket watch.

"Nearly midnight," he confirmed.

Between the soot and the cigarette smoke, the room was shrouded in fumes.

"I realize that opening the window is impossible," Holmes said, "but perhaps we can open the door."

"At *this* hour? Not worth the trouble," Douglas responded, "as we would be consumed by mosquitos and gnats. Besides which, I shall not be responsible for Emanuel's catching a draft." With that in mind, he walked over, removed a blanket from a second mattress, and laid it on top of Emanuel's thin one—then resumed his perch across from his friend.

"I'm astonished he can breathe at all," Holmes quipped. "Or that we can." Nevertheless, he rolled a second cigarette, marveling how good the rancid tobacco tasted, despite the burn.

"Any thoughts?" Douglas asked, indicating the letters.

Holmes shrugged.

"One or two," he said. "Why would the slavers suddenly feel at their leisure to wander about their former ports of call?" he asked, and then he answered his own question. "I posit that their goal," he began, "is not numbers at all. Think of it, Douglas—once a man is willing to entertain the *notion* of selling a human being, never mind actually doing so, in a country where such activity has been declared illegal, he becomes complicit.

"At this juncture," he continued, "it seems likely that enough former owners have entertained the notion—or perhaps taken actual money—that the slavers feel safe to wander about their former hunting grounds."

"Let me be sure I have it correct," Douglas said. "You posit that they never actually *intended* to kidnap ex-slaves in such high numbers—that the purpose of kidnapping is to keep ex-owners quiet and complicit. Their intent, in other words, has always been to import slaves from slave-trading countries, where it's much less costly."

"Precisely," Holmes said.

"But surely the ex-owners are not fools," Douglas protested. "Surely they have done their own due diligence and have discerned whether or not those slavers have the resources to purchase all those slaves. That would require an awful lot of money in the bank, Holmes."

The latter nodded. "True, but in the latter case, the resources are simply a front. A wealthy investor puts up money, knowing he won't have to spend it all. The slavers kidnap just enough ex-slaves here and there to keep the locals complicit and therefore docile. In the meantime, our villains simply wait for an opportune time to import slaves en masse, and for much lower sums, from countries that still trade, moving them through the ports of countries that still allow slaving ships to dock at their shores." He counted off on his fingers: "Puerto Rico, Portugal, Brazil—"

"Yes, yes," Douglas interrupted impatiently. "Thirty countries worldwide, so quite a few to choose from. With a looming war in Europe, and the United States busy with its own recovery, the slavers simply have to wait a few more months. No one will be paying this the least mind."

He flicked nervously at his cigarette. "But why come here?" he wondered. "Why Trinidad?"

Holmes shrugged. "Oil," he speculated. "And coal."

"But the Amerindians are already serving as very cheap labor for both," Douglas countered.

"Nothing is cheaper than free," Holmes replied. "In any case, it is hard to fathom that men would go to all this trouble for oil, or even coal…"

"…or caulking."

"You are referring to Pitch Lake?" Holmes asked.

Douglas nodded. "Most of the ships in the area purchase the sludge as caulking material."

Holmes put out his cigarette and plucked some errant tobacco from the tip of his tongue.

"And not a peep about any of this at the War Office," he exclaimed. "Which certainly unsettles me, though it does remind me—when we hail to Port of Spain once again, we shall have to go by the post office. I sternly charged Parfitt to send me anything of pertinence."

"Little Huan is collecting the post for the Chinese

district," Douglas said. "I shall ask him to collect your letters, as well." He looked distracted, and frowned. "The most pertinent question remains. If this is all true, can anything be done? Can these people be stopped?"

Holmes shrugged again.

"Britain has no jurisdiction over slave-trading countries at all," he said somberly.

"And escape would be a constant threat," Douglas added. "How do the slavers manage it? It's not like the days when nearly every country had its own slave trade, and freedom was prohibitively distant."

"Where can they locate land that is at once safe from mutiny *and* beyond the reach of national laws?" Holmes asked.

Douglas shook his head. *Yet another dilemma*, he thought, *on an endless list.*

As Holmes inhaled a few more puffs, he suddenly recalled something Mrs. Sutton had said.

"Mr. Sutton, God rest his soul, decided to go a different way, purchasing land off the coast..." He sifted her words through his brain—

And then it came to him.

"Douglas!" he practically shouted it. *"Islands!"*

In the corner bed, Emanuel chuckled and snorted in his sleep.

31

HOLMES WAS MORE THAN PRIMED TO RIDE BACK TO THE governor's office immediately.

"If we leave now," he insisted, "we could easily make it to Port of Spain by early morning. They will have maps of nearby islands, indicating which are located in international waters, while still being close enough to Trinidad to be practical for exchanges. There we can also find ledgers of sale."

Douglas—though every bit as anxious as Holmes—would not forsake Emanuel.

"I will not have him wake up alone," he declared.

The two fashioned a compromise. They would set off at dawn the following day, to arrive at the governor's office by mid-afternoon.

While Douglas stretched out on one of the little beds, Holmes declined to lie down at all, preferring to remain seated at the table, to smoke what was left of the rank tobacco, and to stare periodically at the window for any sign of light.

By the time they had deposited Emanuel safely in San Fernando, then made their circuitous way back to Port of Spain, the sun was beginning its unflagging drop from the sky.

Worse still, when Holmes dismounted, his tired nag missed her step and landed a front hoof neatly on his right foot. As pain shot through him, he cursed the horse, the toes, and "the whole bloody mess." Then he dug Sherlock's walking stick out of his bag and, while Douglas procured water for the horses, did his best to navigate the stairs to the governor's front door, continuing the imprecations the entire way.

When he finally reached the top landing, he noticed three men standing guard outside the closed door. They were large, sullen, and pasty-white, like the professional fishermen he had seen on the Liverpool docks—the ones who sailed on Russian whaling ships.

Holmes approached them with as much gravitas as he could muster under the circumstances. When he announced himself, however, they seemed neither to care about his credentials, nor about any emergency that might involve the governor's time and attention.

"*Nyet, nyet!*" they said when he insisted he be allowed inside—thus confirming their nationality. When he didn't depart, the portliest of the lot balled up his fist and threatened him with it—specifically indicating that he would like nothing better than to leave its imprint on Holmes's sole unmarked cheek.

He was further demoralized to note that the man's substantial fingers were decorated with an array of cheap rings, and he worried that another scar might be in his very near future.

A second brute—this one with a door-knocker beard and a chewed-up toothpick which he bounced from one side of his mouth to the other—growled, "No more governor!" in a thick accent.

"No more governor?" Holmes repeated. "Surely you don't mean he is deceased…?"

The man didn't answer, and the three of them simply fingered the long pistols hanging at their thighs, drawing closer to him, making their resolve quite clear.

Holmes hobbled his way back down the stairs and intercepted a very surprised Douglas, who was making his way up. Quickly he explained the dilemma.

"As determined as we are to get in, they seem even more determined to keep us out," Holmes concluded.

Douglas peered up at the men.

"Could this be a misunderstanding?" he asked.

"No misunderstanding at all," Holmes said. They've simply been instructed to keep people out of the office, and that's what they'll bloody well do. The good news, I suppose, is that it's not personal. They've not been warned about *us*, per se."

"Whether personal or not," Douglas interjected, "it would not do to waylay the governor's guards. And in any case, we are in no condition to take them on."

"Then what are our options?" Holmes asked, not really expecting an answer.

Douglas frowned again at the guards, then made his way back down the stairs, motioning for his friend to follow. He led Holmes around the back of the edifice, to the five-finger tree that they had seen from the governor's window. It was rich and lush, with outstretched branches that grew up past the balcony. Its star fruit left a trail of sticky juice on the ground and the leaves, making them shimmer.

"You cannot be serious," Holmes said. "I've two toes sprained to a fare-thee-well…"

"It is a dramatic approach, I grant you," Douglas replied. "But at least no heads need be broken in the process."

Holmes looked at the tree, then back at Douglas.

"Other than mine, you mean," he muttered.

Without another word, Douglas began to climb.

Damning his weariness and his aches, Holmes followed suit, flinging himself onto the lowest branches. While Douglas's greater reach gave him a distinct advantage, Holmes used Sherlock's walking stick to good effect, hooking upper branches to propel himself ever higher.

In a matter of minutes, they climbed to the edge of the balcony. Douglas leapt across the railing, while Holmes more or less stumbled over it, but both results were the same, and they found themselves at the office's balcony door.

It was unlocked.

The two brushed themselves off and were just praising their own cleverness when they realized that the room was occupied, but not with the governor. Inside, half a dozen Amerindian workers were in the midst of packing up what looked like the governor's personal belongings.

They stopped their labors and stared.

Before Holmes or Douglas could utter a sound, the governor's smug young aide, Beauchamp, strode in. He seemed taken aback to see them, but quickly recovered.

"May I *help* you?" he inquired contemptuously.

Holmes, still out of breath from the climb, took the lead.

"We are here to meet with Governor Hamilton-Gordon," he said in his finest "official" tone.

Beauchamp just smiled thinly. "Sir Hamilton-Gordon has left for Mauritius."

"I see," Holmes said, trying to sound nonchalant. "And when is he scheduled to return?"

"He is not," the aide said.

"Is that a fact?" Holmes said, not yet quite believing it. "And just what is he doing in Mauritius?"

"Oh, did he not inform you, then?" Beauchamp responded. "On the twenty-fifth of June, the governorship is to be turned over to one Sir James Robert Longden. I am afraid that whatever... *plans* you made with the governor, you shall have to revisit with his successor."

"But the governor said he would help us," Douglas interjected, brushing aside Holmes's small attempts to quell him. "He gave us his solemn word."

"Did he?" The aide allowed himself a condescending grin. "Well then, were I you, I would board the first boat to Mauritius to inquire if you heard correctly."

The workers tittered at this last, before resuming their packing.

"Mr. Holmes," the aide said as he pointedly turned away from Douglas, "though you did not ask my advice, I shall now offer it. Your issue, as I understand it, is with a few missing Negroes. But you must understand that Caribbean society has complex, overlapping divisions of castes and classes. Frankly, the Negro is the last thing in the world anyone cares about."

Beauchamp opened the door. His expression was cold,

his intent clear. With no other options, the two men started out. Just as he passed, Douglas turned and cold-cocked the little aide in the jaw, dropping him neatly to the ground.

The workers said not a word, but continued their efforts.

As Douglas shook out his fist, he and Holmes strode out of the office and down the stairs to where the Russians still stood guard.

When the sentries saw Holmes and Douglas again, their laconic expressions gave way to puzzlement, as if the two had simply materialized out of thin air. One muttered something to another in Russian, but they showed no signs of making a move.

They simply watched Holmes and Douglas walk past.

As the two friends untied their nags, Douglas whispered to Holmes.

"I *infer* by this that you were correct—that they were hired specifically to guard against strangers entering through the front door. Since we did not, in fact, enter through the front door, it seems as if we did not fall within their purview."

Holmes nodded.

"Next time," he said as he began to mount, "they should be paid enough to guard the perimeter, as well." He clicked his tongue at his nag. As the barn-sour horses began their plodding way toward the road, Holmes sighed deeply.

"In any case, we must return and scout around," he said. "Somehow I doubt that these men will be quite so accommodating when they see us again." He grimaced as pain shot through his foot.

"Huan," Douglas said, eyeing his friend, "can have someone take a look at your toes. They most likely can be persuaded back into service."

"You mean through some sort of Chinese mumbo-jumbo?" Holmes asked, not in the mood. "No, thank you."

"Perhaps I should venture back here alone, then," Douglas replied, "as your limping about might impede our progress."

"No one knows their way around an office better than I, Douglas," Holmes replied. "It would be like keeping a duck from water. Though if you insist on utilizing your Chinese friends, I wouldn't mind it if a handful stood sentry for us."

Douglas shook his head.

"They are tenuous residents here in Port of Spain," he said, "with families and livelihoods. They don't need any problems with the governor's office, though I am sure they would be glad to help in other ways."

Holmes nodded unhappily.

Finally out of the path of pedestrians, the men tapped the horses' flanks and headed back to the Chinese quarter, to wait out what Holmes hoped would be an uneventful evening, before they returned to the governor's office.

32

HOLMES LAY ON HIS BACK, STARING AT THE WOODEN SLATS OF HIS hovel and waiting for one a.m., the assigned hour that he and Douglas were to venture back to the governor's office. He hoped that their opposition remained unaware of their goal—the land claims—and had not already spirited away pertinent documents.

And what an opposition they are, he thought with chagrin. *People so vile that they would whistle away someone's life, simply for their own gain.*

And Georgiana is among their ranks.

She had ceased, in his mind, to be Georgiana. She had fully become some other creature entirely. She had become Anabel Lynch.

Or perhaps he had separated the two so as to keep a bit of his sanity.

In any event, Georgiana was the lovely, caring creature with whom he had fallen in love back in England, when the most exotic thing in his life was the jumbie bead bracelet she wore on her right wrist. Anabel Lynch was another sort of creature entirely—frightening and unpredictable, who had made certain that he and Douglas would survive the journey to Trinidad, though not precisely in one piece.

She was the one who had lied repeatedly, who had been at least partway responsible for heaven-only-knew how many deaths—while at the same time had felt qualms enough to hide Douglas's letters so that her fellow conspirators might be found out.

He stretched out on the hard, prickly straw, testing both his emotions and his physicality as one might test an unfamiliar object that held some interest, though was not particularly dear.

It no longer felt as if wolves were tearing at his throat each time he thought of her; and although his toes were certainly smarting, physical discomfort did not seem to matter as much as it once had. Aches and pains had become a part of him.

Though at three and twenty, he mused wryly, *I should not be feeling quite so many.*

Something else was occurring, as well, something that seemed foreign to anything he had assumed about himself to this point. He recalled the nightmares he'd had on the ship, and before that the chills he'd felt up his spine at the sight of that false sailor, spitting out of the wrong side of his mouth, and the mutes guarding the house of death.

What would Sherlock say, he wondered suddenly, *if he knew his older brother had given himself over to phantoms and premonitions?*

Whatever this was, this otherworldly sensation, he sincerely hoped it would dissipate. The last thing he needed was to fancy himself a mystic.

He heard the dissonant sound of a nightingale-thrush sing somewhere nearby, and realized that in spite of the ache in his foot, the terrible burden of memories, and a sort of a chronic bone-weariness, he felt strangely lulled inside this little lean-to in the Chinese quarter.

It was more than mere relief.

It was affection.

He marveled at how different Port of Spain was from noisy, congested London. By nightfall, all one could hear was the sound of drums in the distance, the occasional lilting laughter, the soft, warm wind blowing through the cracks and the crevices of the town, which sounded like a child's unconsciously carefree hum.

He catalogued those factors that had troubled him so much at first: the dark and strangely brooding neighborhood with its mucky avenues, its beehive work ethic, and its exotic smells. The lean-to itself, with its well-used straw mattress, grease candles that pooled more than they burned, and the tattered King James Bible... not to mention the thin course of effluence that ran mid-street, and served as the neighborhood toilet.

It all felt familiar to him now, as if he'd lived here for years.

On the other hand, he was still too tightly wound, even at rest. He had always been rather strong and in good form, but now his shoulders, biceps, back, and abdomen were more suited to an adventurer than to a secretary in a stuffy London office. The culprits were a lack of food and constant exertion, to be sure. But this new musculature, plus the scar upon his cheek and the various and sundry wounds upon his body, did make him wonder how he'd be received back in England—if anyone would recognize him at all.

England, he thought. *England without Georgiana.* It seemed impossible to fathom.

He heard a knock upon the crossbeam outside, and then Huan's voice announcing his presence.

"Come in," Holmes said, readjusting his leg so that his foot was elevated.

Huan peeked in, with the usual grin on his face and a letter in his hand.

"Cyrus, he asked Little Huan to check the post today," he said. "And so he did. Though please forgive how late the hour, as he has only just returned…"

"Thank you," Holmes said, taking the letter. "Quite kind of your boy."

The envelope bore the stamp of the War Office, along with Parfitt's ornate schoolboy hand, and Holmes frowned.

"Would you like me to fetch Cyrus?" Huan asked, eyeing the letter.

"That won't be necessary," Holmes assured him.

He pictured Douglas as he had left him an hour before: engrossed in a Chinese game that involved a grid of black lines, and black and white stones. Holmes had watched for a few moments in order to pick up the fundamentals, but as he had never cared for table games, he had quickly lost interest. Douglas, on the other hand, had seemed engrossed and at ease with his old friends—there was no use spoiling his moment of leisure before their next foray into danger.

He pulled his mind back to the present, and found Huan staring at his bare foot.

"Your toes are the size of pecans," he scolded.

"I am aware of that," Holmes said tightly.

Huan shook his head disapprovingly and disappeared again, closing the curtain as he went. The small, soft breeze caused the candle to gutter and go out. Holmes felt around for the matches and relit it.

As he did so, he wondered at his own sense of the dramatic. The trip back to the governor's office did carry a certain amount of risk, but was it truly a "foray into danger"?

You are being excessive, Holmes, he cautioned himself. *Let us attempt to keep a clear head about it all.* He moved as close to the flame as was reasonable, cut open the envelope, took out the letter and read.

My dear Mr. Holmes,

I hope that this letter finds you in excellent health!

Holmes laughed aloud.

If Parfitt only knew.

As he continued, the awkward graciousness and banal niceties of Parfitt's words reminded him of his former life—and so he read the following paragraphs with pleasure and a touch of homesickness.

I am aggrieved to report that our esteemed employer, the Honorable Edward Cardwell, has not been so ~ in excellent health, that is ~ but has been plagued by a recurrence of gout. However, as he does not wish that you should fret yourself on his behalf, it would have been wiser for me to remain mum on the subject, as I am certain you have much to concern yourself and do not need to be troubled with more. Therefore, I pray you erase this sad news from your mind, though I do not, by this, mean to issue orders to my superior and esteemed benefactor!

Dear heavens, man! Holmes thought with a hint of a smile, *get on with it!*

Though of course I desire to impart a cheery hallo! ~ as does my aunt, who always refers to you as a top-shelf tenant and sends her warmest wishes ~ the real reason for my missive regards that most curious series of withdrawals and then deposits which you had mentioned before your departure.

In brief, our tenuous political climate has made it so that I have been <u>officially</u> entrusted with monitoring any unusual monetary exchanges from or to Prussia or France by way of the Bank of England. In that regard, I report to you now that the series of sums that originate in Luxembourg through our own Bank of England, and that from there are deposited in Jamaica, have escalated both in sum and in frequency.

Though there is no direct link between Jamaica and Trinidad, there are oddities nevertheless. The first is that the sums, which were once negligible, are now rather substantial: up to thirty thousand British pounds per deposit. The second is that the sums never rest in England but are spirited off quickly to Jamaica.

The third is the signatory. This appears to be Count Wolfgang Hohenlohe-Langenburg, related to Her Majesty the Queen in that he is first cousin to Ernst, Prince of Hohenlohe-Langenburg, who is in turn married to Feodora, Her Majesty's half-sister. I am afraid I cannot account for the origin of the funds, nor state how they were utilized, and this last is troubling. I have done the requisite research on the Count, and he has no employment to speak of, nor any lands to administer. He seems wholly dependent on Her Majesty the Queen, who is also generous toward her half-sister Feodora.

Holmes rubbed his eyes, and read the pertinent part again. This could be the monetary link to the purchase of islands—if indeed they existed—and to the slaves. If so, it would prove to be an almost insurmountable scandal for the Crown, were it to surface publicly.

Whatever small sense of safety Holmes had entertained, it instantly dissipated. He and Douglas would have to get to those ledgers in any way they could manage.

At that moment, there was another knock upon the cross frame outside.

"Come in," Holmes said.

The curtain parted. It was Huan again, this time shadowed by the hunched little man with the saipan on his head, who served drinks and dumplings each night at the long table.

"Charlie Woo," Huan said. "Meet Mycroft Holmes."

The little man bowed, and then rose again, as eager and vibrating as a squirrel. He carried a carpetbag in his hand.

"He will fix your toes," Huan said, smiling.

Holmes stared at them both.

"I don't mean to be rude," he said to Huan, "but he will do no such thing. I have never had anyone handle my toes, and I am not about to start now."

"Mycroft Holmes!" Huan said crossly and—in Holmes's estimation—a bit too loudly. "You are free to do as you wish for your own sake, but I will not have you putting my dear and good friend Cyrus Douglas in danger because you are unable to run, or to fight! You *will* put your toes in his very capable hands, and we will hear no more about it."

With that, Huan closed the curtain behind him, doing so with a flourish, leaving Holmes alone with the small, hunched man—who bowed again, and opened his bag.

33

AT ONE A.M., AS THEY RODE AS NEAR TO THE GOVERNOR'S office as they dared, Holmes apprised Douglas of Parfitt's letter.

"Count Wolfgang Hohenlohe-Langenburg," Holmes recounted. "It seems he is vaguely related to the Queen in that he is first cousin to Feodora's husband, Ernst."

Douglas could not help but laugh.

"*Vaguely?* In royal circles, the two may as well be twins!"

"Yes, it was facetious," Holmes said, smiling.

"And are you thinking he factors in, in some manner?"

"Not yet," Holmes admitted. "I know only that the money trail is suspicious indeed."

Putting that particular query aside, they dismounted, and made their way on foot to the back of the building. Seeing not a soul, they scaled the selfsame tree, with Holmes making good use of his cane, and vaulted onto the balcony again.

In truth, he didn't need the cane at all, for reasons he couldn't understand. Back at the lean-to, the stooped little man had worked quickly. First, he had laid his hand flat against Holmes's chest.

"Will that heal my toes?" Holmes had asked sarcastically,

but Charlie Woo had ignored him. Instead, he'd lifted his hand from Holmes's chest, had pointed to his heart, and then had wagged his finger at him in a manner that Holmes did not appreciate at all—as if he were scolding him for being a naughty boy. But before he could protest, Woo had moved on. He had placed needles into Holmes's skin—none on the broken toes themselves, nor even on his chest—rather at the top of his foot, at his ankle, even at his temple. Though he had expected the needles to hurt, they had not...

What had ached, and substantially, were points of pressure in his hand, neck, and shoulders where Woo had pressed down with a two-fingered grip that brought to mind a seventeenth-century vise.

One spot in particular, in Holmes's right hand—the soft flesh between the metacarpal and the phalanges—had caused his head to pound so intensely that he'd feared an aneurysm. He very nearly told the man to cease this madness and be gone, but his curiosity bested him. And so he'd remained quiet, squeezing his eyes shut and grimacing until the pain had dissipated.

At that juncture, he had been shocked to find that not only had the ache in his head disappeared, but so had the ache in his toes—along with the little man in the *saipan*. He had left without a sound.

While Douglas had surely realized that Holmes was no longer limping, he'd said not a word about it. Holmes, for his part, had remained equally mum—he would not give Douglas the satisfaction—though he did notice a small smile playing at the corners of his friend's lips each time he chanced a look down at Holmes's foot.

* * *

The balcony door was secured this time, but Douglas administered a deft kick to the handle, and the thing groaned open.

Once inside, Holmes jammed the walking stick against the door to prevent unwanted visitors. Douglas found a couple of small candles and put them into service, and they set about scouting for the sales ledgers. Practiced in the bureaucratic arts, Holmes quickly located them inside a locked bookcase, its miniscule key still fitted neatly inside the lock.

"Their security is not the best," he sniffed.

"Few things on the island are," Douglas noted.

Thankfully, the ledgers were in perfect order, catalogued and cross-referenced by years and locations.

"Now let us see which have changed hands in the last ten years or so," Holmes muttered, and he handed one to his friend. As Douglas labored through his first record book, he eyed Holmes speeding through half a dozen.

"With two hundred and thirty unnamed islands to scan," Douglas muttered, "I shall never make fun of your quick reading skills again."

They searched in silence for a while, acutely aware of any noises that came from outside.

Holmes found three islands, equidistant from Venezuela and Trinidad, that had been sold in 1868 and 1869, and he quoted the ledger number to Douglas, who nodded.

"Here's one," Douglas replied, "sold in March 1860. It sits close to those you've found, according to mark on the map and sale number."

Holmes sighed. "Now I see why no one bothered to hide these. There is nothing contested here, not one nefarious thing—all these sales are legitimate. There is no mention of the terrain, either. What could grow there? Sugar? Cotton? In a climate like this, with such varied topography, it could be anything."

Douglas picked up the only ledger that remained to be perused, while Holmes walked into the little antechamber where Beauchamp, the governor's aide, kept his desk. It was locked, but he picked up a paper cutter, jammed the point at just the right angle between the drawer and the frame, and it quickly gave way.

Among various files of little interest, he found a large sealed envelope. On the envelope itself were numbers, written in a prim, neat hand. They matched those of the islands that had been bought.

Inside was a promotional pamphlet that was every bit as well executed and costly as the *Sultana*'s. But rather than praise a steamship, this one advertised human beings.

The daguerreotype showed a group of thirty or so Africans in an idyllic island setting, posed on the sand in three rows. The first row was comprised of children, most between eight and twelve—an age where they could begin to earn their keep. They were smiling and appeared to be well cared for.

The second consisted of florid young women with strong thighs and good hips, nearly all of childbearing age. And the back row featured men, solidly constructed and able-bodied, with their arms slung about each other's necks and grinning at the camera obscura, as if they had just enjoyed a spirited game of rounders.

Behind them, in the gleaming water, was moored the very same steamship featured in the flier that had been slipped into the unmarked envelope at Emanuel's house.

Holmes turned to the back of the pamphlet—and felt his legs go limp. He sat down hard at Beauchamp's desk.

It was another daguerreotype, this one of a handsome couple standing side by side and smiling at the photographer: Georgiana and the American, Adam McGuire. The advertisement read:

BEG RESPECTFULLY TO INVITE THE ATTENTION OF ALL INTERESTED PERSONS

For the past Four Years, Adam McGuire, Esquire, and Miss Anabel Lynch, an Educated Woman, have Served as the New Countenances of the Trade. They and other Investors Hailing from the Four Corners of the Globe, from Luxembourg to the United States and from South Africa to Timbuktu, Solicit Your kind Participation in Same.

(Meetings shall take place in London at prearranged and agreed-upon times.)

Holmes shook off the horror he felt.

"Luxembourg," he said aloud. "And South Africa."

Douglas came to stand behind him and stared over his shoulder. He noticed the likenesses of Georgiana and McGuire.

"There they are," Holmes murmured. "The faces of the 'new slavery.'"

"I am profoundly sorry, old friend," Douglas replied.

Holmes marveled how often, on their journey, words had proved lacking, but how—in the last analysis—words were all that people had to try to comfort one another. How strange it was that the mere knowledge of Douglas's friendship mitigated the pain somewhat.

"I understand why Luxembourg should prove suspicious," Douglas said, changing the subject. "But why South Africa?"

Holmes recounted Georgiana's keen interest in the diamond mines on land owned by those Dutch farmers, the de Beers.

"One year ago, on the day of our engagement," he concluded, "it seems that she was…" He paused there, for the truth was entirely ironic. "…otherwise engaged. Clearly, she used the knowledge I'd given her for the cause—"

They heard a rattle at the door. Someone on the other side was turning the doorknob, but to no avail.

They had been discovered.

Then, the pounding and pushing began, along with imprecations in Russian. Douglas quickly stowed the books in their original bookcase, locked it again, and moved for the balcony.

On impulse Holmes grabbed a ledger entitled "Waterways 1580 to Present," and followed Douglas out. The two threw themselves over the railing and onto the tree, clambering down as quickly as they could—only to find two of the three pasty-skinned security guards waiting for them at the bottom.

34

BY THE TIME HOLMES'S FEET HIT THE GROUND, HE WAS so undone that he could barely face this new and deadly challenge. He would have liked nothing better than to raise his hands in defeat, but the Russians did not seem to be interested in prisoners, but rather victims.

Douglas was to be their first. After a brief scuffle, he had dispatched one guard with a forceful kick to the throat; but now his partner seemed intent on making him pay for that infraction. He had a gun pointed at Douglas's temple.

"You die!" he raged, his hand shaking.

That flair for the dramatic was the pause that Holmes needed. In a split second he unsheathed the walking stick, revealing a long, sharp knife. With his last burst of energy, he raised it up and charged at the man, stabbing him through the chest with such force that it pushed him backward against the five-finger tree and impaled him there.

Holmes stared, immobilized by what he had just done.

By then the guard on the ground was beginning to recover his senses. With one move, Douglas yanked the long knife out of the Russian's chest. The body fell to the ground like a marionette whose strings had been cut.

Douglas then spun the knife around and pointed it at

the prone guard's throat. The man froze, then lay flat on the ground with his hands upraised.

"Go," Douglas commanded, stepping back.

No translation was needed. The guard stumbled to his feet and ran off.

Holmes just stood there glued to the spot, still clutching the portion of the cane that formed the sheath. He watched the blood trickle from the open wound in the dead man's chest. His eyes were open and seemed to be staring at Holmes, their gazes locked.

Douglas grabbed him by the arm, and dragged him away.

By the time they'd reached the horses, Holmes was pointing back at the dead guard and trembling.

"Why in heaven's name did you pull out the knife?" he whispered to Douglas. "The man might've lived if you hadn't."

"He was already dead," Douglas asserted, "and you know that as well as I. When I removed the blade, blood did not spurt out, because there was no longer a heartbeat to propel it." With that, Douglas wiped the blade on his horse's blanket and handed it back to Holmes—who fell back and refused to accept it.

"No, I do not want it!" Holmes protested. His voice choking. He began to mount. "I never wish to see it again."

"Nonsense," Douglas stated. "You must have a weapon, and this is as good as any."

"And I tell you *I do not want it*!" Holmes insisted.

"Now you are giving in to histrionics," Douglas declared with an upraised eyebrow. "You are not unacquainted with death—what has possessed you?"

Holmes glanced over his shoulder at the corpse. Crumpled at the base of the tree, it was no longer staring at him.

"I have never killed a man before," he confessed.

"I see," Douglas replied quietly.

"I do not want the knife," Holmes insisted again, and Douglas nodded.

"I understand," he said. "But do try and recall that you used it to save my life."

Holmes hesitated a moment longer.

Then he took the knife and placed it back in its sheath.

Later that night, a despondent Holmes sat at the long table in the Chinese section. This time, the dumplings and liquor did nothing to quench the emptiness in his belly. Not even a good cigar—Douglas had managed to pick up a handful of *Fundadores* from one of the Chinese traders—could ease the ache he felt.

And for once, it had nothing to do with Georgiana.

Douglas was right, of course. The deed had had to be done. And he had seen death—plenty of it—not only working for Dr. Bell, but simply by way of being a Londoner.

Of course, though one could argue that England was a civilized country, there had been public hangings for most of Holmes's life—they hadn't been banned until he was nigh on twenty years of age. And there were poor unfortunates who occasionally dropped dead in the streets from cold, or hunger, or disease.

Yet he had never been the cause of another human being's demise.

I am barely out of adolescence, Holmes reminded himself in what sounded suspiciously like Douglas's voice. *And have lived a rather sheltered existence.*

"Holmes?" he heard Douglas say, speaking beside him. "What do you think?"

"Of what?" Holmes asked.

Douglas and Huan had been sitting to his right and discussing what their next steps might be. Huan had departed without a sound, but Holmes had begun to grow accustomed to members of the Harmonious Fists appearing and disappearing with uncanny speed, even if it meant a rather wanton disregard of protocol.

"Should we investigate the islands in question?" Douglas began, though without much conviction. "After all, we know where they are located."

"You mean *go* there?" Holmes said, as if he couldn't believe what he was hearing. "The two of us, in our present condition, against what is undoubtedly an army?"

"Might I remind you," Douglas parried, "that the Harmonious Fists are ready and willing to fight on our account? In all, they comprise more than three hundred fighting men. And there are the Merikens…"

"The Americans?" he repeated, puzzled.

Behind him, a woman's soft voice corrected him, one he knew all too well:

"Not the Americans, my love," she said. "Merikens."

Holmes turned around.

Huan and Little Huan were holding Georgiana between them. Or rather, they were holding her upright, for she looked so frail that she could barely stand on her feet. Her rosy color was gone. Her lips were cracked and dry, but she tried to smile as she met his shocked gaze.

"Merikens," she repeated in a voice that was a wisp of what it had once been. "Colonial Marines. I thought for certain you'd have heard of them.

"Then again," she added, "I suppose no one can know *everything.* Not even *you*, my dearest."

35

IN THOSE FIRST FEW SECONDS THAT HE STOOD BEFORE her, Holmes conjured up his entire lifetime yet to come. The three children he'd always dreamed they'd have. Their small but lovely terraced home in Pimlico, and if all went well, St. John's Wood. The Christmases and Easters and birthdays they would celebrate as a family. The flaxen-haired, rosy-cheeked grandchildren he'd someday bounce upon his knee.

All of it blown to smithereens in the span of a heartbeat.

How slight a thing will disturb the equanimity of our fair minds, he thought, although he could not recall, at the moment, who had written those words.

Austen, perhaps? Or Dickens?

One thing was certain. Georgiana, that slight and delicate thing, had always disturbed the equanimity of his mind. And this day was no exception. But, God's bones, how frail she looked—how weak! Her skin was the color of... what? Even ivory seemed too dark an assignation, and snow too robust, too cheery, parchment too yellow.

She is of the palest gray, he realized. *The color of tombstone.* But on the heels of that thought came another.

Do not pity her.

She deserved no pity, he knew that—not so much as a solitary glance her way. And yet, he could not help but look at her—though he sincerely hoped that this look did not appear so bare and wounded as it felt to him from the inside.

Thank heavens I am no longer mad with grief. That had been excised by the deaths of innocents and miscreants alike, by the many mishaps he and Douglas had endured at her hands. What he felt at the moment was more akin to a dull pain, as if he'd been hit unflaggingly in the same spot for so long that it no longer felt a part of him.

Then, surprisingly, he began to move toward her.

No, Holmes! he thought fiercely to himself.

How, then, was he within inches of her, gazing into her eyes as if he were some poor, hapless serpent that she had charmed? Those eyes were still so lovely—fathomless, guileless.

"*Search* her!" he heard Douglas say behind him. "If you do not, I shall."

He was about to protest, but one glance back dissuaded him. Douglas's expression communicated, in no uncertain terms, that his dear, kind, and closest friend was easily capable of killing her with his own two hands. And so while Huan and his son held her upright, he did as he was instructed. He gently patted her down.

"She is not armed," he mumbled to Douglas. Then he asked Huan, "Where did you find her?"

"She found us," Huan responded. "She begged us to bring her to you."

Little Huan confirmed his father's words with a solemn nod.

Georgiana raised her hand and placed it lightly upon Holmes's arm, as she had the last time he had seen her. And as usual, he felt that absurd desire to please her. Then he noticed the jumbie bracelet on her right wrist.

Half its beads were gone.

"Where are the rest of them, Georgiana?"

"I begged you not to follow me," she whispered.

"You could not have used more than two on me," he insisted. "Where are the rest?"

She said nothing.

"Georgiana!" Holmes shouted at her. "*Where are the rest?*"

"I ate them," she said. "Two days ago."

He did not recall crying out, but he must have, because there was a movement like a fluttering of birds around him. The Harmonious Fists were there, hovering, assuming their fighting stance, in case there should be trouble.

And then he was shaking her.

"*What did you do?*" he screamed, as though somehow it could be undone by force of will.

Once again, it was Douglas who intervened.

"It's no good, Holmes," he said. "She is dying. You can do nothing for her… not now."

As Douglas stepped away, Holmes stared at her.

"But *why*?" he asked in a wavering voice. "Why *any* of this?"

She looked up at Huan, who was still holding her.

"Might I perchance… sit down?" she said as agreeably as if she were requesting a cup of tea.

* * *

Huan and Little Huan escorted her to a bench in front of a flowering *poui* tree. Georgiana sat slowly, like someone who had aged fifty years in a few weeks. Then she grasped the sides of the bench as though determination alone would keep her upright.

Father and son moved some distance away, where they could watch the goings-on without eavesdropping. Douglas planted himself closer by, his arms crossed tightly at his chest, his expression furious.

As for Holmes, he found himself squatting on one knee before her, like a man about to propose, though he could not say how he got there.

"You came to me to unburden yourself," he said gently. "I pray you do so now."

She stared down at him, and nodded

"I… was recruited years ago," she began softly, "before I ever left Port of Spain. My father was an… early investor."

A coughing fit assailed her, but she struggled on.

"You saw our plantation," she said. "Everything my family had worked so hard for—gone. They assured us that nothing so demeaning would ever again happen to another hard-working family. And it was to be indenture, not slavery. My own ancestors were indentured, as you know, and… if we kept workers a mere five years and… and if we gave them something for their trouble—"

"Something for their *trouble?*" Douglas interrupted. "What, their liberty for a loaf of bread?"

She turned and looked at Douglas. "And what of *me?*" she said. "Am I to do nothing while former slaves are given more rights in England than I as a woman will ever hope to achieve? The right to *vote*, Mycroft!" she added piteously, turning back to him. "How long have I been dreaming of that?"

"It is an unfair world," Douglas interjected coldly.

"Douglas, please…" Holmes muttered. But he had questions of his own.

"Why bring the boy with you?"

"The boy." Georgiana sighed. "He was my special project. A budding poet. I gave him a small writing desk. When I announced to my charges that I was leaving, he followed me—and stowed aboard."

"And when you realized that I, too, was aboard, you used him."

"Yes," she said. "We used anything and everything to dissuade you. I cannot even tell you where he is now. Ran off, I believe," she added vaguely, sounding a bit like her addled mother.

Holmes flinched, wishing with all his heart that Duffer *had* run off.

"And what of the other children?" he asked. "The ones massacred along the shore, Georgiana. How did you justify that?"

"I didn't *know* about the children!" she cried, suddenly agitated. "I thought the talk of phantoms was just to frighten them, to keep people from the water."

"Why the water?"

"Because of… of the effluence," she said vaguely, as if she did not quite understand it herself. "The effluence that would occur once we began to dig—it all had to be settled, you see, before we made it public."

She reached for Holmes's hand. When she found it, he could feel hers trembling.

"It was all moving forward as planned, or so I thought," she continued. "Then, back in London, when you said the children were dying, I… well, I could not fathom it. Who would *do* such a thing? I had to see for myself."

"And when you arrived, what did you find?" he asked her as equitably as he could manage.

"At first, everything appeared as it should," she said. "But then…" She looked away. Her eyes filled with tears.

"I felt as if I had entered a nightmare. But I… I pretended to go along, do you see? Then, the moment I could get away, I went to find the letters, and while the fire was being set, I stowed them in the chute. I knew you'd be smart enough to find them, my darling, and put an end to this!"

She was gripped by another fit of coughing so violent that it seemed as if it would rend her in two. Holmes pulled his handkerchief out of his pocket and proffered it. She accepted it, and thanked him.

"Georgiana," he asked. "Did you ever love me?"

She managed a smile.

"How like a man," she said in a wisp of a voice, "to turn the conversation back to himself."

"Did you ever *love* me?" he asked again, searching her face.

She stared back at him and sighed.

"But how can I know… such things, Mycroft? When one is raised to view men as commodities—this one provides an income, that one a title—how could I step outside my own sex and class to know what I felt?"

"So you chose me because of the position I held," Holmes declared bitterly. "And what of McGuire?" he asked, though it felt as if it were tearing him in two. "Are you in love with him?"

Georgiana laughed softly and shook her head.

"I was married… to a cause. For four long years. Did I love him?" She shrugged. "Until women are granted lives independent from those we marry, most of us are as free to choose a mate as a dog in a kennel is free to choose its master."

Still he peered at her intently.

She shrank away from his gaze.

"Do not look at me that way, dearest," she said softly. "I cannot *bear* it."

"Where are they now, Georgiana?" Douglas interrupted. "Your compatriots?"

Georgiana seemed as if she could not utter one more word. But Douglas was insistent.

"I… I heard that some slaves were taken to First Island in the Bocas del Dragón," she told him. "But I don't know why…"

"The Dragon's Mouths?" he translated. "And which is First Island?"

She gave him the coordinates, reciting them from memory.

"There are guards there," she added. "Mercenaries, forty or so…"

"What sorts of weapons do they possess?" Douglas continued, moving toward her as he spoke.

"I…" She tried to speak but could not, then began to

rise. Her eyes looked dilated. She stared at Holmes as if she were seeing a ghost.

"Dearest," she cried out. "Guard your heart!"

And with that, she drew one more ragged breath and sank back against the *poui* tree. Her face relaxed. Her expression became almost peaceful.

She was gone.

Holmes dropped down on both knees and might have remained there for eternity, were it not for a strong black hand that yanked him up gruffly by the collar.

"No!" Douglas said. "I will *not* allow you to mourn her, and so disdain the lives she has already ruined."

"I cannot simply leave her!" Holmes protested.

Huan came up alongside him.

"We will see to her," he offered. "We will give her a decent burial, for your sake, for we are fond of you and have no wish to see you suffer."

Holmes nodded his thanks. Then he studied her face for one last time. He heard the tune in his head—the one Sherlock had hummed to tease him, the one he himself had hummed as they were heading to the plantation.

> *La donna è mobile, qual piuma al vento…*
> *Woman is as changeable as a feather in the wind.*
> *Lighthearted, easy to love…*
> *Whether in tears or laughter, she deceives.*
> *Always miserable is he who trusts her…*

He reached out and pressed her eyelids closed. Douglas put an arm around him, and Holmes allowed his friend to lead him away.

He did not look back, even once.

36

THAT NIGHT, HOLMES AND DOUGLAS SECURED THE AID of the Sacred Order of the Harmonious Fists. And when Holmes made it clear that it was a foray into the unknown, and insisted that the fighters be at least eighteen years of age, there were still three hundred who volunteered.

"Since we do not even know what we are seeking or what we shall find," Holmes opined, "we must approach this as a scouting expedition, and not an invasion. Though I am grateful for your support, Huan, and that of your men, we must rely on the element of surprise.

"Our group should be small."

"I agree in principle," Douglas said, "but allow me to play devil's advocate. With an invasion, we would have numbers on our side. And while subterfuge has its advantages, we leave ourselves open to ambush, most likely with no survivors."

"True," Holmes acknowledged, "but the result would be the deaths of a dozen men, and not of hundreds."

As the war council continued, Douglas and Holmes lit the last two cigars that Douglas had purchased, and Huan put a match to his long clay pipe.

"A great wrong must be righted," Huan said, exhaling a

cloud of white smoke. "Whether a dozen or hundreds, my men will do as they must. But one thing is sure," he added. "If we should die on that island, three hundred *will* go there, and they will avenge our deaths." He punctuated this last with another cloud of white smoke, and his cheerful grin.

"Well," Holmes declared, "I sincerely hope that won't be necessary."

The next morning, just before light, Huan and Little Huan drove Holmes and Douglas to the seven Company Villages of the Merikens. Following behind were two more carts and mules, each carrying five members of the Harmonious Fists.

It was to be another all-day journey, possibly into the night, but the inland road wasn't quite so eroded by wind and water as the coastal route had been. Thus they made very good time.

As they headed toward Moruga at the south-central stretch of the island, Holmes and Douglas took turns telling Little Huan the exploits of the Merikens. For the younger natives in the north, their daring feats were largely unknown.

At first Little Huan listened with half an ear, and then with more and more interest as the tale unfolded of an all-but-forgotten skirmish between Great Britain and a handful of American states. In 1812, when Britain invaded the Atlantic coast of North America for what would be a brief but bloody conflict, the Crown promised freedom to any American slave who'd join her ranks.

At the risk of their lives, thousands left their shackles

behind and escaped to the British lines. Many were routed off to the Royal Navy or the West India regiments, but eight hundred or so remained to do battle on American soil. They renamed themselves the Corps of Colonial Marines, and fought valiantly alongside the British, bearing arms against their former masters.

When after nearly three years the conflict ended, with Britain sadly vanquished, the Crown realized that these warriors who had so nobly served would face a grim future in their own country. Thus, they were given free passage to various British holdings, including Trinidad.

There, around Moruga, these former slaves founded what came to be known as the seven Company Villages. In spite of all they had been through, however, they never disavowed their American heritage. When the locals began to refer to them as "Merikens," they accepted their new name with pride.

"What do we want from them?" Little Huan asked. "Are they to fight alongside us?"

"Most are too old to fight, if they live at all," Holmes responded. "Yet we may enlist the help of their sons and grandsons, yes."

"They have skills that we can use," Douglas added. "Even now, one and two generations removed, the Merikens have kept their reputation as great warriors, swimmers, and saboteurs. But they have never met us—we are strangers to them. So, for them, this will be a foolhardy proposition at best. What we hope is that they will lend us four or five boats, so that we might sail from Moruga to Icacos, and from there to the Bocas del Dragón islands."

Holmes shrugged. "Though why they should do even that much is certainly in question."

"Perhaps you should have mentioned sooner the folly of this venture," Little Huan said with a smile.

Holmes smiled back. It was the most he had ever heard the young man say in one breath, and he was gratified to know that the lad had humor, as well as strength.

"The foolish will tread where the wise will not," Holmes replied. "If we waited for the wisdom of this venture, Douglas and I would still be in London."

"To fools, then!" Little Huan exclaimed.

"To fools!" the others declared.

Night had already fallen by the time their little scouting party arrived at the largest of the seven villages, with Nico braying happily as if he were leading a parade. The presence of strangers thus announced, men and women, boys and girls quickly gravitated toward the newcomers, most greeting them like old acquaintances, though they had no idea why these men had come, or who they might be.

Others arrived from nearby villages, and soon the welcoming committee had swelled to nearly four hundred. The local women brought sustenance—plates and platters of fried chicken, pan-fried pork, okra, grits, shoofly pie, and other culinary delights that had been handed down through the generations—while the men provided ale and musical instruments, including guitars and drums.

Holmes, focused on his mission and desperate to get on with it, looked askance at the festivities, while Douglas,

Huan, and Little Huan took it all in their stride.

"What a sour countenance," Douglas declared. "Might I remind you of certain protocols that you yourself attended to with the governor before we could even mention the business at hand?"

"I will grant you tea and small talk, yes," Holmes objected in a whisper, "but not a bacchanal! How long is this to last?"

Douglas simply rolled his eyes, and clapped along with the music.

Objections notwithstanding, Holmes sat on the ground, and listened and watched politely. After a while he found himself, if not joining in with the singing and the dancing, then certainly clapping along.

Douglas was gratified that his friend seemed to be on the mend.

After the music died off, and everyone had eaten their fill, a large group settled down and listened dutifully to the point of the visit. It fell to Douglas to rise to his feet and deliver the unhappy news—that a group of white men was attempting to reinstitute slavery, right under their noses, and that their little scouting party was seeking the Merikens' help.

"We have three hundred fighting men—" Douglas announced.

"I see only ten," someone called out. "No more drinks for you, brother!" he concluded while others laughed.

Douglas smiled gamely and cleared his throat.

"As I was saying," he continued. "We have three hundred fighting men available, if need be, but our mission at the moment is to get a group of scouts onto First Island so that we might discern who these enemies are, and what their plans might be. To do that, we must have vessels. We realize that you make your livelihood on the sea, and that four or five boats is a sacrifice indeed, but that is what we require."

The raucous gathering became ominously silent.

Holmes, Douglas, and Huan waited in the unnatural stillness for someone to say something—anything at all.

Finally, one of the elders, halt and nearly blind—but who wore the decorations of his former glory upon his cap—crossed his arms at his chest and shook his head no as vehemently as he could manage.

"This is a suicide mission," he called out in a quaking voice. "You shall all die... and lose our boats into the bargain."

Holmes shook off the shudder that went through him.

A moment later, an older woman spoke.

"You are asking us to lend you our boats," she opined, "even though you admit you do not know, other than some forty men on shore, how many other enemies there might be. You do not even know if anyone on the island needs to be freed at all."

"That is a fact," Douglas admitted. "We know only that a group of investors has bought some islands, and we know its intent. We do not know how far it has gone to execute it."

"Or even if," a man called out.

"But let me say again," Douglas continued, "that we

have three hundred Chinese brothers who are prepared to follow us there, and to die, if need be. These ten have come as potential lambs to the slaughter." He pointed to the Harmonious Fists who stood in regal dignity on the sidelines.

"All for a cause that, frankly, is not theirs at all—but ours! Yes, this is *our* cause," he said, his voice growing in conviction. "Yours and mine! And so I am asking you, as brothers and sisters who share the same skin color, to supply us with what we need so that we might do what needs to be done, and do away with this scourge once and for all!"

"Hear, hear!" Holmes said aloud, but nobody joined him. The large group behaved as if they were a large flower, shutting down for the night. There was hardly the sound of breath in the air.

He was trying to think of what the deuce he could say that could move them, if Douglas hadn't, when a young man rose to his feet. He was perhaps twenty years of age, with the bearing and the direct gaze of a born soldier.

"For those who don't know me, my name is Jessup Jones," he declared in an accent that was a mix of American and Trinidad patois. "Grandson of the Noah Jones as fought in First Company alongside the Britishers. My grandpa was my age when he ran away from the plantation. Didn't have no shoes on his feet, had never shot no musket. But he volunteered just the same, because he knew what was right.

"And the Britishers took him, because that's how desperate they was."

The assembled crowd chuckled at this.

"When he left the American states back in 1812, my grandpa Jones was one of a million slaves. He died right here in this village, ten years back, and on the day he died, the number of slaves in America had grown to four and a half million."

He paused and let the words sink in.

Murmurs of disapproval rippled through the crowd.

"We know how quick things can go bad," he went on. "Look what happened in less than one man's lifetime. Now these good folks—" He pointed to Douglas and the Harmonious Fists "—have come to try to stop the bad before it starts."

Holmes noticed as a few glances of respect, however reluctant, turned their way.

"Your livelihood depends on the good Lord giving you fish so you can feed your families," the boy reminded them. "How many fish you think the good Lord's gonna give you if you turn your back on your brothers in chains? So I say, whatever we can do, that's what we do. If it be boats, then boats! If it be lives, then lives! Who knows but that we have been chosen for such a time as this," he concluded to the rousing cheers and "amens" of those present.

"He paraphrased the Book of Esther," Holmes whispered to Douglas.

"A good touch," Douglas admitted with a slight nod. "Wish I'd thought of it."

From that moment on, there were many volunteers, buoyed by the women's blessings and promises of bounteous treats to take along—accompanied by threats of hungry bellies if they were to refuse.

It was all Douglas and Holmes could do to choose the hardiest of the lot to join them. As it turned out, that was no easy task. Hardiness seemed to be part of the Merikens' heritage.

Finally, Douglas begged them to decide amongst themselves, and so the elders—some of whom had done their stint as colonial marines—made the final choice. Ten of their ablest men were picked to join the newly formed ranks, including the young orator Jessup Jones.

Douglas, Holmes and Huan spent the rest of the night going over a battle plan, such as it was—given that they knew neither the topography of the island nor who might be protecting it.

As the Merikens cleaned and oiled their weapons like people born to it, the women continued to ply them with food enough for a king's feast, though the ale had been cut off and replaced with a bitter-sweet ginger brew that eased the spiciness somewhat. Nevertheless, for the duration of the meal Holmes's tongue was definitely on fire, and remained that way.

Try to enjoy it, Holmes, he reminded himself. *It will be the last respite you shall see in a while.*

37

AT FIRST LIGHT THE FOLLOWING DAY, THE FIVE FINEST
boats were selected for the journey; a remarkable sacrifice
for the community, as they would most likely not return.

Nevertheless, the ancient colonial marine, led by two
younger men, hobbled up to Holmes. He said not a word,
but handed him a gift—a gleaming spyglass.

"He had it since he was a young man himself," Jessup
Jones whispered.

"I am honored," Holmes responded.

The old man brought his gnarled and trembling hand
to his forehead and saluted smartly before being led off.

The three commanders—Holmes, Douglas, and
Huan—surveyed the tiny force who had been willing,
upon their word alone, to follow them into what could
be a slaughter, along with hundreds of others who were
supporting them with encouragement, equipment, victuals,
and prayer. For the first time since their journey began,
Douglas's eyes grew moist, and he stifled a sob.

"Pray hush now…" Holmes started to say, but before it
had quite left his lips, he felt his own throat catch.

Douglas took a deep breath—the sort that let Holmes
know just how much responsibility his friend was placing

upon his own shoulders. They climbed into the boat alongside Huan, Little Huan, and Jessup Jones, and set off out of the bay, then into the open waters. The other four boats carried nine Merikens and ten Harmonious Fists, numbering twenty-four fighters in all. As they made their way through the Columbus Channel into the Gulf of Paria, the late April heat was already descending upon them even before the sun had fully risen.

It was an inspiring sight, black and Chinese fighters sitting shoulder to shoulder as they set off for a speck of land halfway between Trinidad and Venezuela, each of them willing to die so that they might free a group of men they had never even met.

So as not to think about the trial ahead, Douglas focused instead upon all the changes that had transpired in such a relatively brief span of time. Since their adventure had begun, he himself had not altered much—or, not in any significant manner, as even his bruises had all but healed.

Holmes, on the other hand, was not the same young man who had left the Liverpool docks almost three weeks before, a bit pampered, a bit spoiled, a bit too cocky for his own good, too conscious of status and of the secure and pleasant future he had mapped out. This new Holmes had a long straight scar that ran down one cheek. He was balanced on the prow of his boat like a taller, sun-washed Napoleon, his skin burnished by the sun, his hair tousled, and his muscles hardened by use.

The most important alteration, however, was not in his

physique but in his eyes. Wisdom lingered there now, as well as a deep sadness—far more than a boy-man of three and twenty should know.

Douglas wondered if his friend would make it out of this alive. He realized, not for the first time, that life or death was not the most important thing. The most important thing was the mission, their own small attempt to "proclaim liberty to the captives," as the Book of Isaiah had commanded nearly three thousand years before. To engage in a war where there would be no material benefit for the victor other than the liberation of oppressed and victimized human beings.

This is a holy war, he thought.

And every so often, holy wars must be fought.

The group of five boats reached First Island around noon. Even from afar, the speck of land offered no solace to their group. Its foliage was dense, and its interior hilly, automatically pressing the advantage to whomever had gotten there first.

Holmes called the others to a halt just more than a mile from shore. He pulled out the precious spyglass and surveyed the land. Off to one side, a clump of reeds swayed in the hot wind—but on the banks he could see some forty guards, their sole purpose to prevent intruders.

Georgiana's warning had been accurate. From what he could make out, they did appear to be mercenaries. Only a dozen or so wielded rifles, and most were far from watchful, but were instead lounging about, laughing, talking, drinking, and even napping.

He handed the spyglass to Douglas, who quickly verified his impressions.

"The possibility of attack was clearly an afterthought," the latter mused aloud.

Holmes nodded. "Either that, or the guards are only the first obstacle." Both men fervently hoped that this was not a premonition.

By this time, a small storm was brewing. Within the span of minutes, the wind picked up considerably and a light rain began to fall, turning the water brackish and churning the seaweed to the top, which was to their advantage. But it also meant that the slack tide would be against them, pushing them away from shore rather than closer in.

Eleven men, including Douglas and Jessup Jones, were ready to make use of their first vital weapon.

An equal number of crocodile lungs—eleven—had been wrapped in dried seaweed, and then sealed with a smattering of pitch so that the air became locked inside. They were the handiwork of the Meriken women, designed to keep fishermen alive, should their vessels sink or capsize. The men pulled the lungs from the boat, where they had been stacked like so many oversized pillows, and threw them into the water.

They then jumped in, positioned the objects underneath their chests and rode them, thereby keeping themselves buoyant and their weapons dry.

Back on board, Holmes read the water's pull, its temperature, and the Merikens' average weight, and estimated their time to the breakwater as between sixty and sixty-two minutes.

Here and there, fishing boats large and small dotted the landscape. Holmes and the Harmonious Fists took advantage of this cover, venturing as close to the mercenaries as they dared.

The water was cool, a relief from the mugginess of the day. That much was a blessing, Douglas mused as he fought past the initial shock of what he had volunteered to do. At first, it was difficult to keep his mind from wandering, or from giving in to anxiety.

Why on earth did I not allow a younger man to take my place? he scolded himself. *Even if I make it to shore, if I am too exhausted to fight, what earthly good will I be?*

After a few minutes he relaxed and thought only of keeping his feet kicking evenly and smoothly, and as close to the surface as possible in order to preserve energy.

He could feel his gun where he had put it, strapped between his shoulder blades, still dry and protected against his skin. And when he looked around, he was gratified to learn that he was still neck and neck with the Merikens, every one of them younger than he by a decade, at least.

The men were perfectly equidistant from each other. If all continued well, they would surround the beach, surprising and disarming the guards.

As the group of swimmers approached the breakwater, Douglas had no idea how long it had taken them, as he had left his timepiece, most of his clothing, and other belongings back on board. From the soft play of light behind the cover of clouds, he assumed that Holmes's estimation of one hour had been accurate, and that the boats would soon be joining them in their first salvo.

The closer he came, the more he sacrificed form for determined effort as he fought hard against a strong current. His legs felt like rubber. Above him, the light rain kept trickling down, which was quite useful in keeping visibility low.

He noticed that the mercenaries had taken shelter from the wet under a canopy of trees. The moisture-drenched air, which carried every sound, was carrying the growl of snoring. They seemed so relaxed that Douglas was concerned that this was indeed a ruse—until he reminded himself about men for hire.

Unless they believed in whatever cause they had been engaged to uphold, such men did not often make the best combatants, as they were rarely willing to sacrifice their lives for the handful of shillings they would receive—usually at the end of their service, and not before.

I hope they have been promised very little pay indeed, he thought ruefully. With that he pulled himself up out of the water, keeping low while hastening to his agreed-upon hiding place.

Then he waited for the others to get into position.

As he fought his own exhaustion, he thought of the men who were to join him in securing the beachhead. In particular, he thought of Jessup Jones, saying a silent prayer for him and the other youngsters, asking that their youth, determination, and idealism would preserve them intact.

On the beach, the sleepy and distracted guards were completely shocked to see men rising up out of the water from all directions, like fully armed phoenixes raking them with bullets. Then, not a moment after, a dozen warriors in very peculiar clothing scrambled out of fishing boats anchored nearby and propelled themselves forward at inhuman speeds, their bodies contorting and twisting in impossible directions.

From his vantage point, Holmes saw unmitigated panic in the guards' eyes, and he recalled Douglas's words.

There is nothing quite so frightening as to have the human body come at you in some unexpected way.

It seemed the mercenaries indeed had nothing to prove, and no one for whom they would lay down their lives. They immediately dropped their weapons, raised their hands in the air and fled, hastening onto half a dozen small boats that had been pulled ashore, or diving into the water fully clothed and swimming frantically away.

Rather than pursue them, Holmes, Douglas and the emboldened men gathered up the abandoned weapons, and pushed onward toward the island's interior.

38

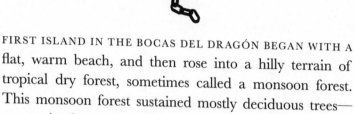

FIRST ISLAND IN THE BOCAS DEL DRAGÓN BEGAN WITH A flat, warm beach, and then rose into a hilly terrain of tropical dry forest, sometimes called a monsoon forest. This monsoon forest sustained mostly deciduous trees— mountain ebony and teak, the sorts of growth that thrived in an uninviting and sandy soil.

The forest did not rise up in the center of the island in a neat and orderly fashion. Instead, it seemed as if it had been crushed and pushed to one side, allowing the large crescent of beach below.

In its long history, the misshapen island had seen few humans. It was normally alive with the cries of parrots and monkeys, and the rustle of big cats that moved so stealthily through the green that they were all but invisible. Those sounds had been stilled by another, a foreign one that cut most unpleasantly through the air.

It was the zing of bullets bursting out of unseen chambers in rapid succession, as deadly as the deadliest cat and flying by at unmatchable speeds.

Holmes, Douglas, and the Merikens had left the expanse and easy sightlines of the beach crescent and begun their trek up through the scrub. Walking at the head of the pack,

Holmes caught a glimpse of a human-made structure at the promontory, though with the low-lying clouds and the drizzling rain, it was impossible to tell if it was a ruin or something of more recent vintage.

He was pointing it out to Douglas when the shooting began.

The men dove for cover as best they could while firing back at their targets, very nearly blindly. This time it wasn't just a handful of quickly vanquished opponents, as they'd encountered upon landing, but seemingly hundreds of unseen enemies—all so well armed that reloading was not a concern, as there were few intervals in the deadly volley.

Within moments, a thick cloud of gunpowder had insinuated its way from amongst the trees and into the atmosphere. In the wet and humid air, it spread and settled and formed a canopy over the entire area, so that pinpointing the shooters' locations proved futile.

Holmes crouched in a groove in the brush. He had been provided with a weapon but, unlike Douglas, he was not a brilliant shot, as he had never had much cause to practice. He was even less adept when he could not see the target.

So, instead of firing back, he did the next best thing.

He began to listen, as if to a strange, discordant melody, to the pings of ammunition in the trees and the rocks and the dirt. As firepower continued to assail them from the hills, he noticed something altogether unusual.

"Douglas!" he called.

But his friend could not hear. He was some fifty feet away, and so intent on preserving the lives of those around him that the cry dissipated into the air.

So there was no alternative but to test his theory on his own. Before anyone could stop him, he rose from his cover, the cane clutched firmly in his fist, and moved quickly toward the shooters while bullets hummed on either side of his head.

Douglas gaped at his friend, then he called out for the Merikens to cover this recklessness, which they did, shooting back as best they could. Suddenly Holmes turned and headed back the same way he had come.

"Drop and hold!" Holmes thundered to the Merikens as he slid back into his crevice. The command made its way down the chain. The men ceased fire as bullets from the hills continued to whiz and ping against every rock, tree and stump.

Holmes waited a moment to catch his breath; then he crawled upon his belly the fifty feet toward Douglas.

"Gatling guns!" he proclaimed, enthused.

Douglas stared at him, incredulous.

"You *saw* one?" he asked.

"No, but I witnessed their effect! The Union put them into service during the American Civil War, but just this year, Mr. Gatling brought their manufacture to the United States. Their value is quite underestimated, Douglas! You may buy one for seven hundred pounds, even less if—"

"Holmes, *please*..." Douglas said through gritted teeth.

Holmes scooted closer to him, very nearly giddy with the joy of discovery, all sense of danger apparently forgotten.

"Their gravity feed reloading system allows even the untrained to fire some two hundred rounds per minute! The Gatlings are the reason there seem to be a hundred men under cover, and why they have no need to reload."

"A Gatling can still kill you," Douglas objected vehemently, "so why on earth would you run into the line of fire?"

"I did no such thing! I ran *between* the lines of fire, do you see? My guess is they have…"

He listened to the bullets vibrating through the atmosphere, then landing, and he began to estimate.

"…three Gatlings. With slaves at each."

"*Slaves?*" Douglas repeated, aghast.

"Of course! Certainly, it *must* be. Who else? Because whoever is manning the guns is doing us no harm, but rather coming to our rescue!"

"Holmes," Douglas warned. "Do not force me to commit violence."

"Douglas," Holmes exclaimed in return, "do you not see? Someone is turning the crank of the guns, but not altering their positions, thus allowing us set rows in which to advance. Listen!"

He pointed to the brush and trees around them. As the volley of bullets continued unabated, Douglas attempted to do what Holmes had requested, though it was no easy task.

"There are no orders being issued," he said at last. "No commands to flank the guns right, left, up or down!"

"And here's something else," Holmes added, looking up the hill. "My assumption is that the slavers are no longer on this island. They left their captives behind to defend against us, perhaps with a warning of some sort that would force them to comply. My guess is, the slaves believe the slavers can still hear them—and so they continue to shoot."

"Yet they are creating a clear path for us—is that it?" Douglas pressed.

Holmes nodded. "Perhaps they hope that, whoever we are, we are preferable to what came before."

Huan made his way over, and Douglas's own excitement was beginning to percolate:

"Holmes believes that there are Gatlings," he told Huan, "manned by slaves, and that they are simply shooting straight ahead. Which means that whatever space is formed between the guns themselves are byways, of sorts—paths we can utilize to make our advance up the hill. Is it worth the risk?" he added, for the Harmonious Fists were unarmed, and so were particularly vulnerable.

Huan stared at both of them.

"You are certain of this?" he asked.

"No, but it is what we surmise," Holmes replied.

"We must test your theory, must we not?" Little Huan said to Holmes, joining in. "I can take the path you took, make sure it holds, before we put other men in danger."

"I will not permit this," his father responded. But when Little Huan could not be persuaded to stand down, the older man looked at Douglas.

"Then I go with him," he said.

"You cannot *both* go!" Douglas protested.

"Fathers should not outlive their sons," Huan said with a shrug.

"Fine," Douglas said. "Then I will go with you."

"Perfect," Holmes cried, and he grimaced. "Then if I am wrong, I lose the three of you!"

"But you are never wrong, are you, Holmes?" Douglas said.

"I have never hoped for more from my own intellect," Holmes declared, "than I do now."

Little Huan smiled shyly.

"To fools," he cried out.

"To fools!" the others exclaimed.

The three men followed the selfsame path that Holmes had taken. In spite of the hail of bullets whizzing by them, they remained unscathed.

Holmes's theory stood fast.

At his direction, the rest of the men regrouped in single file behind the initial three and began their march up the hill.

As they climbed, the Merikens shot into the air as infrequently as they could without arousing suspicion, should the slavers still be listening. They made their way past the lower brush and toward the trees, where the smoke from the Gatling guns was most dense.

At last Huan and Little Huan, at the front of the line, caught the glint of the Gatlings' burnished gold barrels among the green.

A moment later, they were greeted by a most terrible sight.

39

THERE WERE INDEED THREE GATLING GUNS, AS HOLMES
had predicted. From the looks of it, they had been set up
to protect a crumbling edifice that stood in a clearing at
the pinnacle of the hill. The Gatlings had been positioned
equidistant from each other in such a way that the barrels,
when turning, could cover the entire terrain, thus easily
felling anyone foolhardy enough to attempt an ascent.

As his men reached the guns, the Merikens continued
to shoot sporadically into the air, while the slaves continued
to fire into the brush below. The din was overwhelming.

Holmes peered around cautiously. If the slavers were
indeed close enough to monitor the engagement, he saw
no one.

"Huan!" he said. "Have your men scout about and see
if anyone is still within hearing range."

Huan and his men immediately complied, while
Holmes turned back to the terrible sight before him.

Twelve black men had been shackled four to a gun.
Each of them had a clamp about their necks, with chains
that held them fast so that they could move less than a
foot in either direction. Their clothing was threadbare—
moth-eaten and torn, and the holes revealed bruises from

beatings, along with the deep and ugly gashes that only whips could bestow. They had no water to drink. They'd been starved to skin and bones.

It was the inhumanity that was anathema to Holmes, something he could not have fathomed.

Even Douglas, who had witnessed his share of evil, stood dumbfounded in the face of it.

The prisoners kept at their labors, though they were barely able to stand. At each gun, one man dutifully soaked fibrous matting in water to cool down the barrels. The water had been dosed with sulfur, from the smell of it, so as to make it undrinkable. A second man was stationed to the left of the gun, while to his right were stacked dozens of boxes of cartridges. Every three seconds he'd pick up a box and place it in the rails, which automatically discharged the cartridges. Spring-loading the rails with his thumb would drop the cartridges down into the hopper. By repeating that sequence over and over, the six barrels at his command could each shoot two hundred rounds per minute.

A third man turned the crank that shot the bullets, while the fourth was tasked to position the gun left, right, up or down, depending on the location of the enemy. At each gun, it was this fourth operative who had purposely shirked his duty, thus giving Holmes and his men a way to reach them.

The captives stared at the newcomers with the wide-eyed, nearly innocent gaze of human beings who had nothing left to sustain them, while the Merikens stood back in respectful silence, their eyes downcast.

Holmes, feeling the burden of leadership, began to move

toward them, his mouth rising into a badly formed smile.

"Do you speak English?" he called out over the cacophony.

They cowered, then dutifully continued their assigned tasks.

Douglas laid a restraining hand on his friend, but there was hardly the need. Holmes himself had ceased mid-stride, struck with the realization that perhaps a white man with a cane in his hand wasn't a wholesome sight, no matter how friendly his smile might appear.

After that, Douglas calmly attempted, in Spanish, and then in Portuguese, to communicate that they'd come in friendship, and to be of aid. Most of the slaves looked at him, uncomprehending. But one, the man on the central gun, lifted up a hand. His weapon fell silent, though the other two weapons continued their din.

He was a big man, easily as tall as Douglas but thicker, though his muscles were beginning to atrophy. His head had been shaved, and he still bore the wounds of a haphazard and unfriendly blade. His gaze was coal black and piercing, and the other men eyed him with deference.

"I am Tomas," the big man told Douglas in halting Portuguese. "You understood our trick."

"*He* did," Douglas said, indicating Holmes. "He is useful on occasion. They call me Cyrus. I thank you for saving our lives—now we wish to return the favor. Might you allow it?"

Tomas translated Douglas's words for the others. As two Gatling guns continued to fire—and the Merikens fired back just enough for effect—the captives nodded agreement. Several Merikens finally approached them and offered them water from their flasks. Then they picked up large rocks and used them, along with knives, to crack the links of the shackles.

"Where are you from?" Douglas shouted to Tomas.

"The Gold Coast," he replied as a couple of men worked to free him. "White men caught us, put us into a boat."

"How many were caught?"

"Forgive me. I cannot count," Tomas told him. "But many. Like small fish in a very large net."

"You were on the water for a very long time?" Douglas asked, though he knew the answer.

"Yes," Tomas confirmed. "We lay on our backs side by side on the boat, not much food, almost no water."

"Did many die?"

"Oh, yes. Many. One dies, one lives, one dies… like that."

"And you did not see what they did with the bodies," Douglas assumed.

"No," Tomas replied. "I was inside the belly of the boat. Most likely, the bodies fed the sharks." He stumbled a bit for want of strength but quickly regained himself, and indicated to Douglas that he could go on.

"When you first reached land," Douglas asked, "did you hear the name of the place?"

"No. Though a few of the white men spoke Portuguese, they were careful around me…"

Huan's men returned with their report.

"We cannot say for certain that the island is deserted," Little Huan announced, "but there is no organized force. Or if there is, they cannot reach us quickly enough to do damage."

Douglas translated this last for Tomas, who did the same for his men. Then he lifted up a shackled hand—and the firing suddenly ceased.

The captives looked around warily, as if expecting retribution to rain down from the skies at any moment. When it did not, they gratefully accepted more water and allowed Holmes's men to proceed with the task of freeing them from their chains.

"From there," Tomas continued, "they took us to another island nearby. Bigger. Not many trees. The white men, they were building something, but I cannot say what, for I do not know. They put us into groups. Women and children, too."

"Did they tell you what you were to do there?" Douglas asked.

"They told us nothing," he said. He flinched from the strikes as the men continued to try to break the bolt that held the neck brace in place.

"Then, something happened," he went on. "They take some of us, some who still look strong—men, women, children. They clean us, remove chains, cover us with clothes—good soft clothes. Some white men even take off their own clothes to give us. All of it quick. So many unhappy faces! I tell my people, 'Someone comes that they did not expect.'"

He stopped as the chain jerked, pulling at his neck. Douglas reached over to hold the collar steady while the others continued to hammer at the links.

"So we do what they want," Tomas continued. "We

stand in our new clothes, and a boat arrives, with a woman. With hair like his."

And he pointed to Holmes.

"Was there a man with her?" Douglas asked. "Green eyes? Mustache?"

"Yes," Tomas said. "We had seen him before. He was quick to hit, that one! And he never smiled. But this day, he was smiling.

"First, he takes her to what they are building," he went on. "She seems happy. Then he brings her to us. And she greets us. And we sing a welcome to her in our own tongue, as they told us to—but behind us, we have a surprise."

One last blow, and his neck brace finally fell to the ground with a soft thud. All around them, more shackles fell the same way. Tomas rubbed his neck—but gently, for the bruises were large and painful. He drank a bit more water as slowly as he could manage, considering his great thirst.

"We had hidden a young boy behind us. When she is there, looking so happy, we step aside."

"Holmes?" Douglas called to him. He recounted what Tomas had told him thus far. Then, as Tomas continued his story, Douglas translated.

"The slaves parted to reveal the boy. He was stripped to the waist. He'd been beaten, with old scars crisscrossed under the fresh ones."

Douglas paused, then continued.

"He fell to his knees before her, while the others began to plead with her, in their own tongues, to help them…"

"She starts to cry," Tomas said. "And the white men, they yell and beat the ones who hid the boy. And the man with the green eyes, he is very angry. He pulls her away."

"Did she go?" Douglas asked.

"Oh, yes. Still crying," Tomas told him. "In the morning they moved a great many prisoners to boats, and from there back to the ship. And they left us" —he motioned to the men around him— "here to fight."

Douglas quietly finished his translation. Holmes took a deep breath.

If these men can endure the horrors they've been through, he thought to himself, *surely my own sorrows are of little consequence.*

"And what's that?" Douglas asked, motioning to the remnants of the building at the pinnacle of the hill.

"Again," Tomas said, "there is much that I don't know."

As the last shackle fell, a rousing cheer filled the air, one that took nothing into consideration—not the danger the men were in, nor the ordeal the slaves themselves had suffered.

The Merikens quickly dismantled the Gatlings, separating the barrels from the carriages so that they could be easily pulled along. And while the Harmonious Fists took the guns and the desiccated slaves back down the hill toward the boats, the Merikens, Holmes, and Douglas prepared to climb the remainder of the way to the crumbling building.

"Let me go with you!" Tomas beseeched Douglas in Portuguese, as he was too mindful of rank to join without permission.

Douglas turned and stared at him. He understood the man's good intentions, along with his need to remain viable in his people's eyes. Yet he was reluctant to allow it. Though still a strapping man, Tomas could barely stand.

He had been so maligned that he would be more hindrance than asset.

He conferred with Holmes, who was of another opinion.

"This man is a born leader," he declared. "To send him down with the others is to demean him further."

"Let us hasten him to safety, then, to restore him sufficiently," Douglas countered, "after which he'll be of more service to them, and to his cause."

Still Holmes insisted.

"He must be allowed his dignity, no matter how untimely it may seem.

"Permit it, Douglas," he said.

Douglas sighed.

In spite of his every instinct to the contrary, he beckoned Tomas up the hill.

40

THE GROUP CONTINUED THEIR DILIGENT CLIMB TO THE summit. Tomas, by some miracle—or perhaps through sheer force of will—kept up with the others.

At the pinnacle was the ramshackle old structure. It seemed to have been abandoned years before. The large door swung off its hinges. Boards covered rectangular holes where windows once had been. The only thing to recommend it was that its entrance faced the expanse of the hill, while behind it lay a precipitous drop to the ocean, waves beating against the rocks below.

It would have made a good fortress, a good lookout. But it was none of those things at present.

And yet, the Gatlings were set up to protect it, Holmes mused.

A cry rose up from the beach below, as various voices called out:

"Huo yao!"

"It means 'fire medicine,'" Douglas translated, "though I can't imagine what they are referring to." He and the others looked around to ensure that they were not being ambushed before making their cautious way forward.

The Merikens, weapons out, surrounded the building from all sides, while Holmes, Douglas and Tomas ventured within. Even as their eyes adjusted, with no windows and only one door to provide feeble light, the men struggled to discern anything within that could be of worth.

"*Huo yao,*" Douglas repeated, and he pointed at the ground just outside of the door. There was a sprinkling of something dark, as if someone had spilled a line of pepper upon the ground.

Holmes hurried over, bent down and put a speck of it on his tongue. Then he lifted his eyes up and to the right, as if tasting a complex wine.

"Equal parts sulfur and charcoal," he mused. "French blend, from the Essonne outside Paris. Best gunpowder in the world, reasonably priced, does not absorb moisture. This is either spillage from a weapon, or…"

He stared at Douglas.

"Get the men away from here!" he commanded. "Get everyone back down the hill. *Now!* They have rigged this thing to blow!"

Douglas rounded up several of the Merikens, including Jessup Jones, and pushed them outside. Holmes was about to follow when he noticed that Tomas, instead of leaving with the rest, was peering intently at something in a dark corner and walking slowly toward it.

"*Mera hai, jee nahin! Jee nahin, mera hai…*" he said, his voice pleading.

"What is it, Tomas?" Holmes asked. "What do you see? *Que ves?*" he added as an afterthought, remonstrating himself that it was Spanish and not Portuguese. But Tomas did not respond and did not turn. Instead, he moved more quickly toward the crevice, repeating the same words as before. Holmes wondered if it might be a religious plea of some sort.

Then he saw a light from a match, as well as the shadow of the depraved soul who set it. It appeared to be a young slave, so starved and maligned that he looked half-mad.

Then came the sound of popping, like Chinese firecrackers all around them, growing in volume.

Then Holmes felt a trembling under his feet.

After that, a deafening explosion, and the crumbling walls of the building burst open. Holmes felt himself rising up out of that darkness like a demented jack-in-the-box.

His ears were ringing like a thousand church bells, and though the sensation of weightlessness was terrifying, he hurtled along so smoothly and so effortlessly that he wondered for a moment if he might already be dead.

He almost felt as if he could put his arms out and glide, as in a dream. At first, there were other objects moving alongside him—planks, boards, possibly even other men. Then in another moment, he was alone.

Suddenly, it was over. He was falling—no longer in slow motion, but with terrible and determined speed.

He did the only thing he knew to do.

Rather than fight it, he relaxed, tucked into himself like a snail in its shell, and protected his head.

The water, when he hit it, felt like iron.

* * *

He must have passed out ever so briefly, but when he came to, he was already plunging down toward the depths.

He looked up. The water was sealed tight above him, as if not permitting a return voyage to the land of the living. Then his watery world began to pitch and to spin.

Within seconds he no longer knew which way was north, and he could not afford to lose what little air he still held in his lungs so as to find out. Trying to remain calm, he pulled open his pants pockets and observed the direction of the bubbles. Now he knew which way the surface lay, but to no avail. Though it was only twelve feet or so, it may as well have been twenty fathoms, rather than two.

He would never make it.

He cursed the added muscle weight that was keeping him from rising more easily.

Not for the first time in this adventure, but very possibly for the last, he prepared to die.

Then he spied beside him an unnerving sight.

Whatever else had transpired in Tomas's life—however brutal the blows and ill use he had suffered, however piteous the want of food, or the too-intimate brush with wickedness—Holmes could only pray that some portion of an earlier time had brought him joy. Because, whatever was to occur from this juncture on, one thing was certain.

Tomas's life was done.

He had an enormous gash at his temple. His left arm had been blown clean off, and he was dropping down past Holmes, uncaring in the least.

Out of some reservoir of sentimentality, or perhaps in the assailing madness that strikes when one is faced with unexpected and unwelcome death, Holmes grabbed onto Tomas as he sank, and held him fast.

Better to perish with human company beside me than all alone, he thought fleetingly.

But not a half-second later, a terrible sense of self-preservation overtook him, and he knew what he must do. He wrapped his arms tighter about Tomas's waist, placed his mouth on the other man's mouth and—using the poor man as a sort of "bellows"—squeezed him around the middle and breathed in his breath.

Air filled Holmes's lungs, and he held it fast.

I hope that means, Holmes thought, *that Tomas was still airborne when his breath ceased forever. It would have been a less painful death.* He quietly thanked the big man for saving his life yet again.

The impulse to bring him along to the surface was so strong as to feel like an ache in his soul, but Holmes knew full well that he'd have neither the strength nor the oxygen to succeed. Even if he did, it would change nothing. Air, wind, sun, and even chains held no power over Tomas now.

He was free.

41

HOLMES BROKE THE SURFACE SPUTTERING AND coughing, choking and vomiting. As helpless as a cod with a hook in its mouth, he strained and jerked against the reality of his circumstances. At first he attempted to distance himself from his own agonized heaves with scientific observation.

They are the result of the aspiration of fluids into air passages, he thought frantically. Yet he found it nigh on impossible to remain clinically detached while expelling the contents of his stomach all the way down to the lining.

Suddenly it seemed as if a freight train was powering through his skull. His energy was spent. He bobbed like a cork in the waves, his thoughts spinning.

The slavers had baited a booby trap, and he and his men had taken the bait. There was no telling who lived, and who had died. Tomas was dead. His best friend on earth, Cyrus Douglas, most likely was dead. But what of Jessup Jones? What of Huan, Little Huan, and the other Harmonious Fists?

The odds were long. There had been enough firepower in the shack to obliterate half the hilltop. He himself had fallen from a great height, catapulted up into the air and away from the shrapnel and the debris that had felled Tomas. For all practical purposes, he should not have survived.

Which meant that his very existence—the thing that had followed him around for the past twenty-three years like an obedient dog—was no longer his at all.

His hearing seemed peculiarly sound. The initial roar had disappeared. There was nothing left but a slight ringing.

He looked up.

The rain had abated. Behind the clouds, the first brushstrokes of dusk were painting the sky. The vividness, the sheer exuberance of it, was too much.

He closed his eyes.

I should not be alive, he insisted. *I should not be alive to see this when all the others—nearly everyone I care about—are more than likely dead.* He felt the slack tide tugging at him, insisting he give in. A few more pulls, and he would be too far from shore to ever hope to make it back.

Even now, the carbon dioxide in my blood and tissues is most likely high enough that I would not even need to go under, he speculated. *Three large gulps of water would do the trick.*

After that, cerebral hypoxia.

The end.

Yet something was niggling at him, something foreign, outside his muddle-headed thoughts. Lightly at first, and then more and more insistently, like a pesky gnat.

You are alive, it said. *And you ought not to be.*

The words repeated until he'd had quite enough.

"You needn't remind me!" he screamed to no one in particular. But his voice, rather than roar, came out strangled and hoarse.

For a while, no other thoughts came.

Then he heard another voice—one that was endearing and familiar, if rather snooty.

"The last thing you would want is to lose a limb, or to perish in some freakish manner..."

"Sherlock?"

Holmes said it aloud and glanced about, as if his brother might be bobbing by his side, one eyebrow lifted in scorn and perhaps a dollop of pity. This struck him as so absurd that he began to laugh until tears came to his eyes.

A moment later, he found himself bellowing to the skies.

"No! I will *not* permit you to do away with me, to discard me as if I were nothing!" Once again, it sounded like the call of a dead man to an impassive and indifferent universe. He had no concept as to who might be incurring his wrath, but it did occur to him that, just possibly...

He had a reason to live.

It was something tangible, something that he wanted more than anything he had ever wanted in his life. More than friendship or acclaim, more than the maternal warmth that had eluded him as a child. More than the oxygen that he was drawing in by the lungful, as if the supply might dissipate at any moment.

"Revenge."

He said the word out loud, tasting it. It radiated through him like a fire. He yearned for it more than he had ever yearned for Georgiana... and that was the most sinister shock of all.

She seemed now like a childish fantasy, the product of

stardust and naiveté. The way a small boy might dream of becoming both a scientist and a renowned cricket player. It wasn't simply Georgiana he would have to release, but the whole silly notion of *happily ever after*. He, of all people, should have realized some time ago that it did not exist.

He sucked in a few more blessed, luxurious breaths—this time without guilt or recriminations. Then, as much as it pained him to do so, he slipped under the water again.

Since he was resolved to swim back to shore and take on whatever came next, he did not wish his head to become a target for some newly emboldened mercenary. Rage released in him newfound strength. He recalled the clump of native reeds, tall and hollow, perfect for his purposes. He swam back down and against the current to where he'd last seen them.

They were swaying languidly about, as if this were any ordinary day. He propelled himself back to the surface for another few breaths and then, utilizing a broken clamshell that had gotten enmeshed in the clump, he chose a reed that would suit his purposes, and began to cut.

Finally, he flipped onto his back, put one end of the reed into his mouth and the other in the air, and began stroking slowly but relentlessly toward shore.

By the time Holmes reached the breakwater, dusk was on full and glorious display. The entire island seemed as if it had been infused with it. He heard no sound, other than the occasional quizzical chirping of a bird and the ebb and flow of the tide. It was as if the events of the day had already been swallowed up and forgotten.

He dragged himself out of the water and stood on the sand for a moment, keen-eyed and alert, catching his breath. As an afterthought, he felt for the pistol he had been given, removing it from the holster strapped to his leg.

Waterlogged, of course.

If it had been very nearly useless before, as he was an inept shot, it was completely so now. Nevertheless, he shook out as much seawater as he could. Although he was keenly aware that it could no longer be pressed into service, he saw no reason to inform his enemies of that fact.

Looking down the shore, he noticed that someone had pushed the Merikens' boats back into the sea. Whatever else transpired, he was stranded here. He moved stealthily onto the sand, looking all about, not yet relying on his reverberating ears to guide him.

At first, everything was so peaceful it seemed as if all his efforts at subterfuge were for naught.

Then, he noticed the bodies.

Some were exposed, others half-hidden. Still others were strewn along the shore like discarded petals, tangled in the brush, or broken and still bleeding upon the rocks.

He staggered, sickened by the carnage, not caring a whit whether or not he could be seen, since he was all but certain that there was no one left alive to see him. As he went from one to the other, he attempted to identify each poor soul as best he could. It wasn't an easy task. A handful of victims had holes where their faces had been. Other bodies had already swelled and bloated, rendering them all but unrecognizable.

Two were former slaves, while two others were members of the Harmonious Fists. And every one of the nine Merikens who had joined them in the expedition was dead.

Including the young orator, Jessup Jones.

The boy lay on his back upon a rock, his body still intact. His eyes and mouth were open in an exclamation of surprise. Holmes posited that Jones had been expelled by the force of the blast and had flown through the air, his landing brutal but quick—and that his lethal injuries were internal.

He knelt down beside him and mouthed a silent prayer for Jones and for his family. Then he pressed down on the lids and shut the boy's eyes.

He had not yet located Douglas among the dead, at least not among the poor unfortunates who had perished on the beach, but Douglas had been with Jessup Jones. So if he had not been catapulted by the blast, as the boy had, he was most likely up in the hills, blown to pieces.

The thought was too much to bear.

He left Jones's side and focused again on the two Harmonious Fists and two slaves. The former had been so damaged that they were all but unrecognizable. He scrutinized their hands and was grateful for his own keen memory— neither of the corpses could possibly be Huan or his boy. As for the two slaves, they had been chained to the third Gatling, and had been the most abused of the lot—so weak they could barely drop the cartridge boxes or man the crank.

"If anyone ever deserved to rest in peace," he said quietly, "it is you."

When he was done scanning the vicinity, he counted the possible survivors. Huan and Little Huan, along with eight more Harmonious Fists and nine former slaves. If they were still alive, where in the world could they be?

Then he noticed something that made him shake his head in wonder.

Half buried in the sand, with the water sloshing over it, was Sherlock's walking stick. He staggered toward it, if for no other reason to be reunited with something familiar. He had just laid his hands on it and was tugging it out of the wet sand when he heard an unfamiliar voice call out behind him.

"Mycroft Holmes!"

42

WHEN HOLMES TURNED AROUND, HE SAW A ROWBOAT pull to shore, as another floated a short distance away. Two mercenaries—they did not look familiar, so they'd not been among the guards on the beach—leapt from it into ankle-deep water. Wielding rifles, they wrestled the thing further up the sand. Then they turned and, with bored but dutiful countenances, trained their weapons on him.

Yet this barely resonated in Holmes's mind, for the boat carried two other individuals, and it was they who commanded his full attention. One was Adam McGuire. He leapt gingerly onto dry land, peering at Holmes as if he were a curiosity and this entire endeavor a chore. Beside him came Douglas. McGuire was pulling him along by one arm like a recalcitrant child, while pressing a gun against his temple.

He is alive! Holmes thought joyfully. *Douglas is alive!*

And if his friend was alive, there was hope!

As McGuire and his captive drew closer, it became apparent that Douglas was badly hurt. He had an ugly gash atop his skull, and another down his shoulder, which still bled through the tear in his shirt. Most likely injuries from the blast, he posited.

Both his eyes were swollen nearly shut, and his lower lip was split. These were secondary traumas whose cause was no doubt a recent beating. Yet what struck Holmes like a sledgehammer was to see his friend with his head bowed low—he would not look up. It wasn't submission—that would not have suited Douglas, even if half dead—but it could be a sign of a concussion, perhaps even cranial damage that was beyond repair.

McGuire halted some forty feet away.

"Mycroft Holmes!" he called out a second time. "You, sir, are a thorn in my side."

"As you are in mine," Holmes called back, though his voice sounded, to his own ears, feeble and raw. Just then, the next boat arrived. Two more armed mercenaries jumped out, dragging the bow up onto the beach.

Four mercenaries, four rifles, Holmes thought. The newfound hope began to bead off of him like water upon an oilskin.

This second boat held additional passengers. They stood up on shaky legs and stepped onto the sticky wet sand, trying in vain to brush it off their pant legs as they walked on to join McGuire.

Holmes recognized them all.

None was a surprise.

One was the governor's former aide, the pasty-faced young Beauchamp, whose preternatural smugness looked as if it had been seasoned by trepidation—as if he were not quite certain that the earth upon which he stood was firm. The others were three of the "government types" who had sailed in on the *Sultana.* Judging by their middle-of-the-road sartorial choices and demeanor, not a man among them was the person who'd funded this enterprise. And none—with the exception of McGuire—had the steel-eyed resolve of a trained killer.

So why bring bureaucrats along on such a dangerous journey? Holmes wondered.

McGuire interrupted his speculations.

"I am not keen to shoot an unarmed white man," he said, "but as you are trespassing, I would be well within my rights."

"Why not shoot me, then?" Holmes inquired calmly.

"It's not so simple, Mr. Holmes. I take it you've been in communication by post with your employer?"

"And who, pray, informed you of that?" Holmes asked, well aware that he had done no such thing.

"Your—ah—your *associate* here… though he was not immediately forthcoming."

Douglas lied, Holmes thought, relieved. *He lied… which means he still has his wits about him.*

Or had, he was forced to amend.

"Now if Cardwell should take it upon himself to search you out," McGuire went on, "that would be a burden indeed."

"Oh, to be sure!" Holmes replied. "Beaten, emaciated creatures are hardly the image of the 'new slavery' you wish to present to the world." He skimmed the comment like a pebble across the surface of a pond, and watched the ripples. It wasn't McGuire's reaction he coveted, however, but the others'. In the time it took them to breathe in and then out again, he appraised them.

Three mercenaries remained flint-eyed and poker-faced—they were clearly the finest of their kind, and most likely the deadliest. But the fourth, a pockmarked chap whose physique was covered with a fine layer of flab, licked his lips—a sign of a conscience, or of fear. Yet this indicated that he was not strong-minded, nor resolute enough to go against the others.

He would be useless.

As for the functionaries, the youngest—freckle-faced and snub-nosed, with a slight overbite—shifted weight from one foot to the other. The second, balding and middle-aged, tapped two nicotine-stained fingers against his lips. Beauchamp, the smug little aide, laid his left hand on his right elbow, half-crossing his arms.

Each was a gesture of weakness. But it was the fourth man, a fifty-year-old with a shock of white hair, a florid gut and rheumy eyes, who interested Holmes the most. He blinked a few times, and then glanced to McGuire for guidance.

There *is my pigeon,* Holmes told himself. *The one who will startle first, and cause the rest to scatter.*

Or so he hoped.

He pressed his advantage:

"Isn't that what you promised them, McGuire? A new sort of slavery, one that is more civilized? What a bitter disappointment it must be for your investors."

McGuire didn't even flinch. He ambled closer, dragging Douglas along with him, while the others followed behind like baby chicks.

"You have raised an issue, Mr. Holmes, that we are in

the process of addressing. Beyond that, you have nothing. You cannot link us to nefarious deeds in Trinidad, and nothing we do *here* is illegal. So my best advice is that you take one of those two boats you see there—" he gestured, "—and *git*."

The men chuckled at that. Laughter dispelled tension, which was the last thing Holmes wanted.

He motioned to the bodies strewn on the beach, still all too visible in spite of the gathering darkness.

"What about them?" he asked. "Should I blithely return to England and say nothing about them?"

McGuire had a ready reply:

"Scofflaws!" he declared, his eyes cold. "Malcontents trespassin' on private property. Radicals who do not cotton to a man's right to do business his own way." The bureaucrats grumbled their assent. They were of one mind about this, at least.

"No sense in looking at me like that, Mr. Holmes," McGuire went on. "We lost two hundred and fifty-eight thousand of our finest young men in the war. Believe you me, this handful of corpses is a picnic in comparison. So I ask you again… nicely, sir… to git."

Once more his men chuckled, and then they glared at Holmes—a bit of their bravado restored, while McGuire continued to eye him curiously, as if waiting for him to perform some magic trick or other. In that, he reminded Holmes of "Mycroft's Minions." This last seemed peculiar until he realized that, however unintentionally, he'd been giving this man useful tips for a year, possibly more.

McGuire was no doubt wondering how much longer

he could be useful. Which meant that Holmes would have to play this well.

"Mechanical engineer?" he asked pleasantly.

"Beg pardon…?"

"Your profession. You are a mechanical engineer, are you not?" When McGuire looked appropriately taken aback, Holmes pressed on.

"A handy profession in the South, what with the sudden dearth of slaves. Whoever can keep perfecting the manufacture of cotton stands to gain and you, Mr. McGuire, look to me like someone who knows well how to gain. Beyond that, your placement of the Gatling guns was precision itself. How ironic, given the fact that you were outsmarted by men whom you view as less than chattel."

McGuire jammed the barrel of his gun in Douglas's ear.

"Careful what you say, Mr. Holmes," he growled. "I am not given to humor at the moment."

"Well then, here is a statement you might prefer," he replied. "Let us go, and I shall let *you* go!"

"No, Holmes!" Douglas cried out, glancing up at last.

McGuire's reaction was quick. He cracked his prisoner on the back of the head with the butt of his gun. Douglas crumpled to his knees on the sand.

Then, without missing a beat, McGuire turned back to Holmes.

"I got nothing against your boy here," he said, indicating Douglas. "I just think he oughta speak when he's spoken to."

Holmes strove to keep his focus on McGuire, rather

than on the specter of Douglas struggling to rise, and failing. He noticed that the bureaucrats were equally endeavoring not to look at Douglas. It seemed that violence disquieted them—perhaps they'd had their fill of it.

"I say it again, McGuire," Holmes called out. "Let us go, and you shall be released, as well."

Beauchamp began to snicker, but one look from McGuire quieted him.

"When you say you will 'let' me go," he replied, "I assume you've got somethin' with which to barter?"

"I do indeed!" Holmes replied almost cheerfully.

43

DOUGLAS CEASED HIS STRUGGLE TO RISE. HE LAY ON THE ground, his body as loose as a rag doll, but Holmes could tell he was listening intently. His head was leaning upon his right shoulder, his neck slightly twisted toward the speakers.

"As my associate there at your feet informed you," Holmes said, "a letter was sent to my employer, Edward Cardwell, Secretary of State for War, delineating this entire endeavor."

McGuire sighed all at once, like a deflated balloon. Perhaps he had been expecting Holmes to perform a better magic trick than that.

"So long as what we're doing here is legal," he responded dully, "and so long as we're not competin' with neighboring countries by growing tobacco or sugar, it's our land, our rules."

"That is a sad fact, Mr. McGuire," Holmes acknowledged. "But from what I understand, the large majority of the slaves are no longer *on* your land. When we interfered with your plan, you moved them back to the 'safety' of your ship, did you not? Possibly to fatten them up, make them a trifle more presentable? So how do you propose to get them on shore again?"

"Same way we got 'em there the first time," he said with a shrug. "By ship."

Holmes indicated his walking stick.

"May I?" he inquired politely.

McGuire let his curiosity get the better of him—he allowed it.

A lapse in judgment, Holmes mused. *For if there is one language at which I excel, it is bureaucratese.*

With the tip of his stick, he drew a rough map of Venezuela and the islands. He put a great big X across a major waterway that very nearly touched both shores.

"Perhaps Captain Miles failed to alert you," Holmes said, "or, you may've got rid of him too quickly, but there's a narrow passage between Venezuela and these islands that Britain has claimed as security against Spain…"

Beauchamp and the others chuckled at this.

McGuire held up his hand for silence.

"First off, we had nothin' to do with the poor captain," he said. "It was a terrible accident…"

His associates nodded somberly, and Holmes wondered if they were truly that naïve, or had convinced themselves of their own innocence in the matter.

"Secondly, are you referring to rights of passage datin' back to the fifteenth century?" he asked.

"A long-dormant issue to be sure," Holmes admitted, "but one that's certain to stir sentiments when my letter arrives."

"Oh for the love of God, Mr. Holmes!" McGuire exclaimed. "I tell you again, we have violated no laws…"

"Not yet!" Holmes declared. "But now the British government is aware of your… *business* ventures, and when provoked, a long-dormant issue has a way of rearing its head. Now, I suppose you could moor your ships here,"— he tapped a location with his walking stick—"and row your merchandise in. Rowboats are not subject to censure, and are small enough not to encroach upon Britannia's waters.

"Yet that, of course, would be wildly impractical," he continued, "as the ship would have to disgorge her… passengers… quite a distance from your islands. And if you think that fattening them up is costing you a pretty penny now, just think how hearty and hale they shall have to appear if you plan to row them to shore, thus exposing them to public scrutiny."

He had them now. They were all leaning in, staring at the map—even the mercenaries.

"And so you see, it is only a matter of time until you shall be constrained to test Britain's waterways, as well as her injunctions against slavery. And the moment you do, you *shall* be punished—Her Majesty will see to that. So while you might have a viable business—what you lack is viable transport!"

He let that settle, then he stared at the men with intent. He had one more move. It was extreme, and he was certain that Douglas not only would disapprove, but that it might well terminate their friendship. Nevertheless, to save them both, he had no other option.

"However," he braved on, "if you cease this course of action immediately, and allow the two of us to leave this island unmolested, I shall stand down. And if you know anything about me, Mr. McGuire—and I know you do— then you know that I am a man of my word!"

In the stillness, a voice rang out.

"No, Holmes!"

It was Douglas, hazarding to rise. McGuire kicked him once in the gut, then a second time for good measure. He rolled into a fetal position on the sand and lay there, unmoving.

Holmes felt a white-hot rush of anger racing up his neck to the top of his skull.

Revenge!

But he kept it in check.

"You are not comporting yourself as a gentleman, McGuire," he said through clenched teeth.

"Yes," the rheumy-eyed businessman said mildly, albeit loudly enough for Holmes to hear. "This constant violence, it accomplishes nothing." Holmes could place his accent immediately. The man was Swiss. And with that, another piece of the puzzle fell into place.

"You have my terms!" he called out to McGuire.

Then he turned to the men.

"You can tell your employers that the land they purchased, along with the steamship, shall continue as assets. And Mr. Ellensberg..." Holmes addressed the rheumy-eyed man, who stared at him in dismay. "You *are* Nestor Ellensberg, are you not?" he asked him pleasantly. "Were I you, I should inform my employer that while funds shall be lost in the short run, there is hardly a nascent business that does not encounter a few early snags. Perhaps *that* might quiet him."

Ellensberg began to vibrate like a tuning fork, setting off a chain reaction among the group. McGuire noticed this, and again he sighed unhappily.

"Mr. Holmes," he said, cocking his head to one side. "You are free to go, as I do not happily shoot my own kind. As I said, however, we must be allowed to conduct business in a manner—"

"And as *I* said, you shall release us both," Holmes exclaimed coldly. "Or you may kill me now, and the devil take the hindmost!"

The diffused light that had been lurking behind rain clouds all afternoon had fled. Night was falling quickly. The mercenaries hadn't moved from their armed vigil over Holmes. Douglas was still in a fetal position on the sand, too coiled into himself for Holmes to gauge whether or not he was still viable.

The functionaries had gathered in a tight little knot around McGuire and had remained there—from Holmes's estimation—for a good quarter-hour. Though speaking too softly for him to hear, he assumed that they were debating their diminishing options. And though McGuire's handsome face showed discomfort, he could tell the American was trying to regain the upper hand.

He was striving to turn the tables yet again.

Georgiana may have died an ideologue, Holmes knew, but McGuire was no such animal. He was an entrepreneur, although one who happened to believe in the superiority of the white race, and who was not above killing to make certain his goals were achieved.

He is Prichard's theory of moral insanity come to life, he mused. *A human being devoid of the common thread of human decency.*

He wondered if McGuire was aware that Georgiana was dead, or if he cared.

"Blast that darkness!" McGuire exclaimed suddenly, glancing up at the sky as if it had chosen to plague him specifically. "Fetch the lanterns from out the boat!" he commanded gruffly. "Get two, bring 'em here now."

A mercenary with flinty eyes hastened to the boat, then back with the lanterns, which he quickly lit.

"Hold the damned things up," McGuire barked to the man. "I need to see who in hell I'm talkin' to!"

The guard held up the lights like Diogenes searching for an upright man.

I can save you the trouble, Holmes thought. *There is only one upright man here, and he is crumpled at your master's feet.*

"Mr. Holmes?" McGuire inquired mildly. Holmes did not care at all for the tone of his voice, nor for the looks of unsettled fear that were at once too visible in the bureaucrats' eyes.

"Though I assumed you to be a reasonable man, and true to your word, I cannot say the same for your... associate here. Negroes are emotional creatures, childish and irrational. If there is breath left in him, he will stop at nothing to get his pound of flesh, and I have worked too hard on this enterprise to allow a Negro with ties to the British government to plague me.

"And though I've given you ample opportunity to reverse your stance, still you insist on saving him. That, sir, is an irrational act on *your* part that makes me question the rest of my assumptions about you."

"Be that as it may," Holmes countered, "Edward

Cardwell will still be fully apprised of the situation here, and as I am the only one who can assure him that nothing is amiss—"

"I realize that," McGuire interrupted with a shrug, "and I agree that it is a powerful obstacle. Nevertheless, Mr. Holmes, if my only choice is to kill you, then that is the choice I'll have to make."

With that, he raised his gun and aimed it directly at Holmes's head.

44

MYCROFT HOLMES COULD ASSESS ANY SITUATION IN THE time it took McGuire to lift the gun and aim. Unfortunately, there was little to assess.

McGuire was an expert shot. This, Holmes had determined by his gaze, his stance, and the ease with which he handled the weapon. He had grown up shooting small, quick game, Holmes surmised, like squirrel, and had parlayed that to his stint in the war, graduating to killing Union soldiers with the cool detachment of a sniper. Extinguishing a man some forty yards away would be child's play.

Then too, the four mercenaries had rifles pointed at Holmes, as well. It seemed excessively cautious, but if by some minuscule chance McGuire missed his shot, they would do the honors. And although McGuire's two lamps did little more than cast long, grotesque shadows over the sand, they did enlighten one salient fact—it was Douglas's revolver that McGuire held in his hand. The top-break, single-action Smith & Wesson Model 3.

Holmes was about to be felled by the very implement that he'd hoped would keep them safe. His best friend's gun.

The four bureaucrats, dandies all, looked miserable. What had undoubtedly been described to them as a working man's holiday had turned into a nightmare of violence, especially now that McGuire had marked yet another stranger for death—this one a British functionary, who was about to be butchered in front of them.

They were so easy to read that Holmes felt almost guilty—it was tantamount to perusing a young girl's diary. At the moment of impact, two would scrunch their faces like matching accordions and squint their eyes shut. Ellensberg—who was already gazing blankly, his head slightly forward—would quickly turn away to protect his delicate constitution. As for Beauchamp, he had already squared his jaw and planted his feet to prove he was impervious to bloodshed—which of course he was not.

Not yet.

But practice, Holmes thought bitterly, *makes perfect.*

Of a truth, it made scant difference whether these four watched or did not. They were pawns. As a French journalist had written in the *Père Duchesne* nearly one hundred years before, theirs was "a new form of servitude," however voluntary. They would trail whomever they perceived held the power, hoping that by doing so they could snag a piece of it for themselves.

He was starting to comprehend who the real pawnbroker might be—though he would not live long enough to do a thing about it. He had played his finest hand and had been beaten, if not fairly, then thoroughly. With nothing more to be done, he was preparing to die.

Rather wearily, he thought, *for it is the second time this day.*

McGuire had his arm stretched out and was cocking the hammer when the clump upon the ground flipped into a handstand, pushed off from there, and propelled itself feet-first into the back of McGuire's skull.

By what strange chemical occurrence does time, under excessive stress, manage to warp and to slow down?

The question had always intrigued Holmes, and though he was not about to realize the answer at that moment, he found that he was fascinated by the process when it happened to him.

It was a ferocious kick that would have undone most men. As McGuire tottered forward a few steps, Douglas reached down, wrenched the gun from his hand and turned it on him… while Holmes had the presence of mind to draw his own useless weapon.

McGuire wobbled to his hands and knees and remained there, unmoving. Holmes waited for Douglas to take charge, but that impressive bit of gymnastics seemed to have sapped whatever strength his friend had mustered.

He was struggling to stand on his feet.

"Hands up!" Holmes commanded the bureaucrats.

"Guns down!" he barked to the mercenaries, all the while praying that telltale seawater would not burble out of the barrel and drip down his arm. The dandies obeyed instantly, but the guards were not so easily cowed. Two kept their rifles trained on Holmes, while the other two trained theirs on Douglas.

It was a standoff.

Douglas was blinking hard to keep his swollen eyes focused on McGuire.

"Take my offer," Holmes called out to the men, "and we shall all live to fight another day!"

"Holmes! You cannot do this!" Douglas protested in a weak but emphatic voice.

This made Ellensberg flush crimson. "Do as you intend!" he said to Holmes. "For you are the only sane man here.

"*Um Gottes willen!*" he screeched at the guards. "No more shooting! We leave this place now. Enough!"

For a moment, the four stymied guards had the look of dogs attempting fractions. They glanced at the red-faced Ellensberg, then at their downed employer. Finally, they lowered their weapons and slowly backed away.

"You may take one boat," Holmes said. "Leave the other for us."

"We are too many," Beauchamp protested. "It is engineered for eight."

"Do not fret, Beauchamp," Holmes exclaimed. "McGuire shall remain with us. And keep your hands where I can see them!"

The guards and the bureaucrats, hands raised, moved warily toward the boats.

"You *cannot* let them go!" Douglas pleaded, but even he knew it was over. Until McGuire began to crawl forward and slightly to the side, as if trying to get away.

"Turn around!" Douglas commanded.

McGuire paid him no mind. He just kept crawling forward and to the side like a fiddler crab.

Holmes had to keep his useless gun trained on the departing men. It would be up to Douglas to pursue their leader. But how could he do so, when he could not even walk?

"Turn around!" Douglas repeated to no avail.

"*Shoot* him!" Holmes vented. Then he realized that Douglas was incapable of it. He would never shoot a man in the back.

Yet what his friend could not make out in the dark, with his tortured eyes, Holmes saw all too clearly.

The crab-like motion had a purpose.

McGuire was reaching for a holster at his ankle.

"Douglas!" Holmes cried out. "He has a gun!"

It was a small two-bullet derringer. McGuire dipped down onto one elbow, turned to the side… and shot Douglas twice in the chest.

Douglas collapsed.

Holmes rushed at McGuire, his walking stick brandished above his head, and beat him with it while the guards flew back to his side. One grabbed Holmes's upraised arm as the doughy-faced guard wrapped a beefy bicep about his neck and yanked him away.

The two others helped a bleeding McGuire to his feet.

His head lolling slightly, McGuire indicated the walking stick in Holmes's upraised hand.

"Bring it here," he told the men who held Holmes. "I aim to beat him to death with it."

The guard on Holmes's left tried to yank the walking stick out of his hand. It was a pathetically easy feat for Holmes to reach up with his right arm, pull the knife from its sheath, and fling it. The blade spun end over end, glinting like gold in the light before finding its mark in McGuire's throat.

He stared quizzically at Holmes, as if this were a chess move he had not yet contemplated. He opened his mouth to speak, but only blood came out. He fumbled for the handle, yet had no strength left to pull it out. His hand rested on it limply, almost as if he were posing for a portrait.

McGuire jerked away from the guards, took a few enraged steps toward Holmes, collapsed to his knees, and fell face first upon the ground. The heel of the knife made contact with the hard earth and buried the blade further into his trachea, all the way up to the hilt.

That was when the shooting began.

Holmes instantly recognized the sound. So did the mercenaries. They dropped to the ground and covered their heads. The startled businessmen did the same, though they fumbled their way down—Beauchamp did not duck at all.

Losing did not appear to be a part of the destiny the young aide-de-camp had carved out for himself. He glanced crossly toward the brush from whence the shooting came—and was strafed by a dozen bullets. He lurched about like a marionette and was dead before he hit the sand.

Holmes wasn't the least concerned about the pings that were raising little whorls of dust all around him. He had but one goal—to get to Douglas. Keeping a straight path between himself and his mark, he bolted toward his fallen friend.

As he did so, he drew the surprised attention of one of the guards—the one with the flinty eyes. The man had no notion as to who might be shooting at him, or why. He knew only that a designated enemy was running away. He dutifully rose up on his elbows, took aim at Holmes's back... and was terminated by a volley of metal.

Holmes, in the meantime, reached Douglas and scooped him up in his arms.

His eyes were closed. He was not breathing.

Holmes frantically felt for a pulse at Douglas's wrist, then at his neck.

Nothing.

"Help me!" he cried. "Someone help me, please!"

45

THE SHADOWS CAST BY THE LAMPLIGHTS SPRANG TO life, or so it seemed. They danced and leapt through the hail of bullets. By the time the firing ceased, the shadows had the surviving bureaucrats and the guards surrounded, and were quickly bringing them into mute and awed compliance.

Holmes absorbed these facts as he did everything around him—but opaquely. His focus was on Douglas. He had him in his arms and was rocking him back and forth. If imprecations to the skies could revive the dead, his friend surely would have risen there and then.

The derringer that McGuire had used was a small caliber weapon, one more suited to hand-to-hand combat than to a shootout at greater distance. Were its bullets to have lodged in the thigh or the hip, they would have packed little more than a nasty sting. It was only McGuire's expertise with firearms that elevated that miniscule piece of hot metal into something lethal.

Holmes ripped open his friend's shirt and with his thumb began to frantically measure the entry points.

"Help me, please…" he repeated softly, not certain that he was finding what he sought. He measured again, and then again, just to be sure.

The night was growing chilly. A persistent wind buffeted the clouds, revealing a moon as large and as round as the driving wheel of an old locomotive. The gunfire had ceased entirely. As the Harmonious Fists escorted their captives toward McGuire's boats, Holmes saw the remaining slaves emerge from the brush. This was no surprise to him—he had realized from the first that the volleys were coming from two of three Gatling guns. None but the captives could have mounted them so quickly and efficiently. What did surprise him was how thoroughly their countenances had changed. Though they were no heartier than before—privation had reduced them too much for that—there was a gleam of hope in their eyes. They were at long last on the side of the angels.

But the sense of vindication he felt on their behalf was subsumed by the imposing task before him. Douglas's color was sallow, his jaw lax. Holmes packed the wounds with what he could find. Soft wet sand to cleanse, spider webs to stanch the flow of blood.

Huan and Little Huan appeared by his side. Huan put a comforting hand on his shoulder, but Holmes shook it away.

"Please, my friend," Huan said. "You are torturing yourself…"

Holmes would not hear it. He gave Huan a withering look.

"And what of your healers?" he growled. "Capable of mending crushed toes with the touch of a needle—surely there is one among you who can work a small miracle!"

"Only God can revive the dead," Huan said.

"Stay with him!" Holmes commanded as he rose to gather up seaweed.

Huan lifted Douglas's limp arm and felt perfunctorily for a pulse. He glanced at his son and shook his head. Little Huan bit his lip to hold back tears, stared for a moment at Douglas, then abruptly stood and walked off.

Holmes returned with the seaweed and began to wrap it around Douglas's torso, cursing the pieces that tore in twain before he could finish.

Huan attempted to talk some sense into him.

"He has no pulse," he said.

"Taking his pulse is all but useless!" Holmes snapped. "Trauma has forced his body into a systemic coma to prevent it from perishing in earnest, with breath so shallow that the movement of the chest is all but indiscernible. As for his heart… it is playing a similar trick of hide and go seek."

"Mycroft, we all loved Cyrus," Huan responded. "But we have living folk to care for."

"Go and care for them, then," Holmes said. "Did you not hear me? I will not leave him here!"

The Harmonious Fists had pushed the two boats knee-deep into the water. Huan went to assist Little Huan, who was shepherding the freed slaves, the three surviving functionaries, and the three surviving guards, moving them into the vessels. They sat numbly side by side, black with white, at long last united under one common objective.

To get off that cursed island.

When the Harmonious Fists climbed aboard, the vessels dipped precariously low into the water.

Holmes watched them, impassive.

Twenty-three men had boarded: eleven in one boat, twelve in the other, on vessels built to carry eight apiece at most. As configured, he put their odds of reaching Trinidad at twenty-three to twenty-five percent.

"Mycroft!" Huan waved and called out. "My brother, you must come aboard now!"

Holmes stood up. Clasping Douglas underneath his arms, he began to drag the body inch by inch along the beach toward the boats.

"Come help!" he called out to Huan.

"We must save room for survivors!" Huan called back. "We will return with proper shovels and bury our dead!"

"*He is not dead!*" Holmes insisted.

Little Huan was just stepping into the vessel when he abruptly changed course and set foot on the beach again.

"He has no heartbeat, he is not breathing," Huan quietly admonished his son.

Little Huan nodded. "I know," he said, "but still we must return him to Trinidad. We must bring him home. If we drown, we drown together. 'To fools,' remember?"

Huan shook his head, exasperated. "We are certainly that," he muttered under his breath as he followed his son down the beach.

"Take his other arm," Holmes commanded the moment they joined him. "Gentle! Move more slowly—keep his torso upraised."

The pockmarked guard shook his big head as he watched the men drag Douglas's body along, inch by torturous inch.

"McGuire, he do not miss," he said in a thick Russian accent. "If your friend is alive, it is… *stikhiynoye bedstviye.*"

The two guards in the other boat nodded solemnly.

Besides Douglas, the passengers aboard Holmes's boat were Huan and Little Huan, two Harmonious Fists, the three surviving bureaucrats, the pockmarked guard, and three ex-slaves. The latter were so thin that the outlines of their bones were visible through their threadbare clothes, casting shadows in the lamplight. They were shivering in the night air, but there was no more clothing to be had, so Huan gave them the burlap tarp that covered the boat when it was moored. They gratefully huddled together and wrapped themselves in it.

Holmes, at the prow, arranged Douglas as best he could, his head resting against a seat, his long legs stretched out before him.

As they prepared to shove off, he stared at the third-quarter moon. He gauged that detail, along with the temper of the ocean.

A fair fight was what he needed.

A fair fight, he told himself by rote, *is the essence of competition.*

He turned to Huan.

"If we are to stand a chance against the waves all the way to Port of Spain," he said, "we must balance the vessels."

"To Port of Spain?" Huan said. "We cannot go so far. We must touch down in Moruga."

"There are no proper physicians in Moruga," Holmes objected.

Huan shook his head. "Mycroft…"

"*Huan.* With the way you have arranged things, your odds of drowning are seventy-five percent. If you let me help, even sailing further, you greatly decrease those odds."

"Are you saying you will not help, and increase our odds, if we go only to Moruga?"

"I appreciate that there are lives aboard, and I am quite fond of you and your son. But I must also say that your lives, to me, are not worth his, and, since everything has a price…"

Huan hesitated only a moment. Then he gave him leave. Holmes calculated individual and combined mass and rearranged the passengers accordingly. And although they all did as they were told, minutes still flew by—precious minutes that he knew were of the essence for Douglas.

The tiny vessels shoved off. Holmes could have done better if he had had more time, but their odds of survival had increased by some fifty percent.

It would have to do.

And still he could not rest.

"Mycroft," Huan whispered as the latter began to systematically massage Douglas's hands and feet. "My brother!" he insisted when Holmes appeared not to be listening. "That devil pierced his heart. Even a heart as big as Douglas's must cease when two bullets enter in."

Holmes did not reply but kept up his toil and silent vigil.

* * *

The wind was blowing in their favor, the moon creating a passable light by which to see. The four designated rowers on Holmes's boat—Little Huan, his father, and two Harmonious Fists—were moving the vessel away from the coastline at no contemptible speed, considering the added weight.

When they reached open ocean, though conditions were still favorable, Holmes's vessel began to take on water. Not enough to drown them all, but enough to be of alarm. It was no easy feat to bail her out while attempting to keep her steady. Passengers passed the buckets back and forth as delicately as could be managed.

Only Holmes abstained, continuing to work on Douglas.

The pockmarked guard glanced over at him.

"Why you not help?" he asked in his thick Russian accent, indicating the buckets.

"His blood is not circulating properly," Holmes muttered. "This is the only way to preserve his extremities. You understand?"

The guard looked at him cynically.

"*Nyet.* If he lives… *stikhiynoye bedstviye!*" he exclaimed.

Holmes had had enough.

"I have no notion what you mean by that," he snapped.

A voice beside him rasped out the translation.

"Act… of… God…"

Within minutes, Douglas's breath had grown discernible. His chest was rising and falling—if not altogether smoothly, then at least consistently. The other passengers' initial shock and elation aboard gave way to puzzlement.

"How is this possible?" Huan asked. "It is true, then—it is an act of God!"

"It was not an act of God," Holmes replied. "It was a kick to the head!"

Then he turned to Douglas and whispered, "Very good, Douglas. You are breathing quite well. Now pray keep it up, for I shall not return to England without you."

46

THERE WERE NO PROPER HOSPITALS IN PORT OF SPAIN—
not in Holmes's estimation—nor surgeons competent to do
the fine work of extracting bullets from so precarious an area
of the body. Those little pellets of lead and death would have
to remain where they were, in Douglas's chest, as mementos
of a terrible time.

Holmes paid for a comfortable room, along with
twice-daily visits from a well-regarded local physician, Dr.
George Curlew. As there was still danger of infection, or
of bullets migrating and causing additional damage, he
kept a personal vigil and left his friend's bedside only when
strictly necessary.

While Douglas recuperated, Huan and Little Huan led
a contingent of Harmonious Fists and Merikens—relatives
of those who had perished upon the island—to a steamship
that had been abandoned at its mooring off the coast of
Venezuela. With permission from the government, which
Holmes had secured, they clambered aboard and led more
than two hundred emaciated men, women, and children
down the gangway to safety.

The rescue took place on the fifth day of Douglas's
convalescence. When Holmes told Douglas the story, he

sat up in bed for the first time.

"What on earth are you doing?" Holmes scolded as he bolted from his chair, arms out, as if to catch his friend mid-fall.

Douglas shook his head.

"Holmes, please," he remonstrated. "I am not scaling the wall hand over hand, I am simply sitting upright."

"Are you certain you feel hale enough?" Holmes asked, appraising him doubtfully.

"I feel hale enough to do a jig," he replied, smiling.

From that day forward, Holmes allowed visitors to the sickbed. They always came bearing gifts, from tea and herbs to a quotation from a book to be read aloud, to "the smallest taste" of *callaloo*, *pelau* and other treats that made Holmes's eyes burn simply to hear them named. Afterward, they would collect themselves in an anxious little clutch to debate whether or not this day brought a healthier hue to Douglas's countenance, or a heartier glimmer to his eye, or whether his tone when he said hello had about it the ring of recovery.

Most times they would depart encouraged.

"It was not an act of God, it was a kick to the head!"

On several occasions, Holmes heard Huan in the corridor outside the sickroom, regaling others with the story of Douglas's miraculous healing, parroting Holmes's words down to the intonation, whilst tossing in some words of his own.

"Before he was shot," Huan would recount, "our Cyrus dealt a savage blow to the back of McGuire's skull. This savage blow, it caused that demon's brain to 'float back in his spinal fluid'—isn't that right, Mycroft? It floated, yes? And this floating, it blurred that demon's vision! So that he missed Douglas's heart by a millimeter."

Douglas's friends could not get enough of that story—it always ended in cheers and applause. And although Holmes would shake his head and feign annoyance, in truth he could have heard it a thousand times more.

By week two of his convalescence, Douglas was regaining his old humor. He had taken to calling Dr. Curlew "the Saint Nick of the West Indies," for that was whom the man resembled—a rotund, jolly sort who would smile and pat the girth around his middle while making the most onerous pronouncements. He let it be known that, whether Douglas lived or died, he would no longer be what he once was.

"The *mano a mano*," he said, chortling. "The sparring, at the advanced age of forty, like a young buck… things of the past! Travels, too, for what could be a negligible infection for a hale man can prove fatal to you, Cyrus. *Fatal.* Never forget that you still have two bullets lodged in your chest."

"I would be hard pressed to do that," Douglas grumbled, "with you and Holmes reminding me every quarter-hour."

"Yes, *ha-ha*, quite! 'Travels bring travails'—that should be your motto. And though I grant you there are benefits to smoking, including the relief of asthma, I agree with my esteemed colleague Doctor George Sigmond, who conducted quite a study of it some years back, proving that tobacco is no friend to the ailing heart. Therefore, whatever else transpires, you must never, ever smoke again."

That last caused Douglas to groan like a condemned man.

"A tobacco seller who does not smoke!" he cried to Holmes. "What sort of odd beast would that be, I wonder?"

Holmes wondered that, too.

"Not to worry, Douglas. Once back in London, we shall get a second opinion, and a third—"

"And a tenth, I suppose," he interrupted, "until they tell us what we want to hear."

"Has there been something you have cared to do?" Holmes asked discreetly. "Apart from what you do, I mean…"

"If you are asking if I've ever had a yen to play the piano, or to garden, the answer is no," his friend said. He was sitting at the window. As he spoke, he kept turning his head like a sunflower to the spot of light that glowed through the curtains. Then—out of politeness, Holmes supposed—he would turn back to his interlocutor.

"I do not mean to be flippant about my own life," he assured Holmes. "In truth, there is no lack of people in dire need, and I always assumed that if I could but earn enough, I might be of some assistance—to children in particular."

He sighed. "Now, it appears that was a pipe dream… along with the pipe, I suppose. From what Saint Nick tells me, I could not even have gone along to help Huan and Little Huan liberate those poor souls, for it involved travel. And you, Holmes! You are a madman for remaining here with me, when you could have participated in such an event."

Holmes shrugged. "I saw a portion of it. I watched from the wharf as some went home to their families here, while others boarded the ship for Sierra Leone. I can only hope that, whatever hardships they might endure from here on, freedom shall forever taste sweet."

Douglas nodded, then turned away again.

Holmes felt a twinge of guilt. Though they had spoken of many things since his recovery, they had not yet discussed the "deal" that he had struck to free them. Nevertheless, he knew full well that it had disturbed Douglas's faith in him.

"Bargain with the devil, and you are no better than he is," he had mumbled on that first night of recovery, when the pain was excruciating, and his social graces severely wanting.

Holmes had at long last apprised his employer, Edward Cardwell, of what had transpired—though he made it appear as if the entire adventure had been an unpleasant surprise that had torn his attention from investigating the French Creole issue. In the last two weeks he had also read every available book, manuscript, and newspaper article that had to do with the history of the West Indies, to try to make sense of what those islands represented, and what could possibly be harvested that was worth so many human lives.

This knowledge, married to the sorry events he had witnessed, caused him to realign his priorities, to take a different view of social structure… one might even call it a long view.

More than anything, he wished to discuss those changes with Douglas. To deliver his soul, as it were, and perhaps to justify his actions, just a little. He rehearsed what he would say.

Catching a criminal in the act is nowhere near as important as closing the loopholes that allow one to act the criminal in the first instance, he longed to explain. *That means affecting laws, it means bargaining in a way that there will always be checks and balances in place. At the moment, will it always seem right or even fair? Of course not—*

In his mind, he heard Douglas interrupting, most likely with something about ends never justifying means.

I no longer think that is true, Holmes protested in turn.

Douglas, seated in the chair in the sun, nodded as if he had heard.

"Yes. Perhaps something to do with children," he mused.

Holmes ran a hand through his hair. The philosophical—and thus far imaginary—conversation with Douglas would have to wait. At the moment, whether for ultimate good or ill, there was a bit more bargaining to be done.

It included a visit to Nestor Ellensberg.

"Mr. Holmes...?"

Ellensberg stood at the door of his rented room. A stickpin on his lapel bore the flag of Switzerland. On an end table sat a well-brushed Tyrolean hat. He was dressed for travel, a detail of which Holmes was already aware, as he had been demanding that a passenger list of departing ships be messengered to him each night for the past week.

In the light of day, standing so near him, Holmes could see red glints in Ellensberg's white hair.

Redheads! he mused. *They have presaged bad luck from start to finish.*

"Of a truth, I thought you would have us arrested the

moment we arrived at Port of Spain," Ellensberg said, inviting him inside.

"Of a truth, I would have," Holmes told him pleasantly, "if I had any hope that the charges would stick."

"Be that as it may, you have stood by your word."

Ellensberg indicated a chair, and they sat—discreetly appraising one another across the small but well-appointed chamber.

"It is not as if I suddenly disagree with indenture," Ellensberg exclaimed. "I am most profoundly in favor of it, as commerce would be quite lost without it. But the manner in which it was done, no, no—that was wrong."

"Mr. Ellensberg," Holmes interrupted, "I am not here to debate the philosophical merits of…'indenture.' I am more concerned with your employer."

Ellensberg sighed. "I am, as of this juncture, no longer in his employ, as I have found out that he, too, is… nefarious? Is that the correct word?"

"It is, if that is what you mean," Holmes said. "To leave his employ—was that your choice, or his?"

"Very much mine!" Ellensberg sputtered. "I do a proper job, Mr. Holmes! I am not the sort to be terminated. But these are *evil* men, who think only of enriching themselves…"

"Whereas you—" Holmes began wryly, but Ellensberg cut him off.

"They made us all, how do you say, part of it!"

"Complicit?"

"Yes, complicit! So we are frightened to say anything, because we have seen too much." He shook his head sorrowfully. "I am simply an intermediary for money. My employer, he makes an investment, and I go to see that it is as they advertise—no more, no less. Of the product, what do *I* know? It could be race horses, or…"

"…humans?" Holmes finished the phrase for him, though he was certain it was not at all what the man had intended.

Ellensberg joined his hands together as if in prayer, and looked away.

"But the humans that were purchased," Holmes went on, "are only the material, the ancillary product. The *tools*," he added when it was clear that Ellensberg did not follow. "They were tantamount to having a fine pen with which to compose a book. The question is, what is the book about?"

Ellensberg remained mute.

Holmes sighed. It was time to redirect the conversation to his purposes.

"I posit that the 'book' is pitch oil," he said. "The so-called Second and Third Islands carry seeps of pitch oil, do they not?"

"You saw it?" Ellensberg asked, wide-eyed.

"No. I read of it in a local newspaper article, dated June 1862. By some reckonings, pitch oil is valuable, or soon will be."

Ellensberg shrugged. "Yes, that is what my employer told me. It seems Mr. Adam McGuire had struck a deal with several gas light companies, including the North American Kerosene Gas Light Company at Long Island, New York. They provide kerosene for lamps, but the demand now far exceeds their capacity to produce."

"The North American Kerosene Gas Light Company did not, however, realize there would be slaves involved," Holmes interrupted. "Did they?"

"No," Ellensberg admitted, "they did not."

"And so your employer elicited money from investors all over the world for this new endeavor in Trinidad," Holmes said.

Ellensberg nodded. "He carries quite a bit of clout. It is my opinion that McGuire was fooled by him, as well," he said quietly.

"In other words, McGuire thought he'd be in the business of... 'indentured servants' who'd extract oil from the earth. So, to keep other speculators away, he had to ensure that locals would not notice errant seep washing up on the southern shores of Trinidad. Which meant he further had to ensure that the locals would be terrified to walk their own beaches."

Ellensberg nodded again.

"But, in spite of investors, money in the bank, and all that preparation, you never even dug the first well," Holmes declared. "Is that correct?"

Ellensberg swallowed hard. "Yes. That is when I realized that my employer had no intent of making it a real business, but to take away all the investments for himself." He looked so out of sorts that Holmes almost felt sorry for him.

"But he has not yet absconded with the investors' money," Holmes said.

"Not yet, no."

"And when he does, no one will say a word of it,

because no one wants to admit that they were involved in such a dirty business."

"If the workers had been in good condition, as advertised," Ellensberg protested, "then perhaps the investors would not be so ashamed. But now…?"

"Might your employer have done it on purpose?" Holmes asked. He watched the pinkish hue drain from the other man's face, until he looked very much as if he would faint.

"That is purely speculative on my part, Mr. Ellensberg," he added quickly. "Although, if my intent had been to make the investors complicit, and to steal their money all along, then it follows that a sadist like McGuire—who was sure to ill-treat the slaves—would be very useful."

Ellensberg stared at Holmes, aghast.

"Duplicity!" he spat. "From first to last!"

"It appears that way," Holmes said with understatement. "I am equally certain that you have asked yourself why workers would be put in place before there was work to be done. Did you see drilling equipment? The newest methods drill, they do not dig; they use a steam engine…"

"Poland and Romania still hand-dig their wells and are quite successful," Ellensberg countered. "Even so, I saw nothing," he admitted, "though I visited all the islands."

"Equipment costs money," Holmes declared. "And, unlike slaves, it is harder to dispose of when it proves inconvenient or outdated."

"Mr. Holmes, please." Ellensberg looked near tears. "As I said, I was a middle operative, not a mastermind."

"No. But you were the keeper of the funds. You made sure that the currency from half a dozen countries would be moved around, not enough to cause alarm, but enough to be—let us say 'liquid.' The final move would be to deposit it all in *one* bank—to be quickly picked up and carried off, with no one the wiser."

Ellensberg hesitated. "Yes," he said at last.

"And now that you have been found out, are you willing to suffer the fall?"

Ellensberg wrung his hands. "My employer is a very powerful, well-connected man. What choice do I have? I am sorry, Mr. Holmes. Regardless of the disdain I feel, or the fear for myself, I cannot give you his name." With that, he resolutely crossed his legs at the ankle and set his rather well-fed jaw into place.

"Oh, I do not need his name," Holmes assured him. "He is Count Wolfgang Hohenlohe-Langenburg."

Ellensberg stared at Holmes, open-mouthed. Abruptly he stood, his florid face so engorged with blood that Holmes feared a cardiac episode might be imminent.

"Mr. Ellensberg," Holmes said soothingly. "Sit, sir. I am not a constable, nor am I judge or executioner. I am here neither to arrest nor dispatch you."

"Then, what is it you wish?" Ellensberg bleated, as he shakily resumed his seat.

47

HOLMES AND DOUGLAS'S JOURNEY BACK TO ENGLAND proved blessedly uneventful. There were no storms or other calamities, and the mid-sized ship, with the felicitous name of *Constance*, had the wind at her back—another good omen.

When she made her first port of call, a few hours' dalliance in the nearly landlocked Kingston Harbor, Holmes first ensured that Douglas was happily convalescing in the grand saloon over a game of whist, in the company of businessmen from Cuba and Cameroon. Then, without a word to anyone, he quickly disembarked. At the wharf he rented a horse and driver, paying handsomely so that man and beast would make haste to the island's dilapidated capital, Spanish Town.

The carriage had barely drawn to a halt when he leapt out, dismissed the cab, and marched through the doors of Jamaica's most prestigious monetary institution, the Colonial Bank. Though a bit shabby, it still had the air of self-importance, as of a nobleman gone to seed.

Besides his own credentials, he carried a signed fiduciary letter that gave the bearer the right to withdraw funds from a series of numbered accounts. These accounts held various currencies—British stock, British and South African pounds, Swiss francs, Cuban, Puerto Rican and Venezuelan pesos, and the gold *quadruple pistole*—or doubloon—that Jamaica had been circulating since the seventeenth century. Holmes imagined from the first that it would be a healthy dose of monies. After all, a relative of the Queen was not likely to cause so much double-cross and human misery over a pittance.

But by the time the clerk sent for a manager, who in turn beckoned a supervisor, who—in hushed whispers— begged the pardon of the bank president who hurried over to scrutinize Holmes, he realized that the sum might be a bit more tidy than he had imagined.

The president, a pinched and persnickety sort who would have felt quite at home at any sacred institution of funds in London, first ascertained that Holmes was indeed a member of the esteemed British government. Then he and his minions, hand wringers all, painstakingly compared Holmes's fiduciary letter to previous signatures of one Nestor Ellensberg.

The bank president, in Holmes's estimation, seemed not at all gratified to discover that everything was aboveboard, and that this young man—with his sun-burnished skin, an impressive scar upon his cheek, and a roguish air—had every right to the funds in question. Amidst stares and clenched-jaw whispers, with the minions at his heels like so many anxious ducklings, at long last the august head of the bank was obligated to release the combined sums into Holmes's care.

* * *

The British cache alone was extraordinary—1.2 million pounds sterling in five-pound notes.

The rest, taken together, equaled it.

Two guards placed the money, stock, and coins in an enormous leather travel case that had been left by Ellensberg for just such purpose. The bank then provided, in addition to the guards, a driver, a carriage, and a horse. With great dispatch, these returned both Holmes and the suitcase to the *Constance* a quarter of an hour before it was scheduled to leave port. Rather than allow the retinue to accompany him aboard like a sullen parade, Holmes dismissed them all.

Once they had departed, a few shillings persuaded two local lads to drag the suitcase up the gangway. The pieces of eight were the true burden, as most everything else was made of paper.

It was only upon seeing a puzzled Douglas peering at him from the observation deck that Holmes realized he would have to come clean sooner, rather than later.

Once back on British soil, the first thing Holmes did was to ride Abie, so as to experience the freedom and exhilaration that only a fine horse—one who is an exquisite fit for its master—can provide. He was gratified to see that Parfitt had indeed taken very good care of him.

Parfitt returned him with many thanks, along with the requisite amount of wistfulness, as Abie was a horse that one thoroughly enjoyed and therefore tended to miss.

Abie, in turn, nuzzled Parfitt's neck to show that he

understood the boy's dedication, and that the affection was reciprocal.

Holmes had messengered a note to Sherlock to meet him on the banks of the Thames, and so he rode Abie to the designated spot. Then, a few moments before his brother was to arrive, he reached into his pocket and extracted two items.

One was Georgiana's likeness.

The other was the pair of little backward-facing feet.

He looked at them both, nestled in the palm of his hand. Complicit, somehow, belonging one to the other. Then, without recriminations or indeed much thought at all, he walked to the river's edge, let them fall into the water, and watched them sink out of sight.

"Brother mine!" Sherlock said, walking up behind him. "What strange, exotic ritual is this? And what has happened? I hardly recognize you!"

Sherlock had guessed, from his stance alone, that something profound had altered him irrevocably. He turned and smiled, enjoying the look of utter shock on his brother's face.

"Sit down, Sherlock," he said, "for I have much to recount."

48

SUMMER HAD VERY NEARLY OVERTAKEN THE BRITISH isles when Holmes and Douglas arrived at the village of Ascot, in Berkshire. A mere six miles from Windsor Castle, it was a healthy green swath of British countryside belonging to the Crown. For the past one hundred sixty years, the seventeenth day of June had—give or take a few intervals—seen the running of the horses in the Trial Stakes, the first race of the flat season.

The royal carriages, which held Her Majesty the Queen and the royal party, made their formal procession up the Straight Mile. The spectators who had gathered to watch— some hundred thousand, by Holmes's speculations—were beautifully turned out and eager. Perhaps not so much for the race to start, as to see and be seen.

"Ascot," Holmes quipped to Douglas, "is a social event with racing as an addendum." He wore a gray morning coat and matching top hat, both purchased on Jermyn Street, and both so fine as to shame the topcoat that Georgiana had once favored. Though he was no longer saving for marriage, and though the money was now abundant, nevertheless he had blanched at the cost.

He was finally persuaded to indulge by his distinguished

dark-skinned "butler." "Since you have been given access to the Royal Enclosure, perhaps a bit of extra decorum is warranted," Douglas had reminded him wryly.

Holmes conceded the point, calculating that if he could but utilize the outfit for twenty occasions or more, he could justify the exorbitant expense.

As he had requested permission for Douglas to accompany him, he had also selected a double-breasted waistcoat with a turnover of quilted silk and an overcoat trimmed in fur. In truth, Douglas's outfit had cost more than his, but it had seemed somehow less ostentatious. And since a black man not of royal blood could not attend a series of fittings for such a fine set of clothes, he had even hired a man of Douglas's height and size to serve as mannequin, so that the tailoring would be as near perfect as could be managed.

"Fur lining might be a bit excessive for a gentleman's gentleman," Douglas had mocked when he'd first laid eyes on it. "You have me gussied up like an Ethiopian princeling!"

"Since we have been given access to the Royal Enclosure, perhaps a bit of extra decorum is warranted," Holmes retorted with a grin.

Regardless, Douglas wore it as he did his own more modest outfits, with an easy grace that belied any sense of discomfort he might have felt. After the Queen's procession, the two men made their way to the Royal Enclosure, where Holmes showed his badge, as well as Douglas's, signifying the Queen's permission to enter.

They were now among the most elite of the elite.

A few moments later, Queen Victoria—in her usual

mourning black and accompanied by her faithful Scottish manservant—arrived amid great pomp and took a seat at her private box. Sitting behind her was an array of lords and ladies, beautifully turned out. Beside her, by special invitation, was her rather delicate half-sister, Princess Feodora of Leiningen, on one of her rare visits to London.

And on her other side—gazing on the still-empty racecourse as if he could not be bothered to engage with mere mortals—sat Count Wolfgang Hohenlohe-Langenburg.

He was some fifty years of age, well dressed, bearded and portly, with a settled, self-satisfied countenance which said that the world belonged to him, and nothing could alter that fact.

To accuse such a man of misdeeds is to court disbelief, if not outright hostility, Holmes mused, eyeing him.

Moments before the first race was to commence, the Queen's manservant, John Brown, glanced over at Holmes and nodded discreetly. Holmes rose and made his way to the Queen's private section. When a guard stepped in his path, Brown signaled that Holmes be permitted into the inner sanctum.

He bowed to Victoria as he passed. She dipped her head but did not look him in the eye. Then he went and stood directly in front of Hohenlohe-Langenburg, blocking his sightline and his light.

The latter looked up at him mildly and blinked a few times, as if not altogether certain that he was real. He glanced at Victoria, but as she paid neither him nor the blond chap any mind, he turned back to Holmes.

"Have I the pleasure of your acquaintance?" he asked icily.

"Not at all," Holmes said equitably, "but I believe you were very well acquainted with Adam McGuire, who met an unfortunate end. And you are also acquainted with Nestor Ellensberg. He has returned to Zurich, there to remain unmolested.

"The Crown is now richer by 1.2 million pounds," he continued, "a sum that you should consider well spent, as it prevents you from wasting the rest of your natural life in confinement."

The older man blanched. He glanced again at the Queen, but she sat ramrod straight and did not deign to give him even the smallest glance.

Feodora looked over, curious.

"You will also be gratified to note," Holmes went on, "that the remainder, in various currencies—since they cannot be easily returned—shall be well spent on operations of mercy and the like. Of course, should you attempt to claim any portion thereof, I have it on good authority that the confinement you have thus far avoided shall be awaiting you.

"And now," he concluded, "I very much hope you enjoy the freedom that a fortune of birth has granted you, for surely others would never be so lucky."

Holmes was about to walk away when he was called over by an unmistakable brogue.

"Mr. Holmes…"

John Brown beckoned him to Victoria's side.

Holmes went to the Queen, and bowed low.

She glanced at him with her indecipherable shoe-button eyes, and then leaned toward her half-sister.

"Feodora," she said languidly. "May I present Mycroft Holmes…"

As Holmes bowed again, and Feodora dutifully extended her hand in greeting, the Queen raised her voice so that it could clearly be heard.

"Mr. Holmes was able to recover more than one million pounds in five-pound notes that were somehow… misplaced."

"Oh!" Feodora said. "That is quite a large sum to go missing, is it not, Wolfgang?" she said, in an attempt to include her cousin in the conversation, for it appeared to her that he was being left out.

Hohenlohe-Langenburg tried to speak, but the words seemed to stick in his throat. He could manage little more than a nod.

"Mr. Holmes is a man whom I hope to convince to come and work for the Crown, for he has our highest trust and esteem," declared the Queen.

"I cannot imagine I shall be very hard to convince, Your Majesty," Holmes said with a smile. Then, as the first race of the season was about to commence, the Queen excused him from the Royal Presence and he resumed his seat next to his friend.

"Satisfying?" Douglas whispered.

"Beyond," Holmes whispered back.

Revenge, he thought. *Not ethically sound, perhaps. But sweet.*

He could purchase the building outright, he speculated as he watched the horses run—the one that housed his beloved Regents Tobaccos. And although Douglas had already paid to restore his family home, why not provide funds for Douglas to start a colored orphanage in London, one named after his wife and child.

After all, the Pennywhistles could run the shop. What need was there for Douglas to torture himself day in and day out with the smell of tobacco? At least until they found a physician who was more to their liking.

"You are humming to yourself, Holmes," Douglas interrupted.

"Not 'La Donna è Mobile,' I hope," Holmes asked with trepidation.

"No. More like Bach's *Mass in B Minor*. 'Gloria,'" he responded with a laugh.

Holmes laughed too, and turned his attention back to the race.

The horses were all fleet of foot, but in the end, Green Riband took the prize.

Everyone applauded.

Holmes sighed contentedly.

He had not bet this time. He'd had no need.

One of those buildings, he mused, could be near his present abode—he had seen a nice one for sale, if in need of renovation, on Baker Street. His brother Sherlock would soon graduate and might require a pied-à-terre in London, family life being what it was.

And of course, Mrs. Hudson would make a very fine landlady…

ACKNOWLEDGMENTS

THE AUTHORS WISH TO ACKNOWLEDGE THE FOLLOWING for their invaluable help in bringing this project to fruition:

Deborah Morales, intrepid and fearless producer (and all-around mensch); Steve Saffel, whose editorial skills (and patience) are nonpareil; Miranda Jewess, for her marvelous attention to detail; and Leslie Klinger, for his love of Sherlock Holmes and his persistence in freeing him.

We would also like to thank the Titan team for going above and beyond for us: Nick Landau, Vivian Cheung, Laura Price, Alice Nightingale, Emma Smith, Julia Lloyd, Paul Gill, Chris McLane, Ella Bowman, Katharine Carroll, and Hayley Shepherd.

KAREEM ABDUL-JABBAR

AT 7' 2" TALL, KAREEM ABDUL-JABBAR IS A HUGE holmesian in every way. An English and History graduate of UCLA, he first read the Doyle stories early in his basketball career, and adapted Holmes's powers of observation to the game in order to gain an edge over his opponents. He played basketball for the Milwaukee Bucks (1969–1975) and the Los Angeles Lakers (1975–1989), scoring 38,387 points to become the National Basketball Association's all-time leading scorer. Kareem was inducted into the Basketball Hall of Fame in 1995. Since retiring, he has been an actor, producer, a coach, and a *New York Times* best-selling author with writings focused on history. His previous books include *Giant Steps, Kareem, Black Profiles in Courage, A Season on the Reservation, Brothers in Arms, On the Shoulders of Giants: My Journey Through the Harlem Renaissance*, and the children's books *Streetball Crew: Sasquatch in the Paint, Stealing the Game*, and *What Color is My World?*—which won the NAACP Award for "Best Children's Book." In 2012 he was selected as a U.S. Cultural Ambassador by former Secretary of State Hillary Rodham Clinton. Currently he is chairman of the Skyhook Foundation and a columnist for *Time* magazine.

ANNA WATERHOUSE

A PROFESSIONAL SCREENWRITER AND SCRIPT CONSULTANT, Anna Waterhouse has worked alongside film and TV legends to repair structure and dialogue. She has consulted for premium cable miniseries and basic cable series, co-producing a feature-length documentary for Mandalay/HBO. She was supervising producer and co-writer (with Kareem Abdul-Jabbar) of the critically acclaimed feature-length documentary *On the Shoulders of Giants* which won the "Best Documentary" NAACP Image Award and two Telly awards in 2012. She has written several how-to screenwriting seminars for *Writers Digest* and teaches screenwriting at Chapman University in Southern California.

Sherlock Holmes
THE PATCHWORK DEVIL

BY CAVAN SCOTT

It is 1919, and while the world celebrates the signing of the Treaty of Versailles, Holmes and Watson are called to a grisly discovery. A severed hand has been found on the bank of the Thames, a hand belonging to a soldier who supposedly died in the trenches two years previously. But the hand is fresh, and shows signs that it was recently amputated. So how has it ended up back in London two years after its owner was killed in France? Warned by Sherlock's brother Mycroft to cease their investigation, and only barely surviving an attack by a superhuman creature, Holmes and Watson begin to suspect a conspiracy at the very heart of the British government…

TITAN BOOKS

Sherlock Holmes
THE THINKING ENGINE

BY JAMES LOVEGROVE

It is 1895, and Sherlock Holmes is settling back into life as a consulting detective at 221B baker street, when he and Watson learn of strange goings-on amidst the dreaming spires of Oxford. A Professor Quantock has built a wondrous computational device, which he claims is capable of analytical thought to rival the cleverest men alive. Naturally Sherlock Holmes cannot ignore this challenge. He and Watson travel to Oxford, where a battle of wits ensues between the great detective and his mechanical counterpart as they compete to see which of them can be first to solve a series of crimes, from a bloody murder to a missing athlete. But as man and machine vie for supremacy, it becomes clear that the Thinking Engine has its own agenda…

TITAN BOOKS

THE FURTHER ADVENTURES OF
Sherlock Holmes
THE WHITE WORM

BY SAM SICILIANO

Sherlock Holmes and his cousin, Dr Henry Vernier, travel to Whitby, to investigate a curious case on behalf of a client. He has fallen in love, but a mysterious letter has warned him of the dangers of such a romance. The object of his affection is said to be under a thousand-year-old druidic curse, doomed to take the form of a gigantic snake. Locals speak of a green glow in the woods at night, and a white apparition amongst the trees. Is there sorcery at work, or is a human hand behind the terrors of Diana's Grove?

THE FURTHER ADVENTURES OF
Sherlock Holmes
THE RIPPER LEGACY

BY DAVID STUART DAVIES

Sherlock Holmes and Doctor Watson investigate the
case of a kidnapped child. With no ransom note,
and a sinister connection to the highest echelons of
Victorian society, the companions' lives are in danger.
What is the child's true heritage? And what is the
connection with the vicious Whitechapel murders?

AVAILABLE IN JULY 2016.

TITAN BOOKS

For more fantastic fiction, author events, competitions,
limited editions and more

VISIT OUR WEBSITE
titanbooks.com

LIKE US ON FACEBOOK
facebook.com/titanbooks

FOLLOW US ON TWITTER
@TitanBooks

EMAIL US
readerfeedback@titanemail.com